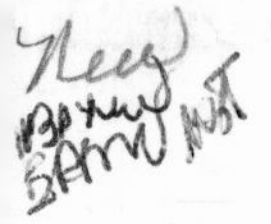

RANDOM
HOUSE
LARGE
PRINT

NANCY THAYER

THE HOT FLASH CLUB

The Hot Flash Club is a work of fiction.
Names, places, and incidents either are a
product of the author's imagination
or are used fictitiously.

Published in the United States of America by
Random House Large Print in association
with Ballantine Books, New York, and
simultaneously in Canada by Random House
of Canada Limited, Toronto.
Distributed by Random House, Inc.,
New York.

*The Library of Congress has established a
Cataloging-in-Publication record for this title*

0-375-43355-4

www.randomlargeprint.com

FIRST LARGE PRINT EDITION

10 9 8 7 6 5 4 3 2 1

This Large Print edition published in accord
with the standards of the N.A.V.H.

FOR

Deborah Beale, Mimi Beman,
Charlotte Maison, and Pam Pindell
Je t'adore!

Enormous thanks to my agent Meg Ruley, my editor Linda Marrow, my brain trust and inspiration Josh Thayer, Casey Sayre, Sam Wilde, David Gillum, and Jill Hunter Wickes, and my steady light, Charley Walters.

THE HOT FLASH CLUB

1 FAYE

It was while Faye was gathering donations for the community tag sale that she realized, with a shock, that any stranger going through her house would think she was obsessive, anal-retentive, or, at the very least, eccentric.

Although, if the stranger were a female around Faye's age—fifty-five—*she* would probably understand what could appear to others as an unhealthy mania for clothes.

Naturally, Faye's clothing hung in the large walk-in closet of her bedroom.

Also, in the guest bedroom closet.

And in the closet of her daughter's bedroom, for Laura was twenty-eight, married, and had left only a few of her favorite childhood things at home.

Faye's clothes did *not* hang in the attic, because when she and Jack bought the house thirty years ago, they converted the attic into a studio where Faye painted. But *more* of

Faye's clothes were hung, folded, or bundled in plastic wardrobes in the spacious linen closet at the end of the hall.

So much clothing!

She felt appalled, and slightly guilty.

It wasn't just that Faye, like most women, changed her wardrobe for summer and winter and fall, or that, like many other women, she had casual clothes for daily life and some elegant suits for the various committees she sat on, and a few gorgeous dresses for the events she had attended with Jack, a corporate lawyer and head of his own prestigious Boston firm. It wasn't only that she had Christmas sweaters and tennis skirts and the black velvet evening cloak that had been *her* mother's, so how could she possibly part with it? Or that she'd kept the expensive, elegant raincoat she'd bought on a trip to London with Jack, where she'd torn the hem, stepping out of a black cab on the way home from the theater. She intended to mend it, but she hadn't yet found time to do so. In the meantime, she'd bought another raincoat or two, to serve until she mended the London one. It wasn't that during this long, gloomy spring, she'd bought, on an impulse, *another* raincoat, a rain slicker of cheery, cherry red.

It was that she had so many clothes for so

many seasons and reasons in so many different sizes.

The size 12s were in Laura's bedroom.

The size 14s were in the guest bedroom.

The size 16s were in the linen closet.

The size 18s were in her own closet, right next to her husband's clothing. It was *his* clothing that had gotten her started on this spree in the first place.

One long year ago, Jack, her darling Jack, had died of a sudden heart attack, at the age of sixty-four.

In the middle of the night, Jack had sat up in bed, turned on the light, and said to Faye, "Don't forget—" then clutched his chest and fallen on the floor.

Don't forget *what*? Faye wondered. It kept her awake at night, it made her walk right past her townhouse, it bit at her thoughts like a tack in her shoe. Don't forget I love you? Don't forget to tell Laura I love her? Don't forget to look in the secret door in the Chippendale cabinet? (She'd looked there and found nothing.)

"He was sleeping," her son-in-law Lars assured her. "He might have been dreaming. He might have been thinking something nonsensical, the way dreams can be, like don't forget to feed the giraffe."

Now, a year after his death, her friends, and Laura, too, insisted that it really was time to part with his things. Laura and Lars had taken what they wanted. The rest, they reminded her, should not languish in her house when they could be useful to so many others. So Faye was diligently preparing to donate his clothes to the community fair. Most of them, anyway. She would keep a few items: his old robe, worn at the elbows, no good to anyone else, and so comforting to her, and the blue Brooks Brothers shirt he looked so handsome in. The rest she really would give away.

And she *absolutely* would give away some of her own clothing, too. At least the size 10s.

Although, Faye wondered, collapsing on the carpet and leaning against the bedpost—because her bedroom chairs and the bed were covered with clothing she'd sorted through—would giving away the size 10s be admitting she'd never be that size again? Would it be like *giving up*?

All her life, her weight had gone up and down more than the scales of a Tchaikovsky concerto.

Well, more up than down.

Faye *loved* to eat and never lost weight without fierce determination and control. Usually she weighed the most in early January, after the ounces and inches from the feasts and celebrations of Thanksgiving, Christmas, and New Year's had accumulated, like a confetti of cellulite, onto her hips. She weighed the least in the summer, when the combination of dread of appearing in public in a bathing suit, and anticipation of light, floaty summer dresses, had driven her to diet down a size or two.

But three years ago, she'd had a hysterectomy for fibroid tumors—that had been wonderful, she'd lost several pounds while lying down! On her doctor's advice, she took the hormone replacement therapy that had been touted as a wonder drug until, a year ago, the same HRT was suddenly reviled as toxic by a hysterical press. She stopped using it, and now she weighed as much as she had when she was nine months' pregnant.

She hadn't been eating more than usual or exercising less. Just the opposite: Determined not to go creakily into old age, she exercised regularly. In general, she led an active life. In spite of that, and her increasing attention to what she ate, fat collected around her arms and thighs, under her chin, on her bottom and hips, and rose on her stomach, warm and rounded, like a freshly baked loaf of bread.

Long ago, Faye had vowed not to compare

her physique to the skeletal models in magazines—her healthy body provided her with so many pleasures, why should she criticize it? She decided she'd try to cut down on fats and eat more veggies.

And she was trying.

But another loss had struck her, hard. Faye hadn't told anyone about this, not Laura or her closest friends, because speaking of it might make it *real*, might make it lasting.

For thirty years, Faye had been a talented, respected artist whose contemporary Impressionist still lifes sold as fast as she could finish them, making her quite well off, which she didn't even need to be, since Jack, a successful corporate attorney, made more than enough money. It wasn't the money that mattered anyway, it was the work, it was the daily mix of discipline, inspiration, knowledge, and risk that made painting so important to her. Through her painting, she interpreted the world. Through her painting, she expressed her gratitude for the luminous mysteries of any normal day.

Nine months after Jack's death, Faye decided she must put an end to her grieving and try to paint again. After all, painting was one of the joys of her life. Jack would want her to paint. So she climbed the stairs to her third floor studio, set up a still life of red pears in a silver bowl, pulled on her smock, readied her paints, and lifted her brush. Several hours later, she stood perplexed and more than a little frightened by what she saw on the canvas. It was muddy, thick, dull.

She waited a few days, then tried again. But for the first time ever, painting was *work*, and at the end of the day, what she'd accomplished was not even mediocre.

Have patience, she told herself. Her mind needed time to remember its talents.

But time didn't help, nor did patience. Playing Rachmaninoff in her studio didn't help, nor did so many infusions of ginseng and other helpful herbs that she expected little green twigs to curl out her ears. The gift of painting, which had sustained her all her life, had simply vanished, and she had no idea whether it would ever return.

She refused to believe this loss was connected to Jack's death. Her love for Jack had been the main catalyst for her work. Even though he was gone, her love for him remained as constant as it had when he was alive, and she believed that somewhere he knew this and continued to love her, too.

No. She was certain the loss was connected to her age, to her failing hormones, to the same physiological changes that added weight to her body and blotted her memory like random whiteouts of Liquid Paper.

Because she believed that happiness was at least in some part simply a choice, she refused to mope about it, she didn't mention it to anyone, and she kept trying, climbing up to her studio, standing in front of a canvas with her paints. She could joke about the changes in her appearance—the increasingly white hair, thinning lips, and her weight—but her inability to paint was a real source of concern. Was her artistic talent shrinking, shriveling, curling up and dying, like a brilliant older friend of theirs crippled with Parkinson's? If she couldn't paint, she couldn't be herself, Faye. It was a terrifying thought.

Shortly after she stopped hormone replacement therapy, a new torment appeared in her life. Hot flashes. At unexpected times of the day, an invisible match slashed up her body, igniting her into such incandescence she was always surprised smoke didn't come out her ears. It also fried her brain, disconnecting reason from emotion. No matter how firmly her mind assured her it would pass, her instincts told her she would detonate unless she ripped all her clothes off *now.* During the day she dressed in loose layers of cotton she could tear off in a moment, and in the winter, she often stepped out on her back porch in her cotton tank top, luxuriating in the freezing air.

It happened at night, too. She'd awake in a panic of heat, and after she'd thrown off the covers and flung off her nightgown, she'd lie there panting, waiting to explode. Later, when she'd cooled off, she'd lie staring at the other side of the bed, where Jack had lain, his reliable bulk rising before her like a shield against the dark night. She'd pull his pillow to her and fall asleep, hugging it tight.

Perhaps that explained her sudden inability to paint. Perhaps her mind was overwhelmed from loneliness, lack of sleep, and a general hormonal storm.

She wished she could talk this over with her husband. Jack had loved her passionately, no matter what she weighed. Jack had been Faye's best friend, her favorite companion. He'd made her *think*. He'd made her laugh. After thirty-five years of marriage, he'd still been able to make her breathless in bed. He'd made her want to paint. He'd supported—he'd *championed* her painting.

In her grief after his death, weight had fallen from Faye like her tears. But over the past long, brutally severe winter, she'd gained it all back, and more. The nights were lonely, and a box of chocolates, or a plate of buttery cinnamon toast, were good company. The coldest days were warmed by a bowl of homemade clam chowder and a piece, or two, of apple pie, or a cheese omelet with bacon, hash browns, biscuits, and honey.

So here she was, at the end of March, wearing her largest size—and finding it too tight.

Still, *no self-pity*! Faye ordered herself. She had so much to be thankful for. Her health, her friends, and especially, above all, her lovely daughter, wonderful son-in-law, and adorable granddaughter. She knew she was fortunate to be so close to them.

So she pulled herself to her feet, turned her attention to her bed, and diligently, mercilessly, sorted through her clothes.

Her thoughts were interrupted by a pounding. She hurried down the stairs, smoothing her white hair back into its low ponytail, and opened the front door.

Her daughter stood there, with Megan in her arms and tears pouring down her face.

"Laura!" Faye exclaimed. "What's happened? Is Megan all right?"

Laura reeled into the front hall, the diaper bag swinging from her arm, her thick dark hair tumbling around her shoulders, her nose bright red. Baby Megan's knitted cap had slipped down, covering one eye and part of her face. Her lower lip was quivering.

"Laura!" Faye said. "Tell me! What's wrong?"

"It's Lars!" Laura cried. "I think he's having an affair! Oh, Mommy, I just want to *die*!"

A powerful punch of emotions—relief, anger, sympathy—knocked the wind right out of Faye. When she could get her breath, she said, "Let me have Megan." Lifting her granddaughter into her arms, she led the way into the living room and, settling on a sofa, began unwrapping the baby from her fleecy snowsuit.

Laura collapsed on the other side of the coffee table, slender shoulders shaking as she sobbed. "It hurts so much, Mommy!"

Faye made Megan a safe little nest in the corner of the sofa, surrounded by cushions, handed her the TV remote control to play with, then rose and poured her daughter a glass of sherry.

"Drink this."

"I don't want—"

"Drink it, Laura. You've got to calm down. You'll frighten Megan."

Laura took a sip and choked.

"Take a deep breath," Faye suggested, making her voice nursery-stern even though she felt like weeping herself.

Her poor daughter looked absolutely wretched, her eyes and nose swollen, her skin blotchy.

Lars, having an affair? Faye couldn't believe it. Lars was *wonderful*. Jack had loved Lars, and Jack had been an acute judge of character. Jack would be pleased to know how helpful and patient and understanding Lars had been over the past year. Holding Laura in his arms as she wept and wept. Standing strong and silent between Faye and Laura at the funeral, a ready shoulder for either woman. Never once complaining when Laura's visits to her mother turned into overnight stays in those early weeks when Faye couldn't bear to be alone in an empty home. Welcoming Faye into their house so she could help cook and keep things running the first week after Megan's birth. Oh, how Faye wished Jack had lived long enough to see his beautiful baby granddaughter.

"Take another sip of sherry," Faye said. Pulling an armchair close to the sofa, she sat at right angles to Laura and took her hand. "Sweetie. Why do you think he's having an affair?"

"For weeks, when I called his office or his

cell phone, he hasn't picked up. He's had to 'work late' almost every night. He sneaks in when he thinks I'm asleep and takes a shower before getting into bed. He always used to shower in the morning!"

This didn't sound good, Faye silently agreed. She made cooing noises at Megan, who was deep in baby-fierce concentration, attempting to get the remote control to her mouth.

"Sometimes I can smell perfume on him."

"Have you asked him about it?"

"Once. A week ago. He denied it. But if he is—oh, Mommy," Laura cried. "What am I going to do?"

"Sweetie." Faye moved across to wrap her lovely daughter in her arms. "You haven't been getting much sleep lately, being up all hours with Megan. Maybe you're overreacting."

"I just found *this*," Laura said. From her purse, she took out what looked like a plastic playing card.

"What is it?"

"A 'key' to a hotel room." Laura handed it to her.

Faye studied it. A magnetic strip on one side, the Ritz-Carlton logo on the other.

"The Ritz is close to his office," Laura said.

Grimly she continued, "I know who it is. The receptionist. Jennifer D'Annucio. I saw the way she looked at him at the office Christmas and New Year's parties. She gave him a Hermès tie for Christmas."

"How can you be sure it was she—?"

"I asked him! He said when everyone in the office drew 'Secret Santas,' Jennifer D'Annucio got his name. He said she has a cousin who works at Hermès, and she got a discount."

"That's all possible, Laura."

"Mom, I looked through his credit card receipts. In December he charged a gold bracelet at Cartier. *I* didn't get a gold bracelet!" Laura pounded her fists on her knees. "I *hate* him!" She jumped up and paced the room. "I'll show him! I'll sleep with Joe Foster."

"Joe Foster?"

"Another lawyer in his office. They hate each other. They're terrible rivals. Joe always flirts with me at parties. He's a slimy sleazy little weasel."

"Then why would you want to sleep with him?"

"Because it's the worst thing I can imagine doing to Lars."

"Sounds like the worst thing you could do to yourself." Faye took a deep breath. "All right, now. Let's be sensible. You don't want to have sex with a slimy sleazy little weasel, Laura. You don't want to do anything until you're *sure* that Lars is fooling around."

"And when I get proof"—Laura's eyes filled with tears—"I'll file for divorce."

"Hold on a minute. Let's take one step at a time. You've got to think of Megan."

Laura looked over at her baby, propped in the corner of the sofa. Megan leaned forward, mouth open and drooling, brought the remote control toward her mouth with both hands and great concentration, and whacked herself on the nose. Turning crimson, she wailed.

"Poor baby," Faye cooed, gathering her grandchild in her arms.

"She does this every night." Laura sighed, and tossed back the rest of her sherry.

"Hits herself in the face with a remote control?"

"No, goes into a two-hour tantrum."

"This is the beginning of a two-hour tantrum?"

Laura nodded miserably. "I've called the pediatrician. He said it might be colic, although at four months she's a little old for colic. She had a checkup just last week, and she's in perfect health. But every evening she does this for two hours. Then she falls asleep, and I can't wake her. She sleeps until two or three in the morning, then wakes up and is bright and chipper and won't go back to sleep until six, when Lars is waking up. I feel like a zombie."

"Oh, my poor darling," Faye said. Rising, she brought the scream-ing baby to her shoulder and walked her, patting her back, an instinctive act that had undoubtedly been passed down through the genes since primitive woman. "Why didn't you tell me about this before now, Laura?"

"Because you've already helped so much! I'm an *adult*! I should be able to solve my problems myself!" She stamped her foot, looking terribly young and vulnerable.

Faye moved Megan to the other shoulder. "Does Lars help with Megan?"

"She screams even louder with Lars. I think she's hurt his feelings."

"At least his eardrums," Faye muttered wryly.

"What?"

"You slept through the night when you were a month old," Faye admitted, feeling irrationally guilty for having had it so easy.

"I know! So what am I doing wrong?"

"It's not a question of—"

"I shouldn't blame Lars if he is having an affair." Laura's tears started up again. "My breasts hang, I haven't had the time to shave my legs since Megan was born, and all I can talk about is the color of her poop. I've gotten all saggy and boring! Probably not even Joe Foster would want me now."

"Nonsense," Faye said briskly. "You're the same beautiful, wonderful girl you've always been. All young mothers feel this way, overwhelmed and exhausted. It will get better. You'll see."

"How can it get better if Lars is having an affair?" Laura wept.

"Darling," Faye said, raising her voice to make herself heard over Megan's wailing, "you don't *know* he's having an affair." Her heart broke in half as she looked at her daughter. Laura *did* look saggy—she *sagged* as she sat there, weeping. Never had Laura looked so terrible, and pity moved through Faye's heart like a rumbling, rolling boulder, weighing her down so heavily that she slumped into an armchair, unable to stand.

Megan wailed even louder.

If only Jack were still alive. He would know exactly what to do. Faye knew she had to do *something*. But what?

2 SHIRLEY

The bedroom was quiet except for piano music trickling like water over pebbles. The air smelled of apples and roses. On the massage table, the older woman lay, facedown, completely relaxed and, for a while, free from the arthritic pain that plagued her.

Shirley moved around the massage table like a white dove. She was barefoot, dressed in loose white pants, and a loose white cotton jacket, tied at the waist. Her long, vibrant, red hair was caught up in a clip. Silver moons dangled from her ears, a silver bracelet circled one ankle, and every finger and thumb wore a ring. The stones—moonstone, garnet, opal, cat's-eye—winked at her as she worked, drawing her hands in long, deep strokes down Nora Salter's back.

She concluded the massage with brief gentle touches on her client's coccyx, shoulders, and head, just as the alarm clock buzzed.

"Oh, my." Nora Salter sighed. "That was wonderful."

"I'm glad." Shirley went into the bathroom to get Nora a glass of water, and to allow her a moment to rise and pull on a robe.

"Here you are," she said, handing Nora the glass. "Drink it all, now."

The older woman obeyed with an almost childlike meekness. Nora Salter was in her seventies, and her wealth attracted many admirers, and she was suspicious of them all. Her children lived in other parts of the world, her husband was dead, and like many older people, she went through her days without even the most brief human touch. Shirley knew her massages nourished the other woman's soul as much as they relaxed and comforted her body.

Shirley gathered her CD player, scented candle, balms, and oils, and slid them into a purple batik tote bag. She folded up the massage table, tucked it into its thick canvas carrying case, and hoisted the strap onto her shoulder.

"I'll see you next week," she told Nora, hugging the older woman.

"All right, dear," Nora said. "Thank you."

As Shirley had lugged her bag of paraphernalia and the heavy massage table down the hall, she felt her own body slump. She was exhausted. Good thing, she thought as she pulled on her coat, hat, and mittens, Nora Salter's house was grand enough to possess a staff elevator.

Shirley was sixty years old. Too old, really, to be doing this kind of strenuous work. But she couldn't afford to quit. Three disastrous marriages, all ending in divorce—not to mention an excess of other stupid life choices—had left her scrambling. Over the years, she'd built up a good, reliable clientele, earning enough to keep up the mortgage payments on her sweet little house. Besides, she loved her work.

She trudged out of the house and down the drive, opened the hatch of her ancient VW Rabbit, and wrestled the table inside. She wished she could, at least, cancel all the clients who wouldn't come to her home for their massages, but she couldn't afford even that. Most wanted her to come to them. Because it took time to drive to their homes, sometimes as much as an hour, she charged twenty dollars more for a house call. But that didn't make up for the massages she'd have been able to give if she'd stayed in her house.

But enough negativity, she decided. Between massages she did what she could to restore her natural high spirits. Sometimes she used the drive to listen to inspirational tapes. Today, she parked by Fresh Pond, locked her car, and hit the trail for a twenty-minute jog, her Discman firmly attached to her belt. The music she played for her clients had to be mellow: Enya, Celtic musical, classical. To infuse her with the energy to give the massages, she listened to rock as she ran. Mostly Aerosmith, whom she adored. Good old Boston boys who'd sunk as low as she once had, then recovered, blasting into the stratosphere, now and forever more, the best rock band in the world.

It was her addiction to Aerosmith, and her collection of CDs by Bob Segar, U2, Tom Petty, and ZZ Top that made her current lover, Jimmy, believe she was younger than she was. She'd never lied to him, but she'd never told him her age, either, and most days she felt that somehow she actually *was* younger than sixty. Her lush red hair, curling past her shoulders, her large blue eyes accentuated by violet shadow, her vegetarian diet, her twenty-year abstinence from cigarettes and booze, her naturally slender, lithe body—the package fooled everyone else, and the mirror fooled her, too.

But days like today, when the March wind blew bitterly, and the sky was shrouded with gray, when her knees creaked in protest as she ran, and her entire body yearned for a nap, just a little catnap—days like today made her feel *ancient.*

She walked back to her car. As she fastened her seat belt, the gremlins who still hid deep in the recesses of her brain tempted her with visions of NoDoz, or anything she could buy over the counter that would provide her with the energy to work one more hour.

Shrugging back the demons, Shirley unscrewed the lid from her Thermos and poured herself a cup of Lemon Lift tea, which she drank as she drove.

Her next client was shy, nervous, clever Julie Martin. Julie spent her entire life in her house with the curtains drawn so that no light would streak the radiant machines that had become her family and her friends. Julie played the stock market. Julie *lived* to play the stock market. At all times she had two computers buzzing, and two televisions, one tuned to CNN, one to CNBC. A millionaire several times over, she lived an austere life.

Shirley let herself into the house with a key, stepped into the living room, and found Julie tapping away on her computer.

"Hi, Julie," she called out.

Julie didn't turn her head. "Just a minute, Shirl."

Shirley removed her coat and went into the downstairs bathroom to tug off the T-shirt she wore for jogging and slip into her white jacket. With everyone else, her appearance had to be exactly right, but Julie never noticed that sort of thing. Shirley thought Julie probably wouldn't be able to tell anyone what color Shirley's hair was, and few could miss Shirley's hair, long, curly, and blazing red like Bonnie Raitt's.

Julie's own hair was stringy and lank. Clad in sweatpants and a wrinkled flannel shirt, Julie was still tapping away when Shirley went back to the living room. Shirley turned off the televisions and one computer, opened the drapes, and let the evening's blue light fill the room.

"All right," Shirley said. "Time to unplug yourself." Standing behind the other woman, she put her hands on her thin shoulders. "Tense today."

"I just need to finish—"

"That can wait," Shirley insisted. "Turn it off. Now, Julie."

"I don't want to."

"Turn off your computer, hon, or I'll have to."

Julie typed a few instructions, and the screen went dark. “It’s been an awful day. The stock market—”

“Sssh,” Shirley said. “Bend your head. I’m going to do Raiki on you.”

Dutifully, Julie obeyed. Shirley put both hands on the woman’s skull and concentrated. She was channeling the energy of the universe into this skittish, lonely woman, so she thought of healthy animals and their spirits. Swans gliding. Cows standing trancelike in the sun. Horses running like silk. Dolphins leaping in the sea.

Beneath her hands, Julie’s shoulders relaxed. Her woodlike neck warmed and softened. Shirley sighed with pleasure; she had no children of her own, and Shirley felt very motherly toward this eccentric young woman.

“Now,” Shirley said, softly, “let’s do some stretches.”

A year ago a combination of mild illnesses had sent Julie to a doctor. She ached all over, all the time, she was often dizzy, often depressed. Often frightened. She cried a lot. She believed she was dying of a life-threatening disease. After a thorough physical and scores of lab tests, the doctor asked Julie to tell him about her daily life, then recommended that she begin regular exercise, perhaps yoga, and find a personal trainer and a masseuse.

Julie was twenty-nine, overweight, out of shape, and lonely. Because she could make money sitting at home playing the market from her computer, she'd stopped going out. Now she was almost agoraphobic. She lived on boxes of Cheez-Its and chocolate doughnuts. She didn't own a cat or dog. The concept of coordinating sheets, comforter, and curtains had never occurred to her, nor had the thought of artwork for her walls. She was too timid to join a health club, too shy to dream of working with a personal trainer, but when she'd read in Shirley's on-line ad that Shirley made house calls, she summoned her courage and phoned. Shirley gave Julie a few weeks of massage, then decided that the younger woman needed gentle but firm guidance toward a healthier lifestyle.

One day, instead of giving Julie a massage, Shirley sat Julie down and talked with her. By the end of the hour, Julie had agreed to let Shirley order a week's groceries to be delivered, and she promised to eat them. After a few more weeks, Shirley learned that Julie wouldn't actually get around to preparing a salad, so lettuces wilted, unnoticed. So Shirley ordered finger foods on which Julie could munch while typing: little carrots, radishes, apples, bananas. Julie would microwave food; in fact, Julie *liked* to microwave food; it fit into her understanding of how the world worked. Shirley ordered pots of ramen noodles, and vegetable soups, and tofu-rich casseroles. And after a while, Julie reported she felt better.

Shirley's goal was to help Julie realize that her body was more than a brain with two eyes and ten typing fingers. She designed a series of daily stretching exercises for Julie, who *said* she did them, but most probably she was lying, if the tension in her back was any indication.

Now Shirley switched on her CD player, and gentle music filled the air. They both sat, cross-legged, on the living room floor as Shirley led the other woman through some simple exercises, saddened at how disconnected Julie was from her body. Shirley climbed onto the sofa behind Julie, who was supposed to be stretching both arms high above her head, and who *was* trying, but lethargically. Shirley pulled Julie's arms up high, then opened her fists and pulled her fingers up and out.

"Extend," she told Julie. "Be a cat. Be a tigress flexing her paws."

After twenty minutes of stretching, they sat

facing each other while Shirley talked Julie through deep breathing and simple meditation. When the weather was warm, Shirley opened the windows to let fresh air in, and she was certain she could feel all the sharp electronic molecules crackle out the window, leaving the air fresh.

She ended the hour with a brief massage of Julie's neck, shoulders, and arms, accompanied by one of her little pep talks. Over the past year she'd learned that Julie's parents were dead, her brother lived in Japan, and whatever friends she'd had once had dropped her because of her habit of forgetting social engagements. Sometimes during a massage, Julie would begin crying, in high little squeaks, her throat tight with embarrassment as she nearly hyperventilated. This was good, Shirley assured her miserable client. She was releasing toxic emotions and opening her chakras.

Sometimes, like today, Julie actually *communicated.*

"I can't imagine my life without you." Julie's voice was almost a whisper. "You make me feel like a human being."

"I'm so glad, honey. I'll see you next week."

As she steered her coughing old car through the congested streets to her home in the crowded Boston suburb of Somerville, Shirley indulged in her favorite daydream: One day she'd establish a retreat for people like Julie, a beautiful space where people could come to rest and rejuvenate their spirits. Her clients would listen to music, do yoga and tai chi, hear lectures on spirituality and health, learn how to cook healthy, delicious meals; they'd learn to laugh again, to move gently with the harmonies of the universe. Shirley knew exactly what the rooms would look like, how the air would smell, which plants she'd nurture, the way she'd organize her staff—

Her *staff*! Who was she kidding? She didn't have the money to pay for a new muffler, never mind a *staff*. Her idea was good, she knew that, but the practical considerations were daunting, and she had no ninety-seven-year-old maiden aunt who was about to die and leave her a fortune.

Her retreat was only a dream.

And some nights, like tonight, when the wind was picking up, battering the loose shutter on her kitchen window, when her refrigerator held only a cold slab of tofu and a lonely orange, when her boyfriend had left a note on the table, telling her he was going down to the bar to have a drink with friends, sometimes the siren song of alcohol sang to her of exquisite comforts. Sometimes she longed to join

Jimmy at the pub, where a whiskey would warm her, soothe her aches, and hush the clock ticking away her years.

Sometimes, like tonight, it was nearly impossible to stay home and stay sober.

3 MARILYN

As Marilyn steered her Subaru toward Logan Airport, her mind was fractured in three directions. First, she had to concentrate on driving; second, she yearned to be back in the lab; third, she was overwhelmed with emotion because her beloved older sister was leaving after a week's visit, and she didn't know whether she was more sad than glad.

She loved Sharon—she *adored* her. She always had. But Sharon was so bossy and judgmental! And Sharon had something on her mind—Marilyn could tell. As a paleobiologist, Marilyn could usually hide from the modern world, but she could never escape her sister's opinions.

Sure enough, from the passenger seat, Sharon announced, "Marilyn, I have something to say to you."

"So," Marilyn said, "say it." Inwardly, she sighed. Probably, Sharon was going to criticize the way Marilyn looked. *Sharon* looked fabulous, with her hair tinted blond and sliced in a chic blunt bob. Her black pantsuit was flattering and smart, her nails professionally shaped and French-tipped. Marilyn's dowdy academic appearance made Sharon *crazy*, Marilyn knew, but the ancient, long-dead creatures she loved to study didn't care that her gray hair was yanked back into a practical bun, nor that her sweater and slacks were twenty—or was it thirty?—years old. From Marilyn's scholarly perspective, thirty years was brand-new.

Sharon shifted in her seat to face Marilyn. "Frankly, I'm worried about Teddy."

"Teddy!" Marilyn glanced at her sister in alarm. "Why?"

"I don't like his fiancée. I don't trust her. I think she's after Teddy for his money."

Relief made Marilyn laugh. "Don't be ridiculous. Lila's father's a successful plastic surgeon! He's got his own clinic just west of Boston!"

"Marilyn. Listen to me. You know I love Teddy. But have you *looked* at him?"

"Of course I have! I look at him all the time!"

"All right, then, picture him in your mind's eye. Then picture Lila. What's wrong with this picture?"

Marilyn thought. "Nothing. Lila's a lovely girl."

"No, Marilyn. Lila's not a 'lovely girl.' Lila is a drop-dead knockout beauty who wears Versace and Manolo Blahniks."

"What's your point?"

"Oh, honey—" There was genuine anguish in Sharon's voice.

They reached the airline terminal. Marilyn found a space at the departure curb and angled into it. "Want me to come in with you?"

"No. Just *listen*." Sharon unfastened her seat belt and aimed her determined glare at her sister. "Marilyn. I love Teddy. I *adore* Teddy. But, honey, Teddy is—" She took a deep breath.

"What? Teddy's *what*?"

"A geek. Teddy is a geek."

Marilyn stared at her sister, a red tide flushing her face.

"A nerd," Sharon said. "A twerp."

"All right, all right, I get the point." Marilyn chewed her lip, then brightened. "But you know, Sharon, Teddy looks *just* like his father, and I fell in love with Theodore."

Sharon closed her eyes, seeming to pray for courage. When she opened them, she reached out and angled the rearview mirror toward Marilyn. "Yes. That's true. And look at yourself."

Marilyn stared at her reflection, puzzled.

"And please recall what you've spent your life looking at," Sharon continued, reaching over the backseat to gather up her scarf, purse, and overnight bag. *"Dead bugs."*

"Trilobites," Marilyn corrected with quiet dignity. Sharon never had respected her life's work. Opening her door, she said, "I'll get your suitcase from the trunk."

Standing behind the car, buffeted by fumes of passing buses, taxis, and cars, the two sisters scowled at each other.

"I know you're angry with me," Sharon said. "But I had to say this. I'm afraid Lila's marrying Teddy for his money."

"I've told you. Lila's family has plenty of money."

"Do they? Perhaps they did, but do they now?"

"What do you mean?"

"I mean that a lot of people have lost a ton of money in the stock market in the past year. I mean that you and Teddy and Theodore think that it's normal to sit around the dinner table discussing genetic alterations that will make the corn borer's stomach explode, but in fact, that's not what most people consider dinner conversation. I mean that you fell in love with Theodore even though he's short and fat and bald, because you truly live the life of the mind and don't realize you go around looking like an extra from *Lord of the Rings*. I mean you love Theodore because you understand and admire his work. But Lila Eastbrook doesn't have a *clue* about Teddy's work, and she never will. Her deepest thought's about Chanel's newest lipstick shade. Marilyn, if you don't watch out, your son and my nephew will get his darling heart broken, *and* Lila will make off with a lot of that lovely money you've forgotten you have."

"You've been here one week, you've seen Lila and Teddy two times, and you've deduced all that?"

"Honey, I'm a headhunter. It's my business to size people up quickly."

"Well, what can I *do*?"

"Stall when they talk about the wedding. Convince them that next spring would be better than this fall. Get on the Internet, check out how Eastbrook's clinic's doing. Discuss it at dinner some night with Lila, see how she reacts. I'll think about it and call you when I come up with some better ideas."

"I just can't believe this." Marilyn twisted her hands together.

"Don't look so worried. We'll work it out. I wouldn't mention it if I didn't love Teddy so much. I want only the best for him. You've got to admit that your marriage with Theodore has lasted so well because you're both scientists. Don't you want a marriage like yours for Teddy? I mean, just imagine. Once they're past the first sexual frenzy, what will Lila and Teddy even be able to talk about?" Sharon glanced at her watch. "I've got to run, or I'll miss my plane. I'll call you tonight. Love you." She hugged her sister tightly, kissed her cheek, then grabbed her suitcases and rushed into the terminal.

Marilyn stood gaping as her sister strode away. All human DNA was 99 percent the same. Only 1 percent of one's DNA was different from any other human on the earth. How could it be, then, that she and Sharon, who shared not only the nature of DNA but the nurture of the same parents, the same home, the same education, could have turned out so differently? Life was such a mystery. In a microscope—

A horn blasted through her thoughts.

"Lady! You gonna stand there all day?" an irate cabby yelled.

Marilyn blinked. What? Where? Forcing herself to focus, she remembered where she was and what she had to do. She got into her car and drove away from the terminal. She longed to head for the university and the refuge of the lab, where she was working on the meticulous extraction of a trilobite from a slab of Ordovician shale.

Instead, she drove to the Isabella Stewart Gardner Museum. Its hushed, eccentric opulence always provided an atmosphere where she could think.

As she drove she tried to look at the situation logically. First of all, she reminded herself, consider the source: Sharon was a loving sister, married for years, with her own thriving business and two grown, married children. She loved Marilyn and her family, so it was not with malicious intent that Sharon had stirred up this hornet's nest in Marilyn's heart.

Blunt, practical, and honest, Sharon was a superb problem solver. Marilyn, in contrast, was dreamy-minded in an intellectual way. She tended to let the teakettle rattle dry as she stood two feet away, field glasses in her hands, watching crows feed in the backyard. Fortunately, her husband was just as preoccupied with his own thoughts about the mysterious puzzle of genetics. In fact, over the past few months, Theodore had taken to eating most his meals out because it took too much time from his work to drive home to eat. Fine with Marilyn, who was delighted to be released from the kitchen; she had more time for her own research.

Neither Theodore nor Marilyn had ever longed for riches or the luxurious life money could ensure. It was a passion for the scientific process that had driven Theodore to discover how to alter the gene of a parasite that killed expensive exotic fish so that the gene self-destructed before it could harm the fish. When a pharmaceutical company that sold, among other drugs, preventive medicine to the aquarium industry, bought Theodore's formula for a staggering sum, Theodore and Marilyn had laughed and popped a bottle of champagne. Then they'd wandered back to their work, leaving the champagne to go flat. Their colleagues urged them to take a trip to some exotic place, but the thought of being away from their work horrified them, as did the suggestion that they dislodge their books and papers from their Victorian house near the university simply to move to a more prestigious address. They'd spoken, briefly, about hiring a housekeeper, so that Marilyn would have more time for her lab work, but her teaching was only part-time at the most, and they were terrified by the very thought of someone moving their papers and books around. In the end, they decided to send their laundry out and live with dust and clutter.

Teddy took after both of them. When Teddy turned twenty-one, Theodore had given him a seven-figure check, as he did when Teddy won his doctorate in genetic biology at Harvard. Teddy had thanked his father, then stuck the money in the bank and continued to live in a rented apartment near MIT. He was too busy with his own research for frivolous matters, and his parents understood that completely.

Marilyn showed her pass, entered the Gardner, and settled on a bench in the sunny courtyard, filled with statuary and, today, a plethora of lilies and azalea. Hidden deep in the pots, beneath the leaves and showy blossoms, unseen minuscule creatures were busily going about their everyday work, waving their antennae, crawling, chomping, defecating, tunneling, mating—

Teddy. Her son. Her wonderful brilliant son.

What had Sharon called him? A dweeb. A nerd. A *twerp*.

Rather unkind, but not inaccurate. Like his father, Teddy was portly, was losing his hair, and wore heavy, black-rimmed glasses. Yet it had never occurred to any of them that he could be unattractive. He'd always had girlfriends. He'd had a steady girlfriend in high school, dear little Ursula, who *was* ursine in appearance, squat and burly, low to the ground, with beady dark eyes, thick dark hair—on her arms and legs as well as her head—and an incipient mustache. Ursula played field hockey and the violin. Recently she'd married another violinist and moved somewhere in the Midwest.

In college, there had been several girls. Candy had been Marilyn's favorite, and Teddy had seemed very serious about their relationship, but after getting their doctorates, Candy had gone off to work for NASA while Teddy stayed on at MIT.

After Candy, there hadn't been anyone long-lasting until Lila. Even so, Teddy was not *repulsive.* He was not *obese.*

Still, it was possible that Sharon had a point. Marilyn took off her horn-rimmed glasses and chewed on them as she thought. All Teddy's former girlfriends had been, if not homely, exactly, then certainly dowdy. Marilyn was dowdy herself, as Sharon never failed to remind her, but she couldn't get her mind to dwell on the mysteries of clothing, hair, and lipstick. Heaven knew that her beloved trilobites, dead in their rock coffins for 500 million years, didn't know or care what Marilyn looked like as she bent over them, abrading away, with exquisite care, the dust of ages from their long, thin, cockroachlike bodies.

Marilyn's fingers twitched, longing to get back to work. She rose and walked through the museum, telling herself to stay on the subject for just a little longer.

Now: Lila. What was different about her from Teddy's other girlfriends?

Most obvious: Lila was really beautiful. Even Marilyn had noticed that. Marilyn looked at the flamenco dancer in Sergeant's painting and decided that Lila, though fair and petite, had the same flashing intensity. Yes, Lila was glamorous, but so what?

True, Teddy hadn't met Lila the same way he'd met his other girlfriends, in a science lab. Where had they met? Marilyn searched her memory. Hadn't they—oh, yes. She remembered. Lila had tripped and fallen in the Bread & Circuses parking lot. She'd been wearing high heels. One of the heels had snapped off. For a moment she thought she'd broken her ankle. Teddy had been on his way to his car, and he'd seen her fall, and helped her up, and taken her for coffee. They'd liked each other at once and started dating, and now they were engaged.

Could Lila have targeted Teddy and fallen on purpose?

That was just ridiculous. She mustn't let Sharon's doubts turn her into a suspicious harpy.

I mean, Marilyn asked herself, how would Lila even know that Teddy was wealthy?

Well, she answered herself, there was that write-up in the *Boston Globe*.

Marilyn paused in front of the tapestry hanging across from the steps to the second floor. Medieval, it depicted a rustic village scene, with peasants and farmers and cows and trees, and at the bottom, a pair of rabbits mating. A lusty scene, and lust was good. Certainly she had enjoyed it all those years ago, when she and Theodore had fallen in love. If they no longer felt lust for each other—and Marilyn couldn't actually remember the last time they'd had intercourse—it could have been years—they always had so much reading piled next to their beds—if they no longer felt lust, they certainly did feel great affection for each other. Marilyn thought she and Theodore had a satisfactory marriage. She'd always assumed the same would be true for Teddy.

Teddy might not be handsome, but he was brilliant, and kind, and good-natured, and sweet, and often funny. He was her darling son, even if he was twenty-nine years old.

What if Sharon was right? What if Lila was after Teddy for his money? What if she was marrying him only to divorce him? Oh, what a dreadful thought. Marilyn knew she mustn't let herself bury her head in the literal sand of her work. Somehow she had to find out about Lila and her family.

But how?

4 ALICE

Alice used to be beautiful, even first thing in the morning, waking up with her cheek creased from the pillow and her hair standing out from her head like a child's drawing of the rays of the sun. She used to be able to sit naked in the full exposure of sunlight, stretching, yawning, her breasts full and high, her tummy sleek as a silk evening bag, every pocket of her body as glistening and fresh as a spring morning.

Knowing this had given her a kind of power that had, along with her intelligence, ambition, and intuition, carried her up the ladder of corporate success. It was important to her work that she be attractive. No one said this, but it was true: The vice president in charge of administration for the TransContinent Insurance Corporation, especially if she was an African-American female, had to look good.

And for years she'd looked *great.* All her life she'd been attractive, until a few years ago, when it began to take some amount of maintenance on her part—exercise, diet, hair color, makeup. After fifty, the effort was almost daunting, but she was determined. She looked more chic than sexy, but chic worked.

Then, suddenly, it seemed, she woke up one morning to discover she was sixty-two.

It was as if she were a tiger, powerful, sinuous, burning bright, padding majestically through the jungle of life. Pausing to look in the mirror, she discovered that somehow, overnight, she'd become a sheep. A gray, common, *creaking* sheep.

Worse, other people saw her as a sheep.

Sheep were easy prey for jackals, lions, and wolves.

She cursed as she dressed for work. Her newest suit, for which she'd paid over a thousand dollars, was too tight at the waist. She could scarcely fasten it. After lunch, she'd be in agony and, unless she was lucky, the button would fly off during a conference and hit one of the new honchos in the eye. It was the style now for younger women to wear their shirts out over the waist rather than tucked in. When Alice tried it, she felt chubby and sloppy, and she remembered all those years of telling her sons to tuck their shirts in. Still, she left her white shirt out, pulled the suit jacket on, and left it unbuttoned. Not the best of looks, but it would do.

As long as she didn't have to raise her arms. The sleeves were suddenly too tight, pulling at her shoulders. It seemed, these days, she gained weight while simply breathing air.

Now, shoes. The pair that coordinated with the suit had cost over four hundred dollars. Black, with a boxy three-inch heel, they made her legs look fabulous. The pleasure she got from the other corporate heads stealing glimpses of her legs almost offset the sheer torture of wearing them.

God, she was vain, and she knew it! However, her vanity was not just a personal flaw, it was also a professional tool. Three months ago, TransContinent merged with Champion Insurance and became TransWorld. Its new, glittering headquarters towered in the heart of downtown Boston, only minutes from Alice's condo on Boston Harbor. She could walk there easily, but she wasn't going to today. Not in these shoes. She headed out to her sleek black Audi and entered the early-morning traffic.

Alice's job was to develop and implement umbrella policies for management information procedures, employee benefit policies, and human resource plans in and among the complicated network of offices.

A lovely, fit, energetic, brilliant, cocky, *younger* woman had come from Champion to work with Alice as assistant to the vice president in charge of administration.

Alison Cummings. Thirty-two, unmarried, no children, a Harvard MBA.

It bit Alice's ass that this young princess was named Alison. Until her arrival, everyone had called Alice by the shortened version of her name. Going by Al had endowed her with the power of masculinity in written communications and on-line, as well as providing a slight frisson of sexuality in face-to-face meetings, because she was so obviously female. It had *worked* for her. But Alison also went by Al, and during their first superficially pleasant and deeply cold-blooded meeting, the two women had agreed with gritted teeth that both would give up the nickname and go by their full names, to avoid confusion. Alice had thought Alison should, because of Alice's seniority, be respectful and extend to Alice the right to go by Al, but that thought didn't seem to cross anywhere near the younger woman's mind. She'd been more interested in measuring Alice's corner office with calculating eyes. Her own office down the hall was almost as large, but not as prestigious.

Alice steered her way into the TransWorld garage, parked in her reserved spot, and took the elevator to the thirtieth floor. Ruefully, she recalled that Alison Cummings had one thing working for her, literally: She'd brought her secretary with her during the merger. She had *her* guardian in place.

Alice did not. Her own loyal and circumspect secretary, Eloise, in spite of Alice's desperate pleas, had retired, leaving Alice personally bereft and professionally endangered. Eloise had been Alice's watchdog and secret agent; Eloise could sense an office intrigue the moment it glinted in the conspirators' eyes. Eloise would have helped Alice figure out just how determined Alison Cummings was to undermine her.

Since Eloise's defection, Alice was scrambling to find a new secretary, but it was tough. Enough drastic changes were taking place with the merger; Alice didn't want to raid a junior officer's staff and provoke someone's resentment, but she didn't want to have to train someone totally new to the industry, either. Right now Alice had a temp from the office secretarial pool.

It was this secretary who greeted Alice as

she entered her office. Diane was competent, but she was also thirty-five, divorced, man-hungry, and swooningly eager to work with Cummings's secretary, a fortyish man named Barton Baker.

Though Alice knew she could expect no loyalty from Diane, she still stopped at Diane's desk to chat a few moments, trying to build some kind of camaraderie. Briefly they discussed weather, the latest news on Stan's health, and commiserated on the chaos the new merger and acquisitions were causing the company.

When Alice headed into the inner sanctum of her own office, Diane followed her.

"Could I bring you a cup of coffee?"

"Thanks, Diane. I'd love a cup of decaf."

How far would it go toward engendering a close relationship, Alice wondered, if she confessed to the secretary that these days coffee gave her acid indigestion and heart palpitations? Bad idea. Diane was too young; she'd see any weaknesses on Alice's part as signs of imminent disability and death, and she'd leak it to the rest of the secretaries, and before she knew it, the jackals would be at Alice's heels.

Settling at her desk, Alice booted up her computer, scanned her schedule, and checked out the TransWorld interoffice daily report. As she waited for her computer to access her e-mail, she eased her feet out of her gorgeous shoes, knowing she was trading immediate comfort for the eventual necessary agony of compressing her feet back in. Diane brought her decaf. Alice stirred artificial sweetener into it and sipped as she blasted directives, responses, and suggestions off into the Internet ether. Five minutes later, the waistband of her skirt was slicing into her skin. What was up with that? Did she have some mysterious illness that made her bloat like an elephant? With the help of estrogen patches and occasional diuretics, she'd pretty much sailed through menopause, and she'd thought by now the worst was over.

The truth was, she now realized, the worst was never over. She was sixty-two, and the worst was inexorably heading her way. What had sagged would never rise again. She'd get back her twenty-two-inch waist only at her deathbed or in the grave. She couldn't afford time off from work to have plastic surgery, and now that Eloise was gone, she couldn't even relax her arthritic back with the little secret catnaps she'd stolen every afternoon while Eloise guarded her door.

To add indignity to infirmity, she'd been in her office only twenty minutes and already she had to pee. As senior vice president, she had her own bathroom off her office, but she was painfully aware that out at her desk, Diane would be able to hear the toilet flush. She would be, even unconsciously, alerted to the frequency with which Alice went to the john. For all she knew, Diane was at heart a kind woman, but Alice had to consider her one of the jackals. Alice dare not betray the slightest sign of weakness.

She *had* to get her own secretary. ASAP.

Among the professional e-mails were two brief blips from her sons: Alan in Houston and Steven in Oregon. She adored them and took pleasure in the knowledge of their continuing health and happiness and that of their wives and children, but she'd never been a warm-and-fuzzy woman, except perhaps the first few years when her boys were babies. She loved her work, and she was damned good at it.

She'd been with TransContinent for thirty-six years. In a way, it was her true home. She'd been a lowly receptionist when Arthur Hudson founded the company in Kansas in 1966. Her sons had been in elementary school then, and she'd been married to her high school sweetheart, Mack Flynn. Women didn't work so much back then, but Mack had less talent and persistence for keeping jobs than for playing football, and the family needed her income. Eventually Mack got a steady job delivering Coca-Cola, but he was a handsome, good-natured womanizer, and the job provided lots of opportunities to meet women.

When Mack divorced her to go out with someone else, TransContinent provided stability and support. With her boss's urging, Alice continued working during the day while taking classes toward a master's in administration at night. Slowly she'd climbed the corporate ladder, becoming administrative assistant to the vice president in charge of personnel and administration. By the time her sons went off to college, she was able—*just*—to pay their tuition: good thing, too, since their father couldn't.

When she was thirty-five, she made the mistake she most regretted: She'd had an affair with Bill Weaver, her immediate superior. He was in charge of personnel, and he taught her everything about the job. Founded on mutual respect, their relationship had deepened as the company grew and the stresses mounted. Their sexual affair seemed a natural outcome of the long hours they spent working into the night, night after night after night. But Bill had a wife he loved; he'd never misled Alice about that, and she had thought for a long while that what she had with Bill was sufficient for her life. She *had* no other life, really. During other holidays when Bill was at home, she was perfectly happy, and even sometimes relieved, to have the time to herself. Often she simply spent the time in bed alone, catching up on hours and hours of lost sleep.

After five years, Bill's wife discovered their affair. Around the same time, the home offices of the company were moved to Boston. Bill remained, but Alice made the move with them, though it meant leaving behind her home and a scattering of old friends she seldom saw. She'd been forty-one years old.

Since then, she'd been celibate, and the truth was, that was fine. All the passion, energy, and devotion she'd given Bill she now channeled into her work, and it had paid off, finally: At fifty-one, she was made a senior vice president of the company. The only woman vice president. The only woman officer, *period*.

Alice had seen the company grow from three hundred to over five thousand employees. She'd been personally responsible for researching, targeting, and implementing the personnel programs and benefits that made TransContinent a company where everyone wanted to work. Her office walls were hung with awards presented to her from within the company and from national organizations, for her innovative work in providing all the employees of TransContinent with excellent benefit packages and superior working conditions. Because of her work, TransContinent had been one of the first corporations in the country to provide in-house day care; her system had been used as a model all over the nation.

Now she faced a new challenge: developing human resources guidelines for a multinational organization. It would be a bitch of a job.

No, she had to do the job with a bitch.

During the preliminary conference call with their immediate superior, Melvin Watertown, Alice sketched out an overview for integrating the human resources policies and employment benefit programs, including a humanitarian plan for day-care centers for the workers, and health clinics, and possible educational opportunities for the employees in the new operations.

Alison Cummings had scoffed. "Your ideas are sweet, Alice, but financially unsound."

Alice snapped back, "The majority of our shareholders are interested in optimizing the environment for the workers."

"No, most of our shareholders are interested in profit. We're not a charity."

"In the long run," Alice argued, "employee benefits pay off."

"Our newer shareholders don't care about the long run," Cummings shot back. "They're young, they're in a hurry, they want to see profits fast."

Alice had thought the young were supposed to be idealistic! Obviously, this was not a quality Alison cherished, nor did she show any respect for a woman who had struggled through the early years of feminism so some sleek cookie like Alison could step into a high-ranking job.

"Why don't you formulate an employee package you both can live with and get back to us," Melvin had growled, and signed off.

True, Alice had rushed things. She knew that conditions and needs had to be studied and humanitarianism needed to be balanced against profit and loss. Some of their new facilities weren't operational yet. In some project areas further exploration had to be done before the size of the necessary workforce could be estimated. She'd attempted a preemptive strike, wanting to prove she had the overview and didn't need Alison, and Alison had struck back, hard and fast, instead of making a conciliatory gesture such as suggesting they discuss it.

Alice was glad for the warning. She'd always intended to stay at TransContinent until she was forced to retire, and just a few years ago the company got rid of its mandatory age sixty-five retirement policy. She had the acumen, knowledge, and experience the company needed. This company was her home, her family, and her friends. She planned to work here until she was carried out in her coffin.

She'd be damned if she'd let Alison Cummings change that.

5 FAYE

The sound of the mail falling through the brass mail slot was so familiar that Faye believed she could hear it from wherever she was in the house. If she couldn't actually *hear* it, certainly she could sense its arrival.

She was still in her turquoise kimono when the mail arrived, and, as usual, she took it back to the breakfast room to peruse while lingering over a cup of coffee.

She got a ridiculous number of catalogues. She thought of the waste of trees, and the toll it took on the letter carriers' backs. On the other hand, she did buy a lot from catalogues, and often looked through them as if they were magazines. Her best friends lived in other states, and since Jack's death, some of her married friends had fallen away. The catalogue models' faces were familiar and amiable, and it cheered her lonely days to see them. A free kind of therapy, then.

No bills, but a smattering of ads and a postcard from one of their friends, retired and on a cruise, and—oh! An invitation to a retirement party for Eloise Linley, whose husband Frank had worked at the same law firm as Jack. Over the years, Faye had seen Eloise at Christmas parties and other functions. Occasionally they'd met in smaller groups at private dinner parties in someone's home. Faye had always admired Eloise, who worked as a personal secretary for one of the vice presidents of a colossal corporation. When Jack died a year ago, Eloise had sent her a note of condolence, and when Frank Linley died six months ago, Faye had returned the favor. She'd contemplated calling the other woman to ask her for dinner or tea, but somehow had never gotten around to it. Now Eloise was retiring, and the company was throwing her a party.

Faye was pleased to be invited, but she wouldn't go. She wasn't close to Eloise. She rose to toss the paper into the recycling bag.

"What's that, Mom?" Laura asked, coming into the room. Barefoot, in a robe of Faye's that hung on her, her hair tied back in a ponytail, she looked about twelve years old, except for her swollen breasts in their nursing bra.

Laura and Megan had moved in for a few

days, because Laura had a killer cold that made her sneeze and cough incessantly. When Laura wasn't sneezing, baby Megan was screaming, and Laura was exhausted. Faye was glad to help, and she agreed that Laura wasn't much of a seductive sight at the moment; it might not be a bad thing for her marriage if she and the baby were away from Lars for a few nights. On the other hand, was it wise for Laura to desert her home when she thought her husband might be having an affair?

Laura picked up the invitation. "A party? At the TransWorld building? Cool!" Dropping into a chair, she blew her nose.

Faye poured a glass of fresh orange juice and set it before her daughter. "Oh, honey, I won't know anyone there."

"Thanks, Mom." Laura sipped, then said, "You'll know Eloise. You're bound to know someone else. The munchies should be terrific, and I've heard the building's astounding."

"But I don't have anything to wear," Faye protested. Her honest nature forced her to admit, "Nothing that fits."

"Then *buy* something!" Laura insisted. "You've *got* to go! It will be good for you. You can't just mope around the house for the rest of your life."

That was true, Faye silently agreed. She

leaned against the counter, gazing at her daughter and granddaughter, remembering twenty-eight years ago, when she'd been pregnant with Laura. Then, Faye had *enjoyed* having that extra little basketball-sized attachment on her body. Now, she weighed as much as she had when she was nine months' pregnant. Furthermore, age and hormonal change made weight accumulate not just in her normal belly, but also in a new rotund protrusion between the bottom of her breasts and the top of her waist. It was rather like having a sleeping puppy lying on a pillow on her lap, except that when she stood up, the puppy, pillow, and lap remained. Plus, every day the puppy grew. It had been a dachshund. Now it was more like a bulldog.

Still, Faye resolved to view her changing body in a positive way. After all, her stomachs were rather *companionable.* Like mascots. She could even name them. Honey, for the larger lower one, Bunny for the upper. The thought made her smile.

"Mom?"

Faye forced her thoughts back to the present. She peered into the refrigerator. "Would you like some scrambled eggs? Maybe an omelet?"

"I'd love some, but don't evade the issue. You really should go to this party."

Faye took down her favorite blue-and-white pottery bowl and began to break eggs into it. She and Laura had always given each other good advice. "All right, then, I'll go!"

Then it was her turn to counsel Laura. She only wished she knew what to say.

6 SHIRLEY

All night long, Shirley dreamed she was at a wonderful party. She woke warm and happy, as if she were floating on the memory of her dream.

Later, as she stood at the kitchen window, eating yogurt and granola for breakfast, she saw a bird she'd never seen before fly to the feeder she kept full on the old apple tree in the backyard. Another good omen.

And the day went by flawlessly. All her clients came to her, so she had time to rest and exercise in between. Two of her clients tipped her that day, which was rare. Hiram Folger, who had arthritis, rose from her table saying that was the best massage she'd ever given—he felt like a new man! And poor Betsy Little, who wanted so desperately to get pregnant, only to find herself each month overwhelmed by debilitating cramps, told Shirley she believed she had magic in her hands. Betsy felt she was receiving such good energy from

Shirley that someday her body would surprise them all with a strong, healthy pregnancy.

"You're absolutely right," Shirley affirmed, not because she wanted Betsy to continue coming for her weekly massages, but because she knew that when the body was involved, half the battle was won by one's heart and mind.

When her last client left, Shirley brewed a pot of cranberry tea and curled up in a basket chair to find the movie listings in the newspaper. Jimmy had been in a good mood this morning, as well he should have been, because Shirley, floating on clouds of pleasure from her dream, had surprised him with a blow job he said he'd remember all his life. So perhaps she might be able to persuade him to see a movie with her. Usually he hated movies. Jimmy was a restless man, a man's man, and the only movies he wanted to see were too violent for Shirley. But she felt hopeful this afternoon. There was a movie starring Jack Nicholson that looked good, and Jimmy loved Jack Nicholson. Maybe they'd go out for dinner, too, at the Thai place she loved. Maybe—

The front door slammed, startling Shirley. Jimmy came barreling into the room. He was a big, burly man with a beard that always needed trimming and eyebrows as bushy as his beard. He wore jeans and a studded black leather jacket. His striped T-shirt strained over his beer belly, and his eyes were wild.

"I'm out of here!" he yelled. "I'm blowing this fucking town."

"Jimmy!" Shirley jumped to her feet. "What happened?"

"That fucking wop, that's what happened!" Jimmy said. Turning, he stomped down the hall to their bedroom.

Warily, Shirley followed at a distance. Sometimes, when Jimmy got really steamed, he took his anger out on her. From the hall she watched him yank his duffel bag down from the closet shelf. Jimmy worked at a local discount furniture store, loading and delivering furniture, and his boss, Manny Scillio, was forever riding Jimmy about taking too long to make his deliveries. Manny accused him of stopping by a bar on the way. The fact that Manny's suspicions were true wasn't of interest to Jimmy.

"Jimmy—"

"He fired me! That stupid cocksucking asshole fired *me*!"

"Oh, hon, I'm so sorry. But you know, maybe it's a good thing. You've hated working for Manny. Now you can find another job, a better job, one you enjoy—"

Jimmy yanked his drawer out of the bureau

so hard it fell on the floor, splitting. He shoveled his underwear, socks, and T-shirts into his duffel bag. Jerked the Ralph Lauren Polo button-down shirts she'd bought him for birthdays and Christmas off the hangers and stuffed them into the bag, too.

"No way am I staying in this town. I'm sick of the cold weather, I'm sick of the gray sky and mud. I'm sick of living around wops and gooks. I'm heading south."

"You're leaving?"

"Yeah, I'm leaving, and don't you give me any grief about it, Shirl. You know I've been unhappy here. You know I like Florida. I got friends there."

"Great, friends who sell drugs. Jimmy, you'll get sucked right back in—"

"Don't start with me! Don't even start!" Jimmy brushed past her, into the bathroom to scoop up his toothbrush and Shirley's toothpaste.

"But Jimmy, I thought—"

He stormed down the hall to the front door. "It don't matter what you thought, Shirl. Don't matter what I thought. Things change. I'm gone."

He left, not bothering to close the door behind him. Shirley stood there, watching him mount his Harley-Davidson. He did look bad on that cycle. He roared off down the street, taking the corner fast, leaning sideways the way he liked, looking dangerous and sexy as the devil.

He vanished from sight. The vibrations of his cycle disappeared from the air. Everything was quiet.

Shirley blinked. She couldn't absorb it. She couldn't believe he wouldn't come roaring around the block, and back up into her driveway and her life.

She just stood there, waiting, like a *dope*, until the furnace kicked on, its ancient rattle alerting her: She was freezing and letting cold air into the house. But she felt that if she shut the door, it would be final. Jimmy would really be gone.

Out of the corner of her eye, she spotted her mailbox. Fetching the mail was never fun. All she ever got was bills, and it occurred to her that Jimmy, who didn't help with her mortgage, hadn't paid for last month's share of the groceries and utilities. Again.

Reaching into the rusting metal box, she found three pieces crammed in. As she wrenched them out, the lid broke with a squeak, then just hung there, dangling pathetically by one hinge.

She slammed the front door shut and leaned

against it, drained of energy and hope. Jimmy was gone.

But the familiar old longing returned, the old and powerful craving for that which would fill the emptiness, dull the sorrow, and bring back the sense of joy she'd felt in her dream this morning. Her old friend/demon/enemy: alcohol.

But jeez Louise, no herbal teas or meditations would get her over this pain of Jimmy leaving.

She flopped down on the sofa and tossed the mail on the coffee table. Sure enough, the mortgage bill was there, and the gas bill.

Shirley Gold, welcome to your life. Tears burned her eyes. Dear sweet Jesus, she wanted a drink! Just one. One small scotch, and she'd feel so much better.

Then she saw, through tear-blurred eyes, the third piece of mail. Something handwritten on quality stock. What on earth?

Grabbing it up, she studied the address. It was her name, all right. She ripped open the envelope. It was an invitation to a party for Eloise Linley, one of her massage clients.

Well, hot damn!

Her dream had been prophetic.

This was enough to make her believe in anything.

Maybe she could even believe in herself.

7 MARILYN

Under the buzzing lights of the university lab, Marilyn bent over a table, brushing with meticulous care at a slab of shale.

It was after seven o'clock on Thursday night. Theodore was off at a conference for a week, so she didn't need to worry about fixing dinner for him. She could stop by Martino's, pick up some salads, brew a pot of coffee, spread the newest science journals out on the dining room table, and read.

Faraday McAdam strolled into the room. Faraday was about Marilyn's age, and handsome, if you liked red hair and a ruddy complexion. He wore a heathy tweed jacket and a cheerful tartan vest.

"Marilyn! I'm surprised to see you here."

"Really? Why?" Faraday was a colleague of Marilyn's, a paleobiologist. He was always extremely nice to Marilyn, which proved, her husband Theodore said, that he was jealous of Theodore and trying to weasel the secrets of

Theodore's work from her. Marilyn thought this didn't quite make sense—Theodore was a molecular geneticist, his field different from Faraday's—but as Theodore had pointed out, if Faraday didn't want to pry into Theodore's work, or at least try to hang on his coattails, why did he spend so much time around Marilyn?

Faraday said, his brow furrowed in puzzlement, "I thought you'd be in Hawaii. With Theodore."

So there you are, Marilyn thought. *Theodore.* "It's a scientific conference, Faraday, not a vacation."

"Oh, come on, you know we always mix pleasure with business at these things. Besides, *you* could have had a vacation. You could have gone along and enjoyed some sunshine."

They turned to look at the window, where sleet tapped with an almost musical rhythm.

"I wanted to keep working," she told him truthfully. Well, half-truthfully. It was Marilyn's own intellectual ardor that kept her bent over her work. Faraday didn't need to know that Theodore hadn't invited her to join him on this trip.

"Ah. Well, in that case. But, look. Why not let me take you out to dinner tonight? We'll go to a Polynesian restaurant and indulge in drinks with flowers in them."

For just a moment she was tempted. Then she thought of Theodore; he'd think she was a traitor. "No, thanks, Faraday," she responded. "I have other plans. In fact, I was just getting ready to leave."

"Too bad. Another night, perhaps?"

"Perhaps."

He went off down the hall. The building was silent. Marilyn stretched to ease her aching neck and shoulders, and stood for a moment, looking out. Night had fallen, but the university lights backlit the sleet as it gyred in the wind. Nature liked spirals. The sleet sparkled in the night, each tiny bead alive and dancing.

In contrast, Marilyn felt heavy and leaden as she pulled on her camel hair coat and her wool cap and gloves. Wrapping her wool muffler around her neck, she crossed it over her chest, buttoned her coat to the neck, hefted her bags, locked her office, and trudged down the hall and out the door to the parking lot.

Marilyn had listened to the weather report that morning, and dressed with according caution. It was the end of March, so one could expect a day that started off in relative warmth to end that way, but winter was not through with them yet. She could see that not all of her colleagues had been prepared for the barometric plunge.

At the far end of the lot, Cynthia Wang, the new biology assistant, was whooping with laughter as she slipped and slid across the slick pavement. Her gentleman friend reached out to help her, and they both went down in a flurry of legs. Marilyn waited to see whether someone was hurt. Should she help them up? But Cynthia and her friend rolled on the ice, hysterical with laughter. So, Marilyn thought, they'd be all right.

She had been smart enough to wear her thick-soled, high-ankled, leather walking boots to work, and as she settled in her old Subaru, she tried to feel appropriately self-satisfied. Instead, she felt melancholy. She couldn't remember when she'd last laughed as she slipped across the ice. Had she, ever?

If you're born a cockroach, you will not evolve into a butterfly. Marilyn had always found great comfort in the reliability of nature. Early on she'd found her niche, and her life had been tranquil because of it.

But sometimes—

Theodore had left today, to attend a weeklong conference on genetics and the sea. She wouldn't miss him very much. She always rather enjoyed it when he was gone. She ate odd meals at odd hours: two hard-boiled eggs with lots of salt and four pieces of toast smothered with expensive Dutch raspberry jam, that sort of thing. At night she watched television for irresponsible hours, and not just the news and the Discovery Channel, but old unabashedly romantic black-and-white movies that often reduced her to inexplicable tears.

She'd been weeping more and more, ever since, a few days ago, she'd inadvertently overheard her son and her husband fighting. Teddy had stopped by, as he often did, to join them for drinks and a brief discussion of the latest scientific news or office politics. Marilyn had stepped into the kitchen to put together a tray of cheese and crackers. Did they want pickles? she wondered. Salami? She'd hurried down the hall to ask them, but froze at the sound of her son's voice. It was low and angry.

"I don't understand why you don't arrange to take Mom with you!"

Silence. Marilyn knew that Theodore was lighting his pipe, an activity that enabled him to gather his thoughts.

"Why should I take her with me?" Theodore asked in a reasonable voice.

"Because it's in Hawaii. Because Hawaii's beautiful. Because you are being given free accommodations in a world-class hotel. Because you and Mom haven't been on a vacation together for years."

"May I remind you, this is not a *vacation* for me."

"Oh, come on, Dad. Of course it is. You'll have to give a paper and attend a few seminars and dinners, but you'll have plenty of afternoons to explore and swim—it even says so in the invitation!"

Theodore sighed. "Teddy, I understand your intentions are good. But please remember that I have been married to your mother for thirty years. I know what she likes and doesn't like. More importantly, I know what and who will be helpful to me at a conference. I have a reputation to uphold, remember. Which reminds me. Did you have a chance to read Weingarten's paper?"

Marilyn had slunk back to the kitchen, bowed by the sadness of her son's voice, which exposed clearly the sadness of her marriage.

But she had to focus on the present. With a shake of her head, she saw she'd somehow driven herself to Martino's and parked the car neatly between two others in the parking lot. Right, she told herself. Enough sniveling. She hurried into the restaurant.

To the right lay the dining area; to the left,

the little shop with its deli counter. Theodore was a plain meat-and-potatoes man, so Marilyn indulged now, buying pickled mushrooms and antipasto with fat wrinkled Greek olives and a pasta salad with pesto and roasted red peppers. And bread. And wine.

As she fished in her purse for money, she heard a familiar laugh. Where? Who? She paid, gathered her purchases, and headed to the door, then stopped as she heard the laugh again.

It had to be Lila, Teddy's fiancée. Her laugh was so distinctive. Teddy was in Hawaii with his father. Perhaps Lila was here with her parents. Perhaps Marilyn should say hello—

Peering into the dining room, she spotted Lila immediately. Such beauty. Lila stood out in any crowd. Tonight her hair was pinned up on her head in that careless way young women did it these days, so that the ends fanned out like a turkey's tail. She wore a red dress with a plunging neckline.

She was smiling. She was throwing her beautiful head back in laughter. She was accompanied by a man. A handsome man, with sleek black hair and gangster looks. He put his hand over Lila's.

The two obviously knew each other well, or were going to.

Marilyn told herself she should go over and say hello. Undoubtedly, Lila would explain just who this man was, this man who wasn't Teddy.

"Excuse me."

Marilyn was blocking the door. Two people, arms full of pungent purchases, were trying to get out. Rattled, Marilyn pushed through the door and out into the cold night, and the only reasonable thing to do seemed to be to keep on going to her car.

As she drove home, Sharon seemed to beam herself onto the passenger seat like a hologram, reminding Marilyn of her warning that Lila was interested in Teddy only for his money.

The house loomed empty and dark. The mailbox next to the front door was crammed, as usual. She collected the correspondence and dumped it, with her book bags and food, onto the dining room table, then went up to her bedroom to change into the comfort of a robe. She turned lights on everywhere to make the house feel warm. She wished she had a dog or cat, but Theodore had too many allergies.

Settling in at the table, she began to read, absentmindedly picking at her food, which had lost its savor. She was worried about Teddy, about the strange man with Lila.

She wished she had someone to talk to. *Really* talk to. The truth was, she was lonely. Her life had been devoted to her family and her work. She'd worked hard, juggling the demands of both worlds, until now she'd arrived at a calm lagoon. Her son was a successful scientist about to be married. Marilyn was a tenured professor and a respected authority in her field. She had many acquaintances, but no real friends. True, she could always call her sister. But she didn't think she wanted to hear what Sharon would say.

At nine, she made a cup of instant hot chocolate and curled up on the sofa to watch *The Thin Man*, the perfect antidote for her mood, frivolous, glamorous, silly. When it was over, she felt much better.

Back at the dining room table, she read until the grandfather clock in the front hall chimed midnight. Stretching, she looked down at the pile of mail she hadn't read yet.

Catalogues—toss those. Professional magazines, and *The Smithsonian*, she put aside for herself and Theodore. Bills. And a thick envelope for Dr. and Mrs. Becker. She ripped it open.

An invitation to a party! For Eloise Linley. They used to be close, back when Teddy was in high school with Eloise's son Jason, but Jason went off to college in California, married, and remained on the West Coast, and Marilyn hadn't seen Eloise for years, until the funeral for her husband six months ago. Theodore wouldn't want to go. He considered time spent on anyone but scientific colleagues a waste.

But Marilyn would go, she decided. It was a long time since she'd been to a party. The thought had a kind of frightening allure that made lightning bugs flicker in her heart.

8 ALICE

Arthritis was turning Alice into a stiff-limbed mannequin. At home she sat around on a heating pad, but she didn't dare use one of those at the office, especially now that little Alison was around. So Alice creaked and ached through her day, and after work she drove straight to CVS to buy a cartload of Bufferin.

She was hungry, and cranky, and her feet hurt, so naturally the lines at the cash register were long, and everyone was sneezing or hacking with a late-winter cold. She sighed, letting her eyes rest on a display on a nearby counter. Out of the blue, a truly bizarre craving possessed her.

There, among the chocolate Easter candy, was a rack of plastic beaded bracelets, in a symphonic sherbet of colors: turquoise, pink, pale green, lavender. Suddenly, for no reason, Alice desperately wanted to buy every color and slip them onto her wrist.

It would be like wearing a rainbow.

Still: *plastic* bracelets? For thirty years she'd worn only solid gold jewelry. She considered it a kind of signal: Whatever she touched was only the best. If anyone saw her wearing plastic bracelets—she shuddered, paid for her Bufferin, and hurried to the door, each step a burn of pain. She *had* to get different shoes.

Sleet hit her face as she rushed to her car. Just as she reached it, she slipped on some thin ice coating the pavement. Reaching out to catch herself, she knocked her arm on the hood of her Audi. She had to stop a moment to get her breath. Now her feet hurt, her back hurt, and her arm hurt.

"You okay, ma'am?" A punk kid with spiked hair and more spots on his face than a leopard approached her, sleet slapping against his jeans jacket.

"Of *course* I'm okay!" she snapped.

He held up his hands as if she'd pointed a gun at him. "Sor—*ry*." Loping off, he looked over his shoulder at her. *"Jeez."*

"I am *not* an old woman!" Alice yelled at him, but only in her mind. She wasn't so far gone that she'd taken to yelling at hoodlums in the street, even if she had spoken rudely to him. He'd only been trying to help, and she was appalled at her instinctive fear simply because he was young, tall, and resembled a space alien.

What was happening to her? She watched the boy move off down the street, making a game of sliding on the ice. *Come back,* she wanted to call. *Come back and tell me if I look like an old woman!*

Turning around, she entered the pharmacy, strode up to the counter, and selected seven plastic bracelets.

"For my niece," she informed the salesgirl, needlessly.

"Oh, she'll love these," the girl cooed. "Everyone does. It's the rage right now. They bring you good luck, too."

"They do? How do you know?"

"It says so, right here." The salesgirl pointed to the print on the card behind the rack of bracelets.

ORIENTAL GOOD LUCK BRACELETS
IN REAL FAUX STONES
WILL BRING YOU GOOD LUCK!!
One size fits all.
Stretchable. Made in China.

"Uh-huh." She had respect for *stretchable.* "Thank you." Accepting the paper bag holding the bracelets, she headed back out to her car.

After turning on the engine to warm up the car, she reached into her purse, took the bracelets out, and slipped them onto her wrist. Now her arm looked different. In the dim neon light from the pharmacy, who could tell the beads were plastic? They were cool on her skin and made a companionable rattle as she put the car into drive.

Buying plastic bracelets, for God's sake. Was she losing her mind? They glimmered when she stopped at a red light. If it were summer, they might be appropriate.

But maybe this demented purchase signaled an authentic yearning. It occurred to her, as she drove, that it had been years since she'd bought anything with color in it. Needing to look businesslike and competent, a woman intruding into the old boy network, she'd bought only shades of beige, and gray, and black, and ivory, for years. It simplified her life. It sent the message that although she always looked presentable, even elegant, she didn't waste much time on shopping. Even the clothes she wore at home were in neutral shades, in case someone dropped in unexpectedly.

At the long brick building, a recently restored warehouse running along Boston Harbor, she pulled her mail from the box in the hall, pressed the elevator button, got off on the fifth floor, and let herself into her condo.

When she'd moved here twenty-one years ago, she hadn't wanted to waste time on decorating; there had been so much work to do at the office. Besides, for a woman from the Midwest, the ever-changing display of sailboats, steamers, and massive foreign container ships seemed a luxury she'd never tire of. So she'd had the place done up in cream, beige, and black. Then, she thought it looked sophisticated.

Now she thought it looked dreary. Impersonal. Bland. Even the art she'd chosen for the walls was black-and-white—photographs of different cities at night.

Suddenly, with the same inexplicable craving that had driven her to buy the bright bracelets, Alice wanted to look at flowers. She wanted to cuddle a teddy bear. She wanted to cuddle a real-life, hair-shedding, dander-strewing cat. She wanted to wear a crimson robe while she painted her toenails scarlet.

She looked at the bracelets on her wrist, and smiled.

After changing into the robe she had—caramel, with cream trim—she padded into the kitchen to pour herself a glass of red wine. Then she threw herself onto the sofa and lifted her tired feet, tucking a pillow beneath them. Ah. Bliss.

Her mail lay in the center of the coffee table. Nothing she couldn't wait to check out—except—something heavy, addressed by hand.

She opened it. Oh, yeah, the going-away party for Eloise Linley. The other executive secretaries had organized it, and Alice was glad. Eloise deserved it. Even if Alice felt Eloise was bailing out just when she needed her most, she had to go. It would be churlish not to, plus it might signal a weakness to the new kids on the block. Sighing, Alice turned on her heating pad and lay back on the sofa, staring out into the night.

9

Saturday night as Faye prepared for the party, she put on a CD of Strauss waltzes and concocted a light drink of vodka with cranberry juice, loving the rosy color, which always put her in a festive mood. She showered, pulled on her turquoise kimono, and sat down on the quilted rosewood bench in front of her dressing table.

She looked in the mirror.

A stranger looked back.

She leaned closer, as fascinated with her face as she'd been as a teenager, scrutinizing each pore. Back then, of course, she'd been trying to maximize her sex appeal. Now she wanted only to remain recognizable. Every day it seemed some bit of her skin slipped another millimeter. Her eyes were no longer the same size or shape, and her lids drooped like a pair of ancient panties with stretched elastic waistbands.

Behind her, on a padded hanger, was her

new, loose dress of fawn-colored silk, which, when she'd tried it on in the shop, had seemed dignified and subdued. Hanging from her closet door, it looked more like garment bag than garment.

Not so long ago, a new dress was a cause for excitement. Red dresses especially. She loved red dresses. With their flamboyant *look at me!* intensity, they aroused within her the kind of anticipation she might feel for a lover. A red dress invited the unexpected and promised excitement.

This dress promised comfort.

Not a bad thing. After all, Faye thought, a life, like the earth, has its seasons: the pastel blush of youthful spring, the green luxuriance of fertile summer, then the flames of autumn, in defiance of the approaching colorless winter. Faye was fading into the winter of her life. Her looks and powers were diminishing. She needed glasses, and she was beginning to consider the sense of hearing aids. Her mind, which had once flashed fast, efficient, and bright as a hummingbird, now flapped and squawked like a turkey.

Faye wasn't afraid of the future. She hoped her death would reunite her with Jack. She had wonderful memories of her past: She'd been married to a man with whom she shared a profound love, she had a daughter and a granddaughter, and she had worked, for so many fulfilling years, at her art.

The present baffled her. She knew it was time for others to move into the spotlight. It was time for her *daughter* to wear red dresses. Faye wouldn't change that for the world. But wasn't there something more she could do with her life while she still had health and energy, sporadic as it was?

For starters, she counseled her reflection, she could attend this going-away party for Eloise Linley. Jack would want her to. And it would be a way of celebrating the retirement of a contemporary.

She began to make up her face. She'd never used foundation, but now she wondered whether she should, to even out her skin tones. Or would it emphasize her wrinkles? She made a mental note to buy some new eyeliner shades. The black she'd used for years stood out too harshly against her fading skin, giving her the horrified stare of an extra in a Stephen King movie. As she carefully painted her mouth, she remembered she used to assume old women's lipstick was applied crookedly because they couldn't see well. Now she realized it was the lips themselves that had become uneven, thinned with age and pleated with lines.

Never mind, she soothed herself, as she rose and slipped on the fawn silk dress. It looked elegant, and it felt blissful, sliding over her like water. She draped a long silk scarf swirling with roses around her neck, letting it hang loose almost to her waist—a trick she'd seen on television, this was supposed to elongate her appearance. She rubbed a tissue of fabric softener over her stockings and slip to prevent any static cling that would accentuate her bulges. She used to sprinkle her skirts with water for this purpose, until she realized any wet spots might hint at incontinence. She tucked an extra sheet of softener in her purse, clipped on a pair of gold earrings, stepped into her shoes, and blew her reflection a kiss.

After locking her kitchen door, she settled into the comfort of her BMW. She was just a little nervous as she drove toward downtown Boston and the spectacular new TransWorld building. She still wasn't comfortable going out alone at night.

The traffic heading into Boston was light. She found the TransWorld parking garage, showed her invitation to the guard, and spiraled up to the fifth tier before she found a spot. She locked her car, patted its hood in appreciation of its friendly automotive beep, and headed toward the office complex.

Several others joined her as she entered the vast lobby. They all smiled, but the others were couples, and as they all crowded into the elevator, Faye felt shy. Odd, how when Jack was alive, she'd had no reluctance about entering a crowd by herself. She'd gone off to movies, theater, parties, lectures, without the slightest self-consciousness. She'd had no trouble approaching strangers at these affairs, and now she realized how Jack's existence in her life had accompanied her like a tag on her chest saying *chosen*. She could be independent precisely because she was attached.

The door slid open on the twentieth floor. They stepped out into an enormous ballroom. Chandeliers shimmered. A live band played light rock. Waves of laughter rose and fell as men in tuxes and women in drop-dead dresses floated effortlessly toward one another, animated and glossy with success. As Faye passed through the crowd toward the drinks table, she saw how their glances dismissed her. In this sea of life, they were mermaids, sting rays, and sharks, while she was only a large, homely manatee, the sea's cow.

She took a flute of champagne and a handful of cocktail napkins, then retreated to a corner to look around the room. When she spotted Eloise, she did a double take. Always before, chubby Eloise had been dressed for success in appropriate executive secretarial garb: suits and pantsuits in taupe, navy, and gray. Tonight a dazzling amber-and-gold caftan draped her full figure and set off her hair, newly dyed a shocking saffron and cut short and stiff as a whisk broom.

Eloise was surrounded. She would be all evening, so Faye began to squeeze her way through the crowd.

"Faye!" Eloise bent forward to hug her. "How nice of you to come!"

"You look amazing tonight," Faye told her.

Eloise threw her head back and laughed. "Well, Faye, I feel amazing! I'm so excited about my plans." Linking one arm through Faye's, she pulled her close. "I was just getting ready to tell Marilyn and Shirley what I'm going to do." With her free hand, she gestured, "Faye Vandermeer, meet Marilyn Becker and Shirley Gold. Faye's husband Jack worked in Frank's law firm. Marilyn's son Teddy was my Jason's best friend in high school."

Faye nodded at Marilyn, a thin, scholarly looking woman with gray hair and glasses, clad in red tartan skirt, gray turtleneck, and burgundy plaid blazer.

"And," Eloise continued, "Shirley has quite simply saved my life—she's a masseuse and good witch."

Faye thought Shirley, with her turbulent red tresses, glittering violet eye shadow, voluminous batik trousers, and multicolored scarves looked more like a belly dancer, but she admired her audacity.

Eloise was bubbling over. "Now! Let me tell you my plans! I was so damned sad and lonely in that huge old house after Frank died, I thought I'd go mad. So I sold it, bought myself a cute little Winnebago, worked out a route with the best campsites on Internet maps, and next week I set off to drive all over the United States."

Marilyn's jaw dropped. "By yourself?"

"By myself! Well, I am taking Roger." She paused wickedly, then added, "He's my Rottweiler. He's four years old and the biggest baby on the planet. He wouldn't bite someone stealing his dinner, but he looks ferocious."

Faye asked, "Won't you be lonely?"

Eloise adjusted her gold tortoiseshell glasses as she gave Faye a reprimanding look. "You mean as lonely as I've been in that big old house all by myself? As lonely as I've been working in this corporation that's just merged and the new people assume I'm just a fat old lady?"

"Assume," the academic interjected, "makes an ass of u and me."

"Ha! Precisely!" Eloise chortled. "Look, I've been wanting to do this all my life. I've got stacks of books to read, and the addresses of a ton of old friends and acquaintances to visit, and I bet I'll make a lot of new friends along the way. I'm going to lie on the grass looking up at the stars from every park I can find. I'm going to drive down every side road that catches my fancy and while I drive I'll listen to opera—the entire opera, not just the arias—and country western music, and jazz, whatever I'm in the mood for. I'm going to eat whatever I want and in the evenings, if it's raining, I'll curl up and read scientific essays and adolescent porn. I'm going to explore this country and my own mind. I've spent my whole life paying attention to my outside. Now I'm going to pay attention to my inside."

Faye was speechless. So, it seemed, were Marilyn and Shirley, who stood next to Faye with their mouths hanging open.

"Eloise!" A handsome older couple approached and Eloise turned the radiance of her personality on them.

"Widow's wisdom or menopause madness?" A tall African-American woman in a chic black pantsuit stepped into the gap Eloise left. The three women stared at her with the guilty expressions of choir girls hearing a friend say *Fuck* in chapel—she had said the *M* word in public. A quick look around assured them no one was near enough to hear, and so they relaxed.

"I think Eloise finished with menopause long ago," Shirley whispered.

"But has menopause finished with her?" the tall woman shot back. "I'm Alice Murray, by the way, Eloise's former boss."

Alice looked formidably classy, except—Faye squinted—she wore several bracelets of different hues ringing her arm. The bracelets looked *plastic.* Odd, but they made the regal woman seem approachable.

"Your point is that we've lost control of our destinies, right?" Faye asked.

Alice nodded brusquely. "Absolutely. We can't decide when our bodies will cooperate as they always have—something beyond our control has taken over."

"Our control has always been an illusion," protested Shirley.

Alice's nostrils flared. "No," she insisted, "it *hasn't* been. Until the past year or so, if I controlled what I ate, I lost weight. Now, even if I starve, I gain."

Marilyn stepped closer, nodding so enthusiastically her tortoiseshell glasses slid down her nose. "It's not just weight! When I sneeze or laugh or cough, I pee, no matter now much control I exert."

"And I certainly have no control over the hot flashes that scorch every thought from my head," Faye added.

"I haven't had a hot flash yet," Marilyn admitted.

"Lucky you," Alice said dismissively.

Marilyn experienced the timeless terror of being cut from the popular group. She needed to *offer* them something. "But I can't find my armpits!" she confided urgently.

The other three women looked startled.

Marilyn rushed to explain. "I mean, I don't always shave because I can't see up close like that without my reading glasses, and I can't wear my glasses in the shower, they fog up, you know—"

Alice snorted. "Honey, count yourself lucky to be able to get near your armpits. Mine are lost in the crevices."

"Don't worry about it," Shirley advised. "As you get older, you grow less hair."

Marilyn looked stricken. "Everywhere?"

Shirley nodded. "Everywhere."

"Oh, my." Marilyn's gaze fell downward.

"If that bothers you, you can get a wig for your pubic hair," Shirley told them. "Something called a merkin."

Alice nearly spilled her drink. "You're kidding!"

Fascinated, Faye asked, "How does it work? I mean, wouldn't it come off during, um, any kind of friction? And for heaven's sake, how is it attached? You wouldn't want to use glue down there!"

Marilyn was scribbling into a small leather notebook. "I'll research it," she announced.

A young waitress appeared before them, holding out a doily-covered tray of pleated gray mollusks on beds of curly endive. "Marinated mussels?"

"God, no!" Alice barked, recoiling.

The four women burst out laughing, instant rapport zapping among them like a kind of electric shock.

Looking puzzled, the waitress moved away, while a group of the young and the beautiful cast curious looks at the four older women.

"Want to get out of here?" Alice asked.

"Yes!" Faye said.

"There's a bar just down the street—" Alice began.

"I don't do bars," Shirley interrupted. "I'm a recovering alcoholic."

"Fine," Faye told her. "Anyway, I'm starving."

Alice took charge. "Let's go to Legal Seafoods. Does everyone have her own car? Everyone know where the restaurant is?"

Everyone did. They made a dash for the elevator, giggling and knocking shoulders like schoolgirls sneaking out of class.

"Should we say good-bye to Eloise?" Marilyn whispered just before the doors slid shut.

"I don't think we need to," Faye said. "We've done our duty."

"Hey, I think we're past all that duty crap," Alice said, and the other women looked at her wide-eyed.

At the restaurant Alice requested a booth in the back, and the maitre d' led them to it. The ride in separate cars had cooled their initial affinity and at first, as they studied their menus and ordered, their conversation was stilted. They were, after all, nearly strangers.

Then Alice turned sideways, lifted the hem of her black silk jacket, took hold of the waistband of her trousers, and tugged with both hands. Fabric ripped.

"Are you crazy?" Shirley demanded. "That suit must have cost a thousand dollars!"

"More," Alice retorted calmly. She took a huge, belly-deep breath. "It has an elastic waist and I *still* couldn't breathe! One bite, and I'd pass out, hit my head on the table, and you'd be driving me to the ER."

Faye laughed. "I know just how you feel! Why is it that no matter how little I eat during the day, the jeans I can zip in the morning are tight in the afternoon and impossible by evening? I mean, what's the *purpose* of that?"

"I'm still having periods," Marilyn began timidly. "What's the purpose of that? I mean—"

She clamped her mouth shut as the waiter arrived to set their drinks before them: scotch and water for Alice, Perrier for Shirley, a margarita for Faye, and a daiquiri for Marilyn. Alice noticed Shirley chewing her lips as she studied the menu, and announced, "It's my treat tonight."

"That's not necessary," Faye protested.

"No, not necessary, but something I'd like to do, okay?"

"Well, thank you," Faye replied, and Shirley and Marilyn echoed her.

After the waiter went away with their orders, Alice raised her eyebrows at Marilyn. "Periods, still, huh. How old are you?"

"Fifty-two," Marilyn whispered.

"Honey, you're a baby," Alice told her. "I'm sixty-two."

"Sixty," said Shirley.

"Fifty-five," said Faye.

"Okay." Alice looked at Marilyn. "Go on."

"All right. I mean, talk about having no control! Sometimes my periods come every three weeks, sometimes every week! Sometimes they're light and last a few days, other times they're heavy and last three weeks. One day I looked down at my pad and nearly fainted. I thought I'd just lost my liver! So I have to wear Maxi Pads every day, but I have to anyway, because of the peeing thing."

"Incontinence." Alice nodded.

"I'm not *incontinent*!" Marilyn protested. "It's more complicated than that. It doesn't happen all the time, and if I really concentrate, sometimes I can control the leaking. But that requires a monumental effort of will, and that distracts me from my work. The other day I was straining so hard not to pee when I sneezed that I said Mercury, Mars, and *Penis*!"

Faye laughed. "I told someone my favorite Hitchcock film was *Rearview Mirror*."

Alice grinned. "I asked someone if they'd seen the *Vagina Monocles*."

Shirley played with her scarves. "That makes sense, in a way. You'd only need one eye to see inside a vagina."

With a tap of her spoon, Alice got them back on track. "Okay, fine, we all are experiencing minor brain blips, but losing that kind of control doesn't bother me as much as losing control of our lives."

"I agree." Faye sipped her drink, loving the instant hit. "I was thinking earlier tonight that I don't miss being sexy as much as I miss being interesting."

"Hey, we're still sexy!" Shirley protested. "I love sex more now than I did when I was twenty! Then all I could think about was whether I looked beautiful lying there with my knees up to my ears. Now I just turn off the lights."

"I agree that for women sex improves with age," Alice said. "If you can find a man who wants to have sex with you."

Marilyn sipped her drink, which seemed to give her courage. Chin high, she confessed, "I don't care about sex anymore. I'm all dried up down there. I feel sort of like a purse that's been zipped shut."

"But aren't you married?" Shirley nodded toward Marilyn's wedding ring.

"For thirty years. Theodore's a brilliant scientist, but too engrossed with his work to think much about sex." Tugging at the ring, she pulled it off and held it in her hand, a small empty circle. "It doesn't bother me, really, and it doesn't distress me that men don't flirt with me anymore." Dismissively, she slid the ring back on. "What *does* hurt is that I'm invisible to younger women. I've spent so many years learning hard lessons I'd love to pass on."

"Don't talk to me about younger women!" Alice growled. "I'm working with one since my company's merged, and she's about as respectful of my seniority as a Shetland pony is of a Clydesdale. In meetings, I *feel* like a Clydesdale—enormous, plodding, and fat-assed, while she frisks around on her pretty pony legs, shaking her fancy mane. "

"Ladies." The waiter appeared with their orders: salads or broiled fish for three of the women, chocolate cake for Shirley. Alice, Marilyn, and Faye stared at the dessert with surprise.

"Well," Shirley pointed out, "you are all

enjoying alcoholic drinks! I need *some* indulgence!"

"Is it as good as it looks?" Marilyn asked.

Shirley took a bite. A look of utter bliss crossed her face. "It is," she purred.

Three hands shot up in the air. "Waiter!" Alice called.

After they'd ordered their own cake, they concentrated on eating for a few moments, then Faye said, "Alice, about the woman in your office. She can't help it if she's young and pretty and energetic. We were all that way once, too."

"True. But we weren't able to walk right into positions then that young women hold now. Women of *our age* broke through the glass ceiling by bludgeoning their own heads against it. Now young women just swim upward without any problem, yet they don't even *notice* those of us who made it possible. Worse, they want to get rid of us so they can have our jobs."

"Is that what's going on with you?" Shirley asked.

"I'm afraid so." Alice nodded grimly and waved for the waiter. "Take my fish away and bring my cake, now."

"Me, too," echoed Marilyn and Faye.

"And I'll try your chocolate decadent pie,"

Shirley told the waiter. She caught the others' glances. "Hey, chocolate's good for you! Scientists have discovered three foods that keep you young. Fruit, alcohol, and chocolate. And I can't do alcohol!"

Marilyn's brow was furrowed. "You know, I have a problem with a young woman."

"Tell us," Alice urged.

Marilyn squirmed. "Because of Theodore's patented inventions, our family has, um, a fair amount of money. My son Teddy is a brilliant scientist, as his father is, and he's kind and good and funny. But he's not what you'd call conventionally handsome."

"That doesn't matter," Shirley countered. "Women aren't fussy about men's looks."

"I think you're right. But my sister Sharon, who visited recently, told me she doesn't believe my son's fiancée really loves him. Sharon's afraid Lila's marrying him for his money." Tears welled in Marilyn's eyes. "I don't know how to find out the truth! I'm better with dead bugs than with people!"

Shirley and Faye blinked.

"Maybe you'd better elaborate," Alice suggested.

"I mean I'm a paleobiologist. I study trilobites, bugs that lived millions of years ago."

Alice grimaced. *"Uh-huh."*

Faye shuddered.

The waiter set desserts before them. Everyone dug in, murmuring ecstatically.

"Now that I think about it," Faye said, pressing her napkin to her chocolate-rimmed lips, "a younger woman's playing havoc with *my* life! Or rather, with my daughter's."

"Tell us," Alice demanded.

Faye licked chocolate from her lips and put down her fork. "My daughter, Laura, has been married for a year to a wonderful young man, Lars Schneider. He's a lawyer, and absolutely adorable. Laura and Lars were meant for each other, you can tell by their names, for heaven's sake, and they've been so happy together. But then Laura had her baby four months ago, and now it seems that Lars is having an affair with a secretary in his office. Although I can't believe it of him."

"Maybe he's not," Shirley said hopefully.

"Maybe he is," Alice said cynically.

"Oh, dear," said Marilyn. "That's very sad." She took the last bite of her cake. "What else is on the dessert menu?"

They called the waiter over and ordered a chocolate brownie sundae each.

Faye turned to Shirley. "No younger women clouds on your horizon?"

"Nope. Just got the same old hassles—looking for a decent man and trying to pay my bills. Actually," she continued after another bite, "I do have a dream, and I suppose my predicament is, I'm afraid it will never come true."

"A dream!" Marilyn licked her lips. "How wonderful to have a dream at your age."

"Hey, come on!" Shirley said defensively, "I'm not dead yet. Listen, modern nutrition and medicine are prolonging our lives and improving the years we will have. If we keep active, we'll be leading healthy, happy lives in our eighties and nineties."

"Use it or lose it," Alice said.

"Exactly," Shirley agreed.

"Use it or lose it," Marilyn echoed dreamily. "I wonder if that's true about sexual desire."

"Honey, you can get it back," Shirley told her. "You just have to get in touch with yourself again."

"So to speak," Alice quipped dryly.

Marilyn blushed and quickly turned the attention back to Shirley. "What's your dream?"

Shirley sat up straight and adjusted the scarves around her shoulders. "I want to create my own little retreat. I'm a certified masseuse, but I've also studied and read about other kinds of alternative health possibilities, and I'm fascinated by the connection between body, mind, and soul. I want to create a place where people can come with all kinds of problems, from serious health issues to depression to the sort of thing you're talking about, Marilyn, the loss of sexual appetite. We'd work up each person's chart individually and create a program just for them, of massage, aromatherapy, hypnosis, yoga, dance, spiritual explorations, and so on."

"Sounds like a great idea," Faye said.

"It *is* a great idea." Shirley smiled, then sighed. "But, unfortunately, it will never happen."

"Why not?" Marilyn demanded.

"Because I don't have the money. Furthermore, I can plan the retreat, but I'm hopeless at things like legal contracts and bank loans and malpractice insurance. My eyes just cross when I try to read financial documents."

"I think," Alice announced slowly, thinking it out as she spoke, "there's a way we can help one another."

"Really?" Marilyn took off her glasses and stared.

"I need a piece of paper." Alice dug in her purse, retrieving a small leather notebook and a Mont Blanc pen. "And another round of chocolate."

Only one other chocolate dessert was listed on the menu, a chocolate raspberry torte. "Let's each get one," Shirley suggested.

"All right," Alice announced, her pen flashing as she wrote, "we've got four problems. Faye, you want to know whether your son-in-law's having an affair with a secretary at his law firm."

"Right. Jennifer D'Annucio."

"Fine. Shirley, you need help with legal and financial matters."

"Right."

"Third, I want to find out whether the little brat in my office is after my job. And fourth, you, Marilyn, want to know whether or not your son's fiancée—"

"Lila Eastbrook."

"Lila Eastbrook?" Faye interrupted. "She can't be after your son for his money. I mean, the Eastbrook Clinic and Spa are famous!"

"Yeah, and the U.S. government once had a surplus." Alice kept scribbling. "Look, we can each solve someone else's problem. Let's consider the possibilities."

"Oh, this is fun!" Faye cried, fishing an ice cube out of her water glass and rubbing it along her neck, which had suddenly turned red. Seeing the others look at her, she explained, "Hot flash."

"That's it," Alice said. "That's what we are, the Hot Flash Club." She speared a piece of chocolate cake on the end of her fork and lifted it into the air. "A toast, to the Hot Flash Club."

The other three stabbed up a piece of chocolate cake. Tapping them together, they echoed, "To the Hot Flash Club!"

"Ladies"—Alice grinned roguishly—"let's plot."

10

Saturday night, Alice, Shirley, and Faye had ordained that before Marilyn could execute her assignment for the Hot Flash Club, she had to change her image. *Completely.*

Faye had agreed to shepherd Marilyn through Parts One and Two of her transformation. Shirley and Alice both had to work and weren't able to come along, which was fine with Marilyn, who found Faye, of the three other women, most like herself. Shirley, with her violet eye shadow and spangles, was rather startling, while Alice, beautiful, arrogant, and outspoken, terrified Marilyn a bit.

But she trusted their judgment, and so here Marilyn was on Monday morning, sitting in the ophthalmologist's chair, holding her ancient tortoiseshell glasses in her hands while she gazed at her reflection through her new contact lenses.

She was excited and terrified. She felt like a

tiny gastropod being swept away from the sheltered cove of her tidy life in a flash flood of enthusiasm toward—what, exactly? She had no idea. But she'd always enjoyed the challenge of research and discovery, so she tried to think of her own life as a research project, and this gave her courage.

Blinking, she tucked the glasses in her purse and went out to the parking lot where Faye waited, as she'd promised she would be, in her dark green BMW.

"You look great! Your beautiful green eyes look huge now!" Faye told her, as Marilyn slid into the car. "How do the lenses feel?"

"Fine, I guess," Marilyn said. "It's amazing, how little I notice them, and I can see perfectly well."

"Good. On to the hairdresser's." Faye steered the car out of the lot and out into the flow of traffic. Her silver-white hair was caught up in a simple chignon.

"I'm a little anxious about changing my hair," Marilyn confessed meekly.

Faye glanced over with a smile. "Only natural. How long has it been since you've had your hair styled?"

Marilyn cringed as she admitted, "Um, I don't think I've ever had it *styled*. I used to try to curl it, decades ago—"

"Well, who cuts it?" Faye asked.

"I do."

"*You* do!"

"I just pull it over my shoulder and snip off a few inches with my desk scissors whenever it seems to be getting too long."

"Oh, my. Ricky's going to love getting his hands on you."

But the first thing the hairdresser did when Faye and Marilyn walked into the salon was to clap his hands against his face in a gesture of horror.

"¡Madre de Dio!" he cried, circling Marilyn. "Where have you been hiding, under a rock?"

All the other people in the shop turned to gawk at her, but Marilyn liked that he said *rock*, as if he'd received a subliminal message about her profession and passion. "Um, yes, in a way."

Clad in tight black trousers and a black silk shirt open to the waist, Ricky vibrated slightly, like a flamenco dancer ready to spin her off in a tango. And he did take her by the shoulders to guide her, through a haze of perfumes and a glitter of mirrors, into a pink chair. Settling her there, he began to pull out the bobby pins and rubber band that anchored her bun to her head. As her hair fell down around her face, he ran his hands through it.

"Look at thees hair!" he scolded. "Look at thees split ends!" He seemed about to weep. "And look! Eet's all jagged!" Frowning, he demanded, "Have you been cutting your own hair with desk scissors?"

Marilyn nodded, chagrined and yet pleased he was so perceptive. She appreciated professional acumen.

"Aiieeyy," the hairdresser moaned, waving his hands.

"Ricky." Faye intervened, stepping forward. "Marilyn is a professor. She teaches at MIT. She's well respected and very intelligent, and she's never needed to look anything but academic for years. But now she wants to change. That's why we came to you."

Ricky patted his chest, calming down. "Thank God you did!" He ran his hands through Marilyn's hair again. "You have nice thick hair," he decided. "We can do something weeth eet."

"Color it," Faye told him.

"Yes, of course. And I'll style eet. Something easy to care for, I assume?"

"Absolutely," Marilyn agreed.

"Look," Faye said. "I'm going off to do some shopping. I'll be back in a couple of hours."

"Fine," Marilyn said. She allowed herself to

be led off to a cubicle to change into a pink smock. Then she lay back with her head in a sink, closed her eyes, and surrendered herself to the ministrations of strangers.

As Ricky and his elves flitted around her with their bottles, elixirs, brushes, foils, and clips, Marilyn drifted into a reverie, remembering years ago, when her hair was still a deep natural auburn. Theodore had told her to stop wrapping it around fat plastic rollers, trying to make it curl or bounce. "You're just wasting your time," he'd said. "Don't try to look glamorous. You're not the glamorous type."

He hadn't meant to be cruel, simply factual, and back then, when Teddy was an energetic toddler and Theodore worked late at his lab and Marilyn was struggling to write her doctoral dissertation on *Light Isotopes in Phosphatic Fossils,* she'd been so overwhelmed, exhausted, and occupied that she'd received Theodore's verdict with, if not pleasure, certainly relief. It was easy to yank her hair back into a rubber band and skewer the bun to the back of her head where it stayed as she chased after her little boy, and cooked, and cleaned, and did laundry, and sat up late at night bent over her books.

The years had flown by. Teddy grew into a brilliant, curious, optimistic boy who loved playing with microscopes, just like his parents. Theodore taught at MIT and worked on his private research. Marilyn was awarded her Ph.D. and offered a tenured position in the paleobiology department at MIT, and even though Theodore, over in the molecular genetics department, insisted she was given the job in order to keep *him* happy, she ascertained through the way the other professors treated her that she was respected in her field. Certainly her papers were published in scientific journals as often as Theodore's. And her courses were always *packed* with students. In fact, this year she'd taken a sabbatical from teaching, simply to allow herself time to catch her breath and concentrate fully on her own laboratory work with her own fossils.

Ricky's voice brought her back to the present. "Ees okay now to open your eyes."

The tone of his voice telegraphed his delight. She opened her eyes.

At that moment, Faye swept into the salon, a shopping bag in each hand. "Oh, my heavens!" she cried. "Marilyn, I never would have recognized you!"

Staring at her reflection in the mirror, Marilyn was startled into speechlessness. Her new glossy, coppery hair fell about her face in a shaggy jumble ending just below her ears.

Bangs covered up the wrinkles on her forehead. Her eyes looked bigger, her cheekbones more pronounced.

"You look twenty years younger!" Faye exclaimed. "Ricky, it's a miracle!"

"Yes," Ricky agreed, modestly clasping his hands in front of him. "Eet ees."

Faye bent over Marilyn. "Do you like it?"

"I don't know. It's so different."

"*Now*," Ricky announced with a flourish, gesturing toward another cubicle, "for the makeup!"

"Oh, no, please," Marilyn pleaded. "I never could comprehend cosmetics."

"Eet will be simple," Ricky promised. "A little mascara, a little blusher, some leepstick."

"Think of it as a scientific experiment," Faye suggested.

It was after six when Ricky finished. As Faye drove toward Legal Seafoods, Marilyn flipped down the visor and stared into the mirror, completely fascinated by her new self.

"You *are* pleased, aren't you?" Faye asked. "I do hope you are. I know it's unsettling, looking so very different, but trust me, the change is marvelous."

Marilyn nodded.

Still, as they entered the restaurant and walked through the crowded room toward the other two women, already seated at a table, Marilyn felt people's eyes on her. This was new, and unsettling. She was afraid she'd trip over her own feet or clumsily bump into a table. The desire to be invisible resurfaced from her adolescent years as powerfully as ever.

Shirley jumped up, crying, "Jeez Louise, Marilyn, look at you!"

Marilyn wanted to shove the other woman under the table out of sight—and crawl under there with her.

"Don't make a scene," Alice hissed, yanking Shirley back into her chair. "But the change is awesome," Alice continued, as Faye and Marilyn sat down. "And I use that word deliberately."

The waiter arrived, took their orders, and left.

"Let me see what shades of lipstick you bought," Shirley told Marilyn.

"Um, all right." Marilyn brought out her cute little pink-striped cosmetic bag, which, she discovered to her surprise, excited the interest of the other three women as much as a collection of crustaceans would a scientist.

"Those shades are perfect for your complexion," Alice said. "You look beautiful, Marilyn."

"Oh, well, maybe not *beautiful*." Marilyn squirmed, uncomfortable with compliments; they'd been so rare in her life. She missed having her tortoiseshell glasses to fiddle with and gnaw on.

"The way you look now? I guarantee Barton Baker will come on to you," Alice said.

Marilyn chewed her lip. "I don't know. Maybe I do look *better*. But I still don't know how to attract men. The very thought of *trying* to flirt makes me break out in hives!"

"You don't have to *flirt*, honey," Shirley assured her. "Just be friendly, and interested, and caring."

"Just *listen* to him," Alice continued. "He's new to Boston. The company's a minefield since the merger. He might want to talk about Alison Cummings."

"Be *maternal*," Shirley suggested.

Marilyn turned to Shirley gratefully. "What a good idea! I can do *maternal*."

"Now," Alice decreed as their meals were set before them. "For the rest of us."

Relieved to have the attention turned away from her, Marilyn tucked her cosmetic bag into her purse. She noticed how Alice could eat with her left hand and flip through the pages of her notebook with her right, a multitasking skill Marilyn had also developed during the evolution of her career.

Alice said, "Okay. First. Marilyn said the Eastbrooks are advertising for a new housekeeper." She pointed her fork at Faye. "Did you find the ad in the Sunday *Boston Globe*?"

Faye nodded. "I did. I phoned this morning. I've got an appointment to interview for the job on Thursday afternoon."

Marilyn slid a folder toward Faye. "I spoke with Frances Corbett. She's an old friend of mine from college. I told her about my suspicions about Teddy's fiancée. Frances's own wealth has acquainted her with gold diggers, so she said she'd be delighted to help. She promised to give 'Faye Van Dyke' a glowing testimonial if Mrs. Eastbrook calls."

"Fabulous." Faye glanced at the names of her references, then put the folder in her purse. "I'll add this to 'Mrs. Van Dyke's' résumé. A friend of mine, Helen Westchester, also agreed to be a reference, and with Alice's name, that ought to do it."

Alice was squinting at Faye. "Don't wear that suit to the interview. It's too well cut."

"Oh, I know," Faye agreed. Nodding toward her shopping bags, she said, "I bought a few less expensive outfits for the job."

"Good. You've got to look cultured, but financially distressed." Alice checked her notes. "Now, Marilyn, I've made some phone calls about the Eastbrook Clinic," Alice continued, "and everything seems in apple pie order. More clients than they can handle, lots of celebrities, and the Eastbrooks have been generous with charities even during the stock decline, so I can't believe they're in financial difficulties. But you never know what people are hiding."

"If I get the housekeeper's job," Faye cut in, "I'll find out."

"Good." Alice made a check on her list. "Marilyn, you're filling the position as my temporary secretary, which will enable you to infiltrate the new group and find out what Alison is up to."

Marilyn said briskly, "Right."

Alice made another check. "Shirley. I'm helping you with your business planning."

"Yes, and my assignment's to find out whether or not Faye's son-in-law is having an affair." Shirley cleared her throat. "I've come up with two ideas. Well, two variations on one idea: I can offer either Lars Schneider—that's his name, right, Faye?"

"Right."

"—a series of free massages. Or I can offer them to Jennifer D'Annucio."

"How?" Alice asked. "You don't know them."

"Easy," Shirley told her. "I'll tell them their name was entered in a drawing in a store like Filene's or CVS, and she, or he, won."

"Offer it to Jennifer," Faye suggested. "Men are less likely to want massages, I think."

"The kind you offer, anyway," Alice remarked dryly.

"Besides," Faye said, "I don't know how Lars would find the time to have a massage. He works twelve hours a day for the firm."

"That's horrible," Shirley said.

"It's typical," Faye assured her, "for young lawyers trying to make their way in corporate law. Plus, Jack, my husband, Laura's father, was one of the founders and senior partners of the firm, so Lars has a lot to live up to. My husband was brilliant."

Alice asked, "Is Lars?"

"Jack thought he was." Faye thought about it. "He's smart, clever, industrious, but I'm not sure how ambitious he is. I think he went into corporate law because of his admiration for Jack."

"How does he find time to have an affair?" Marilyn wondered aloud.

"Well, Jennifer D'Annucio's the receptionist for the firm," Faye said. "He sees her every day."

"Yeah," Alice added, "and Lars probably feels a woman who works where he does understands the stresses and pressures better than his wife."

"I suppose that's true," Faye agreed. "Laura says they haven't been talking much since the baby was born. When they do talk, it's about Megan—how much weight she's gained, the color of her poop, that sort of thing."

Shirley said, "Well, I'll learn what kind of free time Jennifer has and what she's doing with it."

"Great." With a flourish, Alice slammed her notebook shut. "We're organized."

"Dessert, anyone?" Faye asked.

"Not for me," Alice said. "Not for any of us," she added, checking her watch. "We still have to help Marilyn choose her new wardrobe."

They left the restaurant and whipped to the other end of the mall to Lord & Taylor, which was open until nine. Alice led them to the Better Clothes section, where, it seemed to Marilyn, the other three women fell into a kind of trance, drifting along through the racks of dresses as if stoned on the store's soft music and perfume.

"I feel like Margaret Mead visiting New Guinea," Marilyn whispered.

Shirley quirked an eyebrow. "Lord & Taylor's makes you think of New Guinea?"

Marilyn shook her head. "No, no, I mean, I feel like I'm discovering a tribe with completely different customs from my own."

"Marilyn"—Faye laughed—"your tribe is the female, and believe me, shopping is a universal female instinct."

"With the occasional exception." Shirley looked pointedly at Marilyn.

Alice scrutinized Marilyn. "You're a size ten, so you'll be easy to fit. I suggest we each choose a few outfits for Marilyn to try on. The look should be businesslike, but with sex appeal. Let's meet back here in fifteen minutes."

"Cool!" Shirley said. "It's like a scavenger hunt!"

The other three women vanished among the racks of clothing. Marilyn stood alone and uncertain, in her plaid skirt and blazer, which were perfectly serviceable and had been for years. Think *sexy*, she urged her brain.

Timidly, Marilyn forced herself to move through the racks. Her parents had both been academicians. Her father had loved her mother faithfully for fifty years of marriage, and her mother wore the same sorts of things Marilyn did. She wished her sister Sharon were with her—no, she didn't! Sharon would fall on the floor in a laughing fit if she knew Marilyn was going to try to look *sexy*.

This was so *hard*. But she did like her new hairstyle. And she felt a definite obligation to the group, especially since Faye was going to so much trouble to find out about Lila Eastbrook. Marilyn squinched up her eyes, concentrating.

Fifteen minutes later, she met the other three outside the dressing rooms. Their arms were laden with clothing for Marilyn. They each took a cubicle, hung up their selections, then gathered outside Marilyn's stall.

"Don't try anything on yet, Marilyn," Alice called. "Let's see what you've got, first."

"Um, okay." Marilyn shoved the curtain aside. She took a hanger off the hook and held out a formfitting fuchsia crocheted dress with a halter top and a lace-up back.

"You've got to be kidding," Alice said.

"You said sexy!" Marilyn protested. "Isn't this sexy?"

"Perhaps too sexy for an office," Faye

gently intervened, removing the offending garment. "What else, Marilyn?"

Meekly, Marilyn held up a black gauze top with a plunging neckline and ribbed black trousers with tiers of ruffles at the ankles.

Shirley choked, snorted, and turned away.

"What?" Marilyn demanded.

Faye asked, "Anything else?"

Marilyn brought out her final selection, leopard skin capris with a leopard skin, off-the-shoulder, spandex top.

Alice closed her eyes, leaned against the wall, and muttered a prayer.

"Great!" Faye chirped, wrenching the hanger from Marilyn's hand. "Now, let's see what *we've* chosen for you."

The three other women presented her with a variety of skirts, slacks, and silk tees in harmonizing shades of browns and grays. None of them had plunging necklines or ruffles, none was spandex or body-hugging.

"I don't understand," Marilyn complained, sliding into a pair of loose silk trousers. "I thought you said I should look sexy."

"In an understated way," Alice snapped. "Not like someone applying at Hooters."

Marilyn sighed as she pulled on a loose, silk, long-sleeved shirt. "I'm too old to be sexy, aren't I?"

"Of course not!" Shirley retorted. "I'm older than you are, and *I'm* sexy."

"It's a matter of environment," Faye explained. "Looking *appropriate* for your environment. For TransWorld, you need to look alluring, but elegant." She stepped back, appraising Marilyn. "Well, hey! You look *great* in that. You're so lucky to be so slim."

"Your shoulders are hunched," Shirley told Marilyn. "You need to work on your posture."

Something in Marilyn snapped. "Well, *you* have a whisker on your chin!"

"I do?" Shirley nudged Marilyn aside, to get closer to the fitting room mirror. "Jeez Louise, will you look at that, I do have a whisker. Does anyone have tweezers?"

Faye dug in her purse and handed Shirley her tweezers. Shirley bent toward the glass.

"I thought you said we grew less hair as we grew older," Marilyn reminded Shirley accusingly.

"True," Shirley answered, without moving her lips, concentrating on catching the whisker. "Less hair where we want it. But we do start getting whiskers where we don't want them."

Alice laughed. "I found a whisker on my left breast last week."

"Eeek!" Marilyn cried, lifting the silk top so she could survey her breasts.

"Don't take that top off," Faye cried. "It looks fabulous on you!"

"I agree." Alice looked at her watch. "Marilyn, if you buy those four trousers, and those four tops, and those four jackets, you'll by able to mix and match them any way you want, and look great every time."

"You're right!" Faye flipped through their selections. "Aren't we all clever!"

"Wait!" Shirley cried. "Buy, this, too, Marilyn." She handed her a long swath of lime green. "Toss this over your shoulders. It will give you flash."

11

The Eastbrook mansion towered on a hill in a bucolic suburb thirty miles west of Boston. The drive, thick with pebbles white as snowflakes, led between stone pillars supporting stone urns, around the house to a fountain centered in a parking circle, and back around the other side of the house to complete the loop.

Down the hill, roof just visible from its shelter of birches and spruce, was the Eastbrook Clinic, with its three operating rooms, where wealthy clients paid fortunes to have their faces sculpted, their asses hoisted, and their tummies and backs vacuumed of fat. They recovered in the Eastbrook Spa, a cluster of low white buildings surrounding a courtyard where they could lie on long chairs listening to the melody of the fountain, smelling the multitude of flowers, always present, fresh every day. Elsewhere on the grounds, secluded among trees, were garages for various cars and quarters for some of the staff.

It was in the elegant white French Provincial mansion that Eugenie Eastbrook had her own office. She'd suggested during their telephone conversation that Faye drive around to the back of the house, which would make it easy for her to come to the staff entrance at the back hall. Accordingly, it was there, on Thursday morning, Faye knocked.

Eugenie Eastbrook herself greeted Faye at the front door. For one icy instant, Mrs. Eastbrook scanned Faye up and down. Faye held her breath. Then Mrs. Eastbrook delivered a frosty smile and invited Faye to follow her.

Down a narrow carpeted hall they went, through a door, into the front of the house, a world of pastels, gilt mirrors, chandeliers, and an atmosphere of such serenity Faye wondered if they'd found a way to distill Valium and steam it into the air.

Mrs. Eastbrook's office opened on to the main entrance hall, with doors, discreetly camouflaged by murals, to the living room on one side and to the housekeeper's office on the other. Like the rest of the exquisitely maintained home, this room was decorated, carpeted, and draped in a luminously floral plush luxury Marie Antoinette would have appreciated.

"Beautiful room," Faye murmured.

"Thank you." Mrs. Eastbrook settled behind the delicate ivory desk whose curved legs, inlaid with gilt rosettes, supported a crystal-and-ebony desk set and a state-of-the-art computer. "You brought references?" She held out her hand.

Faye took a sheaf of papers from her purse and gave them to Mrs. Eastbrook, who slipped on her glasses and read.

In the striped silk lute-back chair facing the desk, Faye waited quietly, hands in her lap, ankles crossed in a ladylike manner, covertly scrutinizing Mrs. Eastbrook.

She was a petite woman, and exquisitely beautiful, with large blue eyes and straight blond hair falling crisply just to her collar. She had to be somewhere between forty and fifty, for her daughter Lila was twenty-three, but her skin stretched blandly over her bones, erasing the years. No wrinkle marked her smooth forehead, thanks, Faye assumed, to an injection of botulism, and her lips had the youthful pout of someone recently injected with collagen. She was, of course, thin.

Faye wasn't slender, but she did look *appropriate* in her modest gray suit, low court heels, and single string of pearls. Her white hair, in its usual chignon, was correct. The suit didn't fit as well as her clothes usually did, because in real life, for an occasion of any importance, she used a dressmaker who altered everything exactly. But here she was not supposed to look like someone who could afford to have her clothing perfectly fitted. She was supposed to look like an educated, dignified, and slightly impoverished woman who had worked all her life, and Faye felt she'd accomplished that when she bought the taupe pantsuit with its blessed elastic waist and slimming thigh-length jacket.

Beneath the jacket, Faye's heart did the salsa. Her hands were clammy. Monday night, in the company of the others, Faye had felt brave, even lighthearted. She thought it was rather like joining the CIA but without the danger. But now that she was actually here, under a false name, talking to a real person, her nerves shot hot flashes through her body, one after the other, like Roman candles.

Eugenie Eastbrook murmured, "You worked for thirteen years for the Maine Corbetts."

Faye nodded. "Yes."

Eugenie looked up. "I like that. It speaks

well that you stayed with one family for so long."

"Frances Corbett wanted me to go with her when her parents died, but I preferred to stay in the East," Faye said.

"I see. Well, now." Mrs. Eastbrook leaned back in her leather desk chair. "My husband, as you know, is a plastic surgeon, and the director of the clinic. My daughter and I share the duties of supervising the offices and staff. The housekeeper's duties are confined to the house. We need it to run smoothly, always. We often hold dinner parties for prospective clients to meet satisfied patrons, and occasionally we have potential clients as guests in this house. It goes without saying that discretion is of the utmost importance."

Faye said, "Of course."

"This establishment must run like clockwork," Eugenie Eastbrook said.

"I understand," Faye replied.

"My family works six days a week and are on call for seven." Eugenie Eastbrook punched out her words in sharp verbal bullets. "From time to time your duties will intersect with those of the spa and clinic. The housekeeper must liaise with me, the cook, two maids, two chauffeurs. She must be able to perform some secretarial functions—you do know how to use a computer."

"I do."

"She must be capable of giving orders without hesitation and of receiving orders without resentment. She must look appropriate at all times."

Faye said, "I understand."

"Well, Faye, it looks like you might be just the right person for the job. Can you start right away?"

"Yes."

"Excellent." She rose. "Let me give you a tour of the house."

Faye followed her prospective employer out of the office into the hall, her heels sinking into the plush carpet. It was like walking on marshmallows. The thought made her stomachs perk up.

"Living room, dining room, my office, housekeeper's office, pantry, kitchen, back stairs, elevator," Eugenie Eastbrook announced briskly. "Housekeeper uses back stairs or elevator."

The same plush carpet covered the second floor, except for the bathrooms, which were floored with ceramic tile, all shining. In the master bedroom, a Hispanic maid was making the bed.

"This is Julia," Eugenie Eastbrook announced. "Julia, this is Mrs. Van Dyke, who will be our new housekeeper."

Julia nodded and returned to her work. Her employer ushered Faye through the rest of the bedrooms and the large linen room, where the ironing board, towels, sheets, pillows, quilts, and other household necessities were kept. They returned to the first floor by way of the carpeted front stairs, which curved gracefully down to the entrance hall.

"This is the housekeeper's office." Eugenie Eastbrook threw open a door.

Faye followed the other woman into a small, tidy room, complete with desk, computer, filing cabinets, and a phone with a score of speed-dial buttons.

"This door," Eugenie Eastbrook said, "leads into my office, which, although open during the day, is full of private and confidential information and must be off-limits to almost everyone. At night I lock it."

"I see."

"The housekeeper would enter her office," Eugenie Eastbrook continued, "either directly through this door from the kitchen or the main door from the hall. You only enter my office through this internal door at my request."

"Of course," Faye said.

"All the staff's quarters are out in staff houses on the grounds, except for the housekeeper's, for obvious reasons. These are the housekeeper's rooms."

They had arrived at the far end of the hall. Faye stepped through a door and made a quick glance around the suite: bedroom, sitting room, and bath, pristine and perfectly equipped.

Politely, she murmured, "Very nice."

Mrs. Eastbrook did an about-face that would have impressed a Marine and stalked back to her own office, where she grabbed up a cluster of keys. "One of the housekeeper's responsibilities is to ensure, every night before retiring, that all the doors on this floor are locked."

"Very well."

"I must stress, Mrs. Van Dyke, how essential discretion and security are to this household."

"I understand."

"Unscrupulous journalists have tried to enter this house, hoping to discover the identity of some of our clients. We must be on guard at all times."

"Of course."

Just then the door opened. A gorgeous young woman walked in, her blond hair tumbling down her back, her eyes bright blue, her smile as fresh as summer. No plastic surgery needed there.

"This is my daughter, Lila," Eugenie said. "Lila is my assistant here. Everything I know, she knows; if she asks you to do something, you can assume it came from me. Lila, this is Faye Van Dyke."

Faye smiled. "Hello, Lila." Something about Lila reminded her of her own daughter, perhaps simply the glow of youth. Catching the frown on Eugenie Eastbrook's face, she remembered who she was supposed to be, and added quickly, "Or would you prefer me to call you Miss Eastbrook?"

Lila's mother answered. "Miss Eastbrook. And I am Mrs. Eastbrook. And of course you will call my husband Dr. Eastbrook. We will call you Mrs. Van Dyke. We find this formality preserves a professional tone that is reassuring to our clients."

"Of course." Faye had chosen the pseudonym; it was close enough to her real last name to feel right.

"I believe that's everything then," Mrs. Eastbrook announced. Eugenie handed her a thick folder. "Why don't you read this contract and sign the privacy clause. You'll move in tomorrow, and report here, to my office, at eight o'clock Wednesday morning."

"Very well," Faye said.

She rose. "Welcome aboard, Mrs. Van Dyke."

"Thank you." Faye rose, and shook Mrs. Eastbrook's hand. Mrs. Eastbrook escorted her down the long hall to the staff's door at the back of the house.

On the white circle drive waited her rented Toyota, appropriate for her "new" life. Faye sank into it gratefully. Her suit was drenched with sweat, her limbs trembling with adrenaline, her heart still popping off rockets. She drove away from the house. At the end of the drive, she began to grin. When she reached the highway, she burst out laughing.

12

Most people who entered the offices of the senior executives of the Trans-World Insurance Corporation in downtown Boston were intimidated. That, of course, was the intention. Sleek, glossy, high-tech, the offices were meant to transmit an instantaneous message of power and wealth, just as the enormous windows that walled the corner of Alice's office provided a view of what looked very much like the entire world.

But as Marilyn Becker established herself in the handsome ebony-and-teak office just outside Alice's own, it didn't occur to her to be impressed. Why should an expensive office in a multibillion-dollar international insurance corporation intimidate her? MIT didn't. Nobel Prize–winning scientists didn't. Nothing in the world seemed significant compared to trilobites, those cockroachlike creatures who lived in the earth's mud almost 400 million years ago, who called this planet home for more than 300 million years. They saw continents stir, glaciers clash, volcanoes spew. Compared to that, the human race with all its egotism was little more than the wink of a trilobite's calcite eye.

Marilyn mused on her beloved trilobites while acquainting herself with the piles of folders on the secretary's desk and the files on her computer. At the moment the noncontributory defined benefit retirement plans for what had been TransContinent had to be costed out and scheduled for the newly enlarged company, and possible plans for overseas companies had to be developed and plotted and costed out. That meant gathering actuarial assumptions from various countries, which meant in turn piles of paper and computerized graphs.

It would be a breeze. All these figures were negligible compared to those of paleobiology.

The hardest thing so far that day had been dealing with the damned green scarf Shirley had insisted she wear. Marilyn dutifully wore it to work, sat down at her desk with it fluttering around her, took out a pen, and shut the scarf in her desk drawer, nearly decapitating herself. She removed it immediately.

Now a movement on the computer screen caught her eye—it was her own reflection, ghostlike in the background. It gave Marilyn the strangest impulse. She wanted to take her new compact mirror out of her purse and just gawk at herself. She forced herself to work.

"Hello."

Marilyn looked up. A man stood smiling at her. He had a thatch of black hair that he wore in a kind of scramble, just like hers. This made him look young, but Marilyn guessed this was Barton Baker, Alison Cummings's secretary, who was—Marilyn had read his personnel file—forty-five. His wool suit and pale blue shirt looked hand-tailored to fit his trim hips, muscular chest, and broad shoulders. He was a stunning specimen of *Homo sapiens*.

"Hello," she replied.

He arched an eyebrow. "I heard Alice had a new secretary. I'm Barton Baker. Alison Cummings's executive secretary."

Marilyn shook his hand. "Marilyn Becker." At his touch, something warm surged through her—the infamous hot flash, no doubt.

"Alice's executive secretary?" He lounged against the wall.

"Perhaps. I'm here on a trial basis. For a month."

"Good luck," Barton said.

"I'm going to need it?" Marilyn asked.

Glancing at the closed office door, Barton

leaned close and confided, "She's a smart woman, and principled, but she's got all the personal warmth of an armadillo."

Marilyn smiled at the image. She liked armadillos quite a lot—they were vaguely related to trilobites, but Barton Baker probably didn't know that.

"But to be fair," Barton continued, "it's got to be hard to be a woman, and an African-American, and a vice president in this business. Anyway, I think you'll like it here. Did she show you where the TransWorld restaurant is? It's less expensive than going out."

"She told me I could find directions in the employees' handbook. She takes her lunch in her office while she works."

"Why don't I come back about twelve-thirty and take you down myself? It's cafeteria style, but the food's excellent."

"That would be nice," Marilyn replied coolly.

As Barton walked away, she caught herself staring at his shoulders, and his back, and his tight, taut butt. Butt! She thought *butt*! This man made her have thoughts like that? Should she have lunch with him?

Of course she could! She was a grown-up. She was *maternal*. What could possibly go wrong?

13 ALICE

Shirley lived in Somerville, one of the urban suburbs just across the Charles River from Boston. Friday evening, Alice drove through the maze of one-way streets, through "squares" without trees, benches, or right angles, past triple-decker houses jammed along narrow car-crammed streets, until she turned onto an avenue of modest single-family dwellings with driveways, garages, lawns, and cheerful beds of daffodils and tulips.

She didn't need to use Shirley's directions anymore. Shirley's house *had* to be the one with the WELCOME banner appliquéd with enormous violets hanging above the purple front door, the window boxes bobbing with pansies, the wind chimes made of glittering beads and colorful painted metal angels, and the hand-painted purple mailbox swinging from a nail.

Alice sighed. She'd had a tough day at the

office, she had a pile of defined benefit post-retirement plans in her briefcase to read over the weekend, and she wasn't exactly eager to spend time with Shirley, who seemed to Alice to be rather ditzy and certainly not the best candidate for owning her own business. But she'd agreed to the conditions of the HFC, and she was going to do her part and do it well, because, dammit, that was what Alice Murray was all about.

She knocked on the purple door.

"Hello!" Shirley said with a big bright grin on her face. "Come in!"

Alice stepped inside. "Well," she said, looking around at the candles, pillows, crystals, and Buddhas. "What an amazing room."

"Thanks," Shirley said, taking the remark as a compliment. "Sit down, won't you? I've made us some Red Zinger tea."

"Red Zinger?" Alice repeated warily. She'd never heard of such a thing. If it was anything like this room, it was probably hallucinogenic.

"It's made from hibiscus, rose hips, and lemongrass," Shirley told her. "It promotes energy and—"

"I'd prefer a scotch," Alice said. "I've had a hard day."

"I'm sorry, but I don't keep any alcohol in the house. I'm in AA."

"That's right. How long?"

"Twenty years."

"Impressive," Alice said, and she *was* impressed. She knew from life with Mack how hard it was for an alcoholic to stay sober. In Mack's case, it had been impossible. "In that case, tea will be fine."

"Great."

Shirley poured the ruby liquid into a purple mug. A great many things in Shirley's house were purple.

Alice sipped the tea. It was hot and thin. "I think we should get started," she decided. "Why don't you show me your office."

"My office?" Shirley laughed. "Honey, I don't have an *office*."

"I understood you run your business from your home."

"I do. Let me show you."

Alice set her teacup on the table and followed Shirley down the hall.

Shirley opened the door. "This is my massage studio."

The room was small but, unlike the living room, so free of clutter it felt spacious. A massage table stood in the middle, on an imitation Oriental rug. Instead of curtains, vertical white blinds filtered the early-evening sunlight into stripes that shaded and illuminated the posters on the wall. There were colored charts of "pressure points" on the feet, the muscular system of the body, and something called chakras. A single chair sat in the corner next to a small table, which held a CD player, a stack of CDs, and many vials of oils and lotions.

"Have you ever had a massage?" Shirley inquired.

"No."

"You should try one sometime. I'll give you one."

"How much do you charge?"

"It depends. For new clients, eighty-five for an hour."

"Good. Where do you keep your records?"

"In the kitchen. I don't like anything like that in this room, it might disturb the karma."

"Right. Okay, let's go to the kitchen."

Shirley led Alice into a clean, bright, and lavender, but surprisingly uncluttered, kitchen.

"Sit down." Shirley gestured to a chair next to a small desk and pulled a kitchen chair over to face her. "After a massage, after the client is dressed, I bring her in here and give her a full glass of water. That carries off the toxins released in the massage."

"Never mind about that. Let's focus on the business side of your work."

"Uh, okay. Let's see. Then I ask her—or him—if she wants to come the same time next week, and mark it on this calendar."

"Then you take the payment?" Alice pulled a pad of paper and a calculator from her purse.

"Right."

"And you give a receipt."

"Um, no. Why would I do that?"

"Well, for tax-keeping purposes, for one."

"Taxes! I hate taxes!"

"We all hate taxes, but we still have to pay them." Alice peered worriedly at the other woman. "You *do* pay income tax, don't you?"

"Of course." Shirley shifted nervously on her chair. "A friend helps me."

"This friend told you that you can deduct part of your mortgage and utilities because you run a business in your house?"

Shirley bit her lip. "Someone told me about that, but the thing is, I don't want anyone from the IRS to come check up on me. It would ruin the karma of my house."

Alice took a deep breath. "Okay, let's come at this from another angle. How many massages do you do a week?"

"Between fifteen and twenty."

Alice clicked her calculator. "So you make between sixty-six thousand and eighty-eight thousand dollars a year?"

Shirley gawked. "God, I wish! How did you get to that amount?"

"If you charge eighty-five for a session, times fifteen a week, times fifty-two weeks in a year—"

Shirley laughed. "Wait! I don't charge eighty-five for *every* session!"

"Why not?"

"Well, um, some clients can't afford that much. And some of the others have been with me for a long time, so I have to charge them what we started with."

"Why?"

"Why have they been with me for a long time?"

"Why do you have to accept the original fee?"

"Well"—Shirley's forehead wrinkled as she concentrated—"because I'm doing the same thing I've always done?"

"You're also eating the same food you've always eaten—"

"Not really. I've gotten much more organic—"

"The point is, Shirley," Alice snapped, "even though you're giving the same service, you have to adjust for inflation. If the fuel you use to heat the room where you give your massages cost you ten dollars ten years ago and twenty dollars now, you need to double your rates to help offset the increase in what you pay."

Shirley looked blank.

"Shirley." Alice sighed, shaking her head. "How could you possibly think you could run an entire business?"

Shirley crossed her arms defensively. "Why, I'd hire someone else to do the paperwork."

"Yes, but if *you* don't know the fundamentals, you'll get in a terrible mess."

Shirley looked crestfallen. "You mean you don't think I'll ever be able to have it?"

"No, I don't mean that at all. You're an intelligent, competent woman. You just need to learn a few basics. And that's why I'm here. Okay?"

"Okay."

"Let's start with the records you do keep. Receipts for gas, for example."

"For gas?"

"Don't you drive to some of your clients' homes?"

"Yes—"

"What percentage do you drive to? Half? One-fourth?"

"I'd say half."

"So you can deduct the gas you use driving to and from their homes, and a portion of your auto insurance and excise tax and automotive repair expenses."

"Oooh," Shirley said. "Wow." She smiled. "This could be fun!"

Later, as Alice drove back toward her condo on the Boston harbor, she realized she felt refreshed. *Invigorated.* Shirley might be naive about certain bookkeeping matters, but she was smart enough, and quick, and remarkably, for someone her age, *eager* to learn. And she made no secret of her admiration for Alice's business acumen or her awe at Alice's long and steady history with one company.

It felt nice. These days, at TransWorld, as in the corporate world in general, experience, wisdom, institutional memory meant nothing. The world had moved on, was moving, thanks to computers, at speeds Arthur Hudson couldn't have predicted when he founded the company thirty-five years ago. The world had changed, and so had Alice, but the world was new each day, while Alice only grew older.

Now TransWorld executives commuted between Asia and California, between South America and Africa. TransWorld dealt with countries Alice had grown up fearing, countries with communist-sounding names like Azerbaijan or bizarre names like Jabung, which sounded like something her boys, as children, would have named one of their space toys. What she hadn't realized before was that at some point in her life the entire map of the world had internalized itself in her mind, heart, and soul, and like a complex pinball machine, certain names, when hit, lighted up and binged, sending spurts of fear or distress through her intelligence. She could relearn the world map with its fractured new countries, its unstable political structures, and she *would*, but the harder work would be disconnecting old emotions.

It would help if she had more amiable colleagues instead of the Champion jackals drooling and licking their chops at her heels. It would help if she believed in what she was doing, the way Shirley believed in her retreat. Once, not even so long ago, Alice had felt *good*, pulling together a package of benefits that would slide right into the company's budget while at the same time providing serious security for the thousands of company employees. Now the bottom line was company profit, and she was supposed to be just one of the clever schemers employed to provide the least in order to save the company money, and employees beware.

Shirley was always babbling on about *balance*. Well, perhaps Alice could improve the balance of her own life.

She'd start, she decided, parking her car in its reserved spot at the side of the long brick building extending out into the harbor, with her own home. The second bedroom of her condo was a home office, stacked with charts, reports, and other TransWorld material. Letting herself into the foyer, she checked her mailbox, stuffed the envelopes into her bag, and, too wired to wait for the elevator, clipped up the steps to the third floor. She would clear a space next to her computer for Shirley's center. She'd pour a glass of sherry and spend a couple of hours working up a dynamite preliminary précis that would have investors fighting to write Shirley checks. Unlocking the door of her condo, she decided she could also check the Internet and pull together some figures about the increasing popularity of holistic—

She dropped her bag on the entrance hall table, walked into her living room, and shrieked.

Alan, her oldest son, her pride and joy, was lying on the sofa, watching TV. Alan had actually listened to his mama and gotten an MBA, so when he applied at a Houston oil corporation, he walked right in at managerial level. At thirty, he pulled in a salary that rivaled Alice's and allowed him to dress his big handsome college football fullback body in the finest suits and shirts and ties money could buy.

"Alan!" *What was he doing here?*

She rushed over to hug him till they both were out of breath. "Darling, how wonderful to see you! Have you got conferences in Boston?"

"Uh-uh." He wouldn't look her in the eye.

She studied her boy. Alan had lost at least fifty pounds since the last time she had seen him. His clothes hung off his scrawny body. He needed a haircut and a shave, hell, the boy needed antibiotics, it looked like, the way the whites of his eyes were red.

"What's going on?" she asked, worries banging around in her head like bumper cars at a carnival.

Alan ran his hands through his hair. "Well, a lot. You could say a lot has happened."

"Genevieve Anne?" Alice had never liked his wife, a gorgeous beauty queen who intimidated everyone with her slinky long body and African princess cheekbones. Alice thought the woman shallow and pretentious, but she always took pains to hide her opinion, realizing that not only was her son wild about her, he also was lucky to have someone with him who could work the cocktail party crowd as well as Genevieve Anne.

"Yes, Genevieve Anne. She left me for someone else. But also, Mama, I lost my job and had a kind of nervous breakdown."

"Oh, honey." She sank down on the sofa next to him.

"I'm on antidepressants, but I need some time to get my shit together so I can start over. I was thinking maybe I could stay here with you for a while."

"Of course you can," she assured him. "You can have the guest bedroom." Her thoughts whirled.

She would have to move her computer and desk and papers and reports into her bedroom, open up the sofa bed, and turn her second bedroom into Alan's room. Just for a while.

14

Monday morning Jennifer D'Annucio was tapping away at her computer when her office door opened and a woman entered.

The woman didn't look like anyone their firm would have dealings with. She wore purple leather boots, and a purple cape, with a magenta shawl blazing with astrological signs over her shoulders. She had curly red hair, and violet eye shadow, and silver planets dangling from her earlobes.

"Jennifer D'Annucio?" the woman asked.

"Yes," Jennifer admitted warily.

"Hello, Jennifer." The woman approached the desk, her cape falling open to reveal layers of nearly fluorescent fabric. "I'm Shirley Gold, and I'm happy to inform you that you've been given the gift of six absolutely free weeks of massage therapy."

Jennifer's jaw dropped. "What?"

Shirley had this part memorized—with expression. “As a thank-you to their customers, a number of Boston merchants, hairstylists, and health clubs have held a drawing for a variety of excellent prizes!”

“I didn’t enter any contest.”

“Well, either you entered your name or perhaps one of your friends did, because you have won six weeks of massage therapy from me, Shirley Gold.”

“I’m not sure I want—”

“No problem!” With a great big smile on her face, Shirley turned to leave. “We can just draw another name—”

“No, wait.” Jennifer stood up. “It’s just such a surprise.”

“I am, by the way,” Shirley plunked a handsome business card down on the desk, “an accredited masseuse, a member of the American Massage Therapist Association, and also a member of the Associated Body Work and Massage Professionals. If you want any references, I’ve got my résumé right here, and you’ll notice that several physicians in the greater Boston area recommend my services.”

Jennifer looked at the card. “I’m awfully busy—”

“I can come in the evenings or on weekends. Each session lasts an hour. Since you’re so young and fit, you probably aren't experiencing much tension—"

"Oh, but I am!" Jennifer exclaimed. "I really am! My life is so complicated—" She darted nervous glances at the doors leading into the lawyers' offices.

"Massage is also good for muscle toning and firming," Shirley added. "Not, of course, that *you* need that."

"But I *do*. My thighs are just out of control."

Since Jennifer looked to be about a size 10, Shirley doubted *that*, but she said, "We can work on that problem area. I have a special heat balm that helps bring blood to the surface, which in turn carries fat away, but I shouldn't get so technical here. We can schedule an intake appointment for you now, or I'll just leave my number, and you can phone me to arrange something."

Just then a man absolutely steaming with vigor strode through the door. He wore a pin-striped suit that was probably worth more than Shirley's old car, and he carried a heavy leather briefcase. He was a handsome young urban professional, and Shirley could tell by the way he held his shoulders that he carried enough tension there to drop an elephant.

"I need to go over the Phillips contract with you," he said to Jennifer.

"Right away, Mr. Schneider." Jennifer's voice was cool, but a blush crept up her neck when she looked at him.

Mr. Schneider went into an office, slamming the door behind him.

"I've got to go," Jennifer told Shirley.

"How about Saturday morning, nine o'clock?" Shirley asked. "I'd like to schedule it in now before I make my other calls."

"Saturday at nine, fine," Jennifer said. "Shall I come to your office?"

"I think it's more relaxing for the client if I come to their home," Shirley said smoothly. "I have a portable table."

"Fine. See you then," Jennifer said. She scribbled her address on a piece of paper and gave it to Shirley.

"Yes," Shirley said, smiling. "See you then."

15

Monday night, Faye and Marilyn were the first to arrive at Legal Seafoods. Shirley came next, in a flash of purple scarves. They'd just settled in at a table when they saw Alice stalking toward them, looking furious.

"Waiter," Alice called as she sat down. "Double martini, please."

"Alice," Faye asked. "What's wrong?"

"See that guy over there?" Alice jerked her head to the left.

"The man in the suit and tie?"

"Yeah. The arrogant bastard opened the door for me."

The other three stared.

Marilyn said, "Um, Alice, aren't men supposed to open doors for women?"

"Yeah," Alice responded, "to be polite. Not because the woman is old and too feeble to open it herself."

"How old was he?" Marilyn asked, then explained, "Older men tend to be more formal. Younger men are often afraid their behavior will be interpreted as sexist."

"Yeah," Shirley chimed in. "How do you know he wasn't just being polite?"

Alice looked sulky. "I could just tell. Come on, a woman can always tell these things."

"Alice, I think you're overreacting," Faye said.

"Oh, really?" Alice snapped. "You've never had this happen?"

Faye took a moment to think about it. "Not about opening doors specifically, but I do know what you mean." She sighed and signaled the waiter to order her own martini. "It used to be, when I stood in line at the post office, or the grocery store, wherever, I could feel men's eyes scan my body and face, up and down, quick as a laser. I always pretended I didn't notice, but now, my God, how I miss it. I'd swear to a panel of medical experts those glances provided me with a good healthy dose of vitamin D, like a flash of sunlight."

"Yeah." Alice nodded ruefully. "Clerks were always quick to serve me, and when they did, they *looked* at me. They *smiled*. Now they act like I'm scarcely worthy of their efforts. Or like that puffed-up turkey who opened the door for me, acting so damned *kindly*."

"But Alice," Marilyn protested, "you're so beautiful! And so are you, Faye!"

Alice sniffed. "Not like I once was. Have you heard the joke about the little boy and the little girl sitting in the backyard?"

"If I have, I've forgotten it," Shirley said.

Alice took a slug of her drink, then folded her arms on the table. "A little boy brags, 'I've got two pennies.'

" '*I've* got three pennies,' the little girl counters.

" 'Well, I've got two lollipops,' boasts the little boy.

" 'I've got two lollipops *and* a candy bar,' the little girl replies.

"The little boy thinks furiously. Then he pulls down his pants and holds out his penis. Triumphantly he announces, '*I've* got one of these!'

"The little girl pulls down her pants and considers a moment. Then she looks back up at the little boy. 'Well, I've got one of *these*,' she responds sweetly, 'and with one of *these* I can get as many of *those* as I want.' "

Shirley and Faye laughed.

Marilyn said, "I don't understand."

"We're talking about power," Faye elucidated. "Our youth gave us power we didn't even think about."

"You, maybe," Marilyn said softly. "Not me."

A handsome young waiter took their orders. He smiled charmingly at Marilyn, Alice, Faye, and Shirley, but as he wrote on his pad, his eyes were drawn by three young women, sleek and flexible as trout, who sped, glimmering, past, to a table where three gorgeous young men rose to greet them.

Faye said softly, "I wouldn't want to be that age again."

"I would!" Alice declared.

"Really? Think about it. They're wondering whether or not those men will marry them, whether or not they'll be faithful, and they'll want to have children, but they might have trouble getting pregnant, then the child might be ADD, and if the child's okay, can they raise him without ruining him and still have a career—"

"Not to mention," Marilyn added, "they have to deal with PMS every month."

"Ugh!" Faye and Shirley said together.

Alice relented. "You do have a point. I'd forgotten. All that reproductive stuff—what a fuss! When I was young, I pitied Mack because he'd never be able to experience the pleasure of pregnancy, or the passion of giving birth. But I *envied* him more, because now he had two sons and the same flawless body he'd started off with, while my overweight body was paisley with stretch marks."

"Oh, Lord, yes," Faye reminisced. "And those first few years, I was always so *exhausted*. Remember those damned Kegel exercises that were supposed to make our inner parts tighten up so we'd be better in bed? I was too tired to do even *those* when Laura was a baby."

"And forget sex," Marilyn added. "*Nothing* could be more attractive than sleep."

Alice noticed how quiet Shirley was. "Shirley? Do you have kids?"

Shirley gave a watery smile. "No. I was married three times, and I had a fair number of, shall we say, careless liaisons, but I never got pregnant."

"Did you mind?" Marilyn asked gently.

"Yeah, I did. It was hard. Probably one of the reasons I became an alcoholic. I felt like a failure. And I felt—*picked on*, by Fate. I mean, every other woman I saw had children, why couldn't I?"

"How did you deal with it?" Faye asked.

"Well, first I went to AA. My sponsor, Courtney Green, was a masseuse, and she offered me a free massage. I loved it, and started my own training, and I've loved being a masseuse. My work kept me steady, no matter how rocky my personal life was."

"That's probably true for all of us," Faye said.

"At the party celebrating the grand opening of my own massage business," Shirley continued, "I asked Courtney, 'What made you offer me a massage that first night? You're not rich, and you knew I couldn't afford to become a paying client.'

"Courtney said she liked to put something positive out into the universe for no reason at all. She called it *Spiritual Frisbee*. So I decided to do the same. For a few months, I volunteered at a hospital for long-term patients, helping brain-damaged children and adults regain some range of motion in their limbs. Then I volunteered at a facility for the elderly, and discovered that was the place for me."

"You like working with old people?" Alice asked.

"I do." Shirley's face glowed and softened as she spoke. "I love their wobbling bald heads and toothless grins. I love how they take such pleasure in something as small as a ten-minute neck and shoulder rub. Their bodies might have shrunk and sagged, been scalpeled open and stitched and stapled shut, but when I walk into their rooms, their faces light up with such *joy*. And I love brushing the old ladies' hair and tying it with pink ribbons, or reading Louis L'Amour to the old guys." Shirley grinned. "So, you see, I've found my own babies."

Marilyn had tears in her eyes. "I hope I know someone like you when I'm old."

"That's lovely, Shirley," Faye agreed.

Embarrassed, Shirley shifted in her chair. "Oh, hey, there are times, when I'm alone, when I imagine having a daughter who'd drop by to chat. We'd do each other's nails, perm each other's hair, and laugh about men. Or, a son would be nice, too. By now he'd be grown, a big, burly, hearty guy who'd fix my transmission, my screen door, and my mailbox." A shadow crossed her face, then she brightened. "Anyway, that's one of the reasons I want to create my retreat. To leave, or at least spread, something of myself in the world. I've wasted too many years enjoying too much booze and too many men, but *damn*, I've learned something along the way! I know how it feels to be down-and-out. I know how it feels to be so lonely I'd long for Mr. Wonderful but settle for Mr. Has a Pulse. And I know what a saving grace the simple human touch can be."

For a moment the others sat in respectful silence.

Then Alice said, "Well, damn, girl. That's cool."

"It is," Faye agreed. "With that kind of passion, you can really make your dreams come true."

"You think?" Shirley asked hopefully.

"I do," Faye said.

"I agree," Marilyn added.

"Me too," Alice said.

A waiter appeared. "Dessert, ladies?"

"Absolutely!" they all agreed.

After they'd ordered, Alice leaned back, and said, thoughtfully, "I'm glad I had my boys. They were—still are—the light of my life. But I can't say that was the greatest part of my life. I prefer logic, order, control—"

"Really?" Shirley made her eyes wide and cocked her head in mock amazement.

Alice cast her an admonishing look. "I love my work, I love the challenge and process and achievement of working. I like being my age, having accumulated so much knowledge and experience."

"I agree with you completely," Marilyn said.

Alice continued, "I don't necessarily want to be lusted after, although I wouldn't mind. I just don't want to be considered some old *hag*."

"Now the word *hag* is interesting," Shirley said. "The word *hagia* comes from the Greek word for *holy*. It was once a title of respect for wise, older women. Through time, it's become *hag*, with disparaging connotations."

Alice looked surprised and impressed. "How do you know that?"

"I know lots of stuff like that," Shirley told her.

"Good for you," Alice said, with feeling.

Faye weighed in. "*I* don't want to be like Jack Nicholson in that movie *About Schmidt*. The guy who retires and is totally lost."

"I loved that movie," Faye said. "Kathy Bates was wonderful."

"Kathy Bates is fabulous in everything she does," Alice agreed.

"If Kathy Bates had a son," Marilyn mused aloud, "and people addressed him formally, they'd call him Master Bates." She grinned and blushed.

Alice laughed. "Good to see you're catching up with the sexual revolution."

The waiter brought their desserts. They'd each ordered something different, and for a few moments they were busy, dividing the desserts into four parts and exchanging bits and pieces. Then they ate for a while in luxurious silence.

Alice got them on track. "All right," she announced, wiping her mouth with her napkin. "Down to business." She took her notebook out of her briefcase. "Faye?"

Faye licked her lips, savoring the final bite of chocolate. "I'm pleased to report I've been offered the job as the Eastbrooks' housekeeper."

"I'm surprised," Marilyn said. "Frances Corbett says the Eastbrooks haven't phoned to ask her for a reference for 'Faye Van Dyke.' "

"They haven't called me, either," Alice said. "But Faye looks trustworthy. They probably took her at face value."

"What's it like out there?" Shirley asked.

Faye thought about it. "Posh. Luxurious. Eugenie Eastbrook looks so perfect, she must make love wearing white gloves. I move in tomorrow morning. I get Mondays and most of my nights free, but some nights I have to help with dinner parties. They're having one tomorrow night."

"I know," said Marilyn. "Theodore, Teddy, and I are invited."

Alice raised a warning finger. "You two can't let on that you know one another."

"We won't," Faye promised. "We'll be as secretive as sphinxes."

"Good." Alice checked her list. "Faye, what kind of car do you drive?"

"A BMW. It was Jack's. But I didn't drive it out for the interview. I rented an old Toyota."

"Smart of you," Alice said. "Look, let's keep you camouflaged as well as possible, to be sure they can't ever track Mrs. Van Dyke down to Mrs. Vandermeer." She tapped her pen against her teeth.

"Don't do that," Shirley warned. "You'll chip a tooth!"

Alice stopped. "Here's what we'll do. My son Alan just moved in with me—"

"What happened?" Marilyn asked.

"Long story, but he's getting a divorce and wants to start over on the East Coast. Anyway, I'll have him rent an old car and get it over to you, Faye, for you to use out at the Eastbrooks."

"Great," Faye said.

"Now, Shirley," Alice continued. "I've got another business meeting with you Wednesday night, right?"

"Right. And Saturday I'm going to Jennifer D'Annucio's to give her her first free massage."

"And I've started temping as Alice's secretary," Marilyn told the others.

"Have you met Alison?" Faye asked.

"Briefly. She *is* an ice queen. But Barton, her secretary, seems rather nice."

"Okay, then," Alice concluded. "Looks like we're on course. See you all again here, next week."

They paid the bill and left their table, striding through the crowded restaurant, smiling and talking as they went. At the door, Marilyn, Faye, and Shirley all stopped dead.

Alice nearly ran right into Shirley's back. "What are you doing?" she asked.

Faye grinned. "We're waiting for you to open the door."

16

Faye—"Mrs. Van Dyke"—sat at her computer, collating a file of dinner guests and their allergies, preferences, and, if they'd eaten at the house before, those menus. She printed it off and went down the hall and into the kitchen.

"Oh, good, you've got the list," Margie Porter said. "Have time for some tea?"

Faye looked at her watch. "Yes, I suppose, while we go over the names."

Margie bustled around, warming the teapot with hot water, then filling it again with tea leaves and fresh water and setting it on the table with the sugar bowls and a milk jug and spoons and a plate of her homemade snickerdoodle cookies. Margie was a great pleasure to be around. Comfortably in her sixties, straightforward, easygoing, she loved to cook and she loved to be around people. She'd been with the Eastbrooks for fifteen years, and her only complaint was that she wasn't allowed to have her cat in the kitchen with her—too much danger, Missus said, of just one floating cat hair getting into the wrong person's soup.

"How are you settling in?" Margie asked, sighing as she sank into a chair.

"I'm doing all right, I think. Mrs. Eastbrook seems to be a perfectionist, but I can handle that."

"Missus has a good heart and Missy is a darling." She held out the plate. "Have a cookie."

"Thanks, not right now." Knowing how important appearances were to the Eastbrooks, Faye had determined not to gain another ounce. Smoothing her silk jacket over her stomachs, Faye looked at one of her lists. "Is it Miss Eastbrook's fiancé and his family who are coming to dinner tonight?"

Margie skimmed the page. "Yes, it is. My goodness, wait till you see them! The Beckers are a real pack of geniuses, all three, absolutely Albert Einsteins. The father's won all kinds of scientific awards, but he can't carry on a normal conversation to save his life. The son, Teddy, now, he's better. Teddy's nice. And the mother's nice, she's the most down-to-earth of the three."

"Is she a scientist, as well?"

"Yup. But not genetics. I think she studies bugs. Dead bugs. If you can imagine. But that's good, that's probably why she doesn't mind her husband's looks. He resembles a bug himself, one of those roly-poly creatures? He's short and plump and bald. He wears thick glasses and mumbles."

"Does Teddy look like that?"

"Well, he's younger, of course. Not fat, yet, but he's short and sturdy, you know that kind of fireplug build. He's got nice thick hair, for now; they say baldness is inherited, though."

"Doesn't seem like the kind of man who would be Miss Eastbrook's match."

"Not superficially, no." Margie set her cup down and aimed a steady gaze at Faye. "What you've got to remember about all the Eastbrooks is that there's more there than meets the eye. They look so perfect they seem like they're all whipped cream and no substance, but the substance is there, believe me." She shook herself. "Enough gossiping. Let's finish the list. Okay. They're having the Daunnises, too. That's good. Mrs. Daunnis is due for another face-lift, I believe, and Mr. Daunnis is planning to run for state representative in his district out in the Berkshires."

"Good heavens, Margie, you know everything about these people!"

"Yes, and you will, too, but no one will

know that, if you do your job right," Margie said.

Later that afternoon, Faye gathered her clipboard and pen and keys and made the rounds of the house. The guest bath had fresh towels and flowers. The downstairs was spotlessly clean. The drinks table in the living room was all set, except for the ice, which one of Margie's girls would put in the silver ice bucket just before seven. A tulip drooped from an arrangement on the mantel. Faye adjusted it.

Missus—as Margie called her—was in her bedroom taking a nap, and Faye assumed that Doctor was, too. He had a busy schedule, operating in the morning, doing rounds the rest of the day, entertaining at night. Faye couldn't understand why these people drove themselves so hard. They scarcely had a minute to enjoy all they had.

Faye walked to the far end of the house opposite from her own quarters, at least sixty feet away. She looked into the family room. A large, sunny room, it held overstuffed sofas, a thirty-six-inch TV, state-of-the-art stereo equipment, an old pinball machine, and a refrigerator full of soft drinks.

Faye had never seen anyone in this room.

On the opposite side of the room there was a door, one she'd never been through. Heaven knew there were enough oddities in the structure of the house. Mrs. Eastbrook had shown her the door leading from her office to a tunnel running between the house and the clinic and the spa, so that Doctor could get from one place to the other in bad weather.

But Mrs. Eastbrook hadn't lingered in the family room during her tour, and Faye had been so overwhelmed with all the rooms that she hadn't remembered to ask about it.

Now she crossed the thick creamy wall-to-wall carpet and put her hand on the doorknob and turned.

It was locked.

She'd seen—she *thought* she'd seen—Lila go through this door, with a tray of food. But where did this door lead?

"Mrs. Van Dyke?"

Faye nearly vaulted straight up into the air, but she kept her cool. "Yes, Miss Eastbrook?"

"Is there something you're looking for?" Lila Eastbrook's voice was cold.

"No. I'm just doing my rounds early this

evening, being sure all the doors are locked." Thank God she had her clipboard with her.

"You never need to check that door," Lila Eastbrook said. "It's always locked." Like her mother, Lila Eastbrook was diminutive and sweet-faced, but her voice was steel.

"Very well." Faye crossed the room, and together both women left the family room and went back to the main hall. "If you don't mind my saying, Miss Eastbrook, your hair looks especially pretty today."

"Really?" At once Lila Eastbrook transformed into an eager, hopeful young woman. "My fiancé's coming to dinner tonight."

"How very nice." Faye stepped into her own office.

"Yes," Lila agreed, a giant smile on her face. "Very nice."

Smiling, Lila Eastbrook went up the stairs toward her bedroom.

She must love him, to smile like that, Faye thought.

Then she settled at her desk and pored over her calendar, trying to find a time when Lila and her mother would be away from the house, so she could take a little stroll around the house to see what kind of addition extended from that door in the family room.

After dinner was over, the Eastbrooks and their guests went into the living room for brandy and coffee. Faye helped the maids snuff the candles and clear the table, then left them in the kitchen with Margie.

Out in the dark night, a brisk wind made the April air seem cold, and Dr. Eastbrook had lit the fire Faye had laid earlier in the day. Silently, on her soft-soled shoes, she went through the hall, blazing with light beneath its crystal chandelier. Through the slightly open door to the living room, she glimpsed the group, relaxed and jovial after a sumptuous meal, laughing and talking as the firelight gave off its golden warmth. Faye was possessed by a childish urge to peek in, catch Marilyn's eye, and wink. She suppressed it.

Slipping past unnoticed, Faye went down the hall to the family room. Her footfalls were absorbed in the thick carpet as she crossed to the wall of bookcases. She was restless—perhaps it was the wind, clattering and fussing nervously at all the windows. She hadn't brought any books with her, but she was sure she'd find something in the family room shelves.

Sufficient light illuminated the room from

the brilliant hallway, so she didn't turn on the overhead light. Just out of curiosity, she tried the handle of the door leading away from the family room. Still locked. She listened. Faint sounds of laughter and chatter filtered through the door. Another party? Some of the staff? But no, the more she listened, the more certain she became that they were only television voices she was hearing.

All at once voices came from another direction. Lila Eastbrook said urgently, "Teddy—in here—quick!"

Faye darted into an alcove with a window seat and heavy curtains and flattened herself against the wall. She dare not let the young woman see her there, so near the forbidden door. She hadn't turned on the light when she entered the room, but when any light came on, it would expose her. What could she say she was doing there in the dark?

Then the door to the hallway shut, blanketing the room in darkness.

Faye heard rustling, and small exhalations, and giggles, and groans.

"God, Lila," Teddy Becker moaned. "We'd better not—"

"Oh, Teddy, I love you so much! I don't want you to go home! I want you to come to bed with me, and sleep all night with me. I want to wake up seeing your face."

"And I want to be with you. And we will be together. Just a few more months."

"I *hate* it that we have to wait."

"I know. I know. But we'll have all of our lives together, Lila. And it means so much to them."

"Oh, Teddy, you're so good, so sweet, so kind, you're my teddy bear—" Lila's murmured endearments were cut short by Teddy's kisses.

"Enough," Teddy panted. "We've got to join them, they'll wonder where we are."

The door to the hall opened. Light spilled into the room. Teddy and Lila went out. Faye snatched a book from the shelf and hurried out into the hall, which was empty. She heard Lila laughing in the living room.

Gliding past, Faye went down the hall to her room, where she would wait with an open door and an attentive ear for sounds that the party was breaking up, that it was time for her to slip down to the entrance hall to open the closet and, modestly, with downcast eyes, hand out the coats.

17

Wednesday evening, Alice sat at the yellow Formica table in Shirley's kitchen, her laptop open before her, and a cardboard box full of old bits of paper—Shirley's record-keeping system—next to her.

Across from her, Shirley bent over a yellow legal pad, the tip of her tongue tucked into the corner of her mouth as she concentrated on making a list of every one of her current clients, how long they'd used her services, their addresses, their physical conditions, and their financial status. If Shirley thought they might be interested in her retreat, she was to put a star by their name.

An icy wind pelted the windows and walls. Frustrating early-April weather. Alice had spent the day laboring away on TransWorld Insurance employment benefit statistics. It helped greatly to have Marilyn in her office; at least she no longer had to worry that her own secretary was collaborating with the enemy. And Marilyn was surprisingly efficient, especially considering she'd never been an executive secretary before.

Still, Alice was exhausted from being on guard around Alison Cummings, plus the cold, wet weather made arthritis rip through her system like a staple gun stabbing her nerves. And, there was Alan. He was so tired, he'd said, from working eighteen-hour days, racing through life, trying to be the best, the richest, the quickest, the smartest. He just wanted to be still for a while. And every day he did look better. He was eating more, reading more, and laughing. Often, when she came home from work, he had meals waiting for her. So Alice was optimistic, but the thought of his sadness shadowed her heart.

Shirley looked comfortable in leggings and a long purple T-shirt. "You look tense," she observed.

"I am tense," Alice agreed, rolling her shoulders. "Look, you've got one piece of torn paper here that says 'ginger-scented candle.' "

"Yes. That promotes health."

"A ginger-scented candle promotes health?" Alice looked skeptical.

"Haven't you ever heard of aromatherapy?"

"Vaguely. Do you always burn candles when you give massages?"

"Sure. Usually."

"So they would be considered a business expense." Alice made a check.

"I guess—it sort of spoils the sense of the thing to think of it that way. Listen, Alice, you look tight as a wire. Let me give you a massage."

"My back does hurt." Alice sighed. "But we've got so much work to do."

"You'll be more productive if you feel better."

"All right. I'll have a massage, but I insist on paying for it."

"Nonsense! You're my friend! Look how you're helping me!"

"Shirley," Alice said firmly. "Right now you need to treat me like a consultant."

Meekly, Shirley nodded. "All right."

"Come on, Shirley," Alice coaxed. "Look at *me. Think.* What kind of car do I drive?"

"Um, a Mercedes?"

"An Audi. And what does that imply about my financial state?"

"You're rich."

"Right. So I can afford to pay top dollar for a massage."

"Yes, but—"

"You've got to start thinking like a businesswoman if you're serious about your retreat."

"Okay. Got it. So do you want a massage now?"

"Yes, all right. And do it exactly as if I were a real customer, okay?"

"Okay." Shirley pushed back her chair. "It will take me a few moments to get the room ready. In the meantime, you can use the bathroom. It's best to use the john before you lie on the table."

As she washed her hands in the bathroom, Alice stared gloomily at her reflection. She knew she was doing the right thing, having a massage, it would help her evaluate Shirley's work, and she would be paying Shirley. But she had so much work to do for TransWorld; it seemed frivolous to be having a massage, *lazy*. Once you started on the slippery slope to indolence, it was hard to retrace your steps. She had to prove to herself and others that she could still keep up with the youngest and fittest.

Still, she plodded down the hall to the massage room and entered.

Shirley had changed into loose white cotton pants and a loose white jacket. "Just put your clothes on that chair," she said. "Lie down on the table, faceup. Cover yourself with this sheet. I'll knock before I enter."

The room was steamy with warmth, and Alice was pleasantly surprised to discover the table was warm, too, and firm, but padded. A scent drifted through the air—cloves? Vanilla? She couldn't make it out. A mobile of the planets hung in one corner of the room, a teardrop of prismed glass dangled by a slender thread in the window.

Shirley knocked, then entered. Humming to herself, she slipped in a CD, and a gentle Bach concerto spun its notes into the room.

An hour later, Shirley said, "Take your time. When you're ready, dress and come to the kitchen."

Alice, facedown, thought she might be able to manage that in a century or so. She was so relaxed her body seemed to float like a bubble on the breath of the universe.

With great determination, she peeled herself off the table, dressed, and went into the kitchen.

"That was wonderful," she told Shirley. "You're amazing."

Shirley smiled. "Thanks." She handed Alice a glass of water.

Alice drank it, then reached into her purse for her wallet.

"I'd really feel better if you didn't pay me," Shirley insisted.

"I'd really feel better if I did," Alice shot back. "I've got the cash—or would you prefer a check?"

"Cash is fine."

Alice handed Shirley a one-hundred-dollar bill.

"I'll see if I have the change."

"I don't want change," Alice said.

"But this is too much!" Shirley declared.

"Shirley." Alice put her hands on her hips. "Isn't your fee eighty-five dollars?"

"Yes."

"So I'm tipping you. A little more than 15 percent. Don't your clients tip you?"

"Um, sometimes. Mostly not."

"It's just normal business to give and receive tips."

"Okay. Thank you."

"All right, then. So I've given you cash. What are you going to do?"

"Um—"

"It's a simple question. Why are you so worried?"

Shirley squared her shoulders. "Grab your coat."

Alice followed the other woman out the kitchen door, through the wind and rain, and into the chilly silence of the garage. Shirley's old VW Rabbit sat in the middle, surrounded by rakes and hoses, terra-cotta pots and an assortment of broken objects—a bike missing one wheel, a rusting toaster oven, a kitchen chair missing its seat.

With a great deal of clunking and clanking, Shirley moved aside the rakes, spades, and half-empty bags of potting soil.

"Usually I have to do this more quietly, but now that Jimmy's gone—" Face red with exertion, Shirley hoisted aside a thirty-pound bag of manure and yanked on an oil- and dirt-encrusted bit of concrete. Beneath it was another bag of manure.

"Look," Shirley said, holding the bag open.

"You want me to look inside a bag of manure?"

"Please."

Alice looked.

"Jesus Christ, Shirley! This bag's full of cash!"

"I knew you'd have a fit."

"But what are you *thinking*, keeping money

out here in the garage where anyone could steal it?"

"Well, it's not as much as you think. I don't think there's another hundred-dollar bill in here."

Alice pulled out a crumpled wad of bills. "But there's a fifty, and plenty of twenties. Let's get this inside."

Back in the kitchen, they cleared a space on one end of the table, dumped out the money, and split it between them, counting the bills as they straightened them out.

"Shirley," Alice grumbled, "don't do it that way."

"Why not?"

"Because it's confusing. Put all the ones in one stack and all the fives in another stack, and all the tens in one stack, and all—"

"Hey, there's more than one way to do things! It will add up the same whether I put them in their own little anal pile or in one great big pile!"

"Shirley. Humor me. You've got a lot of money here, and we're going to need to count it twice. And if you accidentally think a one is a ten, for example, or a five is a fifty—"

"All right, all right."

They added it once, then again. Their hands smelled dark and earthy, and the table was covered with small black crumbs of manure.

The total amount was $3,245.

"Wow!" Shirley said. "This is way more than I thought I had."

Alice washed her hands, then collapsed in a chair. "Why was all this money out in a manure bag in the garage?"

Shirley stuck her chin out defiantly. "For a very good reason. I've kept my savings like this all my life, because of my ex-husbands and my boyfriend Jimmy. If they're low on money, and they always are, they don't think twice about going through my wallet and taking what they want. I tried hiding it in the house one winter, and my second ex-husband sniffed it out like a bloodhound."

"But Shirley, why didn't you put it in a bank?"

"Because this money is just extra cash, tips for a massage, and usually when I got home from work I was too tired to go to a bank, or the bank was closed. Besides, if I'd kept it in my checking account, they'd have found out about it and made me give it to them. We're talking about extremely determined men."

"You could have put it in a savings account. It would have earned interest."

"And the bank would have mailed me a

statement, and Jimmy would have read my mail. He'd have gone apeshit that I was stock-piling money. He'd have gotten it."

"You could have rented a special post office box just for your bank statements."

"I could? What'd ya know. I never thought of that. Anyway, Jimmy's gone, and I've got over three thousand dollars, which no one stole!"

"What were you planning to do with this money?" Alice asked.

Shirley shrugged. "I don't know. Save it for a rainy day. Buy a great dress if I ever met a decent man. Use it in an emergency."

"What are you going to do with it now?"

"Put it in a bank?" Shirley said hopefully.

Alice leaned forward. "Didn't you tell me that one of your customers plays the stock market?"

"Yeah. Julie Martin."

"I think we should go see Julie Martin."

18 MARILYN

Thursday morning, fifteen men and two women sat around a long executive table in the TransWorld conference room for a getting-acquainted, brainstorming session.

Melvin Watertown, senior vice president in charge of international expansion, was holding forth. "—only natural that when two companies merge, positions will overlap. But when you see job cuts in this office, remember we're expanding worldwide, opening offices in Canada, England, Australia, and Belgium and investigating other territories."

Alice Murray had a place at the table. Marilyn sat behind her, taking notes. Alison Cummings was directly across from Alice—by accident or choice, all the TransContinent people were on one side of the table, the new execs from Champion on the other.

Alison was obviously the youngest of them all, and lovely. She radiated enormous energy, even when she wasn't saying a word. Her soft hands, nails tipped with the lightest of pinks, rested on the table, on either side of her pile of folders, but her eyes whipped from speaker to chart to speaker, not losing a syllable. Behind her, her executive secretary, Barton Baker, sat, tapping away at his Palm Pilot. Occasionally he shot Marilyn a quick, cryptic smile that made her toes curl.

Marilyn reminded herself to concentrate on Alice, who held her back so ramrod straight she nearly quivered with the strain. Alice and Alison were responsible for creating a detailed personnel policy to cover new international territories, investigating labor laws in each country, devising an organizational chart, job descriptions, and annual job performance evaluations, formulating an employee handbook to cover job discrimination, personal and health leave, health benefits, salaries, and promotion. It would be a massive undertaking, involving a score of accountants, international law experts, and management specialists.

"Any thoughts, Alice?" Melvin Watertown suddenly barked.

For a terrible moment, Alice didn't reply. She cleared her throat, shifted in her chair, and rifled through the papers in front of her. From where

Marilyn sat, it looked as if Alice was actually *squirming*.

Alison Cummings spoke up. "For our purposes, the British branch will be the model."

When everyone's attention shifted to Alison, Marilyn scribbled a note and slipped it to Alice, who showed no signs of reading it.

"It depends on where they decide to house the headquarters." Alice's voice was firm; she was back in control. "If they choose Manchester, they'll halve the costs."

"Manchester is hardly chic," Alison scoffed.

Alice shrugged. "So they'll put a small image office in London." Her voice grew stronger. "I think Canada will be the model. She's our neighbor. Canadians speak our language. They have a similar economy."

"I think you're right, Alice," Marvin said. "Now about tax laws that impact retirement benefits. Henry?"

Marilyn saw Alice's shoulders relax, just a little.

The rest of the meeting passed without incident.

Afterward, in the sanctity of her office, Alice said to Marilyn, "Thanks for slipping me that note. The frigging underwire in my bra broke loose and jabbed me in the armpit. Kept it up all through the meeting." She tugged angrily through her clothes. "How am I going to get through the day? I can't go without a bra!"

"Take it off," Marilyn told her. "I'll tape the wire back in."

Alice went into the bathroom and shut the door. A few minutes later, she extended her arm, a contraption of spandex and silk hanging from her hand like a collapsed parachute.

Marilyn took it over to the desk, laid it out flat, studied it for a moment, then pushed the offending wire back down into its silken channel, secured it with several strips of fibrous tape, and stapled it all several times for good measure.

"This should last the day," she said, handing it back to Alice.

"Thanks." Through the slightly open door, Alice said, "You're lucky to be so slender. When you're my size, nothing fits. My bras ride up, and my underpants curl down."

Marilyn cocked her head, thinking. "Perhaps if you wore fasteners, like garters, or suspenders, between the two, they'd stay in place."

"More likely they'd break from the strain." But the image made her smile, and she relaxed slightly. "I shouldn't have gone blank in the meeting like that."

"You're under an enormous amount of stress with this merger," Marilyn reminded her.

"That's no excuse." Lowering her voice, she asked, "How are you getting along with Barton?"

"We've been having lunch together, getting to know one another. He's from Texas, he's divorced, he's terribly nice, actually—"

"What does he say about his boss?"

"He thinks Cummings is brilliant. Ambitious."

"Is Barton loyal to Cummings?"

"I'm not sure, but I'll find out."

Marilyn shut off her computer. It was the end of the day, and she was exhausted. The pressure of the two colliding megacompanies made everyone tense, even Marilyn, who didn't even really work there.

Barton Baker appeared in her doorway. "Want to go have a drink?"

"Yes, *please*," Marilyn said.

The new TransWorld building had a cafeteria and a coffee shop, but no bar. Also, there was no anonymity.

"Let's go to the Cottonwood Café and do tequila shots," Barton suggested.

Marilyn had never done tequila shots. "Okay."

"Let's take my car," Barton said.

Marilyn paused. At this time of the evening, city traffic was a nightmare. If she rode with Barton, he'd have to drive her back to her car, but she wasn't in any hurry, and she was supposed to be infiltrating the enemy camp. "Okay."

"What a car!" Marilyn exclaimed when she saw his bright red turbo-charged Miata convertible. He opened the door for her as she slipped in and she noticed how he looked at her legs, which, now that she studied them, appeared sleek in her new expensive stockings, and sexy in heels higher than she'd ever worn before. While Barton went around to the driver's side, Marilyn wondered idly if there were a scientific heel-to-arch ratio to predict how to achieve the sexiest leg.

On the ride, Barton concentrated on navigating through the heavy traffic. "I don't understand why there are so many one-way streets," he grumbled.

"Boston roads were originally cow paths,"

Marilyn told him. She hoped he wouldn't find the ride too distressing. Men found uncertainty so upsetting. Theodore always sulked for days if he'd had to drive along a new route. The first time he drove them out for dinner at the Eastbrooks' home, she'd been afraid he'd have a stroke.

Fortunately, Barton quickly found a parking spot on Newbury Street. They hurried along the crowded sidewalks to the restaurant and were soon seated at a horseshoe-shaped bar. Barton ordered tequila for them both.

"Salud!" he toasted.

"Salud!" she replied. He tossed back the liquor, so she did, too. Her throat burned and heat flashed through her like a lightning bolt. Blood rushed to her cheeks.

"This hits the spot, doesn't it?" Barton said. "What a tough day. Want another?"

Her whole body *tingled*. "Sure," she agreed. "I'll have another."

He ordered. They clicked glasses and drank. The tequila tasted earthy, primal, the way the world must have tasted when it was brand-new. How fascinating. This was what trilobites tasted five million years ago.

"More?" Barton asked.

Marilyn laughed. "More."

The control knob of the universal laws

clicked up a notch. Colors were brighter, sound more intense. The beat of background music, something Mexican, exotic, contagious, bounced off the pulse of her blood. Everyone else in the room looked young, hip, and happy, and for the first time in her life, Marilyn felt young, hip, and happy, too.

She'd never sat at a bar with a man, and she found it a bit terrifying, in an enjoyable way. Her stool had no back, and it swiveled, like something at a playground or amusement park. Across the bar, another man gave her the once-over. Marilyn blushed and wobbled.

Barton put his hand on her back to steady her. His touch loosened every tendon in her body.

"I don't go to bars often," she confessed.

"Me, either," Barton told her. "But I just can't face my pathetic rented apartment just yet."

"Oh, too bad. Where are you living?"

"Arlington. After the merger, I had to find a place fast, just to eat and sleep in. But I'm looking for something a little more comfortable. Where do you live?"

"In Cambridge. A nice old house." She remembered she was supposed to be widowed. "It's too big for me now that my children are grown and my husband's gone."

"Gone?"

"He died, two years ago. Heart attack." She clicked her fingers. "Just like that."

"I'm sorry."

"Thank you." She was slightly appalled at how much she enjoyed being widowed. "It was hard, of course, but the fact is, we hadn't been—close—for years." This was the truth, and it felt fabulous to say it.

"A beautiful woman like you," Barton mused. "What a shame."

More tequila arrived. She tossed it back. "I'm embarrassed I said that. Way too much personal information!"

"I'd like to know everything about you," Barton said, looking warm and sincere. Moving closer, he put his hand on hers.

She stared at their hands. They were emitting a weird kind of heat that lit up her body all the way down to her crotch, which glowed like an outer space alloy. Surreptitiously, she glanced down: Nope, nothing showed.

"It's a hard world we work in," Barton confessed softly. "Competitive and aggressive. We wouldn't be in it if we didn't enjoy the challenge—and the money—but sometimes I think I'd enjoy a less combative kind of work."

"I know exactly what you mean," Marilyn agreed.

"And as much as I admire Alison Cummings," Barton continued, "by the end of the day I find her fairly exhausting."

Why, it was easy, doing this detective work, Marilyn thought. And it was fun!

"I've only worked for Alice for a few days," Marilyn said, "but I have to say I find her rather abrasive." Her elbow almost touched Barton's, and her knee actually did touch his now and then, when her stool swayed a little to the left.

"Hey, they're all abrasive," Barton said. "It comes with the job description. And we like some of it, or we wouldn't be working for them. I certainly want to rise in the company. But for people like you and me, well, with all the stress and pressure, we have to be sure to balance our lives with indulgences. "

"That's very insightful of you." Marilyn studied Barton. How young he was, to be so wise. His dark eyes were liquid, electric, and transfixed on her face.

Barton leaned close to her. "Alison Cummings is a Type A personality: driven, egotistic, obsessed with Champion to the detriment of any private life. That's not what I want for myself. I want success, achievement, but not at the cost of personal pleasures."

"Personal pleasures," Marilyn said seriously, "are very important."

Other people were edging up to the bar, pushing against Marilyn's arm, making it impossible for her to pull away from Barton's powerful sexual force field. She felt like a meteor being pulled into the track of a potent star.

"How'd you like the meeting?" Barton asked.

"I found it fascinating," she answered truthfully.

"You were pretty fabulous, passing that note to Alice Murray."

Bells went off in Marilyn's head. "Note?"

"Don't try to kid me. I saw you."

Perhaps it was the tequila. Marilyn burst out laughing. "God, this sounds just like high school! And the note, for your information, said, 'Alison Cummings is a snot.' "

"Really."

"Really."

"Why? Because she had her fingertips on information your boss didn't know?"

"Listen, Alice knows everything, believe me."

"Hey." Barton put his hand on Marilyn's. "I'm not trying to pick a fight. I didn't mean to insult your boss. It's just that I really did think she was kinda slow off the mark a few times during the meeting."

Marilyn gazed into his dark seductive eyes. *Focus*, she ordered herself. "Well, I'm new at TransWorld, but I think Alice has an incisive mind and an encyclopedic grasp of her field. She's been in this business for a long time, after all—"

"That's just the point."

His hand was still on hers. "What's just the point?"

"She's been in the business too long, perhaps, to deal with a business the size and complexity of TransWorld. She's okay for TransContinent, but too antiquated for TransWorld."

"That's not true!" Marilyn snapped, and to her intense embarrassment, she burst into tears. With a rush of chagrin, she realized she was drunk.

"Oh, God," Barton said. "Oh, Marilyn, I'm so sorry. I didn't mean—"

"Could we leave?"

"Of course."

He threw some bills on the counter and, putting his arm under her elbow, escorted her out of the bar and down the street to his car. He settled her in the passenger seat, went around and got in the driver's seat, and started the engine, but didn't put the car into drive. Marilyn pulled tissues from her purse and wiped her eyes and blew her nose. She wondered if her mascara had run. She wondered what women did when their mascara ran. She wondered if the formula for mascara—

Barton turned toward her. "Marilyn," he said earnestly. "I apologize."

Marilyn looked at Barton. *Antiquated*, she thought. Alice is *antiquated*, and so am I, and that's wonderful if you're a trilobite, but pretty awful if you're a living woman.

Barton looked distressed himself. "I never dreamed I'd upset you so much. Please—" He put his hand on her shoulder. "Marilyn—"

Then, to Marilyn's amazement, Barton had his arms around her. He was kissing her, ravishing, hot, furious kisses, kisses like an astronaut returning from space, a soldier returning from war.

And Marilyn was kissing him back.

19

Saturday morning Shirley drove to Jennifer D'Annucio's home on a tree-lined street in an idyllic neighborhood of Stoneham, all single-family homes, with picket fences and birdhouses and tree houses and trikes and bikes in the driveway.

Jennifer, it turned out, didn't live in one of the houses, but in the apartment over the garage of one of the houses. Shirley groaned. She hated carrying her massage table up stairs. But she was feeling unusually optimistic after her sessions with Alice, so she hoisted the carrying case strap over one arm and her bag of oils and CDs over the other, took a deep breath, and began climbing.

"Hello," Jennifer sang, throwing open the door. "Here, let me help you with that. No, please, I insist."

Shirley nearly fell back down the stairs with shock. Jennifer, sleek slick secretary, wore jeans and a T-shirt, both covered with flour.

Her long black locks were stuck up any which way on the back of her head with several barrettes, and her hair and face were also powdered with flour.

"God, it smells good in here," Shirley said as she stepped inside.

"I know! Isn't it wonderful? I made some pies for a friend's child's day-care's bake sale. Apple, pecan, and peach. Where would you like to put your table? There's more room in the living room."

"Could we close the curtains?" Shirley asked. "Just to dim the light of the room so you can really relax."

"Sure."

Shirley couldn't help but think, as she set up her table and arranged her oils and plugged the electric blanket in to warm the pad, that if she lived here in Jennifer's apartment, she wouldn't need a massage. She hadn't ever seen a more welcoming space. Several ancient silky deep Oriental carpets overlapped one another, obviously covering worn spots. The far wall was entirely covered with shelves, holding all kinds of books, paperbacks mixed in with thicker hardbacks, with brightly framed photos and painted pots and statues tucked in here and there. A fat, ancient sofa, draped in soft shawls and littered with plump cushions, sat near an old trunk serving as a coffee table, holding more books and a low vase of daffodils. Two other chairs, venerable and cozy, bookended the trunk. The window was draped with curtains in rich floral pinks and greens; Shirley could imagine Jennifer closing them against the bitter winter dark, blushing the room with summer. A drop leaf walnut table, much polished, stood in front of the window, a vase of spring flowers on it, and just a few steps away was the kitchen, old-fashioned, the appliances nearly antediluvian, but everything shining clean. And on the counters sat the pies with their beautiful golden crusts.

Jennifer helped Shirley move the chairs and trunk to make room for her massage table, then went off into the bathroom. Shirley set up her CD player and slipped in an Enya CD, then set out her oils and aromatherapy candle. On second thought, she didn't light the candle; the smell of baked pies was therapy enough.

Jennifer came out of the bathroom, a towel wrapped modestly around her torso.

"I'm fat, I know," she said apologetically, "but you see, I love to cook. I love to eat."

"Sweetheart, believe me, you're not fat," Shirley told her. "You've got a fabulous body."

"Thanks, but it's true, I am fat, at least for getting a man. Men want their women lean and muscular these days."

Jennifer lay on the table, and Shirley flicked on the Enya CD and began the massage. Jennifer's skin was as smooth as cream, the flesh beneath it firm. Her hair was silky and luxurious. She carried her tension in her hips and lower back and in the arches of her feet, and as Shirley worked, she felt the young woman's body relax, rock turning to petal.

The phone rang. Shirley's ears perked up.

"Let the machine get it," Jennifer murmured from her deep repose.

"Hi, honey. It's Carol. Adrienne told me I could call you and *beg* you for some cookies for the church spring fair. You know yours sell before anyone else's, and we desperately need new choir robes, so if you could promise us, oh, say, twelve dozen cookies and maybe a pie or cake? Please? It's not *our* fault you're such a good cook."

Interesting, Shirley thought. Jennifer's body didn't tense at the message, but seemed to expand even more into a mellow space.

Jennifer purred. "I love baking," she said. "I'm always so glad when I have a reason to do it."

"They're all lucky to have you bake for them," Shirley said.

As Shirley kneaded the knots in Jennifer's lower back, the phone rang again, and this time a man's voice came into the air. Jennifer's body tensed.

"Hi, Jenn, it's me. I think I can make it tonight. Sevenish. Dinner? I'll bring wine. Okay, then. See you later."

"Your boyfriend?" Shirley asked.

Jennifer sighed. "Kind of." Her muscles, which had been nearly fluid, knotted up as she spoke. "I mean I love him. And he loves me. But he's married."

"Oh, dear."

"And his wife just had a baby."

"Oh."

"You must think I'm a terrible person." Face flat down on the table, Jennifer's voice was muffled.

"No, not at all," Shirley told her honestly.

"I never meant to be a home wrecker."

"I'm sure you didn't." Shirley went to the foot of the table, lifting and arranging the sheet so that Jennifer's left leg was exposed, and worked on her thigh with long, smooth motions.

"He insists he loves me. He says his marriage is just a sham, that all his wife cares about is the baby. She never wants to make love anymore, she never cooks for him, she doesn't care about him, she's always nagging him, they never have fun, she's always running home to her mother and leaving him alone without dinner and all alone all night."

Shirley moved to the other leg. "That must be difficult for him."

"It is! Very! He says if he crawled in the door bleeding one day, she'd just scream, 'For God's sake, take care of the baby for a while, I'm exhausted, I have to have a nap!' And he works so hard; no one works as hard as he does."

"What does he do?"

"He's a lawyer in the firm I work for. He's way junior, so he's like their slave, he has to take what they dump on him, he's given all the shit work. He's a really nice man, he never meant to run around on his wife, but he says she wouldn't even care if she knew, she can't stand to have him touch her, all she wants to do is sleep."

"Well," Shirley said, "it is exhausting, having a newborn baby in the house."

Jennifer tensed all over. "But if it were *my* baby, I wouldn't ignore my husband!"

You're not here to give a lecture, Shirley reminded herself. You don't even know yet who the man is. There must be hundreds of new fathers in the Boston area.

"He must feel like he's entering heaven when he comes over here," Shirley said honestly. "Your home is so welcoming, and I'll bet you make delicious meals for him."

"It's true, I do. He's always so grateful. And so tired. You know, most of the time we don't really have sex. What I think of as sex. We don't actually make love, not very often. He's always in a hurry to get home so his wife won't find out, so usually I just give him a blow job."

Shirley moved to the head of the table. The hour was almost up, and she still didn't know the boyfriend's name. Still, she couldn't help but feel slightly protective of this beautiful young idiot. "Let's see now, you feed him and comfort him and love him and what does he do for you?"

"Why—he loves me!"

"Which he shows, *how*?"

Jennifer's body was a mass of knots all over again. "He tells me he loves me. He sends me flowers. He gave me a beautiful bracelet from Cartier."

"Is he going to leave his family and marry you?"

Jennifer sat up, red-faced, indignant. "Jesus! You sound just like my mother!"

"I'm sorry," Shirley said. "I had no right to ask you that. It was very unprofessional of me. I guess I just got involved."

"That's all right." Jennifer's shoulders slumped. "You're not saying anything I haven't said to myself, believe me."

"Yes, but it's my job to help you relax. You should get up from this table invigorated and refreshed." She smiled. "Next time I come; we won't talk, how's that?"

"All right."

"I usually get my clients a drink of water after a massage," Shirley informed Jennifer. "Would you mind if I get you a glass of water from your kitchen?"

"Why would I mind?"

"I always ask the first time. I never want to overstep any boundaries." In the kitchen, Shirley ran the water, quickly scanning the calendar on the wall for names. She saw hearts drawn next to some dates, but no names. She filled the glass and brought it to Jennifer. "Drink it all down," she instructed. "It will help drain off toxins loosened into your system by the massage."

While Jennifer was dressing in the bathroom, Shirley packed up her gear.

"I do feel more relaxed," Jennifer said. "Especially right in my back. Did you do that thing for my thighs?"

"That thing for your thighs?"

"You said you had a technique to get rid of cellulite."

"Oh. Oh, yes, I did. But for your first time I have to go carefully. I'll work a little harder on that area next time. Is next Saturday okay, same time?"

"Sure. Oh, and um, I know I won these sessions, but I've never had a massage before—um, should I tip you?"

"It's not necessary, hon. And I wouldn't take a tip today. I feel like I upset you rather than calming you down."

"No, honestly, I feel really good now," Jennifer protested. "Look! Would you like a bag of my cookies? I just made some oatmeal-raisin yesterday. Oatmeal and raisins are healthy, right?"

"Jennifer, I would love some of your oatmeal-raisin cookies." And I'd love to know the name of your married boyfriend, but I guess I'll learn that next time, Shirley thought.

At the door, Jennifer surprised Shirley by hugging her. "You're really nice," she said. "I think you bring good energy with you."

"You give off good energy, too," Shirley said, and she meant it.

"Let me help you carry all that down the stairs," Jennifer offered.

"No, I'm fine."

Oh, dear, Shirley thought as she walked to her car. If I were a man, I'd want to be with Jennifer. Jennifer seemed like a nice girl with a lot to give. Shirley would do what she had to do for her HFC assignment, but she knew she also would like to do something to make Jennifer happy.

20

Monday night all four women arrived at Legal Seafoods at exactly the same moment and had time only for a flurry of greetings before the maitre d' said, "Hello, ladies. Nice to see you again."

He ushered them to a table, Faye leading Marilyn and Alice, all three in tidy suits, with Shirley in her gypsy dress with the swirling skirt bringing up the rear. He seated them and handed them menus.

The moment he stepped away, Faye leaned forward. Several curls had escaped from her smooth silver chignon and dangled in rather charming disarray around her face. Unbuttoning the severe suit jacket she'd worn as she left the Eastbrooks' house, she revealed a loose turquoise linen shirt, one of her favorite old garments, comfortable as her skin but too elaborately sensual for her housekeeper's work. Faye announced, "I've got a *lot* to report!"

Alice grinned. "I suspected as much. I was afraid you were going to trample the maitre d'." She took her notebook and pen from her purse.

"Are you kidding?" Faye looked indignant. "I'd never hurt anyone leading me to food."

Alice laughed. "Good policy."

Shirley flung her violet scarf over her shoulder and arranged a silver-and-amethyst pendant against her bosom. "I have a lot to report, as well."

"Great," Alice said.

They waited a beat, then turned expectantly to Marilyn, who had taken her compact out of her purse and was studying her reflection with such fervent intensity, she seemed unaware of the others.

"Marilyn?" Alice prompted.

Marilyn jumped. "What?" she asked, looking around rather wildly.

"Do you have something to report?" Alice asked.

"Yes!" Marilyn responded. "I do!" She blushed scarlet. "But I'd like to order a drink, first."

"Well, well," Faye said, cocking an eyebrow at Marilyn. "How interesting!"

Taking charge, Alice signaled the waiter. Once their drinks arrived, she announced,

"All right. Let's get this meeting of the Hot Flash Club rolling. Faye, want to start?"

"Absolutely! I'm having so much fun at the Eastbrooks!" Faye confessed. "It's like I'm playing house, but with life-sized furniture and people. The place is palatial, isn't it, Marilyn?"

Marilyn was gazing at the ceiling. Shirley nudged her with her elbow. "Um? Oh, yes, palatial," Marilyn agreed.

"But I must say the Eastbrooks all work incredibly hard." Faye wanted to be fair. "I doubt they take time to enjoy the splendor around them. Eugenie Eastbrook is chilly, but Margie says she has a good heart, and I trust her judgment, although I'm not comfortable enough with her yet to ask about the locked door—"

Alice interrupted. "Who's Margie?"

"Wait!" Shirley pleaded. "What locked door?"

"Oh," Faye laughed, "I'm confusing you, aren't I? I'm getting everything all bunched up. Jack called this 'getting tangled up in your underwear.' "

"Men have more openings for that than women do," Shirley said.

"Unless you count bras," Alice added.

"I wouldn't mind getting tangled up in men's underwear," Marilyn said dreamily.

Faye, Shirley, and Alice gawked at Marilyn, who went back to observing the ceiling.

"All righty, then," Faye said, cocking her head in Marilyn's direction.

"Start over," Alice suggested.

"Right." Faye took a deep breath. "The Eastbrook household is completely geared toward Dr. Eastbrook's work, the clinic, their clients, their potential clients. They have two full-time maids in the house who are under my supervision, and a cook. That's Margie. She's been with the family for fifteen years. She's friendly to me but loyal to the Eastbrooks, whom she genuinely admires. She told me the Beckers"—Faye glanced at Marilyn—"are a pack of geniuses, but that the Eastbrooks are also intelligent. Her words, if I remember correctly, were that the Eastbrooks might seem like whipped cream, but the substance is there."

"Whipped cream," Marilyn echoed dreamily.

Faye rolled her eyes and continued. "When the Beckers were there for dinner last week, I happened to overhear Teddy and Lila catching a few stolen moments together. Nothing too intimate! It certainly seemed to me that Lila's genuinely in love with Teddy. But there's a door off the family room that's locked, and it's the one door in that entire, enormous house I'm not allowed to enter, so naturally my curiosity's piqued. I've seen Lila go through the door, and Mrs. Eastbrook, but it's at the other end of the hall from my office, and I don't have much of an opportunity to be in that wing. But, believe me, I'm going to find out what's behind that door!"

"Oooh, that's kind of spooky," Shirley said, rubbing her hands with ghoulish relish. "It's like Mrs. Rochester in the attic in *Jane Eyre*."

"Why was Mrs. Rochester in that attic anyway?" Alice wondered.

"She was mad, the poor old thing," Faye said.

"She was probably just menopausal." Alice laughed, then stopped. "That's not funny, is it?"

Just then, their meals were set before them, and they turned their attention to their food. After a quartet chorus of appreciation, Faye asked, "What have you found out, Shirley?"

Shirley speared a piece of broccoli with her fork, chewed it, then took a sip of water. "I gave Jennifer her first massage on Saturday. Her apartment is the sweetest place, comfortable, charming, and Jennifer's always baking things for friends, so the air smells divine. She's terribly sweet, and really beautiful—"

Noticing how Faye's face sagged at Shirley's report, Alice broke in. "Enough of the praise! We're not here to start the Jennifer D'Annucio fan club. We just want to know if the woman's having an affair with Faye's son-in-law."

"Yes, Generalissima," Shirley retorted. "The answer is, I don't know. I *do* know she's having an affair with a married man, a lawyer, who has a new baby in the house. The wife is always running home to her mother and leaving the husband alone every night—"

"Oh, dear," Faye murmured. "It must be Lars."

"Maybe not!" Shirley reached over to give a consoling pat to Faye's hand. "There must be tons of married men with new babies in the Boston area. Don't fret until we know for sure. I have another appointment with her next Saturday. I'll know more, then."

Faye put down her fork and leaned back in her chair, unable to finish her dinner.

"Oh, dear," Shirley said. "I've depressed you. I'm sorry."

"I'm not depressed," Faye assured her. "Just worried. It's true Laura's been coming home a lot with Megan. I actually thought it was a *good* thing, because I know how hard Lars is working and how impossible it is to get a good night's sleep with a baby waking up every couple of hours. He's stressed out enough as it is. And Laura's nursing, so I've been cooking healthy meals for her."

"How old is Laura?" Shirley asked.

"Twenty-eight."

Shirley looked skeptical. "Isn't she kind of old to be running home to Mama?"

Alice waved her fork at Shirley. "Listen, it's *impossible* to know exactly when to help your kids and when to back off, even when they're adults. Maybe even *especially* when they're adults. I told you, my son Alan's living with me, and he's *thirty*. He's brilliant. He's got an MBA. He was married to a beauty queen. Now he's divorced, without a job, and virtually homeless. And all he's done for the past week is watch television, sleep, and cook."

"Why don't you kick him out?" Shirley asked, with genuine curiosity.

"Because he's her son!" Faye interjected. "Because no matter how old they get, you always want to help your children. It's a natural instinct. Perhaps the most powerful one."

"Add maternal guilt to that," Alice said. "To start with, I married the wrong man, a man who left us when the boys were little and who hasn't seen them since."

"But, hey!" Shirley sputtered. "If that guy hadn't been their father, your boys wouldn't be who they are."

"I understand that. *They* understand that. It helps logically, but not emotionally. I'll never stop feeling guilty for not providing them with a good father. On top of that, I worked full-time from the time my oldest boy was five. I missed so many significant occasions—piano recitals, football games, school plays. Are they traumatized for life? I didn't think so. They both seemed successful in their work and happily married, although I never did like Alan's wife. Now here Alan is, with all the energy of a turtle. Is he chemically depressed? Did I pass some depressed genes on to him? Did I fail to provide him with a model of a good marriage? Was I too ambitious?"

"Oh, Alice"—Faye laughed—"I feel just as guilty as you do. *You* provided your sons with siblings. I had an only child. Does this mean she's never learned to share properly? Is Laura spoiled? Am I smothering her? Did we allow her to be too—I believe the psychological term these days is *enmeshed*—with her father and myself?"

"Each family's different," Alice decided. "We invent the rules for ourselves as we go along. And don't forget, we're part of the world we live in, and that changes all the time, too. Right, Marilyn?"

Marilyn was toying with her food. Hearing her name, she looked up and smiled. "You're right, Alice." It was obvious she had no idea what they'd been discussing.

"Marilyn, *what* is going on with you?" Shirley demanded.

"Yeah, Marilyn," Alice said. "What's your report?"

Marilyn blinked a few times, making a visible effort to pull herself from whatever cloud of fantasy she was floating on, back to the real world. "Well, you all know I'm working as Alice's secretary."

"Yes," Faye said in an encouraging tone. "And Marilyn, may I tell you how fabulous you look these days?"

Marilyn blushed. "Thanks."

"She's right," Shirley agreed. "You've got the glamour thing going."

"Oh, well, maybe not *glamour*," Marilyn demurred modestly.

"So," Alice prompted, "you had drinks with Barton Baker Thursday night—"

"And I was hungover Friday," Marilyn agreed, shuddering at the memory. "It was nice of you, Alice, to let me go home early."

"You kept falling asleep at your desk," Alice reminded her.

"So what did you learn?" Shirley asked.

Marilyn thought about it. "Quite a lot, actually. Barton told me Alison Cummings is ambitious, egotistical, and obsessed with the company."

Alice leaned forward. "Is she sneaky? Is she after my job?"

"I don't know yet," Marilyn told her. "I'll find out as soon as I can."

"Don't be too eager," Faye warned. "You don't want him to suspect what you're up to."

"I can't be too eager, this week," Marilyn said, looking sad. "Barton and Alison are going out of town on business. They've got to go back to the old Champion headquarters."

"Probably just as well," Alice said. "The company frowns on intraoffice dating."

"Oh, dear!" Marilyn looked stricken. "What will I do?"

"Well," Alice said, with a mixture of sweetness and exasperation, "you might remember that you don't really work there. Besides, I'm your 'boss,' so I think I'll be able to ignore this particular office romance."

"Oh, that's good." Marilyn sighed with relief.

"You're hiding something," Shirley said suspiciously. "Why are you so moony?"

Marilyn tilted her head coyly. "I don't know if I should tell you."

"With a come-on like that, you've got to tell us now!" Faye said.

"Well . . ." Marilyn smiled so hard her shoulders rose up to her ears. "Barton and I kissed."

"Really!" Shirley leaned forward. "How was it?"

"Amazing," Marilyn confessed. "I felt as if he were the nucleus of an atom, and I was the electron!"

The other three women stared at her.

"Could you elaborate?" Faye suggested.

"Well," Marilyn flushed and giggled. "I mean, it was as if we were in our own little world, and he was the center of it, and everything in my body was pulling toward him."

"Go on," Shirley said.

Marilyn sighed. "That's all."

"That's all?" Alice echoed.

"I mean, I was so flustered, I told him to stop. He did, right away. He was a perfect gentleman. He drove me back to the TransWorld garage and walked me to my car and we said good night. He told me he'd phone me as soon as he gets back in town."

Alice flipped through her notebook. "The Champion execs will be back next Monday. Which is also, I'm pleased to announce, the first organizational meeting for Golden Moments."

Marilyn looked confused.

"My retreat," Shirley explained. "That's what I've decided to name it. Shirley Gold—Golden Moments, see? Alice and I are inviting just a few potential investors to her condo to begin the fund-raising phase."

"Sounds exciting," Faye said. "I'm sorry I won't be able to come. The Eastbrooks have a large dinner party that night. But good luck, Shirley."

"I might be busy with Barton," Marilyn said dreamily.

Alice snorted. "We'll *try* to carry on without you." She looked at the others. "So our next Hot Flash Club meeting won't be for two weeks, right?"

"Right," Shirley agreed.

"We should have a lot more to report by then," Faye said.

"Oh, yes," Marilyn agreed. "A lot more."

"That's an accurate scientific estimate, right?" Alice asked.

"Absolutely," Marilyn replied.

21

Tuesday night, Faye was especially restless. For once the Eastbrooks had no social functions. Margie had the day off, Dr. Eastbrook was down in the clinic in his office, Lila had driven off to see Teddy, and Mrs. Eastbrook was secluded in her bedroom.

Once her duties were concluded for the day, Faye had to retreat to her living quarters, where she had her own phone, her own television, and even a small microwave and hot plate so she didn't have to make the trek through the vast hall to the kitchen. It was pleasant enough. But it meant she was so isolated from the rest of the house, she was unable to do any proper sleuthing.

She was determined to get behind the mystery door in the family room. She was certain Lila really loved Teddy, but *something* was off-kilter in this family.

She sorted through the twelve keys on the heavy brass ring Mrs. Eastbrook had given her. Each key was rimmed with a colored plastic tab coded to the colors on the list in her leather organizational notebook: Front Entrance, Back Entrance, Private Passageway, and the various bedrooms, offices, and wine cellar. She didn't have a key to the door in the family room, and *The Room* wasn't mentioned on her map of the house and grounds.

Sooner or later, she thought, the Eastbrooks would have to take her completely into their confidence. Already Faye was aware that Lila disappeared through the door in the family room first thing every morning and last thing at night. Mrs. Eastbrook also disappeared through the door several times a day. Dr. Eastbrook never went there, as far as Faye could tell. It was possible, of course, that some wildly famous celebrity was tucked away there, but Faye doubted it. There were private cottages on the grounds for people of that ilk.

One more try before she gave up for the day. She would—she would go to her office, and if anyone asked what she was doing, she'd say she'd left her reading glasses there.

Still clad in her gray pantsuit, Faye slipped from her room, headed down the hall, unlocked her office door, stepped inside, and shut her door.

Her hand was on the light switch when a

drift of fresh air alerted Faye; someone had come in the front door. Lila must be back from her date.

A bar of light glowed beneath the door connecting her office to Mrs. Eastbrook's. Her steps cushioned by the thick carpet, Faye went to the door, leaned her ear against the wood, and held her breath, listening. It took only a few seconds for her to determine the voices were Mrs. Eastbrook's and Lila's.

"—not fair!" Lila cried.

"Life's not fair, darling." Mrs. Eastbrook sounded weary.

"But Mom, Teddy is a wonderful man. He's kind, he's generous—"

"I know—"

"Then let me *tell* him! He would understand! He wouldn't mind!"

"Lila, we've gone over this before. If just one person knows, everyone knows."

"Teddy can keep a secret! He's absolutely trustworthy!"

"Oh, don't be naive, Lila! You know he'd tell his parents! They're no dummies! They might very well order Teddy to break the engagement. *Then* how would you feel?"

"He wouldn't break off with me, he wouldn't!" Lila broke into sobs so heartrending that on her side of the door Faye felt her own heart swell with sympathy. What was going on?

When Mrs. Eastbrook spoke, her voice was tender. "Darling, wait until after the wedding. Please. It's the right thing to do."

"It's so hard, Mom."

"I know, Lila. It's hard for me, too." Something creaked; Faye recalled how Mrs. Eastbrook's desk chair creaked when she swiveled, and envisioned her employer rising now. A moment later, she heard Mrs. Eastbrook say, "Let's go up to bed. You've had a long day. Tomorrow we've got that senator's wife, and you'll be swamped with work. Take a nice long soak and watch a silly movie, okay?"

"All right, Mom." Lila blew her nose.

The light beneath the connecting doors went out. Faye waited. The carpet's capacity to swallow footsteps helped Faye sneak around, but equally, it kept her from hearing others.

After five full minutes, she opened the door. The hall was empty. She made her rounds, checking to be sure all doors and windows were locked, though she'd checked them only an hour earlier.

The door from the family room was locked tight. Sighing, Faye went back down the hall to her room.

Thursday, Eugenie Eastbrook was giving a luncheon for the board of directors of a Boston-based charity. In the kitchen, Margie rushed about muttering to herself as she created brilliant dishes with a minimum of calories and a maximum of eye appeal.

Faye helped the maids set the dining room table for sixteen. She double-checked the menu with Margie, assured herself that the correct silver had been placed at each setting, removed some wilting leaves from the centerpiece, and ran an eagle eye over the room, looking for the slightest flaw. She adjusted a vase of flowers in the entrance hall and went out to the staff entrance to see whether the dry cleaner's delivery had arrived.

It had. Doctor would need his tux that night, and it was ready, sheathed in plastic, as were several of Mrs. Eastbrook's dresses. Carefully laying them across her arms, she went up the back staircase to the bedrooms. At the master bedroom, she knocked on the door.

"Mrs. Eastbrook?"

"Come in, Faye."

Eugenie Eastbrook lay, fully clothed and meticulously made up, on her vast bed.

"I have your dry cleaning. Dr. Eastbrook's tux is here."

"Good."

Faye hung the clothing in the various closets. "Mrs. Eastbrook, are you all right?"

"I'm fine, Faye. Just tired."

"Is there anything I can bring you? Some tea? A cool washcloth for your forehead?"

"A cool washcloth would be lovely. But no, never mind, I'd have to redo my makeup. No, nothing, thank you."

Faye hesitated. "Perhaps some aspirin?"

"No, Faye. I've set my clock, but in case I doze off, just be sure I'm downstairs when they begin to arrive."

"I will. The dining room looks gorgeous, and the food is heavenly."

"I'm glad. Thank you."

Faye let herself out of the room, shutting the door quietly. She went along the long hallway and into the various bathrooms, gathering towels, washcloths, and discarded laundry. On days when there was a luncheon, the two maids couldn't serve, clear, and keep up with the regular housework, so Faye assisted. She was glad to do it. In the two short weeks she'd worked for the Eastbrooks, she'd become rather protective of them. She didn't know anyone who worked as hard as they did.

If she had to make her report to the Hot Flash Club that day, she would say, without reservation, that Lila Eastbrook genuinely loved Teddy Becker.

And yet. Yet—there was a vein of sadness running through all three of the Eastbrooks, as if their cool reserve was holding back a flood of grief.

Friday, during her lunch hour, Faye chatted with Margie in the kitchen. Trying to appear spontaneous, she said, "It's so lovely out today, I think I'll take a little walk."

"Just don't go down by the spa and clinic," Margie reminded her. "If they saw a stranger walking around down there, they'd think you were a reporter, come to find out who just got a face-lift."

"I'll stay close to the house," Faye promised easily.

She went out the kitchen door to the back, where the delivery trucks parked. Idly, she strolled to the fountain in the center of the circle drive, tilting her head as if pleased with the patter and sparkle of water drops in the sun. She leaned against it and looked up at the sun, letting it warm her face, closing her eyes. She inhaled the fragrance of the hundreds of hyacinths and daffodils bursting up through the green grass where they'd been planted randomly, to appear wild.

Mrs. Eastbrook had gone to the Chestnut Hill Mall to be fitted for some suits, and Faye was pretty sure Lila had left, too, although "Missy" didn't always check in with Faye. Lila's cute little convertible wasn't in the drive, but it could be parked over in one of the garages. Faye didn't think so. The weather had been so nice recently.

Dr. Eastbrook's personal Jaguar was on the circle drive, but the doctor himself was, according to the schedule, down at the clinic. No one was in the living room or dining room. If there were ever a time to check out the house, this was it.

Faye paced the length of the house to the far west side. The driveway circled back to the front of the house, passing along this wall, then there was green grass and flowers and, farther on, a small apple orchard, budding now in a profusion of pink blossoms. Faye ambled toward the orchard and wandered in among the trees.

From there she had a good look at the long west end of the house. She'd opened the curtains herself just that morning, letting sunshine flood into the family room through the high casement windows. Now she could see clearly that a room, about twenty feet wide by forty feet long, was attached to the family room. The single-story extension had one exterior door and several windows. Blinds and curtains blocked off the slightest view of what was inside.

Faye snapped off a small twig thick with pink blossoms, and left the orchard, trying to look dreamy and lost in thought as she headed back to the house. This time, she walked around to the front. When she was near the secret room, she stopped suddenly, balancing on one foot and bending down to remove her shoe, shaking it as if a stone were inside. For just a moment, she rested her hand against the warm stone of the house. With her head so close to the window, she was certain she heard—*crying.*

Someone was crying like a child all alone in the dark.

22

Saturday morning, Shirley drove to Stoneham for her second session with Jennifer D'Annucio. In spite of the rain spilling down, she was cheerful, almost blissful—that afternoon she and that marvelous Alice were meeting with Julie Martin. These April showers would bring flowers, and Shirley's life was flowering, too. Hefting her massage table over her shoulder, she fairly skipped up the wet stairs.

Jennifer threw the door open before Shirley could knock. "Come in out of the rain!" she cried, ushering Shirley into a paradise of baked pastry aromas. Prepared for the massage, Jennifer wore only a red silk kimono over her luscious body, and her black tresses fell loose around her shoulders. "I need to wash my hair," she said, taking Shirley's sodden rain jacket to hang over the bathtub, "but I thought I'd wait until after the massage, because of the oils you use, not that I don't like them, I love them, and my hair isn't dirty, I don't want you to be grossed out, I wash it every morning, but today, since you were coming, I decided not to, I hope that's okay."

Jennifer was happy today, almost giddy, and Shirley was pretty sure it wasn't the weather. "That's fine, hon," she said, setting up the massage table. "Do you need to use the bathroom before you lie down?"

"Oh, well, I suppose that's a good idea—" Jennifer went into the bathroom, shutting the door firmly.

Shirley glanced quickly around the room. A vase of red roses stood on the drop leaf table. She bent over them, inhaling the perfume, checking to see if a card had come with it, with the sender's name written on it. But, no, nothing like that. She took her CD player out of the bag, set it up on the table, and slipped in a Mozart CD.

Jennifer returned, dropped her robe, and stretched out on the table, facedown. "I've been looking forward to this all week," she murmured. "I got to see L—my boyfriend, *three* nights, it was so lovely, but the weekends are always hard, he doesn't go into the office then, so he doesn't have an excuse to spend any time away from his house. Sometimes I get lonely, all by myself. It really cheered me up, knowing you were coming."

Shirley kneaded the young woman's shoulders, wracking her brain for a question that would cause Jennifer to say her lover's name. "Did he send you those beautiful roses?"

"Ummm, yes, he did."

"Any special reason?"

"To let me know he loves me, of course. And to thank me."

"To thank you?"

"For being here. For taking care of him. For not pestering him with chores or money worries, for letting him *rest.* Honestly, that poor man works so hard at the firm, he takes so much shit from the junior partners, he really hates it there, and I don't blame him."

"Why doesn't he quit?"

"Quit! He couldn't possibly. He's got to be a lawyer because Laura's perfect father was a lawyer. *Ouch.*"

"Sorry." Shirley freed her fingers from Jennifer's hair. Hearing Laura's name almost confirmed Shirley's fears.

Innocently, Shirley asked, "Do his in-laws live in Massachusetts?"

Jennifer nodded. "In Newton, only a twenty-minute drive from their apartment in Cambridge. Lars says they're both really nice, but Laura's their only child, and she's spoiled. Her father died last year, so he's automatically Saint Daddy, with whom no man can ever compare, and Laura's always running home to Mommy, she never cooks dinner for him, he feels so alone, and *his* family lives in the western part of the state, he grew up there, his friends live there, he has no one to turn to, really."

Lars, Shirley thought. Jennifer actually said his name. Even though she'd never set eyes on Laura Schneider, she felt her heart kick with pity for the young woman, and for her mother Faye, who seemed so very nice.

"I mean," Jennifer continued, "he gets home from work stone tired, to find the apartment is a complete pigsty, no food on the stove, no food in the refrigerator, and his laundry is never done, and there are no clean towels so he can shower. No one's there to ask him how his day was, and when Laura *is* there, all she does is cry and complain." At Shirley's request, Jennifer flipped over on her back for the last part of the massage. "I'll tell you, if I ever have children, I'll never treat my husband like that!"

"Sssh, now," Shirley whispered. "It's time to relax completely. Drift away a little while I finish your massage."

"All right," Jennifer replied, and dutifully shut her mouth.

All Shirley had to do for the HFC was find out whether or not Lars was having an affair with his secretary. Drawing her hands up and down Jennifer's perfect calves, rubbing her delicate pearl-polished toes, Shirley sighed deeply. She shouldn't have offered six massages. She'd completed her HFC assignment. What on earth would she do with the next four? She felt like a traitor, listening to this sweet girl.

When she was finished, she brought Jennifer a glass of water, then excused herself to use the bathroom, where she changed clothes and combed her hair and redid her lipstick.

"You look great!" Jennifer told her when she came out of the bathroom. "Do you have a lunch date?"

"Not exactly." Her optimism bubbled up irrepressibly. "I've got a business meeting."

"That sounds exciting."

Shirley couldn't resist smiling. "It is, actually. I have some plans for expanding my business, and my financial advisor and I are meeting with some interested clients."

"Well, that's wonderful. Here," Jennifer said, "I made you some cranberry-walnut brownies. Perhaps you can have them at your meeting."

"Oh, honey, you don't have to—"

"But I want to! I love to bake, and since you're giving me these massages free—"

"They're not free. As I said, someone entered your name, and you won them. The, um, store that sponsored the contest paid me for the massages."

"Still, oh, you know what I mean! I don't like to seem ungrateful. I'm enjoying the massage so much, and besides, I feel so much better, talking to you about my—my life. I don't dare tell anyone else about Lars, I moved here from the Cape, you know, but anyway, I don't want to tell my friends down there that I'm in love with a married man, because they'd tell my mother and she'd kill me if she didn't die of shame first! I'm just so grateful to you for listening to me like you do, not judging me, I can't tell you what it means. So please," she finished breathlessly, "take these brownies."

"I will. Thank you, honey."

Jennifer hugged her warmly, then Jennifer opened the door. Shirley hefted her massage table on her right shoulder, balanced her new, invisible, but very real burden of guilt on her left, and hurried back down the stairs and over the driveway to her car.

Oh, Lord, how could this child be so trusting? She looked down at the warm bag of brownies. It was as if she were carrying a bag of guilt in her hands.

23

Alice parked her black Audi behind Shirley's VW Rabbit, tightened the sash of her Burberry raincoat, and stepped out into the rain.

"Hello!" Shirley bounced out of her car, sunny in a yellow rain slicker, holding up an umbrella printed with dogs and cats. "Hey, perfect timing!"

"You did specify one o'clock," Alice reminded her. Shirley needed to get harder-edged if she was going to pull together a business.

"Right." Shirley stared at Alice as they hurried up the walk to Julie Martin's house. "Are you limping?"

"No, I am not limping!" Alice snapped, then sighed. "Sorry, Shirley. I don't mean to bite your head off. Yes, I suppose I am limping. I have arthritis, and the rain exacerbates it, and it seems to be getting worse."

"Massage is great for arthritis, and I can

show you some exercises and recommend some herbal—"

"Maybe later. Let's concentrate on this right now."

"Okay." Shirley unlocked the door, and the two women entered the dark house.

"We're here!" Shirley called. "I've brought a friend, Julie!"

Alice hung up their coats in the hall closet while Shirley whipped through the house, opening curtains, switching off the computers and TV, banging around in the kitchen setting out cups and turning on the burner beneath the teakettle.

A hunched figure swiveled in her desk chair, peering anxiously at Alice, who, knowing her height and general appearance could intimidate, immediately dropped down onto the sofa. She jerked her head toward the kitchen. "She's a regular little tornado, isn't she?"

Julie Martin's mouth quivered in a semblance of a smile.

"I'm Alice, Shirley's friend." She held out her hand.

Julie extended her own as timidly as a fox moving toward a trap. "Julie," she whispered. Her hand was a brittle icicle in Alice's.

"That bull run at the end of trading yesterday was exciting, wasn't it?" Alice asked.

Julie's eyes lighted up. This was language she could recognize. "Yes, it—"

"Great!" Shirley exploded into the room, clapping her hands. "You've introduced yourselves! I've made Tension Tamer tea, which will help us think, and I brought some snacks to munch on while we brainstorm."

"I think we should sit at the dining room table," Alice said.

"Oh, well, I'm not—" Shirley glanced at Julie, who was obviously still mentally attached to her computers. She nodded. "I mean, she doesn't have a dining room table. But I agree, it will be easier to take notes at a table, so let's go in the kitchen."

Julie's eyes widened like a skittish horse, as if Shirley had suggested heading for Antarctica. Noticing, Shirley went over and placed her hands on Julie's shoulders. "I'll just give you a quick little shoulder massage to help you loosen up."

"I'll make the tea." Alice hurried off toward the singing kettle.

Finally, they were all settled around the kitchen table with their tea, their notepads, and pens. They were, Shirley realized, an odd group, Shirley in her best batik blouse and purple velvet gypsy skirt, Alice in her severe taupe suit and boxy power heels, Julie slumped and bulging in sweatpants and a stained T-shirt.

Shirley took a deep breath. "Julie, the reason we asked you to let us meet with you like this is because I've been wanting to open my own little health retreat. It would be a tranquil place, where people could check in a few times a year, as often as needed, to get mentally, physically, and spiritually refreshed. We'd have a nutritionist to draw up healthy, reasonable diets, and a doctor to evaluate your physical health, and therapists to counsel you, and an astrologist—"

Alice tried not to wince.

"—to prepare your astrological chart. We'd have musicians, and aromatherapists, and instructors to teach you yoga, or aikido or tai chi."

Julie's face was a perfect blank.

Alice cleared her throat. "*I* think it's an excellent idea. As vice president in charge of administration at TransWorld Insurance Corporation" —She saw Julie's eyes flicker as she realized the woman in the kitchen with her worked for one of the most dynamic companies on the stock market—"I believe a retreat like Shirley's could be extraordinarily effective at improving executive performance. I'm going to invest some of my own money in Shirley's venture. Next week we're going to have an organizational meeting with several others to discuss fund-raising to start up her retreat."

"Okay," Julie said.

Alice could tell that was, for Julie, a display of wild enthusiasm, so she moved on to the next point. "One of the reasons we've come to you is that Shirley has three thousand dollars of her savings she'd like for you to invest for her in some high-yield, quick-turnover stocks. Of course that's a pittance to start with, but we have to start somewhere, and we're hoping that after the organizational meeting, we'll have more for you to work with." Including some of your own zillions, Alice silently e-mailed her.

"I see." Julie's eyes wiggled like a physicist working through a calculation of Einsteinian proportions as her thoughts latched onto the words *invest*, *stocks*, and *yield*. Shirley and Alice could *see* the moment Julie got it. "Oh. I'd love to make some money for you, Shirley. Let me show you a list of stocks—"

Shirley flinched as if Julie had offered to set her on fire. "No thanks! I don't do stocks. *You* do stocks, and I'll work on ideas, okay?"

"Okay."

"And Julie," Shirley pressed on, "I know how much you hate leaving your house. So I'm wondering whether we could have my organizational meeting here at your house next week. I'd clean up afterward."

Julie looked as if she were about to throw up. "People . . . here?"

"People with money. Potential investors," Alice told her.

"Well . . ."

"It won't be a crowd or anything. Just seven or eight of us."

Julie looked grim.

"Or we could have it at my place," Alice interjected. "I'll pick you up and drive you." She'd suggested this strategy to Shirley before they came in: make Choice A so terrifying, Choice B, which by itself might seem scary, would feel absolutely comfortable.

"Well, that might be okay." Julie sighed and nodded one-half inch, agreeing.

Back outside, Shirley grabbed Alice in a bear hug. "Honey, you're awesome! You speak with such authority! And you got Julie to agree to leave her house!"

Alice laughed. "I'm just a businesswoman, Shirley."

But as she drove back to her waterfront condo, Alice couldn't help smiling. Working on the design and wording of the preliminary brochure was fun, finessing Julie was fun, planning the Golden Moments sales pitch was fun. She was having a great time, and *damn*, it was nice to be appreciated!

24

Over the past several years, Marilyn had enjoyed a lively correspondence with the eminent British paleontologist Richard Fortey. This exchange existed only in her mind, yet it sustained Marilyn through her worst days. She kept copies of two of his books, *Trilobite* and *Life: A Natural History of the First Four Billion Years of Life on Earth*, on her bedside table to read from every night because his belief, couched in elegant prose, that the smallest scientific discovery, linked with others, would eventually lead to a better understanding of the natural world made Marilyn feel less alone, less insignificant.

Now she stood in her lab on Saturday morning, staring down at the trilobite she'd been painstakingly excavating from its shale tomb, waiting for Fortey's consoling words to speak to her.

Instead, she heard Barton Baker whisper, "Oh, dear God, Marilyn, I really want to take you to bed."

She felt so weak in the knees she nearly fell on the floor.

Of course, Barton wasn't there in the MIT lab with her right then any more than Richard Fortey was, but ever since their insane, adolescent make-out session in his car two nights earlier, every word he'd whispered to her ran flashing on a circular loop through her mind like a Times Square streamer ad.

What was happening to her? She didn't even recognize her own *mind*! It was like being on some kind of rare drug; hell, it was like being on another *planet*!

She looked down at the ancient creature resting in its rock coffin. Trilobites had witnessed cataclysmic geographic events, but at this moment the image of a volcano hurling boulders into a steaming sea couldn't compare to the memory of Barton's fingers stroking her neck. His warm mouth, his thrusting tongue, his hot hand on her breast—

This was ridiculous. She was deranged. Clearly she needed to have sexual congress with someone, and since she was married, she'd better have it with her husband. Even if it had been months—years?—even if she'd thought whatever flames once burned between her and Theodore had been extinguished, she still was his wife, and they were both still alive, and she would just go and—why she would just find her husband and seduce him!

Marilyn switched off the light, left the lab, and headed through the maze of corridors to her husband's office.

She'd just entered the biology building when someone tapped her on the shoulder. She turned to see Faraday McAdam.

"Hello, Marilyn! My God, what have you done with yourself! You look gorgeous!"

Faraday looked pretty gorgeous himself, with his blue shirt accentuating his startling blue eyes and his whole huge body radiating good health. Why, Faraday was *sexy*, Marilyn realized, and it was like an epiphany, although a rather uncomfortable one. What was happening to her? Had she become some new kind of sex addict? Was it possible, at her age?

"Hello, Faraday," she said weakly. "I'm just on my way to see Theodore."

Faraday leaned against the wall, blocking her passage. "Oh, well, are you sure he's there? It is Saturday morning."

"Oh, yes. He left a note for me at home this morning saying he had to go to his office. His trip out to Hawaii made him fall behind in his work. But I thought I might be able to grab him for lunch—"

"Why not have lunch with me?" Faraday asked. "I've been wanting to ask you what you thought of Morris's new book."

"I'd love to discuss it with you," Marilyn told him with genuine enthusiasm. "But some other time." She turned away.

To her surprise, Faraday linked his arm through hers. "Well, we can chat while we walk."

"Um, okay." Marilyn allowed him to pull her so close their hips almost touched as they walked.

Faraday said, "I read a new essay on the Trident-bearing trilobite from the Devonian of Morocco—"

Marilyn looked up at the tall Scot. "Faraday, this isn't walking. This isn't even crawling. Are you all right?"

Faraday blushed, which, since his cheeks were already naturally ruddy, turned his entire face crimson. "I'm fine, Marilyn, I just, I suppose, in my excitement over, uh—"

Marilyn narrowed her eyes. It wasn't like

Faraday to stammer. What was going on? She knew Faraday didn't like Theodore. But he seemed to be attempting to keep her from getting to Theodore's office.

With a click, one and one made two.

Marilyn jerked her arm from Faraday's and took off down the hall. She climbed the stairs two at a time, turned right, came to Theodore's door, and turned the knob.

It was locked. But she heard movements inside.

"Theodore?" She rapped on the wood.

"Marilyn, dear," Faraday panted, storming up behind her.

Marilyn grabbed her keys from her purse, found the one to Theodore's study—he'd given it to her several years ago when he sprained an ankle and needed her to fetch some scientific journals for him to read from the comfort of his bed—and opened the door.

There was Theodore, frozen like an exhibit in a glass case: Middle-aged Man Committing Adultery. A woman, younger than she was pretty, lay across Theodore's desk, her head pressed against the computer monitor, her skirt up around her waist. Theodore bent over her, presenting to Marilyn and Faraday the unfortunate view of his naked, sunburned buttocks and the thin white strip of flesh that had been shaded by his Speedo thong.

For several long moments, no one breathed.

Then Theodore commanded, "Shut the door!"

Marilyn obeyed.

25

Sunday morning Faye awoke determined to get into the secret room. It was the best opportunity that had presented itself so far. Margie had the day off and had, after tidying the kitchen Saturday night, gone into Boston to stay with her sister. That morning Faye fulfilled Margie's duties, preparing fresh coffee, bowls of chopped fruit, and slices of dry lite toast for the three Eastbrooks to eat in their bedrooms. Shortly after that, Mrs. Eastbrook informed her that the three of them were off to church, then to the country club for lunch with friends. If Faye would be kind enough to remove the breakfast trays and tidy the kitchen, and also throw together a large salad for the family to have later that evening . . .

Of course, Faye replied. Sunday was not officially her day off, it was Margie's, but Faye's duties were light. Someone had to be at the house, and there was always bookkeeping needing doing, or laundry and ironing.

Faye watched from the kitchen window as the three Eastbrooks settled into the Jaguar and drove away from the house. Hurriedly she fetched the trays, carried them down the back stairs to the kitchen, and did the washing up, her mind buzzing with thoughts as she worked.

On the housekeeper's key ring were all the keys to most rooms of the house, except for the private door off the family room, but Faye *did* have the key to Eugenie's office, and she knew Eugenie kept *her* keys in the right-hand drawer of her desk. Both maids had the day off and would stay down in their quarters in the staff house. Margie and all the Eastbrooks were gone. It was the perfect opportunity.

Faye moved through the house swiftly. The quiet was unnerving. Faye rushed through her Sunday duties, making the beds in the Eastbrooks' rooms, gathering up used towels and putting out fresh ones, collecting used water glasses and setting out fresh ones, double-checking to be sure the Waterford crystal was spotless.

At last she was through. Swiftly she entered her office, slipped through the connecting door to Eugenie's office, crossed to the beautiful ornate desk, and put her hand on the right-hand drawer.

It slid open as easily as if it were made of silk.

Eugenie's set of keys lay glittering, waiting.

Faye snatched them up. Back in her own office, she took the time to compare this set with her own. Eugenie's set held two extra keys, both with ivory plastic covers. Clasping them tightly, Faye hurriedly down the hall and through the family room.

She stopped at the locked door. She took a deep breath. She said a little prayer for courage. She inserted a key—and the lock clicked.

She pushed open the door, feeling like Alice stepping into Wonderland, and to her surprise, what she came upon was rather like Wonderland.

Wide, spacious, decorated in shades of pinks and blues, the room expanded around her. Light filtered rosily through the windows, all curtained with pink-flowered chintz. To her left was a canopy bed, covered with a deeply quilted spread. To her right were a large television set, an old black-and-white movie blaring from it, and shelves of books, toys, games, and puzzles. A table desk stood against the wall, with a computer on it, balloons floating across the screen.

In a wheelchair facing the television sat a young woman, as twisted and bent as a gnome in a fairy tale. No larger than a ten-year-old, she wore a loose caftan sort of garment, striped in pink and white. Short dark curls covered her head, and from the gaunt, skeletal face of an ancient goblin peered the dark, glittering eyes of a young woman.

She said, “Hello.”

Faye gulped. “Hello. Forgive the intrusion, I was just—”

The young woman raised one hand and pressed a button on her wheelchair, which, with an amiable buzzing noise, turned in Faye’s direction. “Come in, please. I’m always bored on Sunday mornings.”

Faye crossed the room and, dropping in a kind of curtsy that brought her to the little woman’s level, offered her hand. “I’m Faye Van Dyke, Mrs. Eastbrook’s new housekeeper.”

Three crooked fingers gripped Faye’s in a surprisingly tight grasp. “I’m Dora Eastbrook. Lila’s younger sister.”

"Hello, Dora," Faye said. "I'm pleased to meet you."

"You look uncomfortable squatting like that. Please sit down." Dora gestured to a chair facing her own.

"Thank you." She couldn't take her eyes from Dora's face, which although set crookedly on her body, radiated intelligence. "I shouldn't be in here," Faye confessed.

"I know!" Dora giggled, her odd little body shaking. "My poor parents. They think it would destroy their business, you see, if people knew the brilliant Dr. Eastbrook has a child who looks like a troll."

Faye cocked her head. "I wouldn't say troll. More like sprite, or fairy."

Dora clapped her hands together. "Yes! I think you're right! And thank you for not condescending to me, for not pretending that I look normal. Believe me, I know how I look. I've had eighteen years to come to terms with it."

"Are you in any pain?"

"Not as long as I take my pills, do my stretching exercises, and try not to do what I know I can't do."

"Do you ever go out?"

Dora shriveled a little. "Not much. Most weather hurts my skin or my lungs, and I'm susceptible to every passing germ, plus I can't bear the looks I get. It's hardest when teenage boys see me. They're either grossed out or they gawk at me like I'm a science experiment."

"I'm sure your father has done everything medically possible for you."

"Oh, God, yes. He and my mother have devoted their lives to me. I was born with spina bifada and a few other interesting physical complications, and I would have died six or seven times during infancy and childhood if not for their knowledge and care. This" —she held up her two deformed hands—"is as good as I'm ever going to get." Before Faye could speak, Dora pushed a button, and her wheelchair spun her around in a complete circle. "Wheeee! But think how fortunate I am to be born to a family with such financial and medical resources! And to have a sister who loves me as much as Lila does. I hardly ever get bored. I have CDs, and the television, and my friends and Internet relationships." A shadow crossed her face. "But sometimes—" Her tilted little head darted forward. "Like to play cards?"

"Why, yes, I do. But" —Faye looked at her watch—"I'm not sure how long I should stay in here. And I'm a little concerned about what

I should do now, I mean, whether I should tell your mother that I've—"

"Oh, you can't tell her. She'd fire you at once. Plus she'd be a nervous wreck, not that she isn't already. She's not unkind, don't misunderstand me, but she's terrified that news of me will leak out. I'd be a great story for the tabloids. *Plastic Surgeon Wizard Hides Ultimate Failure.*"

"That's a terrible thing to say," Faye murmured.

"Perhaps, but true. You could sell my story to someone for a nice pile of money, or you could blackmail my parents."

"I'd never do either one!"

"Well, I hope not. It would be a disaster if you did."

"But why? Surely people—"

"Surely people aren't vain, superficial, and irrational? Please. Look at my father's patients, then look at me! I scare people! If patients even saw me in the house, they'd run for their lives. People are afraid I'm contagious. They don't want to know I exist, and more than that, they don't want to think they could have children who look like me."

"But—"

"And before you get righteous on me, let me tell you something you probably don't know. My father rakes in a ton of money, making handsome people look young, and he needs that money, not just to keep me in all my luxuries, but to take part in DART. Twice a year he flies down to South America to operate on the severely physically handicapped and injured. The cosmetic surgery he does there makes the difference between life and death. He not only does it without salary, he pays for medical supplies, nurses, and the clinic."

"That's wonderful."

"Damn right it's wonderful. So you mustn't endanger it." Dora hit a button on her chair and went zipping across the room to a card table. "Enough about that. Let's play cards. Gin rummy? I play on the computer, but it's more fun with a live human being."

Faye checked her watch. "I suppose I can stay in here for thirty more minutes."

"Great. You deal."

As Faye pulled out the folding chair, settled in at the card table, picked up the pack, shuffled, and dealt, Dora said, "Tell me about yourself, Faye. Where are you from?"

"The Boston area."

"Married?"

"I'm widowed," Faye said. "My husband died just over a year ago."

"I'm sorry. Any kids?"

"A daughter." She couldn't help smiling, "And a granddaughter." Faye waited to see if Dora would need assistance with the cards, but the young woman swiftly snapped them up and arranged them to her satisfaction between the six working fingers of her two hands.

"Names?"

"Laura's my daughter's name. Megan's her daughter's name."

Dora discarded a three of clubs. "Healthy? Happy?"

"Healthy, yes. Happy—" She thought of Laura's tears. "Married life can be difficult for young people, especially with a new baby in the house."

"Well, I think you're wise to take a full-time job out here."

"Oh, why is that?" Faye drew a seven and stuck it between two others.

"I think it's a mistake for parents to get too involved with their grown children's lives. Except for someone like me, of course, but I'm an extreme case. 'Cause it's never just one way, you know."

"What do you mean?" Faye shifted uncomfortably in her chair, sensing she was about to learn something about Lila Eastbrook, and wasn't that why she was there, after all, to find out whether Lila really loved Teddy Becker, or was just after him for his money? She just felt so guilty, hearing secrets from this young woman.

"Well, take Lila, for example. You know how hard she works for the clinic and spa."

"Absolutely."

"What you don't know is beneath her beautiful exterior she's terrified."

"Terrified!"

"Sure. All her life she's been gawked at just as much as I have, and sure, in a nicer way. She's been the Eastbrook Poster Child for Beauty and Perfection. Now she's engaged to this man she's mad about, and she's afraid once he gets past her looks he'll discover she's stupid."

"Is she stupid?"

"No way! But she's never been really *tested*. She's been wrapped up in the family business all her life. She's never held a job anywhere else. She's never even *applied* for a job anywhere else. She got into a decent college, but she's always suspected she was admitted because of our dad's money. She didn't finish college, because they needed her to help out here, that's the story anyway, but she wasn't making good grades, and that might have been because she was spending so much time here helping out, but she'll never know, will she? I love Lila, and I love having her spend time with me, but I'm worried about her. She needs to detach from this family and stand on her own."

"You're very wise for someone so young."

"Hey, I've had a lot of time to listen to Oprah. And by the way, gin." She grinned. "Another game?"

"Sorry. I'd better get back to the rest of the house before they come home." As Faye rose, her eye caught on several cheerful crayon drawings thumbtacked to the wall. "These are great! Did you do them?"

Dora shrugged. "Just kid stuff."

"No." Faye walked closer, bending over, because they were placed at Dora's eye level, and studied the Crayola drawings of tulips, of a snowman, of a cherry tree in blossom, of the fountain at the back of the house. "No, these are quite good, really. Vibrant."

"Thank you." Dora motored next to Faye. "It takes concentration, but I really like doing it."

"I can see that. Have you tried paints? Pastels?"

"You're kidding, right?"

"No. No, I think you should try paints."

"Do you paint?"

"Yes, actually—" Faye's face fell. "I used to." Dora's eyes were gleaming. "I have a book you might be interested in. I'll bring it the next time I see you."

"When will that be?"

"I'm not sure. I'll have to check the calendar to find the next time everyone will be out of the house. But I'll come back as soon as I can." Impulsively, she leaned down and kissed Dora on her slanted pixie cheek.

26

Late Monday afternoon, in the privacy of her TransWorld office, Alice was having trouble concentrating on her Trans-World work.

Because of the merger of Champion and TransContinent, many jobs overlapped, which meant some employees in the two gargantuan corporations had to be laid off. The big boys at the top had already hashed out the major executive positions, but Alice and Alison were charged with cutting twenty to fifty additional jobs on the next rank down. Of course they each wanted to keep their own people, so it was a difficult task, not unlike checking the chads on the Florida presidential ballots. They'd tried to work in a conference room, but that neutral space quickly became radioactive from their disagreements. Finally, they'd decided to work via e-mail from their offices, and they'd improvised a chart comparing several personal variables—title and definition of position, seniority, plus and minuses in personnel files from both senior and junior staff, present salary and benefits.

Alison had just whipped off, at two minutes after five, a new e-mail so dense with figures it spread itself across Alice's screen like a rash of measles. Alice closed it. Her head was swimming. No more for tonight, she thought.

Tonight was the preliminary organizational meeting for Shirley's retreat, and *that* was what Alice wanted to focus on. It would be at Alice's condo, which would inspire more confidence in prospective investors than Shirley's purple palace.

An ulterior motive also weighed in: Alice hoped Alan might get to know Shirley during the conference, and be more amenable to seeing her for massage and other therapies. She was beginning to realize what a breath of fresh air Shirley brought into her own life—even though Shirley was nearly destitute, she was so *buoyant*, so optimistic. Perhaps some of that might *rub off* on Alan, Alice thought, chuckling.

A discreet knock came at her door.

"Yes?"

Marilyn Becker looked in. "I'm leaving now, Mrs. Murray."

Alice grinned, but kept her voice professional. "Step in here for a moment, Marilyn, before you leave."

"Yes, Mrs. Murray." Marilyn retained her professional demeanor as she entered Alice's office, but once she'd shut the door, she giggled and hugged herself. "I think tonight's the night!" she confessed in a triumphant whisper.

"Yes, for the Golden Moments meeting at my condo. Are you coming?"

Marilyn pulled an office chair close to Alice's desk, leaned forward, and whispered wickedly, "I might be coming, but not at your condo!"

Alice laughed. "Why, Marilyn, you saucy thing. Got a date with Barton?"

"He's taking me to dinner."

"Aren't you pleased with yourself?"

Marilyn chewed on the side of her lip. "Yes, but I'm also terrified. God, Alice, I feel about nineteen."

"You *look* about nineteen, too, Marilyn. You're glowing." A thought occurred to Alice, who squinted skeptically at her friend. "You aren't falling in love with Barton, are you?"

"I'm not sure," Marilyn answered truthfully. "I've never felt like this before. When I married Theodore, I wasn't so much in love with him as I was certain that we were meant to live our lives together. It was an intellectual, philosophical kind of thing. With Barton, it's all physical."

"He sure seems attracted to you. He's always hanging around your desk."

"I know. But sometimes it actually has been about work. Even then, just having him so near makes me feel deliciously *melty*." Seeing Alice's expression, Marilyn hastened to add, "But don't worry, Alice. I won't forget my assignment! I intend to be *cunning*. When the time's right, I'll just throw in a few questions." She checked her watch. "I've got to go home and change! I'll see you tomorrow."

"Have fun!"

Alice watched Marilyn fairly prance out of the office. She looked great! It wasn't just the cool new clothes and haircut. Marilyn was having *fun*. She was playing the role of vamp, and loving it. It made Alice remember the years, long ago, when she'd been in love with Bill Weaver. Just passing him in the office had been like plugging into a universal electric source; she'd been jolted by passion, and that energy had energized her work and her entire life.

For a moment, she closed her eyes and let the memories move through her like a favorite song. She would like to fall in love again.

Likely chance. Snapping back to business, Alice wiggled her mouse, clicked her computer, and closed Alison's everlasting e-mail. She'd deal with that tomorrow. She clicked the mouse again and checked her other e-mail.

All boring business-related matters—except for a mysterious surprise: something from "Your Secret Admirer."

Right, Alice thought. I've got a secret admirer. Well, it *was* possible that one of the new executives found her attractive. Stranger things had happened. Look at Marilyn and Barton. She opened the e-mail.

Hey, Beautiful. I'd like to get to know you. Want to get to know me?

Alice hesitated. This was undoubtedly worthless spam.

Still.

She clicked it open. The screen turned pink, filling, as Alice watched, with flashing red hearts.

That was all. No message, no clue about the sender. Whoever her admirer was, he was shy about it. Or maybe just flirtatious?

Enough! Alice turned off her computer and rose, put her hands on her aching back and stretched. Gathering up her Burberry and briefcase, she strode out of her office, down the long corridor to the bank of elevators. As she pressed the DOWN button, her heart rose up.

"Hi, honey. Wow, you look handsome." Alan had showered, shaved, and put on the new white shirt and chinos Alice bought him. "And the room looks perfect."

Alan had moved the kitchen chairs into the living room to form a circle for their guests. He'd fanned brochures out on the coffee table between bowls of nuts and plates of cookies. "I'm leaving to pick up Julie Martin now."

"Great. Be gentle with her. She's neurotically shy."

Alice hopped in the shower, washing with a fragrant soap Shirley had given her. The floral scent lifted her spirits. She dressed in one of her favorite outfits, something too wild ever to wear at work, a turquoise tunic with matching slacks, and she was just loading herself with what she secretly called her war medals, heavy necklaces and bracelets of turquoise and silver, presents she'd given herself for each rise in pay and position, when the doorbell rang.

That would be Shirley, arriving before the others.

Alice greeted Shirley, who swept her up in

a warm hug. "You're so wonderful to do this, to have this here, my God, look at this place! It's awesome!" She turned to Alice. "How do I look?"

Alice had suggested that Shirley tone down her astrologist's appearance and try to present a more businesslike front for this crucial meeting. Accordingly, Shirley had braided her wild red hair and twisted it at the back on her neck, securing it with pins. She'd left off the purple eye shadow and dressed in brown slacks and a white shirt. Then, being Shirley, she'd added a silk shawl swirled with ambers and golds.

"You look perfect," Alice told her.

They sat around the coffee table, going over the packets Shirley and Alice had put together. A handsome brochure announced the opening of "Golden Moments, Spa and Wellness Clinic." Alice still flinched at the word "wellness," but Shirley assured her it was part of the vernacular. On the front of the brochure was a photo of a person receiving a massage, seeming so blissed out that Alice relaxed just looking at it. Inside were the list of treatments the clinic would offer, and on the back the director of the clinic and her board were listed. At the moment, Alice, Julie Martin, and an MD and his aromatherapist were on the board.

Accompanying the brochure was a folder to

be handed to each prospective board member that night when they arrived. Inside, compiled by Alice, were charts costing out the initial investment, the proposed time frame, and the dividends to be, eventually, paid out.

"Looks good, Shirley," Alice said. It should; Alice had put it together on her own laptop. Consulting with Shirley, she'd written every word. And Alice felt as giddily nervous about it as she had when her boys starred in kindergarten plays.

The doorbell rang.

It was an odd group who arrived. Gruff Dr. Peter Donovan, a psychiatrist, grumbled in with his fey aromatherapist wife Reya fluttering around making his scotch and water just the way he liked it, asking in whispers if he needed another pillow for his back. Suzanne West, the astrologist, had a surprisingly gravelly voice for someone dressed in layers of pastel chiffon. Nora Salter, Shirley's wealthy socialite client, made a stately entrance, leaning on a cane.

Tom Warren, a yoga instructor, was Alice's age, and attractive, his bald black head shining, his movements gentle, almost delicate. Shirley thought he might be a prospective beau for Alice, who had insisted she wasn't interested in anything like that, so Alice was amused at her disappointment when she realized he was gay.

Jennifer D'Annucio was invited even though Alice knew the young woman had no money—she needed to meet other people, Shirley had insisted, and Jennifer, delighted to meet a new set of people, had brought along some of her hand-concocted canapés. Fred and Ted, who owned the beauty salon where Alice had her hair done, were also there, at Alice's request. Not only did they have plenty of money, should they want to invest, they also would be great word-of-mouth advertisements for Shirley's retreat.

Alan had picked up Julie, whom he now escorted into the room. Shirley hurried to greet the timid young woman, who had gone wild and pulled on a pair of khakis and a clean, if unironed, blue cotton shirt. She'd even combed her hair.

Shirley put her arm around the young woman. "Julie, you look great! Come sit down here, I've set a chair for you right next to me."

For a while, Alice and Shirley let the others mingle, drinking coffee or tea, admiring the view. Then Alice invited them all to have a seat. She remained standing.

"I want to thank you all for coming this

evening," she said. "As you can see, you're part of a very small group of select individuals. We've invited you here to announce the creation of a new enterprise."

As she spoke, the conversation she'd had two days ago when she and Shirley discussed the sales pitch danced mischievously at the back of her mind. "It's not an *enterprise*!" Shirley had asserted. "It's a retreat, a shelter, a haven, a—"

Alice had interrupted. "Do you want people to invest money?"

"Um, yes."

"It's an *enterprise*."

"Okay."

Alice continued. "We're all aware of the way our lives are changing. Everything moves faster. Music's louder. People want more of our time, our money, our attention. Everything's competitive. Everything's tugging on us. No matter how much we do, we can't get everything done, which makes us move faster and fall farther behind." As Alice spoke, she realized she meant exactly what she said.

"Shirley Gold wants to create a shelter for those of us who are superstressed. She wants to create an environment where we can relax and be refreshed. This is where we, adults who take care of so much, can be taken care of, ourselves. As vice president of TransWorld Insurance Corporation, I find Shirley's idea brilliant. I've spent time with Shirley, having massages, and it's been good for my body and soul."

She paused dramatically. "As a businesswoman, I'm getting in on the ground floor, being one of the first to invest in Golden Moments, because I think it will be good for my checkbook." She smiled around the room. "I'll let Shirley tell you more about her concept."

Shirley stood. At first, she was dry-mouthed and obviously nervous. As she spoke, she became calmer and more assured. Explaining her dream, she was caught up in the excitement of its possibilities, and soon she was waving her hands around, trying to conjure up pictures in the air. She was irrepressible, and Alice felt almost maternal as she watched.

Really, she didn't know when she'd felt so—*content?* Was contentment what she felt? Well, how would she know? She'd never felt it before. Triumph, yes, she'd felt that, many times. Pride, exultation, self-respect, all consequences of her disciplined labors, her self-determination, her ambition to succeed. Of course she'd felt love: carnal and romantic love for her husband, Mack, and her lover, Bill Weaver. And she'd adored her two sons, adored them still, love for them was woven into the matrix of her heart.

But *content.* No, she couldn't remember when she'd felt that. Part of it came, no doubt, from being a component in the creation of a new enterprise. If there were an entrepreneurial gene, it was built into her DNA. She had always thrived on challenge.

But this was different somehow. More personal. More healthy.

More fun.

27

"This is it." Barton Baker unlocked his apartment door and ushered Marilyn inside. "Pretty basic, isn't it?"

The room was small, square, and gray. The gray sectional furniture sat on a gray rug that ran right up to the gray-and-white faux-marble tiles of the chrome-and-gray kitchen.

As far as Marilyn was concerned, the place was done up in leopard skin and fur. However it looked, it was the lair of a single man, a man ten years younger than she was, a man who had just taken her out to a heavenly dinner and kissed her so passionately in the elevator on their way up Marilyn thought her clothes might ignite.

"Nervous?" Barton asked. He ran his hands through his already disheveled black hair, a sign, Marilyn thought, that he was excited.

Marilyn nodded. They were still standing just inside the door. Marilyn's knees were so weak she wasn't sure she could take another step. She hadn't spoken with Theodore since she caught him with the grad student, and just then she didn't care if she ever spoke to her husband again.

"I am, too." His voice cracked endearingly. "I've got some good white wine. Unless you'd prefer cognac?"

"Cognac," Marilyn croaked.

"Hey." Barton put his hands on Marilyn's shoulders. "Don't be afraid. We won't do anything you don't want to do."

His touch was enough to bury her fears in a landslide of lust. Marilyn lifted her head and took a step forward. His arms went around her, his mouth lowered to hers. He pressed his body against hers, and someone moaned. Marilyn was pretty sure it was she.

Barton was taller than Theodore, and both slimmer and more massive. His chest was hard, his stomach flat, his hips, oh Lord, what was that? It had been so long since she and Theodore had made love, and it had been years—decades—since he'd pressed a big long erection against her loins. She'd forgotten how perfectly configured the biological system was, how the circuitry of the human body was wired superbly for this—mating.

"Let's have the cognac later, okay?" Barton

asked, his breath making every little hair on her neck stand at attention and tingle like antennae.

"Okay."

He led her into the bedroom. More gray. He tossed back the duvet and lowered her with him onto the bed. In his hurry, or perhaps out of kindness, he didn't turn on the lamp but let the light from the living room drift in through the open bedroom door to bathe the room in silver. Still, as they removed their clothes, Marilyn felt like the contemporary little pill bug related to the trilobite, who rolled up in a ball whenever frightened. She almost wished she could curl up in a ball herself, defending and hiding her ancient body, so inscribed with the stretch marks of her pregnancy with Teddy, her skin speckled like a duck egg with millions of tiny pink moles that had blossomed all over her during the past two years. Her breasts were full, with unusually wide, dark nipples that resembled those rubber plugs used to stop drains, and that morning in the shower, she'd found several white hairs in her pubic hair. She'd yanked them out, but all day long she'd been so worried about the coming date with Barton she'd probably grown in a new white crop.

But his hands, warm and gentle, slid gently

over her body. His palm brushed one nipple, then the other, then circled down to crush her pubic hair. His hand slipped between her legs. She wanted to pull a pillow over her face and bite it hard. She settled for burrowing her face into his chest. She laced her fingers through the curly hair on his chest, pressed her hands against his ribs, arched like an arbor over his abdomen, which was softer than bone but compact and firm as a carapace, and sliding her hand down, she accidentally touched his swollen penis, and they both gasped.

"I can't wait," Barton said.

"I can't either."

He twisted away from her to open the drawer on his bedside table, and in a flash he took out a foil-wrapped condom, which he ripped apart. He pulled on the condom and rose over her. Marilyn closed her eyes.

He entered her.

She sank down through ocean depths to the soft and unfamiliar muddy floor where the planet's own skin churned, sliding open and apart, while volcanoes thrust lava into the water, hardening, contorting, fracturing into crystals. As the ocean surged and shoved, eyeless creatures were overwhelmed by the roiling elements, squeezed, dissolved, crystallized, and Marilyn was there with them, in that elemental turbulence, she was tossed, raised, and compressed until she was too changed to be Marilyn who was afraid, and she became only a creature subject to nature's gorgeous domination. Her own body fractured open, spilling poppies, lilies, camellias into the sea.

A trilobite crawled up to nibble on a petal.

"Good God," Barton gasped, collapsing next to her.

Marilyn opened her eyes. They were both drenched with sweat. "That was wonderful," Marilyn whispered.

He held her tight. "Amazing."

"I saw a trilobite," she murmured.

"A what?"

"A trilobite. A minute little creature composed of calcite who lived 500 million years ago."

Barton was quiet a moment. "You saw a trilobite while we were making love?"

Marilyn nodded. "It was one of the most glorious experiences of my life."

He raised himself on one elbow and peered down at her. "Um, I'm not sure I understand."

Marilyn stretched luxuriously, still dazed with sexual pleasure.

Barton persisted, "I mean, why would you see a trilo—whatever—when we were making love? Why would you *want* to see one?"

"Because I'm a scientist. I study them." Turning on her side, Marilyn walked her fingertips through the jungle of Barton's chest hair.

"You're a scientist?"

"Well, in my own way," she confessed modestly. "I have a Ph.D. in paleontology, and I'm a professor at MIT."

"Then why," Barton asked gently, "are you working as a secretary?"

Marilyn blinked. The intoxicating nebula of sexual pleasure lifted off, leaving her stranded, naked, and foolish. "Oh, dear."

"What?"

"I've just done something terrible."

"I think you've just done something pretty great, myself," he teased, tracing the circle of her nipples with the tips of his fingers.

Sensations as elementary as the planet's minerals spun through her at his touch. She gazed up at him, amazed at the sheer beauty of his face. His eyes were tender, guileless, and she felt his renewed erection pressing against her thigh.

"I think I'm falling in love with you," Barton said.

Marilyn's entire body flushed with the shock of his words, and when he raised himself up over her once again, a force as powerful as the moon sent tides of pleasure surging through her. She closed her eyes, surrendered, and sank into the subterranean world where fire burst into ocean depths.

After that, they slept for a while. When they awoke, they were both starving, so Barton stalked naked from the room, returning quickly with two glasses of cognac and a bag of potato chips. "Not elegant, but it's all I've got."

Marilyn sat up in bed, pulling the covers up to her breasts. Salt surged into her mouth from the potato chips, it was the most delicious thing she'd ever tasted, she wanted to grab the bag from Barton and cram them into her mouth, she wanted to find the salt shaker and cover her tongue with salt, and when she drank the cognac, she almost wept with delight.

Wide-eyed and addlepated, she turned to Barton. "I think I'm drunk."

"I doubt it. You had only one small glass of wine at dinner."

"Then I'm drunk on sex," she decided.

"Did you see a trilo—whatever this time?"

She smiled. "No. What did you see?" she asked, frivolously.

He put his hand on her face. "You. I saw you."

She almost fainted. Barton's handsome face was soft, his expression so earnest he almost reminded her of her son Teddy, who could be so vulnerable. She was profoundly moved with a desire to protect this sweet man. "Barton, I'm not who you think I am."

"Oh, right. You were going to tell me about that."

"If I tell you," Marilyn said, "you mustn't tell anyone else."

"All right."

She sucked the salt off her fingers, and handed the potato chip bag to Barton.

"No more chips? Must be pretty serious."

"It is. It really is." The words stalled in her mouth. Was this the wrong thing to do? She was supposed to find out whether or not Alison Cummings wanted to edge Alice Murray out and take over her job. Perhaps if she were honest with him, he would be honest with her. He had said he was falling in love with her. He made love to her as if he cared for her. She could trust him. Still, she urged, "Promise me you won't tell anyone else."

"I promise," Barton said.

28

Shirley had the blues.

Sometimes, after a day of good luck—and God knew *those* had been rare enough in the past few years—sometimes, right when you think you're actually going to get your shit together and haul your flat, wrinkled ass a few steps up out of the mire of your life, then it seems the gods look down from where they recline on their clouds, sipping nectar and nibbling pitless peaches, and decide, if not to pull the rug out from under you, at least to jiggle it a bit under your feet, just to remind you they can.

It was one of those days. She awoke, full of optimism and energy, still high on the drug of the previous night's wonderful meeting at Alice's place. She jumped out of bed—well, that was the first disappointment. She only tried to jump. She actually jerked and stumbled, landing on stiff legs, falling sideways, wrenching her spine. Good Goddess! Her back had been bothering her more and more, recently. Wearing those damned high heels to the meeting, instead of her comfortable sneakers or clogs, had pulled something out of alignment. She absolutely *hobbled* into the kitchen, her limbs and joints as brittle and wooden as Pinocchio's.

After a breakfast of cleansing green tea and muesli, she took a hot shower. She still didn't feel up to par, so she broke down and took two aspirin, and as much as she hated to admit it, the damn aspirin helped. Her mood rose.

Then the phone rang.

"It started again," a woman sobbed.

"Oh, honey." Shirley listened while Betsy Little grieved because her period had arrived; once again she'd failed to get pregnant.

"It *will* happen," Shirley promised forcefully. "All your medical reports indicate you're a healthy young woman with no physical problems. You only need to relax—"

"No more!" Betsy wailed. "No more advice, no more massage. I'm canceling, Shirley. Today's session and all future sessions. I've got to find someone else. You're bad luck."

"Betsy, honey—"

But the line went dead.

Shirley clicked her phone off and thumped her forehead down on the kitchen table. She understood that today, probably *nobody* could say anything that would console the other woman. Betsy would just have to walk through her particular pain on her own. Still, it killed Shirley that Betsy thought she was bad luck. It really, really *hurt*.

Plus, there went a chunk of her income.

Before her thoughts began a downward plummet, she slammed the brakes and reminded herself to be positive.

She had to remember: With Alice's help, she'd soon be starting up her retreat. Golden Moments. Now *that* was something to be joyful about! Shirley grabbed the phone and punched out Alice's number, eager to discuss the investors' meeting.

"TransWorld," said the receptionist.

"Alice Murray, please." She wouldn't keep Alice on the phone long. She knew Alice was overwhelmed with work, but she just wanted to hear her voice, to regain that electric connection.

There was a brief silence. Then, "I'm sorry, Alice Murray isn't here."

"Oh." Shirley checked her calendar. It *was* a weekday. "Is her secretary, Marilyn Becker, there?"

There was a pause. "No, I'm sorry, she's

not." The other woman's voice sounded different, *wary.* "Could I take a message?"

"Um, no. No, I'll call later." What was going on? Shirley clicked off, then tried Alice's home phone.

"You have reached Alice Murray. Please leave a message."

"Hi, Alice, it's Shirley. I just wanted to thank you for your help last night, and to talk it all over with you. It was so great! I couldn't reach you at work, but I'll try you at home tonight. Thanks again—a million!"

She tried to sound cheerful, but as she hung up, she felt dissatisfied and irritable—*thwarted.* Jumping up, she checked her calendar—four appointments that day, the last one with Julie. Great! They could talk about Golden Moments. Perhaps cautious Julie would be ready to discuss how much she wanted to invest. Buoyed by this thought, Shirley loaded her Discman, tied on her sneakers, and headed out for a jog—or maybe, she thought as her knees twinged, a brisk walk.

"Hello!" Shirley sang out as she entered Julie Martin's dark house.

"Hey," Julie answered, tapping away on her computer keyboard.

Shirley opened the shades, lighted some cinnamon candles, set up the table, and inserted a CD. "Okay, hon," she said, patting the table.

With docile reluctance, Julie left her computers and lay down for her massage. Shirley worked on Julie's body for a full hour without saying anything that would distract Julie from her relaxation, although she allowed herself to visualize Golden Moments. Why not? Her dreams just might drift into the other woman's mind.

After she brought Julie a glass of cleansing water, Shirley returned to the kitchen to make some tea for both of them. She often spent half an hour or so, just chatting with Julie, and she never charged her for the additional time, even though Shirley knew the comfortable conversation was a kind of therapy for the reclusive young woman. It was always hard work, like trying to make a toad talk. Usually Shirley regaled Julie with tales of celebrity scandals, or recounted more inspirational tales she'd read in some of her massage newsletters.

Instead she decided to talk about Golden Moments.

Heart banging, she carried two mugs into

the living room. Julie, having pulled on her sweatpants and old T-shirt, was looking, longingly, at the computer.

"Sit down a minute, hon," Shirley said. "Let's have some tea."

"All right." Julie slouched over to the end of the sofa and collapsed.

"How was the massage?" Shirley asked, settling at the other end of the sofa.

"It was good." From Julie, this was explosive praise.

Encouraged, Shirley said, "It was great to see you at the Golden Moments meeting last night. Did you enjoy it?"

Julie nodded shyly.

"Well, good! What did you enjoy?"

"Jennifer D'Annucio? She drove me home? She gave me some of her brownies? They're really delicious."

"Hey, that's great!" More than great, Shirley thought; Julie had actually interacted with someone. That was freakin' *miraculous*! "Have you given any thought to Golden Moments?"

Julie shrugged. "It seems like a good idea."

"And also, a pretty exciting investment opportunity?"

"Maybe."

"Just *maybe*?"

"Over half of all new small businesses fail."

"Yeah, well, maybe that's the national average," Shirley protested, "but this will be *my* business."

Julie folded her arms defensively over her chest. "Maybe after it's off the ground, I could invest."

"Hey, Julie," Shirley coaxed. "Haven't you told me you're healthier because of my visits?"

Julie nodded reluctantly.

"Well, then! Other people feel that way, too. You know I could make a success of this. I'm not looking for a huge amount of money from you, just—"

Julie shook her head. "I'm too scared."

"*Scared?* I don't understand. You play the stock market. That takes *lots* of nerve."

"*That's* totally impersonal. I can be ruthless. What if *your* retreat fails? I might hate you for failing to provide me any return on my investment. I'd lose you as a friend. What if it succeeds? I'd lose you as a masseuse."

Shirley hesitated before replying. How easy it would be to say: *Well, you know, you little birdbrain, if you don't invest, you could lose me as a friend* and *as a masseuse!*

But she didn't want to win Julie's investment that way.

"I see where you're coming from, Julie. I

really do. And I won't lie about it. I was counting on you as an investor. But I respect your concerns. Here's what I ask: Please, whatever you decide, don't act from fear. You were so brave, coming out last night. It took a lot of courage. I know it did. So stay strong. Make your decision wisely. Call some of the others, if you want, and talk it over. I'll be your friend whatever you decide. Just don't let fear rule your life."

"Okay," Julie agreed, in a small voice.

"Great. Well, I'd better go." Shirley gathered her stuff, hoisted her table, and said goodbye, giving Julie a hug and a smile, and thinking how easily moods could be transmitted. She hoped she'd cheered Julie up. She herself felt depressed, exhausted, and—after Julie's reluctance to invest in Golden Moments—she felt *scared*.

Back at her house, she dropped everything just inside the door and ran to her answering machine. Surely Alice would have phoned. Or maybe some of the other potential investors—

The message light was blinking! She punched the RETRIEVE MESSAGE button so hard, the machine almost flew off the table.

"Hi, Shirley. It's Faye Vandermeer. I'm just wondering whether you found out anything about—about the situation." The other woman's voice was gentle, but tense.

"Oh, no." Shirley sank onto her sofa and put her head in her hands.

"End of messages," droned the robotic voice.

The last thing in the world she wanted to do was convey bad news to someone else. And this news would set off a chain reaction of misery.

But what could she *do* about it? Her HFC assignment was to find out whether Lars Schneider was having an affair, not to change things. Would it be better if she waited another day to tell Faye, or worse? She felt *terrible*. Jeez Louise, perhaps what Betsy had said that morning was true! Maybe Shirley *was* bad luck. Poor Faye and her poor daughter! Poor sweet, lovestruck Jennifer, for that matter.

Plus, it was after seven, and Alice hadn't called. She couldn't *believe* Alice hadn't called to talk over their successful meeting! She couldn't believe Julie wouldn't invest. Shirley didn't know anyone else who had the kind of money Julie did, not even Nora Salter, and Nora had already suggested how much she was willing to invest. Without Julie's money, Shirley simply couldn't undertake building her retreat.

A muscle in Shirley's back cramped, sending an entire Fourth of July fireworks of pain through her shoulders and neck. As she dug out her electric heating pad, she was dismally lonely. The night before, she'd dressed up and given her all, trying to inspire others with her own plans. And here she was less than twenty-four hours later, all alone and knowing the retreat had failed before it even started.

Her neck pain flared up like a brush fire, but it was the pain in her heart she thought would kill her. It twisted in her chest like a creature splashed with acid. She really didn't think she could bear it.

Vodka would relax her back, and dull all sorts of pain. There was a bar only a few blocks away, a cozy place with low lights, good drinks, and a jukebox playing country songs, all about loss and sorrow. She could almost hear an old cowboy's melancholy twang, and he seemed to be calling her name.

29

When her alarm went off, Alice remained in bed for a while, replaying the Golden Moments meeting in her mind. It had been great! Once Shirley got into the groove, she glowed like a torch, and when she couldn't answer a hard question about finances, Alice stepped in. No doubt about it, the two of them, exuberant, colorful Shirley and practical, executive Alice, had wowed the group. Astonishingly, old Nora Salter had promised to invest right there on the spot, and so had a few of the others. Only Julie Martin, who Shirley had thought would be the first and biggest investor, had stalled, saying she needed time to think about it.

She glanced at the clock, then threw back the covers and began the day. As she showered, she reviewed the preliminary five-year business plan she'd put together for Golden Moments. Tossing back her orange juice, she decided, if she could steal a few moments during lunch, she'd do some more work to detail the plan.

Back in her bedroom, she pulled on her largest skirt. Uh-oh. Too tight. She'd enjoyed too many of Jennifer D'Annucio's brownies. Alice licked her lips. Some of the caramel chip cookies were left over. Alice could take a few to the office for brain food while she worked. She dropped the constricting skirt on her bed and pulled out a pair of loose, elastic-waisted, batik trousers. With a severe brown jacket, they would pass for business wear. She added a heavy set of wooden beads to make it an ensemble. After a moment, she decided on a pair of flat-heeled court shoes, so much more comfortable than her power heels, but what the hell, she had no meetings scheduled.

Outside, the sky floated above her like a great blue balloon, matching her mood as she drove deep into the heart of the Boston business district. Perhaps, when the weather was warmer, she'd ride the T and walk the rest of the way. It couldn't take much longer than sitting in traffic.

It was almost nine o'clock by the time she parked her Audi in the executive garage of the TransWorld building. Usually, she was at her desk by eight. She nodded to Roger at the security desk as she crossed to the executive elevator. She had it all to herself, so she used the shining brass button panel to evaluate her reflection: shorter, wider, because of the flat shoes and the loose trousers, but also less stern, more *interesting*. Here was a woman who might be late for work because she'd spent the night before out dancing.

When *had* she last been out dancing? She couldn't remember.

With a ping, the doors slid open at the fourteenth floor, and Alice stepped out onto the gray carpet.

Frances, who controlled the main reception area, was away from her desk. Unusual. Looking down the corridor, Alice spotted Frances shoulder to shoulder in a tight little gaggle of gabbing secretaries. *Uh-huh, fresh gossip.* When they saw Alice, their eyes widened, and they drew closer to one another. *What?* Could they be gossiping about *her*?

Frances would tell her. The receptionist had been with TransContinent for twenty years, during which time Alice had helped her with no small amount of personal problems. Frances, divorced, had a son with bipolar disorder. Alice had done everything she could to help Frances get decent medical treatment and medical coverage for the boy. He was in a new clinic now, on new medication.

Alice clipped along down the hall. George White's office was empty. Strange. She was certain there were no meetings that morning.

Alison Cummings's office was just before Alice's, guarded by Barton Baker's desk. From the corner of her eye, Alice saw, through the open door, Alison seated at her own desk, eyes glued to her computer screen. On her left, Barton Baker bent toward the computer. George White was on her right, pointing at the screen. The three were too engrossed to notice Alice, but she saw emotion flash over all three faces—and not the same emotion. Suddenly Alison's eyes widened and she covered her mouth with both hands, as if trying to push back a shout of laughter.

What the hell?

Thank God, Marilyn was at her desk, frantically typing.

"Good morning, Marilyn," Alice said. "What's going on?"

Marilyn shot up out of her chair like a rocket, grabbed Alice's arm, yanked her into her office, and shut the door. "We've got a problem."

"Shoot." Alice dumped her briefcase on her desk.

"Your computer caught a virus. It sent e-mails to everyone in your address book."

Alice dropped like a stone into her desk chair and wiggled the mouse to wake her computer up. "Saying what?"

"We're just now finding out, as people come into work and check their e-mail. It seems to be something different for everyone. Some are random statistical charts that won't mean much to anyone without the rest of the information. But some of the personnel info you've been working on with Alison has been sent around. I heard that Jack Foster got Harry Sullivan's personnel file. Now Jack knows Harry makes more than he does, and he's ballistic."

"Damn."

"Also, several people got a copy of your e-mails ordering support panty hose, hemorrhoid cream, and Big Girl's bras."

Alice slapped her forehead. "*Shit.* Okay, what else?"

"I don't know the extent of it yet. Other people got other stuff. Whatever's on your hard drive."

"What a nightmare. How did this happen?" Impatiently, Alice jerked the mouse over its pad.

Marilyn leaned over her shoulder, scanning the screen. "You must have opened an e-mail that carried a virus. I'm sure you've been warned about opening unsolicited e-mail."

"Of course I have!" Alice snapped. "And I *never* open strange e-mail programs!"

"Never?" Marilyn touched the end of a pencil to an icon on the screen. "What's this on your desktop? Card.exe SA?"

"What—Oh, Lord." Alice covered her burning face. "Last night I got an e-mail from a 'Secret Admirer.' I opened it."

"And?"

"It just threw some blinking hearts on the screen. What a moron I am!"

Marilyn gave Alice's shoulder a consoling pat. "Come on, Alice. We all want to open a file from a secret admirer. We'll just get tech support up here to clean your hard drive."

The phone buzzed.

Marilyn grabbed the phone. "Alice Murray's office." Her forehead wrinkled. "Of course, Mr. Watertown. Right away." She hung up the phone. "Mr. Watertown would like to see you in his office ASAP."

Alice groaned. "This stupid Internet is sometimes more trouble than it's worth."

"I'll call tech support now." Marilyn went out to her office.

Alice headed into her private bathroom. She peed, then slipped an antacid into her mouth, swallowing it with the smallest possible amount of water so she wouldn't be tortured with the urge to pee during the chewing out she knew she was about to get. Melvin, like Alice, had been with TransContinent for years. He was a good leader, tough and exacting. She was sure the integration into TransWorld was difficult for Melvin, and she hated it that she'd let down their side, as she thought of it, with this idiotic e-mail business.

Striding down the corridor, Alice sucked in her gut and led with her chin. At the portal to the senior vice president's office, among chrome and glass, sat Elvira Gray, of the gray personality, in her gray suit.

"Hello, Elvira," Alice said, with cool composure.

"Hello, Mrs. Murray." Elvira kept her eyes on her computer. Not a good sign. "He's expecting you. Go on in."

Alice took a deep breath, squared her shoulders, and entered.

Melvin sat at his desk, hunched over a pile of reports. For just a moment as she entered, Alice spotted the top of his head, noticing for the first time how the male-pattern baldness band of white hair around his pink scalp resembled a toilet seat.

Restraining an irreverent giggle, she shut the door firmly. Melvin looked up.

"Alice!" Standing up, his extended his hand over the desk.

So he wasn't going to chew her out. Alice was relieved. When Melvin was angry, he could blast the enamel right off your teeth. She shook his hand.

"Sit down." He gestured to a chair in front of the desk, and returned to his own executive leather chair. He leaned back, put his arms behind his head to stretch his shoulders, and said companionably, "This merger is a bitch, isn't it."

"It's a lot of work for Personnel," Alice admitted.

"Tell me about it." Melvin sighed. "You planning to head off to a resort?"

Alice frowned, puzzled. "No. Why do you ask?"

"It's the only explanation I can come up with for why you'd e-mail me a picture of a naked woman lying on a table."

Alice stared at him, dumbstruck. "You're kidding."

"I'm not kidding."

"A naked wo—Oh, shit, Melvin. That woman's getting a massage. I'm helping a friend put together a brochure for a retreat, and that was one of the photos she e-mailed me as a possibility for the cover. Anyway, *I* didn't send it to you. Somehow a virus got into my computer last night. It's been e-mailing random hits from my computer to everyone on my e-mail list."

"I thought something like that had happened. Couldn't think of any other reason you'd send Jack Foster the details of Harry Sullivan's financial package."

Alice closed her eyes. "Tech support's on its way to clean it up."

"Well, tech support can clean up the virus and stop any new e-mails, but we've got some damage control to do ourselves with what's already gone out."

"I realize that, Melvin. I'll personally speak with Jack about—"

Melvin interrupted. "But let's go back to this naked woman on the table business."

"The photo for the retreat brochure."

"Okay. Whatever." Melvin tilted his head, peering over his glasses at her. "What's that doing on your office computer?"

"Oh, come on, Melvin. You know we all have personal stuff on our office computers. I'm probably the only one in the whole company who doesn't have porn on mine."

Melvin held up his hand like a stop sign.

"Okay. Okay. Still, Alice, it's not like you, to be messing around with something else at the office."

Alice nodded. "You're right. Absolutely. I—"

"Then there's this thing with your secretary, Marilyn—" He snapped his fingers, searching for the name.

"Becker. What about her?"

Melvin dropped forward, his chair squeaking as he moved into a more aggressive position, arms crossed on his desk, head bent low like a charging bull. "You hired her specifically to spy on Alison Cummings."

Alice's jaw sagged. *How in the world—?*

"We have it from the horse's mouth, Alice. Marilyn told Barton Becker last night. He told Alison, who told me this morning, when she got here at six-thirty, as she does."

Alice closed her eyes. Then she scrambled to get on the offensive. "Well, hell, Melvin. Are you surprised? *You* know better than anyone what's going on with this merger. I'm fighting to save as many TransContinent people as possible, and I suppose Alison's trying to do the same for Champion, but frankly, I find her inflexible, cold, and arrogant. You *know* half the office gossip gets carried by the secretaries, and Alison's got her old faithful Barton, while *my* old faithful secretary Eloise retired, leaving me with no protection. What I did was only sensible!"

"No, Alice. What you did was paranoid." Bowing his head, Melvin ran his hands through his white U of fringe, then looked up. "Alice, we go back a long way together, you and I, and I think you know I have always admired the hell out of you."

"I'm aware of that, Melvin, and I appr—"

"So I am just downright sad to see you lose your vision here."

"Lose my—"

"I've felt for a while now, and I speak for the others as well, that you're just not interested in keeping up with the program. You're seeing this merger as a problem, a negative, not a challenge, a positive."

"Come on, Melvin, I—"

"And look what's happened, just in one day. The computer business plus the more serious problem of your paranoia toward a new member of the team. We just can't have this kind of attitude here now. Not with so many enormous new responsibilities."

"Melvin. Listen to—"

"Now, I've talked it over with Bill and Carl, and here's what we've decided." Leaning back in his chair, he held his hands out palms up, as if offering a gift. "We want to give you a nice three-month paid leave. You can go to that massage retreat place you're so interested in. Do whatever you want."

"That's ridiculous. I can't leave when there's so much work—"

He interrupted, very slightly raising his voice. "After that, you can retire with a really first-class settlement package. A golden parachute that will keep your boat afloat in style. Perhaps, if you'd like, a banquet honoring you for all the work you've done for this company over the past thirty years."

"For God's sake, Melvin," Alice said brusquely, "it's Alice you're talking to here. If I'm not working up to expectation, just say so. I'm a big girl. I can handle it. I can—" Then she *saw* the expression on his face. The *compassion* stopped her dead.

For one long, horrible moment, Alice and Melvin stared at each other. She might as well be staring at a doctor who'd just diagnosed her terminally ill, or a judge sentencing her to death. Her heart rattled beneath her ribs like a prisoner shaking iron window bars.

"You're going to force me to retire?" she whispered.

Melvin rearranged his face into a painful rictus of a smile. "Alice, you know I'm your biggest fan. Always have been. I know how much you've put into TransContinent. I know what a hell of a fine worker you've been all these years. To be honest with you, I'd like to see you *enjoy* life a little bit, because that's what you deserve."

Alice pounded her fists on her thighs. "For Christ's sake, Melvin, don't talk down to me."

"I'm not talking down to you, Alice. I'm telling you the God's truth. I want to see you enjoy life, and that's why I've managed to get you a one-million-dollar retirement bonus."

Alice nearly spat. "One million dollars? I make that in three years!"

"But do you want to spend the next three years working with this new team?" Before she could answer, Melvin plowed ahead. "I don't think so, Alice. You haven't given me any signs over the past six months that you'd enjoy the work, or, frankly, that you'd have anything to offer. This is definitely the best solution for everyone involved."

A stinging sensation pushed at the skin of Alice's face. God in heaven, she was going to cry. She was going to *wail.* She was going to fall on her knees, crawl around the desk, kiss the toes of Melvin's shiny wing tips, and beg him not to do this to her.

She swallowed her pride. "TransContinent is my *life*, Melvin."

He shook his head sadly. "It's TransWorld now."

Alice recoiled. Melvin spoke gently, but his words hit her like a blow in the chest. Then, in a flash of mortification, she understood the depth of her own failure, so clearly, *precisely*, betrayed by her use of the name of the former company, the *old* company. TransContinent, and the entire world it represented, had been, like a discontinued item, yanked off the shelf, replaced by a shinier, more efficient, and flashier toy.

"Can I get you something, Alice?" Melvin pulled open a desk drawer and brought out a silver flask. "How about a little brandy?"

Alice shook her head, not trusting her voice not to quaver. She, who had once held the fates of hundreds of people's lives in her hands, was now considered obsolescent, passé—*worthless.*

"A glass of water, then? How about a cup of coffee?"

"No, thank you, Melvin." Long ago, she might have said to Melvin, her old friend and colleague, "Are you kidding? Coffee gives me indigestion and makes me pee like Niagara Falls." Now she could only salvage what little dignity she had left. Clenching her hands and jaw, she rose. She was relieved to find her legs actually supported her; she'd half expected her knees to buckle or shake.

Once again Melvin extended his hand across the desk. "Good luck, Alice. And I'll be in touch."

She could not bring herself to shake his hand. She gave herself that much satisfaction: Head high, she sneered at him, but her insult was lost, because at just that moment, Melvin's eyes flickered down to check his watch. She'd overstayed her allotted time.

Alice pulled Melvin's door shut, firmly, and quietly, but she could tell by Elvira Gray's frozen face that the secretary knew exactly what had just happened. With a flash, Alice realized *everyone* in TransWorld knew about her termination. Her *retirement.*

Melvin couldn't have made the decision alone. He must have discussed it with the other execs, the new TransWorld people and some of Alice's old cronies as well. The thought of *that*, of muttered private discussions about her competence, her failures, her *uselessness*, made her nearly sick with shame.

Briskly she moved down the corridor, face implacable, eyes fixed in front of her to prevent catching even a glimpse of anyone staring at her with amusement or triumph or—*gag*—pity.

"Alice?" Marilyn glanced up from her desk, her face tense. "Tech support came. They took your computer—"

Alice swept past her, shut her office door, rushed into her bathroom, and closed that door. Turning on both faucets full blast, she prayed the noise would cover her sounds as she fell to her knees over the toilet and regurgitated her breakfast. Her heart thumped so rapidly! She was afraid it would explode in her chest, and only the fear of being found dead against the toilet made her lurch to her feet. She rinsed out her mouth, drank some water, and stared at her wide-eyed face in the mirror. Jesus Christ, was this the last time she'd be in this room?

It was.

Frantically she began retrieving personal items from her cabinet. Mouthwash, toothpaste, toothbrush, deodorant, perfume, face cream, all the stuff she needed for working late or rushing off to a business dinner. Under the sink, she found her box of Kotex. She'd finished with periods long ago, but the past ten or so years, whenever she sneezed, coughed, or laughed, she leaked—it was like her damn bladder was attached by a rubber band directly to her nose. How clever she'd thought she was, instead of buying Depends or Poise or any of the other "incontinence" pads, she'd bought sanitary napkins, in case anyone, from the cleaning lady on up, ever looked in her bathroom cabinet. She'd actually thought she'd prevented everyone from knowing she was getting older.

But she *was* older.

And everyone knew.

Clutching the sink, Alice threw her head back and grimaced, expelling a silent howl. She was in so much pain she thought she might die. Perhaps this was how people did die of heart attacks.

She had to keep going. She grabbed the makeup pouch, stuffed with her hygienic needs, and stepped back into her office. Now, to clean out her desk.

Slumping in her chair, she pulled open her drawers, discovering to her shock how little, really, there was for her to take. A roll of breath mints. A handful of change. A zippered leather nail kit. Several emergency packets of panty hose. From the top of her desk, framed photographs of her two sons and their families.

One wall was hung with beautifully framed photos: a black-and-white shot of Alice with Arthur Hudson, in Kansas, in 1966, when he first started the company. Well, Arthur had died two years ago. A color shot of Arthur, Alice, and three other men on the site of the new TransContinent building in '76. Bill Weaver was standing next to her, and after all the intervening years, the radiance of his sexuality still plucked at Alice's nerves like a harpist's fingers. The next shot was taken in 1980, when TransContinent moved to Boston and Alice left Kansas, and Bill Weaver, with his wife, behind. In that photo, Alice looked gaunt. After four years of secret passion, Bill had chosen his wife. Alice had had to move on, and although she smiled, her eyes told of pain.

Several wooden plaques were interspersed among the pictures. The smaller, plainer wooden ones made her smile. Best Secretary of the Year, 1968. Most Valued Employee, 1979. The newer ones, won when TransContinent had grown huge, weren't so meaningful; some motivational type had insisted they give out lots of awards, claiming it would improve company morale. Hell, it had been *her* decision to hire the motivational consultant.

Alice took the earliest two plaques and the

photos down. They left pale rectangles on the wall.

She paused, staring at the small collection of articles. Did she really have so little to carry with her?

Probably there were files on her computer she'd want to copy or send to her laptop. She'd have to wait until tech support cleaned off the virus. How long would that take? Should she wait there?

Doing what?

Dear God, she no longer belonged in her own office! It wasn't *her* office any longer, or it wouldn't be, once she walked out the door. And after she walked out that door—why, her entire life would be over! She'd been married to TransContinent longer than to Mack! Her head held more information about TransContinent personnel than any damned computer—how could they *imagine* they could exist without her?

A tap came at her door, then Marilyn stuck her head in. "Got a moment?"

Alice glared at Marilyn, who looked pretty in a pale rose silk top, not one of the neutral shades the HFC had helped her buy. Did this mean Marilyn had actually gone shopping for herself? Yes, of course, to be more seductive to Barton, who had obviously hypnotized her. Marilyn, whose purpose was to *help* Alice.

"I've got all the time in the world," Alice stated flatly.

Marilyn stepped inside and pulled the door shut behind her. "Tech support—"

Alice cut her off. "You got me fired."

Marilyn blinked. "What?"

Leaning forward, Alice growled, "Oh, not *fired, per se,* they're not about to *fire* an aging African-American female. No, *retired* is the word. Because of *you*, I'm being forced to retire."

Marilyn's mouth fell open.

"You were supposed to *help* me!" As she spoke, all the anger and humiliation of the past hour gathered force inside her, bubbling beneath her breastbone like lava. "Instead, you blabbed my fears about Alison to her *secretary*? Thanks, Marilyn, *thanks a lot.*"

Marilyn went pale. Her eyes filled with tears. "Oh, no," she whispered.

"Oh, no, what? Oh, no, lover boy Barton wouldn't betray you? What did he do, tell you you're beautiful? Did he *make love* to you?" Her voice oozed irony. She could see she was hitting the truth. "He seduced you, didn't he? You told him *everything*, didn't you? And *he* told Alison, who told Melvin Watertown and probably every other executive on this floor. Now *I'm* an object of ridicule, but that's all right, I won't be around to be laughed at, because I've just been handed my walking papers!"

"My God," Marilyn cried, "I'm so sorry! I was sure—"

"You've cost me my job, my income, my reputation. You've ruined my life." Alice had to look away from the other woman's horrified face. She'd be damned if *she*'d be the one to console *her*! With savage movements, she snatched up her photos, her makeup kit, her briefcase. Stalking around the desk, she growled, "Open the door."

Marilyn reached out a shaking hand and pulled the door open. "Alice. Let me—"

Wearily, Alice said, "Go home, Marilyn. It's all over."

To reach the elevators, Alice had to walk by all the other offices and desks, past Alison's office, and Barton Baker's.

She felt like Marie Antoinette being led to the guillotine. Joan of Arc on her way to the stake.

She felt her failure dragging behind her like a piece of toilet paper caught on her shoe.

She hesitated, looking back at Marilyn's desk, hoping to appear as if she'd forgotten something, when in fact she was only stalling. This was going to be the longest walk of her life, and she felt as if she had to do it stark naked. And in a way, this was true, because she had been stripped of all her power, prestige, and pride.

Well, she couldn't stand there all day. Suck it up, she told herself, and began to walk the plank.

As she passed Barton Baker's desk, he rose. "May I help you carry anything?" His voice was greasy with self-satisfaction.

Alice whipped her eyes his way, caught his smug smirk, and saw, behind him, Alison leaning one slender hip against her secretary's desk. Alison wore a red power suit the size of one of Alice's thighs, red heels with points sharp enough to puncture a heart, and a cat-that's-got-the-cream smile.

Without speaking, Alice moved on. All around her, the normal office business noises stopped dead, as if the entire floor had been paralyzed by a rush of toxic gas. Men and women stopped laughing and chatting. They looked up from their desks and stared openly as Alice strode past.

But no one said a word.

When she reached the bank of elevators,

she saw old reliable Frances come around her desk toward her.

"Alice." Frances's voice was rich with sympathy.

Sympathy. That stung worse than snideness. Alice ignored her.

"Could I help you carry anything?" Frances asked.

Brusquely, Alice shook her head. She would *die* if this woman offered one word of pity.

"Alice—I'll miss you so much," Frances said. "Will you call me sometime?"

The elevator doors opened. Alice stepped on and hit the DOWN button without replying. She fixed a look of disdain on her face. At the moment, it was all she could do.

30

Beneath the buzzing light of the MIT lab, the slab of shale lay, gray, mute, and dead. Marilyn sighed as she stared at it. No one knew why, 500 million years ago, all trilobites had been decimated. Other creatures had begun life then, the rugose and tabulate corals, starfishes, even some vertebrates. Time always crept on, carrying nature on its back.

Some trilobites had been able to protect themselves by rolling the ventral side of their tails up to meet the ventral side of their heads, forming little armored balls. She imagined them, curled inside their hard shells, snoozing away in peace.

She wished she were a trilobite.

Marilyn covered her specimen, then reached up and turned off the buzzing light, which crackled accusingly at her. She had accomplished nothing the whole day. That morning she'd hauled her dispirited self to her lab, intending to find comfort and reassurance in her familiar and beloved work, hoping to recover from the terrible shock of Barton's betrayal. But for the first time in her life, fossils could not fascinate. She'd just stood staring, replaying her asinine after-sex chatter that had cost Alice her job.

It was the worst thing Marilyn had ever done in all her life.

And all because she'd been suckered in by Barton, by the way he'd touched her, by the words he'd said—deeper than her guilt was a burning pit of shame at her foolish, *eager* gullibility!

She turned her back on the lab, trudged along the corridor, up the stairs, and through a door to the fresh air. The bright sunlight made her blink, but as she traced a familiar path through the campus, the warmth of the early-spring day gave her no consolation. She was glad to head back down underground to the T.

She slid her token into its slot and plodded along with the anonymous mass, down the steps to the subway stop. She liked being underground, it usually made her feel at home, and as she leaned against the wall, waiting for the train, she thought, not for the first time, how simple life must have been for the trilobites, how uncomplicated! Trilobite mating would have been so easy, so pure, unriddled with doubts about aging or sincerity. *They* never would have used the breeding process for bizarre motives, such as finding out whether one's friend's new assistant was after her job. They *couldn't* have had sexual intercourse for political reasons.

With a roar and a squealing of brakes, her train rumbled into the station. She duly boarded and collapsed in a seat. The train rushed forward. Marilyn watched the windows fill with light and dark and movement, like clips from a jumble of movies. At the Harvard Square stop, she got off, climbing back up to ground level, her heart so heavy she thought she'd have to crawl up the steps to street level on her hands and knees.

On the street, crowds flowed around her, students and professors, salespeople and secretaries, hurrying to and from classes, work, coffee breaks, early lunches. Young women passed by, lithe in their bodies, fresh in their skin, and men, young and old, followed them with their eyes.

At the curb, Marilyn waited for the light to change. Next to her stood a young woman with skin like rare silk, a lacy top ending just below her breasts, her trousers hanging from her hipbones, her sleek belly with its navel ring exposed. Across the street, the glances of men flew toward the young woman's belly button like arrows to a target. An Asian man linked arms with an Asian woman whose face was as perfect as a vase of flowers. Next to him stood a portly, professorial-looking chap with a beret and a tight, smug mouth, accompanied by a gorgeous young woman with wire-rimmed glasses; she was staring up at him as if he were an Adonis.

It took all Marilyn's willpower not to slam her forehead repeatedly against the traffic light pole.

Around there, no one would notice much if she did. But she couldn't take the chance that someone would notice, and call the cops, who would haul her off to a psych ward. Which was probably exactly where she *should* be, for thinking any man on the planet could find her sexually appealing.

Oh, God, oh, God, oh, God. Marilyn squeezed her eyes shut and clenched her fists, trying to block the pain. *How* could she have thought Barton found her desirable? She'd been deranged. She'd been tricked by her new hairstyle, her new cosmetics and clothes, into thinking she was appealing, and then, in an after rush of sexual bliss, she'd blabbed every single thing she knew about Alice Murray.

Alice must *hate* her.

She hated herself.

"Ma'am?"

He said it twice before Marilyn realized he was addressing her. She stared at him in confusion.

"Do you need help crossing the street, ma'am?"

It was only a polite student with backpack and glasses. Marilyn blinked. Across the street, Navel Ring Girl was strutting along in her impossibly high boots. Marilyn must have been standing in one spot for a while.

"I'm fine, thank you," she told the student. "I'm old and unattractive, but I'm fine."

He gaped in surprise, then scuttled away fast.

Of course, Harvard Square had its share of unfortunates, too, and as Marilyn dragged herself across the street, they approached her: the babbling man handing out pamphlets predicting the imminent arrival of aliens. The jittery boys with glassy eyes talking to themselves. The woman who never cut or washed her hair, letting it hang in greasy ropes to her waist. Marilyn stopped and put five dollars in her cup.

"Thank you, my angel," the crazy woman said.

Marilyn walked faster toward her house. At least she wasn't babbling on the street corner, yet. She might not be sexually desirable, but she *was* married, she had been married for twenty-nine years, she—

The last time she'd seen her husband, he'd been having sex in his office on his desk with a grad student.

Marilyn had waited up for him all the previous Saturday night, finally falling asleep on the living room sofa. When she awakened Sunday morning, she discovered Theodore had crept into the house at some point, changed his clothes, gathered some papers, and crept out again.

Well, she would call him when she got home. She would insist he return for a serious talk. She would tell him that *she'd* been unfaithful, too, and now they needed to start over. Sex wasn't so important, after all. Really, it was companionship that mattered, and mutual interests like science. Soon Teddy would be married, and they'd have grandchildren to share.

She smiled to herself. How silly she'd been, letting herself get carried away with such superficial matters as hairstyle and clothing and silly sex! Marriage was a profound matter, and *she* was the only one of the four members of the HFC who was actually still married. That was something.

As she passed through the wrought-iron gate to their yard, the gate creaked anciently and she noticed how the old Victorian looked shabby in the spring sun. It needed painting. Maybe this year she'd actually put flowers in the window boxes.

Theodore's Volvo was in the driveway. Did that mean he was home? Probably. He hated to take the T, and he hated to walk even more. Probably he was home to gather more papers; he seldom had lunch at home anymore.

Maybe he was there to see Marilyn.

She let herself into the house, dumped her purse on the hall table, and went along the hall to the kitchen at the back of the house.

"Marilyn?"

At the sound of her husband's voice, she veered off to the dining room, which Theodore had taken over a few years ago, needing more room for his piles of papers and books. He was there now, seated at the head of the table, scribbling away in a notebook.

"Hello, Theodore," she said quietly.

He jerked his head impatiently the way he always did, because she was *always* an interruption to his work. She stood patiently, waiting for him to finish and address her. His bald head shone, his plump fingers clasped his pen tightly, and beneath his gray corduroy jacket he wore a new green paisley vest. When had he bought the vest? She couldn't remember his caring about such things before.

"There!" Theodore tossed the pen down. He ran his hand over his eyes. "We have to talk," he announced, looking in Marilyn's direction.

"Yes. We do. Would you like some coffee?"

"No. Sit down." He gestured abruptly to a chair. "Let's get this over with."

Marilyn sat down, pushed a pile of papers to the side, and waited. He had said, *Let's get this over with.* So he was going to apologize for his infidelity with that student. That was a start.

Theodore cleared his throat. He picked up his pen, removed the cap, and put the cap back on. "I want a divorce."

"Why, Theodore!" Her hands flew to her heart, she was so surprised.

"I'm sorry you had to see me like that in my office," he continued, "it must have been terrible for you."

"Well, terrible, yes, but," she stammered, her thoughts racing.

"I doubt you can understand." Theodore

rose, clasped his hands behind his back, and paced the room, just as he did when lecturing his students. "You might find solace in reflection on evolution and gender. Males are physically capable of procreating even after fifty, while females are not. Their eggs are old, as you know, and undoubtedly damaged or withered. Ergo, the female sex drive diminishes and disappears. It's only natural."

"Oh, but Theodore!" Marilyn protested, "I still have a *fine* sex drive!" She rose and approached him. "Theodore, *I've* had an affair, too! And I can assure you, my sexuality is still very much in working order!"

Theodore smiled at her gently. "Marilyn, please don't do this."

"Do what?"

"Don't pretend you've had an affair. It's unseemly."

"But I did! And I *enjoyed* it! And he was *younger* than I! And—"

"Marilyn." Theodore removed his glasses, took his handkerchief from his pocket, and polished the lenses. "Don't embarrass yourself further, please."

"Theodore—"

Putting his glasses back on, he aimed a saddened look her way. "My dear. Try to keep your dignity, at least."

"My *dignity*! Theodore, I—"

He came toward her with arms outstretched. Marilyn walked into them. "Oh, Theodore, I still love you—"

But he did not pull her into an embrace. He only clapped her shoulder in a comradely sort of way, as a general might buck up a private. "You were a good wife and mother. Remember that."

Marilyn twitched. "I'm not dead yet!"

"No, no, of *course*, you're not. You have many fine years ahead of you. You still can be useful to the world. There are so many charities that need volunteers. Why, you might consider writing a memoir. About what it was like, being married to me. I'm sure people would love to read about the first half of my life."

Marilyn twisted away from him. "You're serious about a divorce."

"Yes, my dear, I am. I'm going to marry Michelle. Actually"—he arched his neck, preening like a pigeon—"she's pregnant."

"Pregnant!" Marilyn collapsed back into her chair.

"The baby's due in the fall. I've received a Fulbright to Sweden. The baby will be born there."

"Teddy's wedding's in the fall," Marilyn reminded him weakly.

"Yes, well, obviously I won't be able to attend." Theodore strode back to the other end of the dining room.

"You could fly back."

"No, no, I don't think so. I'll need to stay near Michelle, and of course I won't want to take time away from my lab."

"But your son's *wedding*, Theodore! Your only son!"

Theodore stroked his throat. "My *eldest* son."

"Your—" She blinked. Of course, amniocentesis. So Theodore was to have another son. "Still, Theodore—"

"Come now, Marilyn. Teddy's a big boy. He won't care whether I attend his wedding. Anyway, he's bound to take your side in all this. He'll probably be delighted if I keep away."

"Have you told Teddy?"

"Of course not. I wanted to tell you first. It's only kind. I thought *you* might tell Teddy. I've got so many other things to do these days." Theodore dug around in his pockets, looking for his car keys. "I've got a class. I expect you'll want to get a lawyer. I've already spoken with Leonard Darby about this, and

I've told him I want to be generous with the divorce settlement. Of course, you'll understand that we need to sell the house. It will be too big for you, anyway, now that Teddy and I will be gone. And Michelle doesn't care for the house, all the stairs, the gloomy corners—"

"Michelle's been in the house?"

"Oh, now, don't fret. She is *not* critical of you. She understands how someone your age can't manage to keep such a large house in order. But she wants a more modern place. Perhaps more of a showcase, something someone of my stature deserves."

"Your *stature*." Marilyn snorted. "Theodore, you worked on an intestinal fish parasite."

"And we've lived well on the profits," Theodore reminded her. "And you will be awarded your fair share in the divorce." He looked at his watch. "Anything else?"

Marilyn's thoughts moved at Paleozoic speed, stuck in primeval slime.

Theodore continued. "Over the next few days, I'll be moving my clothes, papers, *et cetera,* out of the house. You'll have a year to organize it, sell it, and find a new place. You see, I'm being quite generous." He patted his vest, straightened his jacket, patted the knot on his tie.

Marilyn stood up. “Theodore.”

“Well, I’m glad we got this over with! You’re being a real sport about this, dear.” Briskly he approached her, and rose on tiptoe to peck her forehead, then strutted eagerly out of the room.

Marilyn heard the door close. She gazed around her at the familiar room, which seemed as alien as the moon.

31

Thursday, Dr. and Mrs. Eastbrook drove into Boston to meet prospective patients for lunch, while Lila substituted for the receptionist at the spa who'd come down with a cough.

Margie, the cook, stuck her head around the door of Faye's office. "I'm going back to my apartment for a couple of hours. Dinner's organized. If you want lunch, you can throw something together yourself, okay?"

"Sure," Faye agreed.

Faye finished typing the on-line order for Mrs. Eastbrook's new linens, but her eyes darted frequently to the window. Finally, she saw Margie hurrying along over the gravel, past the fountain, to her apartment in the nearest staff building.

She checked her watch. She should have an hour, at least.

Quickly, she entered into Mrs. Eastbrook's office, opened her desk, and found the key to the family room door. Stashing it in her pocket, she hurried to her own quarters to grab up the book bag she'd brought from home, then flew over the carpet, down the long hall, and into the family room. She unlocked the door.

Dora was slumped in her chair, napping. Faye hesitated. She didn't want to wake the young woman, but who knew when she'd have another chance?

Dora lifted her head. "Is someone there?"

"Dora, it's Faye. The housekeeper."

Dora shifted beneath her tentlike dress, pressed a button on her chair, and turned. Her dear little goblin face brightened. "Oh, Faye! I thought you'd forgotten all about me!"

"Heavens, no, Dora." Faye kissed the young woman on her cheek. "How are you?"

Dora grinned. "Bored to tears! What's in the bag?"

Faye laughed. "I've brought you a present." She went through the large room to the card table at the back and sat down in a folding chair. Dora whirred along right behind in her power chair.

Faye pulled out a large wooden box. She opened it. A rainbow of colors nestled in the divided sections like Easter eggs in a wooden nest.

"These," Faye said, "are soft pastels."

Dora whirred her chair up to the table. She touched the blue pastel, and Faye knew it would feel soft, crumbly, and floury to her fingertips.

"Pretty colors," Dora murmured.

"Yes." Faye took out another box. "These are pastel pencil sticks. They're cleaner to use than the soft pastels, which can crumble and break. These are better for making line sketches, and you can combine the two, of course." She lifted out a loose pile of papers. "These are different papers. Their different textures give different effects. Here, feel." She held out two samples. Dora touched one fingertip to the velvety velour paper, then the harder, watermarked Ingres paper.

Faye brought out a book. "This is a basic beginner's guide to—"

"Are you *nuts*?!" Dora angrily stabbed a button on her chair, which sent her zapping backward. "I can't paint! Or draw! Look at me!"

"I have looked at you," Faye answered calmly. "I watched you play cards, and you held them steady. I looked at your Crayola drawings, and I saw the possibility of talent."

"Right," Dora snorted.

Now Faye took something else from her

bag: a postcard, eight-by-six, a photograph of an elf-sized woman with hands gnarled past recognition seated by a window in a one-room cottage. The sleeves of her green sweater had been rolled up several times to accommodate her short limbs, and over the sweater she wore a pink-and-white flowered apron. Her sparse gray hair was held back by a band, allowing her unusual face to show in all its purity: the nose, a little too large; the chin, nonexistent; the skin, wrinkled and weathered from years of brutal Quebec winters; the eyes, shining with intelligence; the entire face, glowing with a contagious love for life.

Faye held out the card. "Meet Maud Lewis."

Dora whirred closer. "Oh, my," she said softly, for no one could look at this photo of Maud Lewis without smiling back. Dora took the card and studied it. The woman's hands resembled swollen, misshapen feet, the fingers atrophied and shrunk, the knuckles swollen like marbles. "She's beautiful," Dora said.

"Yes." Faye agreed. "You're looking at real beauty there. And look what she has in her hand, and look what's on the wall behind her and on the windows, and on the windowsill."

Dora looked. Behind Maud was a painting, in a cheerful folk style, its flat perspective offset by the bright charm of the colors and the simple, childlike drawing of a black Model T on a road between a bank of yellow and red tulips, and a white house with a bright red roof. On the window next to her was a drawing of two black horses pulling a red sleigh.

"Maud Lewis lived in Quebec," Faye said. "Her family was poor, and when she was a teenager, a disease—I don't know which one—ravaged her body, deforming her face and her hands. But she married when she was eighteen, and lived her whole life with her husband in a one-room house. Well, they did have a loft bedroom, but she eventually was so crippled she couldn't climb the stairs. She painted postcards to sell to make money, then painted all kinds of pictures, all of them vivid with colors and life. Her pictures hang in museums now, one hangs in the White House, a documentary movie has been made of her life, and a book written about her. She's on the Net, too, if you want to see more."

Faye was quiet then, to let Dora contemplate the photo. After a while, she handed her another card, this one of two cows on a green field, framed by pink apple blossoms and a multitude of tulips. The cows wore golden bells and a red wooden yoke and long black girlish lashes framed their beautiful dark eyes.

"Oh, how pretty," Dora cried.

"You could do this," Faye told her. When Dora didn't protest, she continued. "Maud Lewis used paints, and you can, too, eventually, but I thought you might prefer pastels to begin with."

"But I don't know *how* to draw," Dora demurred.

"Maud Lewis never had art instruction," Faye said. "Maud Lewis probably never was able to enter an art museum. But her heart was full of color and beauty, and look, Dora," Faye reached over and picked up one of Dora's drawings of a white rabbit sitting up beneath an apple tree. "*Look.* I can see by the way you've drawn his white ears that he's alert, poised to jump."

"Oh, you're right!"

"If you can make a Crayola drawing that expresses so much, you can do anything you want. And I can help you. I want to help you."

Dora lifted her face to Faye's, and it was shining with hope. "Okay," she whispered. "I guess I can try."

"One more thing." Faye brought out a book, a beginner's guide to painting and drawing. "Scan this. It might give you some ideas."

Dora chewed her lip, suddenly nervous.

"Where will I tell my family I got all these things?"

As housekeeper, Faye knew nothing came in the mail addressed to Dora. She'd given this some thought. "Your parents and your sister are all seldom with you at one time, isn't that so?"

"Yes. Lila comes in the morning and late afternoon, Mother at night. Father, well, he's so busy he seldom comes."

"Then let your mother assume Lila gave these to you, and let Lila assume your mother did. You don't have to lie, you don't have to volunteer anything. When you've figured out which paper you like and whether you want to try paints, you can tell Lila, and she'll pick them up for you."

Dora nodded. "Okay."

"Now. I've got a few minutes more before I need to get back. Let me give you some pointers about line and color."

Friday, Faye's day off, Faye told Margie she was going into Boston to walk through the Public Gardens to see the early daffodils, tulips, and flowering trees. Later, she'd have lunch and a stroll around the MFA.

The truth was, the HFC was meeting that night at Alice's. All their efforts had stirred things up, and the other three were having a crisis.

Faye might very well be having a crisis, too. It all depended on what Shirley found out, which Shirley would report at the meeting.

For the moment, it was enough simply to be on her way home. She longed for her own house as never before. Once inside, she planned to relax in a way she hadn't been able to out at the Eastbrooks, not even in the privacy of her bed or shower. Their relentless compulsion for perfection sapped her of emotional and physical energy, and she was looking forward to moving through her own rooms at her own pace. The HFC meeting didn't start until eight. She would have time to pull on jeans and a flannel shirt, brew a pot of coffee, catch up on her mail and the messages on her answering machine. She'd graze through the new catalogues like a sheep through a pasture. Perhaps she'd snuggle up and nap on the sofa just like Jack used to do. Because she'd given her housecleaning lady the month off, the furniture would be sprinkled with dust, but Faye wouldn't even bother about that. She could live with a little dust.

She turned onto her street. The neighbors'

cherry tree had exploded with masses of pink buds. In all the yards, tulips clustered, erect and blazing, like miniature balloons tethered to the green grass. Sunlight glinted from the windows. The scent of freshly cut grass drifted through the air.

Home.

Her pulse smoothed, her blood pressure dropped.

Then she saw Laura's yellow Saab in her driveway.

She unlocked her door and stepped into the front hall, where she was assailed by a battalion of sounds and odors. The television blared from the back of the house, a sour smell cut through the air, and as she walked through the rooms, too stunned to remember to remove her light spring coat, she tripped over a soft pile consisting of a blanket, a soiled disposable diaper, and her favorite blue cotton sweater, inside out and matted with baby puke.

"Laura?"

She found her daughter in the den. It had always been the favorite room in the house. Jack would stretch out in his recliner while Faye and Laura curled up on the sofa, all of them munching buttered popcorn as they watched a video. On Sunday afternoons there was always time for a board game—Jack inevitably beat them both at Scrabble. When Laura was younger, she held sleepovers there, pushing the bulky recliner against the wall and unfolding the sofa to make a bed, or shoving it away, too, so everyone could curl up in sleeping bags on the floor—not that much sleeping actually happened. The girls would sneak into the kitchen to raid the refrigerator, their high, piercing, giggles rising like bubbles to Faye and Jack in their bedroom. Later, Laura's boyfriends, those she really liked, spent time there, too, watching videos or listening to CDs. Several of them, the *serious* boyfriends, lasted long enough to be invited to play board games on Sunday afternoons. Lars had lasted the longest of them all.

Now the pull-out bed was open, pillows and quilts jumbled all over it, hanging down, dragging onto the floor, mingling with clothes overflowing from several duffel bags dumped around the room. The coffee table, floor, and several shelves were stacked with dirty cups, soda cans, and dishes. In spite of the rock music blaring from MTV, Megan was asleep in the wicker cradle Faye had bought for her grandchild. In the center of the chaos sat Laura, wearing Faye's turquoise kimono, surrounded by her high school yearbooks.

"Oh, Mom, look!" Laura cried. "Look how pretty I was in high school!"

Faye perched on the edge of a chair. "Honey, what are you doing here?"

Laura continued to gaze down at the photos, all the expectant faces caught in their youth. "I don't know, Mom. I guess I just needed a break."

"What about Lars?"

"Oh, who cares about Lars!" Like a petulant child, she stuck out her lower lip.

Faye stood up. "I'm going up to change clothes."

"Mom?" Laura called wistfully. "Do you know what I'd like?"

"What, honey?" Turning, she looked down at her daughter. Laura's hair was lank and greasy, her fingernails a ragged mess.

"I'd love it if you'd make me a plate of cinnamon toast like you used to when I was sick."

Faye took a step back into the room. "Are you sick, Laura?"

"No, Mom. I just would like cinnamon toast."

"Okay. Well, when I come back downstairs—"

Her heart was heavy as she climbed to the second floor, and it dropped like lead when she saw her bedroom. It looked as if it had been ransacked by burglars. Bureau drawers gaped open, spilling out sweaters, lingerie, and scarves in a tangle of silk and wool. Her closet doors stood wide, exposing a visual bedlam of skirts, jackets, dresses, blouses, vests, some dangling by one shoulder off the hangers, others puddling on the floor. Her pretty little slipper chair, the bench at the end of her bed, and most of the floor swirled with more discarded clothing. Her jewelry box was open. Pearls, silver and gold chains, earrings and bracelets twisted together in a glittering jumble.

Faye sank onto the edge of her bed, hands twisting with worry. This was not like Laura, not at all like the young woman who had walked down the aisle on Jack's arm only two years ago, who had smiled up at her husband Lars as if he were the sun. This was not like the good-natured, optimistic child Laura had been or the kindhearted, thoughtful young woman Laura had become. Laura was not lazy, inconsiderate, or spoiled. She married Lars because they were madly in love and wanted to live their lives together. In college, Laura had majored in art history, thinking she might someday work in a gallery or museum or as an art conservationist, but what she really wanted was to have a home, a husband, and lots of children, because as an only child she'd yearned for brothers and sisters. Lars had been an only child, too; they had shared a dream of babies, a house with a white picket fence, and an SUV piled with children and a golden Lab.

What had happened? What had gone wrong?

Faye smoothed the wrinkled sheet. Obviously Laura had slept there last night. Perhaps she'd been there more than one night. Had Lars asked for a divorce? Had Laura left her husband?

"I'm sorry, Mom." Laura stood in the doorway. "I didn't know you'd be here today. I was going to tidy up." She looked fragile and pale in Faye's kimono, her eyes deeply shadowed.

Faye rose and took her daughter in a slightly awkward hug; Laura was taller than she. But except for her breasts, Laura was so thin! At Faye's touch, she crumpled against her mother, weeping.

"I don't know what's wrong with me!" Laura sobbed. "I thought I could be like *you*, I thought I could be *better* than you! I wanted so many children, and now I can't even handle one!"

Faye walked her daughter to the bed, found a tissue for her, then sat beside her, her arm around her. "Have you talked with your doctor about this?"

Laura sniffed. "He says all new mothers are tired."

Faye nodded. "That's true."

"No, actually, it's not!" Laura crushed the tissue in her hand angrily. "Clara's baby is only three months old and already sleeping through the night! Dominique's little boy is six months, and she's already back at work, teaching! And you've always told me what a good little baby I was, you never had any problems at all."

Faye smiled, staring out the window, as if watching the past flash by. "You *were* a good little baby. But I'm sure I had problems, and doubts. I'm sure I was exhausted. As you get older, you remember the good times and the hard times somehow just fade."

"You had Daddy. Daddy always loved you, he never—"

A thin wail from the first floor interrupted Laura, who, to Faye's surprise, clenched her fists tight.

"She's only been asleep for thirty minutes! I can't stand it, Mom! I can't do this, I'm too tired, I'm going to lose my mind!"

Faye was heartsick for her daughter, and she was worried. "Look, honey. Why don't you lie down here and take a long nap? I'll tend to Megan."

"No," Laura sobbed wearily, "I have to

nurse her." She sounded as if she had to walk a hundred miles.

"All right then, nurse her, while I fix you some cinnamon toast."

"Thanks, Mom." Laura pushed her lank hair back from her face and blew her nose.

Faye hurried down to the family room. She snapped off the blaring television, picked up her screaming granddaughter, and carried her, on her hip, into the kitchen. Sorrow and fear for her daughter swamped her. At the same time irritation burned like acid reflux in her throat. Thank God she was going to see the HFC that night.

32

The emergency meeting of the Hot Flash Club convened Friday night in Alice's living room. One by one they arrived, ignoring the spectacular view of Boston Harbor and collapsing on the sofas, as if too exhausted to move a step farther.

Faye was the most presentable, in jeans and flannel shirt stained with baby food. Marilyn's orange turtleneck, burgundy plaid trousers, and sagging pink cardigan hurt the eyes. Shirley was remarkably colorless, in black leggings and a gray T-shirt.

With a thud, Alice set the coffeepot on the coffee table next to the cups, spoons, milk, and sugar she'd already brought out, then dropped into a chair. She knew she looked sloppy in her loose brown sweat suit. She didn't care.

For a moment, no one spoke.

Then Faye asked, "Where's Alan?"

"Out for the evening," Alice murmured.

"How's he doing?" Shirley inquired.

"Better. He's looking for an apartment and checking out job possibilities. With an MBA and all his experience, he won't have to settle for anything but the best."

"He likes the high-power stuff?" Shirley asked.

Alice looked surprised at the question. "Well, of course!"

"So Alan's doing all right. That's *good*." Faye sounded artificially cheerful, like the coach of a losing team.

"Yeah," Alice agreed.

Then they just sat, staring down at the floor. Faye scanned their faces: Alice scowled. Marilyn sagged. Shirley was listless.

Faye tried again. "Hot Flash Club? More like No Clue Club."

No one laughed.

"Okay," Faye said briskly. "I don't know what's going on with the rest of you, but I, for one, have something positive to report!" She turned to the stimulating clash of colors on her right. "Marilyn, I've lived intimately with the Eastbrooks for three weeks now, and I can say with certainty that Lila truly loves your son."

Marilyn perked up. "Really?"

"Really."

"That's wonderful!" Marilyn said, and burst into tears.

Surprised, Faye asked, "Honey, what's wrong?"

Marilyn could hardly speak for sobbing. "I ruined Alice's life!"

Faye glanced at Alice for confirmation.

Alice nodded grimly. "True. She cost me my job."

Astonished, Faye asked, "How?"

Alice jerked her chin toward Marilyn. "She was supposed to get information about Alison from Barton, remember? Instead, she lets Barton seduce her, she tells him *everything*, and *he* tells Alison, who tells my superior, who decides I've 'lost my vision' and *retires* me."

"I'm sorry, Alice. So sorry." Marilyn wept. "I thought he—" She was too humiliated to continue.

"That's terrible," Faye murmured. "Still, we ought to be able to do something about it." She chewed on her thumbnail, thinking.

"I don't have good news, either," Shirley announced somberly.

Faye looked at Shirley.

Shirley nodded. "Sorry. Jennifer D'Annucio *is* having an affair with your son-in-law."

Faye's face crumpled. "I'm not surprised."

Shirley felt tears sting her eyes. "What a mess everything is!"

"But the Golden Moments meeting went off beautifully!" Alice said.

"Yes, but Julie Martin won't invest any money in my retreat!"

"And I—" Marilyn began, but couldn't go on. "Oh, Alice," she wailed, "I'm so sorry!"

Alice took a deep breath. "It's not your fault, Marilyn."

"Of course it is!"

Abruptly, Alice left the room. She returned with a box of tissues she handed to Marilyn. "Come on, Marilyn, cheer up. The truth of the matter is, *I* got myself retired. You're only a human being, Marilyn, and you tried your best, and I *did* find out that Alison wants my job, so you could say you completed your HFC assignment."

"That's very kind of you," Marilyn murmured. "Will you forgive me?"

"I'd better. Life's too short, and I have too few friends to do without you."

"Why, Alice, that's admirable," Faye said.

"And surprising," Shirley added.

"Thanks," Alice said sarcastically, throwing a caustic look Shirley's way.

Shirley just grinned.

Marilyn dried her eyes. "God, what a weight off my mind. And what a relief that Lila loves Teddy."

"But there is a problem." Faye reluctantly admitted. "Well, not a problem. Just a—complication. Or maybe not—"

"Just spit it out," Alice advised.

"Lila has a younger sister confined to a wheelchair and slightly deformed. The Eastbrooks are afraid Teddy won't marry her if he knows."

Marilyn put her hands to her cheeks. "What happened?"

"She was born with spina bifada. Dora's bright, she's good-natured, she's mentally acute. But physically crippled."

"Oh, the poor little thing." A thought struck Marilyn. "Is it my responsibility to inform Teddy?"

"Is it *my* responsibility to inform my daughter that her husband's definitely having an affair with Jennifer D'Annucio?" Faye asked.

Marilyn said, "My son believes we should all live our lives according to *Star Trek*'s Prime Directive."

"Which is what?" Shirley asked.

"Briefly stated, *Do Not Interfere.*"

The four women were quiet for a moment, thinking.

Then Alice slapped her hand on the coffee table, making them all jump.

"Hell, no! We've got over two hundred

years of wisdom in this room. I think the Prime Directive of the Hot Flash Club should be—"

They said it all together. ***"In—ter—fere!"***

They smiled at one another, blasting the mood-swamping emotional fog right out of the room.

"Phase Two begins now," Alice announced decisively. "I'll get my notebook."

Faye stood up, hooking her purse over her shoulder. "And I'm running out to get some chocolate."

"Good idea," Marilyn said. "I'll go with you."

"Me too," Shirley said.

"I'll make a batch of strawberry daiquiris," Alice said. "And for you, Shirley, I'll concoct an alcohol-free Strawberry Slurpy Supreme."

"What's that?" Shirley asked.

"I don't know. I'm going to invent it right now." Alice headed into her kitchen.

The other three women raced away.

Thirty minutes later, Shirley, Faye, and Marilyn returned with their arms full of grocery bags. They set out éclairs, cakes, mousse, pie, cookies, candies, and cartons of ice cream.

They raided Alice's kitchen, carrying out plates, bowls, serving spoons, spoons, forks, and napkins.

Alice presented them with two pitchers of cheery pink drinks and wineglasses misted from the freezer.

For a while, the only sound was the clink of silver against china and contented murmurs.

It was Alice who finally put down her spoon and picked up her pen and pad of paper. "All right, ladies," she said, licking her lips, "let's get to work. And Shirley, don't eat all that Black Forest cake. I haven't had any yet. Try the mousse."

Shirley saluted and obeyed.

"Now." Alice began scribbling. "First. Faye wanted to know whether her son-in-law's having an affair with another woman, and Shirley investigated."

"And she found out," Marilyn added. "She completed her assignment."

"You pulled it off, Shirley," Alice agreed. "Good for you."

"That's right," Faye agreed. "I might not like what she discovered, but she did find out the truth. Thank you, Shirley."

Shirley blinked rapidly, as the information streaked into her brain like light beams. "I did!"

Alice looked at Faye. "So now we have to move on to the next step, which is what to do about it."

"I'm not sure I can blame Lars," Faye told them. "My daughter's depressed. She's not at all like her normal self."

"Postpartum depression perhaps," Marilyn suggested. "Could be treated with drugs, if she's not nursing. Prozac, maybe."

"She's nursing," Faye said.

"So she puts the kid on the bottle," Alice advised briskly.

"She could try herbal remedies," Shirley added.

"She should spend some time alone with her husband." Alice was making notes. "*You've* got money, Faye. Get Laura to a doctor. Get her on some meds. Hire a baby-sitter, send Laura and Lars away for a honeymoon weekend."

"Right," Faye agreed, nodding. "And if Lars wants to tell her about his affair, he can." She looked up at the group. "What if Laura can't accept that he's had an affair?"

"That's up to Laura," Marilyn replied.

"Fine, but he should *end* the affair." Alice tapped her pen like a gavel.

"Absolutely," Faye agreed. "But how—"

"Hey." Shirley moved to the edge of the

sofa. "I have an idea. Jennifer's a nice girl, trust me on this. Why don't we have another little party? For Golden Moments. She came to the last one. She brought those amazing brownies. She drove Julie Martin home. You didn't come to the last Golden Moments meeting, Faye, but come this time, and bring *Megan*. I think when this girl sees the baby, she'll do some serious thinking. Maybe *she'll* dump him!"

"Good idea," Faye said. "But invite lots of people so Jennifer doesn't guess it's a setup."

"Lots of people is great," Shirley added.

"Jennifer and Alan met when she brought the canapés for the Golden Moments meeting. They hit it off. I'll have him invite her." Alice pointed her pen at the other three women. "Each of you contact a few new people and invite them to this meeting." She made a check on her list. "Now. Marilyn. Let's look at—"

"Theodore's having an affair," Marilyn blurted. "That's why I slept with Barton. Well, one reason why. Oh, God, how could I have thought anyone would be attracted to me! I've made a fool of myself!"

"Don't be silly!" Faye chided. "You look gorgeous now, Marilyn. Or at least you did when you wore the clothes we chose for you. This outfit is, well, a little—"

"Repulsive," Shirley mumbled around a spoonful of chocolate.

Marilyn tugged the corner of pink cardigan. "Clothes are that important?"

"Absolutely," Alice said. "They telegraph your identity."

"Cosmetics, too," Faye added. "That shade of lipstick looks great on you, Marilyn, it brightens your face."

Shirley wiped her mouth and turned to Marilyn. "Look at me. If I didn't have my hair colored red, people wouldn't have the same kind of trust in me. Gray tells them I'm old. Red means I'm still vital. I've been coloring my hair for ten years now, and I think it's so important, I carry a note card in my purse with my hairdresser's name and phone number and the formula of the hair product she uses. That way, in case I'm ever hospitalized with my jaw wired shut, people will know what to do to keep me looking good."

Alice laughed. "You know those little silver 'Medic Alert' bracelets people wear in case of emergencies, saying, 'I'm a diabetic,' or 'I'm allergic to penicillin'? We ought to market a 'Cosmetic Alert' bracelet, so if we're ever hospitalized, someone will know our hair color and makeup preferences."

"Good idea," Shirley said.

"But we'll never look *young* again," Marilyn pointed out sensibly.

"And we shouldn't *try* to look young," Alice retorted. "But that doesn't mean we can't look like fabulous women of a certain age."

"Hats," Faye mused, helping herself to another slice of cake. "Remember when women wore hats? My mother had this great little hat, I've seen photos of her in it, it *tilted*, and it had a polka dot net veil. She looked so glamorous!"

"I wore hats when I was younger," Alice reminisced. "Way younger. When I was a little girl, I wore them to church, especially on Easter."

"All the glamorous women wore them when we were young," Faye said. "Jacqueline Kennedy. Myrna Loy."

"Oh, please! Doris Day!" Shirley yelped. "The perpetual virgin! I hated those damned pillboxes. So rigid, so uptight." She stuck her finger in her mouth and made gagging noises. "We all rebelled and let our hair free, and we aren't going back."

"I'm glad I'm not younger now," Marilyn

volunteered. "Forget hats. Look at what young women are wearing these days! Never in my life did I have the kind of belly I'd expose in public, showcased between low riding pants and cropped tops. What do they do when they're bloated with their periods? And how do they keep their underpants on?"

"And what about thongs!" Shirley shrieked.

"Talk about a hair up your ass," Alice muttered.

"I love my stomachs," Faye said in a meditative voice. "When I think of all the good stuff that's gone on there. Carrying my baby." She patted Honey and Bunny fondly. "Eating and drinking. And bad stuff, too, all my painful periods."

"Your second chakra is there," Shirley pointed out.

"Of course it is." Alice rolled her eyes.

"Look," Shirley continued bravely, "the chakras are energy centers in the body. There are seven, and the one located in your abdomen, lower back, and sexual organs control desire, sensations, movement, emotions, and sexuality. It's related to water, and it brings the ability to accept change."

"God knows we need *that*," Alice said.

"We ought to be proud of that chakra," Faye said. "If fashion were designed by older women, we'd wear caftans with gorgeous designs right here over the bellies, and women wouldn't be allowed to wear them until they were fifty."

"But we're back where we started," Marilyn objected. "Women wouldn't wear them because then men wouldn't desire them. They all want young women. They're biologically programmed that way."

Faye wagged her fork at Marilyn. "I disagree. Maybe when they're young, they want young women. Well, maybe all their lives they *want* young women, just like all their lives they basically want to fuck every female they see, but that doesn't mean they act on it. I know Jack wouldn't have chased young women after he turned fifty-five or so. He was too tired. Like me, he often just wanted a back rub."

Shirley hooted. "The last few men I've been with? They've been younger than fifty, for sure, and here's what they like: beer, sports, pizza, and blow jobs, in that order. Hell, they spend more time taking a dump than making love."

Marilyn snickered. "Yes, and they're so serious about their bowel movements. So *proud* of them. Theodore always describes his to me, as if he's just produced a missile for NASA."

"Yeah," Alice added. "You know why?

Because they can't have babies, and they never have periods, and they have to get excited over *something* that comes out of their bodies."

Shirley snorted. "That's why they stand in front of us and fart and belch. That's why they pick their noses like they're mining for plutonium."

Marilyn nodded thoughtfully. "Men are basically very primitive."

"Men are lazy and spoiled," Shirley asserted. "Most of them just want to be serviced. And it doesn't matter who the woman is. I read that *Marilyn Monroe* had to give her lovers blow jobs."

"But some men have problems getting erections," Marilyn interjected. "I mean, Theodore *always* did, even before he turned middle-aged. Oral sex was the only way he could get aroused."

"Honey, there's a bridge I'd like to sell you," Shirley chortled.

"It's true that older guys have a hard time getting erections." Alice smirked at her own inadvertent humor.

"Yeah," Shirley agreed. "Listen, if we're the Hot Flash Club, hell, older men should form the Limp Dick League."

"That's why there's Viagra," Faye said.

"Hey!" Shirley snapped. "Why haven't they made a Viagra for women?"

"They will." Faye spooned more mousse onto her plate. "I think it balances out. Women have vibrators, but men have no electrical substitute."

"That's true," Marilyn said. "They must get tired of their hands."

"An electric vagina," Alice said thoughtfully.

"Sounds scary," Faye said.

"They don't need appliances," Shirley argued. "There are always plenty of women, eager to please any man."

"Maybe women don't need sex the way men do," Faye began.

"*I* certainly do!" Shirley argued.

"Let me finish," said Faye. "My most sexual memories aren't of the orgasms I've had, and I've had plenty. But I remember the first kisses, the intimate glances, the early excitement of laughing at the same jokes. And as I grew older, I didn't stop lusting after Jack, but it wasn't that I wanted to have an orgasm. Why, there were times when I'd watch him undress, and I'd see the red impression where his belt had been too tight because he'd gained weight around his middle, and the way his calves were bald because over the years the socks had worn off the hair, and how his jawline had become a jowl line, and how his chest was kind of growing breasts and his chest hair and pubic hair were turning gray—why, he'd seem so precious to me, then, so vulnerable and beloved, I'd just pull him down on the bed and kiss him all over his body and give him whatever kind of sex he wanted, and scratch his back and the top of his head when we were through, and it was lovelier to me then than any orgasm I'd ever had in my life."

The other three women stared.

Marilyn had tears in her eyes. "You're so lucky."

Faye shrugged. "I'm not so sure. My husband's dead."

Marilyn nodded. "And mine's alive, but I've never felt that way about him. That *tenderness*—I don't think we *ever* had it." She tapped her nail against her coffee cup, took a deep breath, and admitted, "I'm not sure I've ever had an orgasm, either." Blushing crimson, she added softly, "At least not with Theodore. I think I might have, with Barton."

"Well, honey," Faye lifted her coffee cup in a toast, "I'll drink to that!"

Alice cleared her throat. "Let's get back to work."

"That damned Barton." Shirley was licking

her spoon. "I want to get revenge on him. For seducing you and using you."

Marilyn looked confused. "But I was trying to do the same to him!"

"I'm not talking *death* revenge. Just a little mortification."

Marilyn smiled. "That sounds appropriate."

Alice put down her fork, picked up her pen, and scribbled a note on her list.

33

Tuesday night, Barton Baker opened the door to his condo the moment Shirley Gold knocked. For a moment, the two just stood there, taking each other's measure.

She saw a handsome man whose tight blue jeans and white T-shirt displayed a stunning physique, better than that of most men in their twenties. Quite impressive. He was barefoot. His tousled black hair was wet and shining. A towel hung around his neck, testimony to a recent shower. Considerate.

He held out his hand. "Barton Baker."

She took it. "Shirley Gold. Hello." She made her voice brisk, like a German nurse's. To secure an equally hearty, no-nonsense image, she'd tamed her glorious red hair into two taut braids and fastened them over her head like a crown. She wore no makeup, which made her look drab, and she'd borrowed a gray turtleneck from Marilyn to wear with her white tunic and loose white cotton trousers. Her dangling sun and moon earrings, her crystal pendant, her dolphin bracelets, all those she'd left at home. She looked severe, seasoned, and sexless.

"Come in." Barton stepped back from the door. He seemed nervous. "I still haven't been able to discover who entered my name in the drawing."

"It had to be someone at the Chestnut Hill Mall," Shirley lied reassuringly. That was the posh one; the kinds of people Barton knew would shop there. "Here's my card. I am an accredited member of the American Massage Therapist Association."

As she spoke, Shirley studied the room. An open bottle of wine and two glasses waited on the coffee table. Romantic mood music filtered dreamily from the CD player. Her estimate of the man plummeted. It was obvious what kind of massage this guy hoped he was going to get. Thank heavens she had taken pains to look like a masseuse from the Center for the Chronically Chaste.

"If you'd rather not have the massage, you can give it to a friend . . ." She could tell he was reevaluating the situation. When she'd gone to the TransWorld offices, Barton had been in a meeting, so Shirley had spoken with

Frances, the secretary at the main desk, who passed along Shirley's "Congratulations! You've won a free massage!" card. Barton had called to make an appointment that evening. Now he could see that a massage was all he was going to get, and he relaxed—Shirley could read it in his body language. One of the advantages of being sixty was that she could look great when she wanted to, she could even look sexy, but she'd never ever again be considered a *babe*, and sometimes that was very restful for herself and her clients.

Barton cleared his throat and rolled his shoulders. "No. No, I could use a massage. I've been tense lately. Just moved here a month ago, getting used to a new location and all."

"The massage will last forty minutes. I'll set up my table here," Shirley announced bossily. "I'd like to put one of my CDs on. It will help you relax."

"Well, fine." She handed him a disc which he took over to his media center.

As she unfolded her table, Shirley asked, "Have you ever had a massage before?"

"Well—" Looking over his shoulder, he flashed a gorgeous naughty-boy grin. "Maybe not this kind."

Shirley frowned. No doubt about it, Barton

was cute. She could understand how Marilyn would be beguiled by the man. But Shirley resented any sexual innuendoes about her work. She was a health professional, and she wished the rest of the world would get on the same page.

"I need to wash my hands."

"The bathroom's through the bedroom."

"While I'm there, you should undress and lie facedown on the table. Leave your undershorts on," she added, a little more fiercely than she intended.

She passed through the bedroom. Bed, bureau, bedside table. CD speakers. Against the wall, a NordicTrack. No photos. No framed pictures. Nothing out of place. The gray duvet was pulled neatly to meet the gray pillowcases. One book on the bedside table: *Keeping Fit after Forty.*

Well, well.

Marilyn hadn't been optimistic about this little ruse when they first discussed it. "Look," Shirley had insisted, "I'm not going to *harm* the man. He's going to get a free massage! I'm just looking for some kind of weakness, so we can find a way to get revenge on him. You do want revenge, don't you?" Before Marilyn could reply, Shirley snapped, "Hell, *I* want revenge, whether you do or not! Alice has been fabulous with me. She's worked her ass off designing a brochure and talking me through the business process. I'll be damned if I'm going to let some guy ruin her life and humiliate you!"

"But there's nothing in his apartment to *see*," Marilyn had protested. "I was there. It's scarcely furnished! He's just moved in. I can't imagine what you could find."

"Did you look in his medicine cabinet?"

Marilyn had recoiled. "Of course not!"

Now Shirley shut the bathroom door and locked it. On the counter next to the sink stood a bottle of Barbasol and a Gillette razor, a tube of whitening toothpaste and an electric toothbrush. Marilyn said Barton was forty-five; he looked to be in pretty good physical condition. Most men had begun to sag a little, especially guys who spent their time behind desks. Most older men had bellies, or doughnuts around their waists. Yet Barton Baker, however old he really was, obviously understood the importance of looking young, and it was hard to keep up that appearance without cosmetic and often pharmaceutical assistance.

She knew all about pharmaceutical assistance. She opened the medicine cabinet above the sink. She spotted a box of Band-Aids, a tube of first-aid cream. Aspirin. Ben-Gay. A couple of Ace bandages.

And several rows of bottles.

Shirley grinned.

Mega-Man Vitamins with additives promising to reduce fat and increase muscle.

Mega-Man Testosterone Enhancement Capsules.

Mega-Man Arginine to increase sexual satisfaction.

Mega-Man Power Penis Builder, guaranteed to increase both length and width of penis. Funny how the smartest men fell for that scam. Freud had gotten it wrong. It was *men* who had penis envy. An expensive bottle of Armani aftershave next to one of Adonis aftershave, "containing odorless pheromones, guaranteed to attract women and cause them to demand sex."

She shut the cabinet door, flushed the toilet, and turned on the hot water. This was all very interesting, and slightly amusing, but also, Shirley thought, rather endearing. Heaven knew she'd tried a few sexual enhancement capsules in her lifetime, and what were hair coloring, nail polish, and makeup? Some of these pseudo-medications might indicate a naïveté on Barton's part—to think that a pill could enlarge a penis! On the other hand, she had to give him credit for trying.

Back in the living room, she found Barton

stretched out on the massage table, his face down in the well, his long body stretched out like a sunbather's. Soothing classical music drifted through the air, a mixture of Brahms, Schumann, and Bach played with a slightly religious air, which Shirley found helpful for setting the mood with a new client, especially a male.

She lit a candle—vanilla—inhaled deeply, and set to work, taking her time, not bothering to go too deep; after all, this was a freebie, and she didn't plan to see him again, even if he called to schedule appointments. She was there on Marilyn's behalf. As the man relaxed beneath her hands, she thought how easy it would be to inflict physical harm on him—but she shuddered. She didn't like having that sort of thought anywhere near her head. She didn't want to *hurt* him. He was a weasel, not a fiend. She only wanted to embarrass him as he'd embarrassed Marilyn.

When he turned over for the second half of the massage, she discovered her weapon.

Many men who worked with weights shaved their chest hair, but Barton didn't, which was the first clue. Pressing the heels of her palms deep into his pectoral muscles, she encountered an unusually firm resistance. At the same time his eyes flickered, his whole body tensed. He was wary; she was getting close to a secret.

Smoothly she moved her ministrations to his arms, compressing the long triceps, massaging his palms and each finger. With fluid strokes, she moved back to the top of her table, stood behind his head, and pulled both his arms up, extending them in a long stretch that opened up his rib cage and made him breathe deeply.

"That feels great," he murmured.

"Good." She kept the triumph from her voice. No casual observer would notice what she saw, you had to know what you were looking for, really, you had to be an expert to spot the white scars hiding beneath the armpit hair that proved what Shirley's hands told her.

Barton had had silicone implanted in his chest.

That explained why this forty-five-year-old man had the delineated pectoral muscles of a twenty-year-old. It was why Barton's physique was of a vigorous, youthful, powerful male.

It was enough of a secret to embarrass Barton with, but not so terrible that he could be fired over it. It was perfect. She and Marilyn could go to an Internet café somewhere and e-mail everyone in TransWorld. Everyone would smirk when they read that

Barton had silicone pec implants. Barton deserved, at the least, to be smirked at.

She finished the massage and went, automatically, into the kitchen to get him a glass of water, then to the bathroom, to give him time to dress.

"That was wonderful," Barton said when she returned to the living room to pack up. He was stretching his arms, cracking his knuckles.

"Great." Hoisting her table onto her shoulder, she said, "You've got my card, if you ever want another massage or if you want to recommend me to friends, I'd appreciate it."

"Sure." He opened the door to the hall. "Thanks."

She waited to the count of five. Most people who got free massages tipped her something, but Barton was obviously not going to. Well, then, she thought. Now she had *no* qualms about embarrassing him.

34

"Are you going to do it?" Shirley asked.

Marilyn nodded, then realized Shirley couldn't see her over the phone. "I am. Today. I'm going over to MIT now. I'll use one of the lab computers."

"Cool. What are you wearing?"

Marilyn looked down at her body. "My plaid wool robe. It's so cool for Ma—"

"I don't mean what are you wearing now!" Shirley said with laughter in her voice. "I mean, what are you wearing over to MIT?"

"Well . . ." Marilyn twisted the phone cord nervously. She was in the bedroom, and they hadn't gotten around to installing portable phones yet. Now they never would. The house was on the market, and she had to decide what to do with the furniture and all their possessions: towels, sheets, pots, pans, china and silver not used for years . . .

"Marilyn?"

"Oh! Sorry. I was thinking—what did you ask?"

"What you're wearing today. Look, just put on something you bought with the HFC, okay?"

"Well, I'm only going to the lab . . ."

Shirley sighed gustily into the phone. "Marilyn. Your husband's left you for a younger woman. Maybe *you* don't care what you look like, but *I* do. Wear your new clothes and put on some makeup."

"Yes, yes, all right, I will."

Marilyn hung up the phone and hurried to dress before she forgot what Shirley recommended. She had so much to think about these days! The divorce, and the sale of the house, and Barton's treachery, and now this lovely bit of revenge. It would be perfect, embarrassing, but not life-threatening. Hurriedly she dressed, ran a brush through her great hair—short, shaggy hair was so easy to handle!—and rushed out of the house.

Thirty minutes later, she was inside the MIT lab. Just being there whetted her appetite for her own little project. It had been days since she'd devoted any time to her trilobite, and she felt guilty. Still, she had something more important to do first.

She meandered through the building, looking for an abandoned desk. She spotted an open laptop and noticed that a Web browser had been left open on an e-mail page. The sender was listed as "SpyGuy@aol.com." Perfect! She chose the Times New Roman 18 font and typed:

BARTON BAKER
HAS
SILICONE CHEST IMPLANTS!

She addressed the first e-mail to Frances, the receptionist on the tenth floor of Trans-World. Taking her notebook from her purse, she flipped it open to the list of names she'd brainstormed with Alice. Twenty secretaries, ten executives. Fingers flying, she spammed the e-mail to thirty people.

Then she leaned back in her chair and smiled.

She only wished she could be there when everyone read the announcement. No one would suspect Marilyn had sent it. How clever Shirley was, to have spotted those scars. Marilyn had actually been naked with the man and hadn't noticed. Of course, the light had been low, and she'd been preoccupied . . .

In gratitude, she'd promised Shirley she would invest substantially in Golden Moments, but she wouldn't be able to give her an exact figure until she met with her lawyer and had some idea how much money she'd have after the divorce.

"Marilyn?"

She jumped. "Oh, Faraday. Hello."

"What are you doing in this part of the lab?"

"Oh, I, uh, um." Marilyn exited the Internet and stood up. "I was just on my way to my work room, and I remembered something I had to check, so I just, um, used this computer . . ."

"I'm going that way myself. I'll walk with you."

"Oh. Well, good!" she said, flustered.

"You look lovely today, Marilyn."

She glanced up at the tall Scot. "Why, you do, too." And he *did*. His peppery hair, red and white and crisply rising from his head and framing his jaw, made her remember what Shirley said about red hair being *vital*, which made her think of *virile*, which made her blush.

He threw back his head and laughed. "First time I've been called lovely."

His laughter, sonorous and easy, startled her at first. She couldn't remember when she'd last heard a man laugh. It was a wonderful sound, and it made her nipples stand on end, straining for more. She felt them push against her silk blouse and hoped they weren't noticeable.

"Oh, well, I mean, I," she stammered.

He linked arms with her as they strolled along. "*Lovely*'s a fine word, Marilyn. Tell me, how are you?"

"Why, I'm okay."

"You don't seem distressed."

"Oh, you mean about Theodore?" Marilyn cocked her head. "Well, I am sorry, of course, but not actually *distressed*." She looked at Faraday. His blue eyes were so warm, it made her remember how astronomers realized the hottest stars burn with blue light, how in spite of the common perception, blue is hotter than red.

"I'm divorced, you know," Faraday volunteered.

"I didn't know. What happened?" Marilyn tried to remember his wife. Sarah, she thought, a pretty blonde.

"We just grew apart. When the children grew up and left home, we discovered we had nothing to talk about."

"And are *you* distressed?"

"I was at first. It's been several years now. Sarah's remarried, quite happily, to a man who owns an automobile dealership."

"Really!"

Faraday smiled. "Surprising, I suppose, but I'm glad she's happy. She never did understand all the fuss about paleobiology."

"Well, it isn't the sexiest science," Marilyn observed, blushing deeply when she realized she'd said *sex*.

To her surprise, Faraday chuckled, as if she'd said something amusing. "You could be right. What, then, *is* the sexiest science?" He stroked his beard. "In vitro fertilization? Human genome technology? Cloning?"

She'd always loved intellectual discussions. "Space exploration," she eagerly volunteered. "Because of the rocket shooting upward, penetrating space."

This time Faraday didn't laugh. He smiled. He stood right next to her, his body tall, massive, warm, radiant, a Jupiter of a man, and he smiled at her, his blue eyes warm.

"Well, well, Marilyn," he said softly.

Oh, dear, Marilyn thought. He must think she was flirting with him.

Wait a minute, she thought. She *was* flirting with him! Accidentally, perhaps, but she could *feel* a connection between them.

"There's a lecture on the Burgess Shale tomorrow night," Faraday said. "I wonder if you'd like to attend it with me."

"Oh, well, I'd love to do that, Faraday." Her toes curled up in her shoes.

"How about a light dinner before?"

"That would be great." Her heart grabbed her lungs and began to tango.

"Great. Why don't I pick you up at six?"

"Wonderful. See you then." Her mind stuck a rose behind her ear.

She watched him walk away. His shoulders were wonderfully broad. She estimated his height at about six-foot-two. She wondered if there were a correlation between body height and length of penis. Theodore's penis was short and stubby, like him. That might mean that Faraday's was—

"Good morning, Marilyn." A lab assistant hurried past, giving her an odd look.

Marilyn realized she was hugging herself and grinning rather maniacally. She straightened. "Good morning, Ming Chu." She turned to her workstation, bent over her length of shale, picked up her brush, then just stood there, eyes closed, thinking green and succulent thoughts.

Out at the Eastbrooks', Faye was in Dora's room.

"Yes, the pastels are beautiful." Faye snapped one in half. "But they're not sacred. They crumble, they break, and guess what? You can always buy more. You've got to experiment with them, get the feel of them, in your hand, on the different textures of paper. If you don't like the way it looks or feels, we can move to oils or acrylics, but I think you'll get to like pastels."

Dora chose a rose pastel and broke it. "I told my mother that Lila gave me the pastels." She touched the point to the paper fastened on the portable reading stand that now served as an easel.

"Good. Try different strokes," Faye advised. "Long, direct, keeping the same weight. On some papers, the grain will cause the line to break or blur. That's good. Use it." She handed a yellow pastel to Dora. "Now try hatching this color over the rose. You can blend it, you can use your fingers to blur and burnish it. Remember how I showed you to do the main outline? Okay, here's your subject." She placed a green vase of red and yellow tulips on the table. "Loosen up your hand. Play around a bit first. Experiment. If you draw something awful, so what, you've learned something." She checked her watch. "I've got to go, Dora. They'll be back soon."

She kissed Dora on her cheek. At the door, she looked back. The tip of Dora's tongue pressed against the side of her mouth as she bent, rapt, to her work.

Faye went through the door into the family room, double-checking to make certain it was locked. Mrs. Eastbrook and Lila had gone down to the clinic for an organizational meeting, and Margie was in the kitchen preparing a beef Wellington for tonight's dinner party, so Faye had taken the opportunity to see Dora. She did so often, now, with impunity. After all, she'd completed her assignment for the HFC. She could leave anytime. Working for Mrs. Eastbrook was growing tiresome, too; the doctor's wife never eased up, relaxed, laughed, sang, or even stretched and yawned. She was strung tightly as a high-tension wire every minute, and Faye was pretty sure Mrs. Eastbrook hadn't molded herself to fit her professional role. Eugenie Eastbrook would be pretentious in a Turkish prison.

Still, Faye was reluctant to leave Dora. She settled in at her desk to work on household bills. Relegating her personal thoughts to the back of her brain to simmer, she directed the computer to the bookkeeping program.

Her door to the hall was open, but she sensed rather than saw Mrs. Eastbrook and Lila pass. She heard Mrs. Eastbrook's office door slam. From the other side of the wall came voices murmuring fast and low. The voices rose. Faye could understand them without straining.

"—don't *know* how Teddy found out!" Lila's voice was anguished. "It doesn't *matter* how he found out! The point is, he knows about Dora, and he's fine with it. He even suggested she come live with *us* after we're married! You'd like that, wouldn't you?"

"May I remind you, there's more at stake here than you and Dora." Mrs. Eastbrook's voice was cold and brittle.

Lila's tone was placating. "I understand how you feel—"

Mrs. Eastbrook interrupted. "If I agree to let Dora live with you after you've married Teddy, will you stop this foolishness about having Dora attend the wedding?"

"No! Come on, Mom," Lila cried passionately. "Dora's my sister. I love her. I want her at my wedding."

Scornfully, Mrs. Eastbrook commanded, "Be reasonable, Lila. You know how Dora hates crowds. She says it's painful for her to be stared at. It takes her weeks to recover—"

"So I'll have a small wedding. I never wanted a—"

"Oh, please, Lila, don't start this again! We've made all the wedding plans! The invitations have gone out. We can't tell three hundred people we've changed our minds."

"Of course we can, Mom! I don't care about those people! This is my wedding day, and I—"

"*You*'ll be the star," Lila's mother purred. "Your *dress*, sweetheart, think of it! You look *astonishing* in it. This is a *huge* society event, and a crucial moment for your father and me, and for our clinic."

"I don't care about any of that! Not the dress, not society, not the damned clinic!"

"You don't mean what you're saying."

"But I *do*!" Lila pleaded. "Mom, I want my own life. I don't want to be your little showpiece anymore! I *won't* be! I won't be the star of your show, I won't turn my own wedding into a spectacle! I don't care whether Dad loses clients! I want my sister at my wedding!"

"Lila." Eugenie Eastbrook's voice darkened.

"I mean it!"

"I'm finding this very difficult, Lila." Mrs. Eastbrook's words were frosty with precision. "After all we've done for you, you refuse to do this one thing for us."

"Oh, come on, I've done—"

"I think you should leave."

"Leave?" Lila laughed with surprise.

"Leave this house. If you don't care about us or the clinic, if this wonderful life, with every possible luxury, isn't good enough for you, then just leave. *Now.*"

"Mom. Calm down."

"Don't tell me what to do!" Eugenie's words shot like bullets. "Pack a bag. Pack it with whatever you want to take, because you're not returning to this house. Call a cab. And give me the keys."

"What?"

"I want the keys to the house, and the clinic, and I want the keys to your car. If you're too pure to help us, then you're too pure to drive that fabulous little convertible we gave you."

Lila sounded astonished. "Mom. Please. What about Dora?"

"Dora's my daughter. I know what's best for her."

"She's my sister, and I love her!"

Eugenie Eastbrook was adamant. "It's your choice, Lila. Either stay and have the wedding we've planned, or leave."

"You're insane. All the laxatives and injections and diets have finally—"

The slap was loud enough to resonate clearly through the wall.

The silence was louder.

Eugenie Eastbrook's voice was glacial. "Give me the keys to the house and the clinic. All of them. And your car keys. Now, get out."

Mesmerized at her desk, Faye listened. She heard Mrs. Eastbrook's office door slam. She heard Lila sobbing as she ran down the hall and up the stairs. She waited to hear Eugenie Eastbrook cry, but the other room held only silence.

35

The good news was that Alan wasn't lying around the condo like a basset hound on Valium anymore.

The bad news was that Alice was lying around the condo like a basset hound on Valium.

Friday morning, she didn't even wake up until after nine o'clock. Groaning, she wrapped her robe around her and walked into the kitchen to find that her son had already gotten up and quietly slipped out, leaving her a note saying he'd be back that night, and, thoughtfully, a freshly brewed pot of coffee.

She poured herself a cup and carried it into the living room. That in itself was a change. Usually she slurped her morning coffee from a thick rubbery mug with a plastic lid that prevented any liquid from spilling as she rushed around dressing for the day.

Today, she didn't have anything to dress for.

It felt really odd.

Alice had *always* worked. At fourteen, back in Kansas, she'd held her first job as a waitress in Archer's Café; since then, she'd never been without a job. Of course she'd had vacations, and good ones, when she reached the executive level at TransContinent, but the truth was, she'd never really enjoyed them unless she had some work to take along to build her day around. Alice Murray was all about accomplishment, and she had no idea what to do with herself without work.

She was giving another party for Golden Moments a week from Monday, so she wasn't totally useless yet. But that was a long time away. She couldn't get together for a brainstorming session with Shirley that day, because Shirley was doing the rounds of her masseuse jobs. Faye was out at the Eastbrooks. Marilyn was at MIT.

Alice was in her living room.

In her robe.

Well, hell. She might as well eat a pint of ice cream every night and fry bacon and eggs every morning for breakfast and sit around all day watching the hair grow on her legs.

Then she remembered that Esmerelda, the cleaning woman, was due at one. No way Alice could sit in her robe, watching TV, while another woman scrubbed her bathroom floor. No, Alice had to get out and do something.

At the HFC meeting the other night, they'd compiled a list of rules to live by, axioms that they knew from their struggles in the past would help them through the future, things they *knew*, even if they hated knowing them, like eating broccoli is good for the body. These were nutritional hints for the soul, like a kind of spiritual muesli. Near the top of the list was: *If you're depressed, get up, get dressed, and get out of the house.*

So Alice picked up the *Boston Globe* entertainment section and snapped it open, recalling how the three other women had reprimanded her for having lived so long in Boston without ever having taken advantage of its attractions. Dutifully, Alice grabbed a pen and pad and scribbled a list—the physical act immediately cheered her. She loved seeing the words marching in file down the paper, black on white. A kind of exterior order seemed to be lying latent in her interior disarray, and that gave her hope.

Boston Aquarium.

An International Festival of Women's Cinema.

Museum of Fine Arts.

Isabella Stewart Gardner Museum.

Museum of Science.

The Alvin Ailey Dance Theater—that would be interesting. Except it would be at night, and she wasn't sure how she felt about attending theater alone. Might be something she'd have to work up to.

The Boston Philharmonic had matinees on Friday—*well.*

Alice looked at the clock. It was just after nine-thirty. She looked out the window. Sunny day.

The program was Stravinsky and Prokofiev, composers about whom she knew very little. She'd always preferred jazz to classical. But it wouldn't kill her to try something new, and how would she know whether or not she liked the music until she heard it?

She phoned and reserved a ticket at the symphony, but as she showered, her spirits lagged until it was as if she were dragging her own body like a nanny with an incalcitrant child.

"Buck up!" she commanded herself as she opened the doors to her walk-in closet. All her work suits hung there in a gloomy ensemble of black, gray, brown, like shapeless habits for an order of nuns. Just looking at them made her stomach constrict and her breath go shallow.

Well, they no longer fit her body or her life!

She jerked a charcoal crepe suit with its death-grip waistband off the hanger and cast it on the floor. She yanked out a drab olive suit with a skirt that squeezed her stomach like a vise, and tossed it on top of the charcoal. As she added the mouse gray and the dog shit brown, she sensed a new energy flowing through her. Anything the color of ashes, dusk, dust, clouds, feces, or mud was ripped from its hanger and flung out of her life. Her lungs swelled with power as she tugged and tossed, her chest expanded, and she felt like wings were growing from her back, lifting her into the air. She was becoming weightless!

Racing into the kitchen, she grabbed a box of clear plastic bags, took them to her closet, and stuffed them with her clothing. Her business shoes, tight and high and pinching, went into the bags with the clothes. She saved one black suit and a pair of black heels, for funerals.

That finished, she rose and surveyed her closet. She didn't have a whole lot left.

Well, she'd just have to go shopping!

Maybe she'd invite Shirley to come with her.

Until then, she'd wear her loose batik trousers, a long white shirt, and all her turquoise jewelry. And the bright plastic bracelets.

The day was cool, but bright with sun. She set out in her low-heeled cork-soled shoes, striding briskly along the pavement, cutting this way and that through the busy streets, until suddenly she realized there was no need to hurry. The thought was so stunning, she stumbled and almost fell down.

Slowing her pace, she took time to gaze into the windows. She stopped at a bookstore to purchase a paperback novel with a candy box cover, something she'd never permitted herself before in her life, something she'd never before wanted. Before, she'd always read newspapers and *Forbes* and *Money* and other journals, to keep up with the business news. Occasionally, on cross-country flights, she'd skimmed the latest paperback thriller, as long as the plot was so fast she was assured she could finish the book in a minimum amount of time. She'd developed a scheme for judging an airplane book before buying it: the amount of white space on the pages. The more white space, the shorter the paragraphs and sentences, the less the book demanded of her. She could whiz through it without a thought.

What would it be like to read a book she didn't want to *get through*, Alice wondered.

Perhaps she'd find out with this little pink bit of froth. Certainly she'd give it a try. She settled in at a sidewalk café for lunch, intending to read. But the food—a chicken salad with Asian spices and a glass of cool Chardonnay—was so delicious, and the opportunity to eat at her leisure such a novelty, that she put the book back in her purse and concentrated on taste and smell. It was a pleasure, too, overhearing the conversations going on at the tables near hers. People were discussing clothes, movies, music, parties, vacations, and the occasional love complication, but no one was talking about work, and they were of all different ages, in fact, most of them were under sixty. It brightened her day immensely to know that people could build lives around something other than achievement and the battle for success.

Still, she was rather dreading the concert, she decided, as she paid her bill and strolled down Huntington Avenue to the brick concert hall. Because she'd never been to a matinee of anything since local productions of *The Nutcracker* when her boys were young, Alice assumed she would be the youngest person there, surrounded by hordes of doddering little old ladies who would, with much crackling of foil, sneak mints into their mouths throughout the concert.

She was right. When she picked up her ticket at the window and handed it to the usher, the crowd around her was mostly female, and over fifty, and to make matters worse, their hair was coiffed as stiffly as Nancy Reagan's, and they wore expensive, plain wool dresses with a modest diamond pin or gold necklaces. They looked as if they'd all just come from having tea with Barbara Bush. In her flowing batik pants, loose white shirt, and plastic bracelets, Alice was like a parrot among pigeons.

Her seat was in the gallery, toward the side and about halfway back. She slid down the row, found her place, and settled in, pleased by the width of the seat, not so thrilled with the hard wooden bottom.

A skinny young woman with magenta spiked hair, a tattooed necklace, and shitkicker boots slunk down the row and landed next to Alice. I see, Alice thought, they put all the weirdos in the same place.

As she bent her head to study her program, she saw, from the corner of her eye, an African-American man in a silk shirt in stained-glass colors coming down the row. He settled next to her, nodded at Alice, then pulled glasses from his pocket, fitted them over his nose, and turned his attention to the program.

She nodded at him and did the same, but she couldn't concentrate. It wasn't every day an attractive African-American man her age just happened along. She glanced sideways, to see whether or not someone—a wife, a girlfriend—was coming to join him. But the woman who came down the aisle and sat next to him was chattering to her teenage daughter and didn't notice him. Well, then. And he wasn't wearing a wedding ring. My, my.

He cleared his throat. Alice crossed her legs so that her toe pointed at Spike Hair sitting on her left. Spike Hair took a box of mints from her purse and slipped one into her mouth. The scent drifted tantalizingly into the air, making Alice crave a mint. She forced herself to concentrate on her program until the conductor, a Russian with an unpronounceable name, came onstage and the concert began.

It was Stravinsky's *Persephone*, something Alice had never heard before, and something she decided, as the program continued, she didn't need to hear ever again. A swarthy tenor and a pale narrator intoned gloomily in French, as did a despondent chorus, about the underworld and spring. As a violin chord pierced the air, a resounding note pinged in Alice's body.

Uh-oh. She needed to pee, *now.* She shouldn't have had that cup of coffee with lunch, she knew coffee was a diuretic, but it had been such a *small* cup. She recrossed her legs, hoping the change in position would relieve the pressure.

The "Melodrama in Three Tableaux" was long. Persephone was abducted. She was sorry The Shades were so sad. Finally, she was reborn, while flutes and harps plucked strings that resonated up and down Alice's urinary tract.

At last it ended, and after the applause died down, most of the audience rose to stretch during intermission. Some headed out to the rest rooms, which was exactly where Alice was longing to go. She looked to her left. Spike Hair had fallen into a kind of trance, slumped down, head resting on the seat back, eyes closed, legs in their black jeans intersecting in a kind of cat's cradle Alice couldn't possibly step over. To her right, the man was reading his program again.

He noticed Alice looking at him, and lifted his head, giving her a wonderful smile. "That was pretty amazing, wasn't it?"

"I suppose amazing's the right word." Alice

paused, wondering whether or not to be honest. She knew she came off pretty strong. But she admitted, "I found it a bit overwhelming."

"Like a disturbed hornets' nest."

She laughed. "Like that." The slight movement of her torso as she shifted in her seat made a heavy weight press on her bladder.

"My son gave me season tickets," the man confided. He turned toward her. His face was wide, his hair thick, peppery gray, his eyes dark and large. She wouldn't call him fat, but *portly* might work; he clearly enjoyed his food. "I've come regularly the past few months, and I've enjoyed most of the concerts, plus there's something about attending a concert of classical music that makes me feel, well, *virtuous*."

Alice smiled. The man was charming, but he was probably also gay, or a serial killer. If there was one thing she knew for sure in this world, it was that Fate didn't drop an attractive, unattached man almost in your lap every day, or any day. "I know what you mean," she replied, because she couldn't just sit there gawking at him. Her bladder tugged on her attention like a spoiled child.

"I don't believe I've seen you here before," the man volunteered.

She was flattered by the implication that he found her remarkable enough to remember.

"You're right. This is the first time I've been to a concert in years. I am, um, actually, I've recently retired."

"Well, congratulations!" He smiled, showing gorgeous white teeth. "You're about to begin the best period of your life!"

She squinted at him. "Do you really think so?"

He leaned toward her, talking eagerly. "Oh, yes, absolutely. Listen, I was a high school teacher all my life, and I loved my work. Then, five years ago, my wife died, and a few months later, I retired. I thought I'd go nuts. I was afraid I'd end up glued to the sofa, watching old movies and eating too much cold pizza."

Alice smiled. "I've got my own version of that vision."

"Well, I confess I did live that way for a few months. It does take you a while, sometimes, to get back on your feet. But I did. I found—"

"Ssssh!" The woman behind him leaned forward, rapping his shoulder with her program. Only then did Alice realize the conductor had returned to the podium. She exchanged guilty smiles with the man and faced forward, composing herself to listen.

The Prokofiev ballet music was also turbulent and strenuous, but compelling, with occasional comic moments. For minutes at a time,

Alice almost forgot how desperately she needed to pee. She turned, crossed and recrossed her legs, trying to find a position that put the least pressure on her bladder. She didn't succeed. She clenched her toes and bit her lip. The urgency increased. She felt like she was sitting on a burning blade.

As the music billowed with complicated chords and tumult, Alice tried to relax into it, letting the swirling sounds carry her back to the Midwest, where the wind blew ferociously and hail pelted the roofs and torrents of rain—no, she mustn't think about rain. The music thundered to a crescendo. A similar force gathered in Alice's sinuses. She was going to sneeze. And when she sneezed—

Desperately, she pressed her fingers against the bridge of her nose. The music continued to swell and crash. The sneeze died, unexploded. The music ended. The audience applauded wildly. Alice was exhausted.

She planted both feet on the floor, preparing to rise the moment the person on either side did. To her dismay, the conductor strode back onstage, bowed, raised his arms, and turned to conduct an encore.

Sinking back in her seat, Alice thought of deserts. Beaches—whoops, too close to the ocean. Dust. Dust was good.

Finally, the encore ended. After another, less enthusiastic round of applause, the audience began to rise and file out of the auditorium.

When her neighbor stood, she saw that he had broad shoulders and was almost exactly her height. He leaned near, to be heard over the general tumult. "It was nice chatting with you."

"Yes. Nice chatting with you, too." *Move,* she urged him silently. *Go on, you can shove that woman a little, she doesn't look frail, just sluggish.*

"I wonder, would you like to have a cup of coffee?"

"Oh. Well. Yes, that would be nice." He could have asked her if she wanted to go bungee-jumping, and she would have agreed, she could scarcely think, she was becoming nothing but a swollen skin of pressure. At least the row was moving out into the aisle. With each step, Alice's bladder sensed the proximity of relief, and the strain Alice had thought was already at its maximum increased as they slowly crept, along with the crowd, out of the auditorium. "I need to use the ladies' room first," she told him when they finally reached the corridors.

"I'll wait here," he told her.

She raced away.

His name was Gideon Banks. They sat across from each other at a nearby Starbucks, where Alice ordered a cup of decaffeinated coffee and he ordered a bran muffin and a glass of orange juice.

"I'm diabetic," he explained. "Just got that way two years ago; it's called late onset diabetes, and I can control it without insulin if I eat right. I apologize for talking about it, I know it's boring."

"No, not at all," Alice hastened to assure him.

"It's one of the reasons I sort of gave up on dating," Gideon told her. "I mean, you'd think at my age dating would be a relatively simple matter. I'm not looking for a woman to bear my children and share my life, I don't have to worry about liking my in-laws, because they're probably all dead by now, the kids are grown up and on their own, I'm over my midlife crisis. But on the other hand, I find I've become remarkably entrenched in routines. I have to arrange my life around when I eat, what I eat, the damned exercises I ought to do every day. I also know by now that I don't enjoy going to bars, I'm never going to learn to dance, or ride a horse, or scuba dive. So I'm a pretty lame date for most women."

"Oh, I'm sure that's not so." Alice cocked her head as she scrutinized him. He was no Denzel Washington, but then she was no Vanessa Williams. "Most women my age aren't up for scuba diving."

"You'd be surprised. I find your gender much more open to new experiences than mine. Lots of women say there's just one thing they really want to do while they can—climb Mount Saint Helens or see Australia. I'm happy just where I am."

"I've never thought about one thing I want to do before I die," Alice mused. "But then, I thought I'd be working for a few more years."

He inquired about her work, listened attentively, and asked intelligent questions. He had gorgeous teeth, and a dimple in his left cheek when he smiled. *He's got to be a serial killer,* Alice thought. No way can this man be available. But when they left the café to go their separate ways, Gideon asked for her phone number, and Alice gave it to him.

Walking back to her condo, Alice found herself humming a few bars from the encore. The resonance of the sound in her throat felt unusual and pleasant. It surely had been a long time since she'd sung. Well, if this was what retirement was going to be like, then she might be able to welcome it. Certainly she'd enjoyed looking at Gideon Banks. She could imagine accompanying him to movies, dinners, other concerts.

She could even envision—almost—going to bed with the man.

The thought stunned her so completely, she walked right past her condo and had to retrace her steps.

36

Down the stairs of the Eastbrook mansion came Eugenie Eastbrook in a floor-length gown of apricot silk. Her hair, coiled tightly in a chignon, was as pale as the diamonds glittering from her ears and around her neck. Her hips were as narrow as a boy's, her breasts as full and high as a nubile girl's, her stomach flat as a panel of wood. If you didn't know she was the mother of a woman in her twenties, you wouldn't be able to guess her age; nothing gave it away, not the line of her jaw, which was firm and lean, not the lids of her eyes, nor the smooth pane of her brow. This was a woman from a magazine ad, a television ad, from the movies, this was the model for American women of a certain age, the goal to shoot for, the standard by which to compare.

And as Faye stood waiting on the first floor, watching Eugenie Eastbrook descend, she was painfully aware of exactly how she measured up. Beneath her practical navy suit, she felt the width of her hips, the slump of her buttocks, the channels of fat on her back, the flesh kimono swinging from her upper arms, not to mention her stomachs.

But Faye preferred her own body. Her hips had widened from giving birth to Laura. Her weight had accumulated gradually over years of cooking and enjoying delicious food and wine with her family and friends. Her posture and face were marked with grief for the loss of the man who was the love of her life. Why would she want to look as if nothing in life had affected her? Why would anyone? The truth was, Eugenie Eastbrook didn't look young; she looked fake.

Nevertheless, Faye proffered the obligatory compliment. "You look beautiful tonight, Mrs. Eastbrook."

Mrs. Eastbrook unfolded an indigo pashmina shawl and settled it around her shoulders. "Thank you," she said, apathy draining her words of any meaning. For Eugenie Eastbrook, Faye's words were only to be expected, it was what an employee would say, it didn't signify.

Dr. Eastbrook came swiftly down the stairs, sleek in his tux, shooting his cuffs to be sure the heavy links were exposed.

"We'll be late," he warned his wife. He didn't bother to speak to Faye, but strode across the hall, yanking the front door open.

"Lock up after us and set the alarms," Eugenie Eastbrook instructed Faye.

"Of course."

"We won't be back until after midnight, I'm sure. We'll come in the back way. Don't wait up."

Faye nodded. She shut the heavy door and went to the window to look out. She watched the Eastbrooks settle into the Jaguar and, with a spurt that scattered the white gravel, race away from the house.

Faye checked her watch.

The annual Plastic Surgeons of New England Gala had been on the Eastbrooks' calendar for months. It would take forty minutes, more or less, for the Eastbrooks to drive in to the Copley Plaza where the reception, dinner, and dance would begin at seven, so the earliest they could return home would be midnight, and Lila told Faye that in the past few years, her parents had stayed out past two.

So it was safe.

Faye opened the box and switched off all the alarms. She hurried to her room, seized the duffel bag hiding at the back of her closet, and carried it swiftly down the hall to the family room. She unlocked Dora's door and entered.

Dora sat in her wheelchair, rubbing her hands together nervously. "Have they gone?"

"Yes, and they won't be back for hours. We've got all the time in the world. Don't worry. Let's concentrate on you."

Dora giggled. "Sounds like a plan."

"Need the bathroom first?"

"No thanks, I'm set."

Faye unzipped the duffel bag and pulled out a garment of lavender silk and chiffon.

Dora sighed with pleasure. "It's so beautiful." She leaned forward, allowing Faye to undo the Velcro fasteners at her shoulders and lift off the brown dress.

"The dressmaker promised me this would be as soft as an angel's kiss." She shook out the lavender silk, hoping the rustle of the fabric would distract Dora from any embarrassment she might be feeling at having someone new see her bare back, twisted cruelly and laced with scars from operations. Carefully, Faye slid the garment over Dora, clasping the Velcro straps at her shoulders and letting them rest against the young woman's skin.

"Okay?"

Dora smiled, watching herself in the mirror. "Oh, yes."

Faye knelt in front of Dora, tugging the silk, arranging it to fall in little waves to her feet, resting on the wheelchair footrest. "There's more." From the duffel bag, she lifted a swath of chiffon, pale as lilacs, sprinkled with seed pearls and silk violets. This she settled over Dora's shoulders like a shawl. Then she lifted one more thing from the bag, a ring of real violets and pale white baby roses, which she settled on Dora's head.

"Wow!" Dora whispered. Pressing a button, she zoomed forward, getting as close as she could to her reflection.

"Would you like some lipstick?" Faye asked. "I don't think you need blusher, your cheeks are already rosy enough. Maybe mascara?"

Dora nodded eagerly. "Lipstick. Mascara."

Faye knelt next to the young woman and carefully applied the makeup.

Dora's eyes widened. "Why, I'm almost pretty."

"Honey, you *are* pretty," Faye told her. But as she looked at Dora's reflection in the mirror, she saw the young woman's eyes darken, and she knew what Dora was imagining—being healthy, upright, strong, walking arm in arm with a man who couldn't stop looking at her, dancing with a man who would drink in her beauty with his eyes.

Perhaps, Faye thought with a terrible pang in her heart, perhaps she'd been wrong to clothe Dora in such attire, even if only for one night. Perhaps it would make Dora feel more deeply the difference of her own circumscribed circumstances, and grieve for all she would never have.

"Dora!"

Faye and Dora turned—Dora with a whir of her power chair—to see Lila coming through the door from the family room. Lila was radiant in a white silk dress, her blond hair crowned with a halo of baby roses.

Lila rushed to her sister and fell beside her. "Oh, darling, you look so beautiful!" Her love for Dora was like an invisible bridge over the darkness, like a rainbow arching through clouds.

Faye's throat ached with tears as she dug through the duffel bag for her camera. She found it, removed the lens cap, and began snapping photos of the sisters together.

Then Teddy Becker entered the room, debonair in a handsome navy blue suit, white dress shirt, and red tie, a white rose on his lapel.

"Teddy. Come meet my sister," Lila called.

Marilyn Becker, lovely in a pale green suit, arrived next, followed by a tall young woman wearing the white robe and purple stole of a minister, carrying a Bible.

Introductions were made all around, and then the Reverend Smith organized the wedding group into their appropriate places, the bride and groom in front of her, Dora on Lila's left, Marilyn on Teddy's right.

"Dearly beloved," the minister began.

Quietly Faye circled the group, pressing the zoom button, clicking the shot. The modern little camera whirred with exquisite efficiency, its clever digital speed counterpointing the solemnity of the old familiar words.

"For richer, for poorer, in sickness and in health."

Faye remembered the day she married Jack, the gloss and weight of her heavy ivory satin gown, Jack's smile when he saw her come down the aisle, the blur of the minister's words, and most of all, the way Jack took her in his arms and kissed her passionately, right in front of everyone, not for show, because Jack didn't care about shocking his parents or hers, but because he wanted to give her a kiss she'd never forget.

"With this ring I thee wed."

Laura's wedding to Lars had been held on Nantucket in August. Both families had rented several large houses for all the bridesmaids, ushers, friends traveling back from afar, and relatives. Beneath a sunny sky, everyone spent the days before and after the ceremony swimming and sunning on the beach, and the wedding reception took place beneath a tent on a lawn at the edge of the ocean. Strings of white lights had laced the hedges and trees, a small band had played, champagne had flowed, Laura had never been more beautiful, and Lars had blushed the entire time he danced with her.

"Let no man put asunder."

Faye snapped a shot of Marilyn smiling as her son said the venerable words. If Marilyn was pinched by the irony of hearing the words as she stood alone, her husband having filed for divorce, having moved in with a younger woman, she showed no signs. But then Marilyn was a generous-hearted woman. She might be obsessed with the distant past, but she clearly understood that with a wedding, as with a birth, the world begins anew, as fresh and full of hope as the sun rising up to bring a new day.

The ceremony was finished. The groom kissed the bride. Faye zipped down to her own room, wheeling back a cart of champagne, glasses, and clever little canapés. She poured the champagne and handed it around, she passed the canapés on their silver tray, then she took more photographs. She had a glass of champagne herself—she deserved it.

"How can I ever thank you?" Marilyn hugged Faye. "This is the best wedding I've ever attended! And Teddy looks so happy!" She leaned closer, whispering in Faye's ear. "Dora's adorable! How can her parents keep her hidden away like this?"

"It's Dora's choice," Faye told her, turning her back to the young woman to hide her words. "She finds most people's attention too painful to bear. And she tires easily. She likes having this room, everything within reach, nothing surprising, she likes her routines."

Marilyn said, "Teddy told me he and Lila have asked Dora to live with them, but she refused."

"Well, Dora's happy here. She feels safe. And she worships her mother. But I'm sure Dora will want to have Lila and Teddy visit."

Her power chair humming, Dora rolled toward Faye. "I want to give them my present."

"Of course." She handed her glass to Marilyn. "Hold this a moment, will you?" She followed Dora to the back of the room. Hidden behind a bookshelf was the picture Dora had drawn with her pastels. Faye had spirited it out to a shop where it was encased in a beautiful gold frame, and now she slid it from its hiding place and set it on Dora's lap.

"This is my wedding present to you!" Dora called out.

Dora had drawn a yellow vase holding pink tulips on a blue background. The lines were slightly wobbly, and there was no sense of depth, but even so it was a fine and cheerful sight. Faye watched proudly as Lila and Teddy made a great fuss over the drawing, promising to hang it in pride of place above their fireplace in their house.

But Faye noticed how Dora was sagging in her chair, and Dora's face was strained, too; she was becoming tired. Faye caught Lila's eye and cocked her head in Dora's direction. Lila nodded, and soon everyone was hugging and saying good night.

Marilyn and the minister left. Lila stayed to help Dora undress while Teddy and Faye gathered up the champagne glasses and returned the cart back to the kitchen.

"So you still plan to let Dora break the news to the Eastbrooks?" Faye asked, hands deep in soapy water.

Teddy picked up a dish towel. "Lila says it's what Dora wants. She's had so little power in her life, and very few chances to help her sister—it's always been the other way round."

"It's going to be quite explosive around here." Faye carefully rinsed the soap off the last flute and set it in the drainer. "I think Dora's strong enough to take it."

"And you're leaving tonight?"

"I am." Faye dried her hands and looked around the kitchen to be sure everything was in perfect order. "If I thought it would help Dora, I'd stay, of course. But the Eastbrooks will know I'm the one who disarmed the alarms—Dora could have managed to open the front door, but she couldn't have reached the alarm boxes. This way, I'll disappear, and the Eastbrooks can spend their fury trying to trace down a person who doesn't exist."

"Won't they call the people who gave you—who gave 'Mrs. Van Dyke'—references?"

"I doubt it. They never called them when they hired me. Just having the names on my résumé was sufficient."

"What about tracking you through your car?"

"Alan rented it. If the Eastbrooks pursue it that far, they'll have to assume they have the wrong license plate number. But I'm sure they didn't bother to notice the number. They were too busy." Faye flicked off the kitchen lights and led Teddy back down the hall. "They'll be overwhelmed by all this," she told the young man. "I'm glad Lila had Dora with her for your marriage ceremony. I wouldn't have done this if I didn't firmly believe it was the right thing to do. But I wonder whether Lila might reconsider now, and go through with the wedding her mother planned for September."

Teddy tried to look solemn, but he couldn't keep from breaking into a great smile. "I don't think that would work. Lila's pregnant. The baby's due in September."

"Oh, Teddy!" Faye swooped to hug the young man. "Does Dora know?"

"Lila's telling her now."

At eleven o'clock, Faye stood alone in the imposing front hall of the Eastbrook mansion. Everything was quiet; everything was done. She'd stripped her bed and washed the sheets and towels; they were in the laundry room off the kitchen, tumbling in the dryer now. She'd packed her bags and carried them stealthily out to her car. She'd looked in on Dora, who was sleeping soundly in her bed, the circlet of flowers lying on her bedside table, where her mother would see them when she brought Dora breakfast in the morning. Faye could imagine the scene Eugenie Eastbrook would make. Dora's face had glowed mischievously as she assured Faye she was up for shocking her parents. Faye smiled, thinking how everyone should have a chance to rebel at least once in her life.

Checking for the third time to be certain all the alarms were set, Faye laid her house keys on the antique table in the front hall, opened the door, and stepped out into the night. She pulled the door shut firmly behind her and stood for a moment, saying farewell to Mrs. Van Dyke and the life she'd led in this sumptuous place.

She was glad to be leaving. For the first few days it had been amusing, playing at being a housekeeper, and she was glad to have helped Dora, and Lila, and especially Marilyn. But she missed her old life, her real life. Eugenie Eastbrook's world of taut perfection was too chilling, too humorless. Faye was eager to become herself again, and so she hurried over the white gravel to her little rented car and drove away, back toward the comforts of her own home.

37

Who was it who said, "Beware of all ventures that require new clothes?" Shirley wondered, as she dressed for her Saturday seminar in a six-week cram course on business management.

Whoever said it was dead wrong, because Marilyn had bought new clothes to play her part as Alice's secretary, and look at her now, she was a babe.

Today was Shirley's moment of transformation. Her goal was to appear professional, managerial, capable of efficient thought, and Alice and the other HFC'ers—but especially Alice—assured her that her usual wardrobe didn't come within a mile of that image. Marilyn had given some of her suits and dresses to Shirley—they were about the same size—and dutifully, Shirley tried them on in front of a mirror, grimacing at the reflection. In these drab garments, Marilyn might look like a scientist; Shirley looked like a scientific *experiment*.

But that didn't leave much else. She wished she could afford to do what Marilyn did, skip off to the mall on a shopping spree. But she didn't have the money to buy a new shirt. Actually, she did, but she needed to save every penny toward Golden Moments, or Alice would skin her hide.

Finally, she settled on a pair of jeans, her own plain black T-shirt, and a muted heathery tweed jacket of Marilyn's. She still didn't look like herself—the jacket was so rigid, it didn't *flow*. She focused on her face, putting on a minimum of makeup, leaving off the violet eye shadow and toning down her blusher and lipstick. When she was finished, her face had about as much allure as her elbow.

Still, she persisted. She stuck simple silver studs in her ears instead of any of her fabulous earrings. She skinned her hair back from her head into a long fall held by a scrunchie—and nearly gagged at the result. Without the flamboyant cascade of red, every line and wrinkle and sag was visible. How could she walk into a room full of energetic, tech-smart, cellphone-sporting, Palm-Pilot-punching young people, looking like this—*old*?

What had she advised Julie? *Don't let fear*

rule your life? Great advice, but sometimes difficult to follow. Even harder to do it alone. She needed a friendly voice to buck her up and blow away the clouds of self-doubt.

She grabbed up her phone and called Alice. "Alice! I can't go to this seminar! I look old and dried-up!"

"Nonsense," Alice assured her. "You look like Bonnie Raitt."

"More like Willie Nelson."

Alice laughed. "Don't be so hard on yourself. And remember, you're not entering a beauty contest. Neither are the other people at the seminar. They'll be as nervous as you, afraid they won't understand everything, trying to take it all in—they won't even *see* you."

"I suppose you're right. Oh, but Alice, I didn't even go to college!"

"Neither did I, until late in my twenties, and then I put myself through night school."

"Yes, but you're *smart*!"

"So are you."

"No, I'm not! When I read the seminar options, I couldn't understand half of them or pronounce the other half!"

"You're exaggerating."

"I'm not! Listen—what the hell is *macroeconomics*?"

"Well, if micro means small, and macro means big, what do you think?"

Shirley chewed her lip. "The economics of big corporations?"

"Sure. Or even bigger, of nations, of international trade, of the world."

"Oh, jeez," Shirley moaned.

Alice became serious. "Shirley, you don't have to worry about macroeconomics. No one's going to force you to. You need to look at this seminar as a *tool.* Like your massage table's a tool, or your aromatherapy candles. If you want to be the head of your own business, if you want to run Golden Moments properly, so you make a profit, you've just got to get a grasp on certain concepts. And you can do it. I know you can."

"I know I can, too. I just needed to hear someone else say it."

"Well, look," Alice continued. "I'll be glad to help you with the start-up, if you'd like, and I'll get your office in shape for you."

"Oh, Alice, that's so good of you!"

"I'll enjoy doing it. But I wouldn't do anything if I didn't think you were going to make a success of it."

"Thanks, Alice. You're exactly what I needed!"

Buoyed like a kite on a fresh spring breeze,

Shirley grabbed up her notebook and pens, raced to her car, and sped to the Natick Marriott. Borderline late because of her mini nervous breakdown, she ran across the enormous parking lot, checked the room event schedule in the hotel lobby, and, rather than wait for the elevator, took the stairs to the third floor, two at a time.

A pretty young woman at the reception table flashed a smile. "You must be Shirley Gold," she called out. "Here's your name tag and packet. Go right in. They're just about to begin."

"Thanks." Shirley slapped the name tag above her left breast and slipped through the doors into the function room.

Long tables filled the room, facing the front where a white board and a video screen were set up. Every table seated four, and every table was filled to the max.

"Over here," a woman called, gesturing to a place at a table in the corner.

"Thanks," Shirley said to the woman as she took her place.

Maybe fifty people were there, she figured, scanning the room. She saw the backs of everyone's head. White hair, black hair, gray hair, no hair. All ages. All ethnicities—jeez, she never thought of that, of trying to set up a business when English wasn't your first language. At least she knew English. Many of the other students wore jeans and T-shirts, and quite a few of them were overweight and out of shape and, Shirley could tell by their posture, riddled with stress. Yet there they were. She could feel the optimism in the room. If a hope and determination meter existed, this group would send it over the top.

The instructor, Dr. Newcott—but call him "Bob"—was talking, pacing back and forth across the front of the room, slapping his hands together, making jokes, like a coach before a game. He softened them up, whetted their appetites, then hit them with a list of the hard stuff they were going to cover during the day.

Tax laws. Pension and health benefits. Social security taxes. ERA. Job discrimination, federal leave, salaries and promotion, organizational charts, job descriptions, and annual job performance evaluations.

Could it be more boring? To become a certified masseuse, she'd had to learn the names of the skeletal and muscular system in the human body, and at first she hadn't thought she could do it. The words had sounded so silly, and her mind had bubbled with questions like, if fingers were called *phal*anges and the penis a *phal-*

lus, did that mean the penis was a kind of finger, or fingers a kind of penis? Her teacher had stopped calling on her when she raised her hand.

But she'd persevered, and if she could learn all that, she could learn this stuff. Shirley picked up her pen and pressed the point to the first page of her new lavender notebook.

A year. Twelve months. That was how much time Theodore's lawyer told Marilyn she could have to move out of the old Victorian where she'd lived with her husband and son for the past twenty years.

In the grand scheme of things, a year was nothing. If all time were the size of the planet Earth, a year would be a paper clip, an eyelash, a staple. In her own scheme of things, a year was larger, but not quite large enough, Marilyn thought, for the job she had to do.

She wandered through her house like a tourist in a museum gift shop, observing with a ruthless eye what, of all the possessions crowding the rooms, she would like to take with her to her new life.

It was difficult to see the furniture. Most of it was piled with books, and most of the books were Theodore's. Well, then, he could deal with them, he could pack them, or arrange to have them packed. The furniture was a strange mix of dark, heavy oak from his parents' home and sleek teak and chrome they'd bought in their later years when they desperately needed a new chair or bookshelf. She had no use for any of it, he could have it all.

She climbed the stairs to the second floor along a narrow path between more books, journals, and lopsided stacks of clippings from newspapers Theodore had dropped on the stairs, intending to take up later, or, rather, intending for Marilyn to carry up. The hall was lined with bookshelves stuffed to overflowing, as were the two bathrooms and the four bedrooms.

Teddy's room hadn't been changed since he moved into his own apartment. She leaned in the doorway, a slight smile on her face as she remembered how life had once been. You could read the passions of Teddy's life on the walls. Over the childhood dinosaur wallpaper were plastered posters, not of rock stars and blond babes, but charts of the planets, the anatomical structure of the human body, chemical elements, water fleas, flatworms, and gastropods.

Teddy and Lila were in the process of buying a house with rooms for lots of children. Teddy might want these posters, and all the books piled on his desk, bed, chairs, and floor. Well, he could take what he wanted from this room and toss what he didn't. She closed the door and went down the hall.

For the past ten years or so, since Teddy left home, she and Theodore had slept in separate rooms. Though they'd agreed it allowed them to read late into the night without keeping the other awake, Marilyn knew it signaled a turning point in their marriage. Theodore's interest in sex had always been, basically, an urge for something quick, oral, and just for him. Even ten years ago, he hadn't been interested in touching her or looking at her. She'd been only forty-two, but she'd felt much older, her own body as stiff and dusty as a piece of shale, holding only the impression of what once had been a juicy, warm, living woman.

So many wasted years.

Well. She couldn't bear to look at her bedroom, and she wouldn't look at Theodore's. Let him deal with that.

From somewhere in the house, a kind of music floated. After a few moments, Marilyn realized it was the phone ringing. Whisked back to the present, she zipped down the hall to grab the phone in her bedroom.

"Marilyn!" Alice boomed out, nearly breaking her eardrum. "Do you have a moment?"

"Of course." Marilyn sank onto her bed, leaning against the headboard.

"I thought you might be able to help me."

"Well, I'll try." She rearranged the pillows more comfortably. "What's up?"

"It's um, this, um," Alice mumbled.

Mumbling! How out of character for strong, take-charge Alice. *Nothing* intimidated her. Except—"Oh, Alice! Are you worried about tonight? Your date with Gideon?"

"Not *worried*," Alice snapped defensively, then admitted, "More like terrified out of my skin."

Marilyn laughed. "Why? You think he's going to try to get you into bed?"

"Well, maybe."

"Is Alan still living with you?"

"No. He found an apartment in Cambridge."

"So the coast is clear *chez vous*," Marilyn lowered her voice suggestively.

"Clear? For what?"

"What do you think?"

"Oh, Lord. I don't know! This will be our third date, after all, because he took me to the jazz club the other night, and if I count the coffee after the symphony as a date, which probably I shouldn't, but on the other hand, my thinking's old-fashioned, I know young women *do it* on the first date, but what are the *rules*?"

Now Alice was *babbling*. Marilyn laughed indulgently. Their conversation stripped years off her life. She threw herself backward on her bed, sinking into the pillows. "Alice, I don't think there are rules anymore."

"But there *are*. I think someone wrote them down in a book."

"Oh, yes, now I remember. But that's for young women who want to get married. You don't want to get married, do you?"

"I don't know!" Alice wailed. "How can I possibly know what I want? This wasn't in my game plan! It's all happening too fast. I planned to crawl right down into a pit of depression and wallow there for a few months. And look what happened! I never should have left the apartment!"

"Come on, Alice, you've got too much energy to stay depressed. And you like Gideon, right?"

"He's an intelligent, pleasant, attractive man. But—"

Marilyn smiled, twirling the long curly phone cord while she talked. *"But?"*

"But does that mean I want to go to bed with him?"

"You're the only one who knows the answer to that," Marilyn told her.

Alice sighed. "I wish it were that simple."

"It *is* that simple!" Kicking off her moccasins, Marilyn brought her knees to her chest to get a better look at her toenails, which she'd painted a cheerful pink.

"Wait a minute, not so long ago, you said you'd forgotten how to feel sexual desire. Your exact words, if I recall, were that you felt like a purse that was all zipped up."

"That's true. But that was before—" Marilyn choked on her words.

Alice sighed gustily. "Go on. You can say his name. I won't get mad."

"I am so sorry about your job, Alice."

"I know you are. Now forget it. Move on. Was Barton a good lover?"

Marilyn closed her eyes and made a funny noise.

"Marilyn?"

"Sex with Barton was wonderful. Of course it helped that he's so handsome, and he has an amazing body—"

"—and now we know why."

"Well, let me tell you, there was no silicone implant in his penis! It was all real!"

"So how was he on the foreplay?"

"Foreplay?" Marilyn concentrated, mentally beaming herself back to that night. "As I recall, there wasn't anything you could *technically* call *foreplay*. We just kissed, and then we took our clothes off, in the bedroom, of course, and—"

"Wait. Did you leave the lights on?"

"No, but some light came in from the living room. I remember I'd pulled out all my white pubic hairs that morning, but I don't think he even had time to look down there, everything went so fast."

"Did you have an orgasm?"

"I think so. I saw a trilobite."

Alice was silent. Then she said, "You're a little strange, you know?"

"The *point* is," Marilyn began.

Alice interrupted. "I *know* what the point is."

They both laughed. "*My* point is," Marilyn continued, "I'm pretty sure the pleasure I had wasn't because Barton was a good lover. I don't even know what a *good lover* would mean."

"Technically proficient?"

"That might have scared me."

"Romantic?"

"Perhaps, a little." Marilyn tried to remember the evening chronologically, but the memory rushed back in a misty blur, like a fog of perfume saleswomen sprayed in department stores. "Barton told me he was falling in love with me—but that was *after* we made love. No, I don't think my pleasure had as much to do with Barton being a good lover as it did with my being open to the experience."

"So to speak."

Marilyn laughed. "I hadn't made love with Theodore for years, and then it wasn't *making love*, it was me giving him oral sex. He never thought I was pretty. I've never felt pretty, I've never been *sexy*—you know what I look like, a fishing pole. All my life I've been respected for my mind and ignored for everything else. But when I joined the Hot Flash Club, when you three made me get new clothes and a new hairstyle and I saw what I *could* be—it was like I blossomed. I started experiencing life in a different way. Why, suddenly my clothes felt so slinky and silky!"

"That's because they were silk instead of polyester," Alice pointed out.

"And the fragrance of my perfume and makeup and shampoo made me feel like I was always walking through a field of flowers. And all that made me feel sexy, all the time! It's like I'm on some kind of great drug! I'm attracted to almost every man I see these days. I can't *wait* to go to bed with Faraday!"

"Well, I'm happy for you, Marilyn, I really am," Alice said, sounding as if she were about to slit her own throat. "But that doesn't help me. I already wear silk and perfume. And I'm still just downright terrified of letting Gideon see me naked."

"Alice, you're *beautiful*."

"I'm overweight."

"Gideon knows what you look like, doesn't he?" Marilyn pointed out sensibly. It's not like you've been hiding your weight from him."

"As if I could."

"He must have thought you were attractive, or he wouldn't have asked you for coffee after the symphony, and then taken you to the jazz club. Maybe he *likes* plump women. I bet they're more fun to cuddle than a bundle of bones. Besides, you can keep the lights off."

"I suppose," Alice capitulated in a little voice.

Marilyn pressed on. "The question is, are you attracted to him?"

Alice groaned. "I don't know! Honest to God, it's been so long since I've even thought about real sexual attraction without any strings attached, I can't even figure out what I think or how I feel! You say *you* never felt sexy, so you didn't have sexual urges, right? Well, *I* used to feel sexy, and I used it to my advantage, to flirt with a man when I wanted to get my way at work. But I disconnected my own reactions. I never let myself even consider whether or not I felt attracted to a man, because sex was all part of a very competitive game, and I wanted to win."

"Did you go to bed with any of them?"

"I haven't had sex with a man for twenty years."

"Don't you miss sex?"

"I have a vibrator. And I trust it completely. It would never pull the kind of trick on me that Barton pulled on you."

"I know." Marilyn groaned. "But desire is so illogical."

"Where there's a phallus, there's bound to be a fallacy," Alice joked.

Marilyn chortled. "Very funny, in a heady sort of way." They both snickered. Then, turning serious, she said, "Listen. Remember what we talked about in the HFC the other night? We all agreed that whatever we do or don't do, we won't let ourselves be held back by fear. I had a great experience with sex with Barton, and I've got my hopes up about Faraday . . ."

"Have you been to bed with him yet?"

"Not yet. But soon."

"Are you nervous about it?"

"Yeah, kind of. But that's part of the pleasure." Marilyn waved her toes at herself.

"Oh, man." Alice sighed. "You're a natural at this, I guess. I've always played competitive games. I'm not sure how I'll do at a cooperative function."

"It's never too late to learn to share your toys."

"Well, thanks, Marilyn. I wish I could phone you tonight when I get nervous."

"It will come back to you," Marilyn promised. "Just like riding a bike."

38

In a pair of loose canvas trousers and her paint-spattered blue smock, Faye stood in her attic studio, palette in hand. That morning she'd set up a still life of daffodils and tulips in a clear glass vase on a cloth of pale rose. A pretty scene, stimulating and light. She'd clicked on a Gilbert and Sullivan operetta, which always made her smile, and started to work. She stopped for lunch, then returned to her easel. No judgment, she reminded herself. She'd been away from her canvases for a while, she had to cut herself some slack.

The little brass carriage clock chimed four times. Laura and Megan would be there soon. Faye rinsed her brushes and tidied up her studio, then stopped at the door to look back at her work. It was fine. A perfectly decent rendering of spring flowers. People might even want to buy it to hang in their homes—it was cheerful enough. But Faye knew it lacked *heart.* Because her heart wasn't in it. Something about the act of painting itself had changed for her. It was as if she'd spent the day watering a plastic flower.

Perhaps, she admitted, as she turned off the lights and headed down to her bedroom to change clothes, perhaps she found the work lonely. She missed the discreet bustle of the Eastbrooks, tea and scones with Margie, her exciting little visits with Dora, even the ordinary exchange of domestic information with Mrs. Eastbrook and the maids.

Before that, a little more than a year ago, her house had been filled with Laura and Jack; especially Jack. Her studio had been a refuge from the commotion of a busy life crammed with dinners with friends, social engagements related to Jack's firm, and Laura's wedding plans and baby showers. Also, she'd been busy with the normal work of buying the food and preparing healthy, delicious meals for two. Now she was alone in this big old house, and she could easily shop twice a week for groceries. Like her life, the house swelled emptily around her.

Then Laura burst in the front door and Faye hurried down to meet her.

"Megan!" Faye gathered her granddaughter in her arms. "How's my wittle wabbit?" She rubbed noses with Megan, who chortled and clutched a stray lock of Faye's hair.

Faye settled on the sofa with Megan on her lap, untied the baby bonnet, and slipped it off the baby's soft, sweet head. Was there anything more enticing than this warm weight, these bright eyes, this fragrance of baby powder and baby?

Laura rattled around in the kitchen. "Mom!" she yelled. "Didn't you buy any Ben & Jerry's?"

"I haven't had time to go to the grocery store," Faye called back.

Laura entered the room with a box of Wheat Thins in her hands. "You've got to get some decent food in this house."

"I have decent food, darling. Apples. Grapes." She snuggled Megan down among the sofa cushions and handed the baby a fat rubber fish on which Megan immediately began to gnaw.

"They're boring." Laura tossed herself with a thump on the other end of the sofa, tucking her feet up beneath her. "I need comfort food."

"Listen, Laura, I need to discuss something with you."

"Okay." Laura munched a cracker.

Faye turned to the right, toward Megan,

double-checking that the baby was safe and couldn't roll off onto the floor. She turned to the left, toward Laura, and saw how, quite literally, she had once again let herself get right in the middle of this little family.

She moved to the sofa on the other side of the coffee table. That was good. She could look her daughter right in the eye, without straining her own neck. "I'm going to put the house on the market."

Cracker crumbs flew. "Mom! No!"

"Darling, I have to."

"You can't!" Laura protested.

Megan's lower lip quivered.

"Don't frighten your daughter," Faye advised in a singsong voice that would calm Megan.

"Okay," Laura sang back. She reached over to Megan and smiled. "Who's got a rubber fishy?" Megan rewarded her with a grin that sent drool down her chin. "Mom, you can't sell the house," Laura said to Faye with nursery rhyme tones.

"It's too big for me now—"

"But it's *my* home, too!" Laura protested.

Faye peered steadily at her daughter without speaking.

"Oh." Laura sank back in the cushions.

"Oh, okay, I see what you're saying. You're saying I spend too much time over here."

"I'm saying I need to start over, Laura. I've got many years of life left, I hope, and I want to live them happily, not stuck in the past. I think your father would expect that much of me."

Laura's face took on a melancholy cast, and she began to chew on her index finger. Faye watched her daughter regress to this old habit, the sign of stress Laura had displayed during her childhood and adolescence. Laura looked very young, her long dark hair falling around her face, her finger in her mouth, and also older than Faye had ever seen her before, her lovely skin engraved with lines around the eyes and mouth, lines earned by sleepless nights walking the baby, by lonely nights wondering where her husband was. Every single instinct in Faye's heart burned and tugged and strained and longed to fix things for Laura, to offer her complete shelter here in this house, to keep the house exactly as it was so her child did not have to suffer yet one more loss.

She dug her fingernails into the palms of her hands, to keep herself from speaking.

At last Laura raised her sad eyes to Faye. "And what would Daddy expect of me?"

Faye took a deep breath. "I think he'd want

you to create your own home, Laura. Either with Lars or by yourself."

Laura nodded. "I know. You're right, Mom. I'm to blame for—"

Faye lifted her hand. "No need to talk of blame. I needed you so much when your father died, and you helped me by staying here. Who's to blame for that? It doesn't matter. What does matter is that you need to start fresh now, and so do I, and I can't do it here."

"But, Mom, where will you go?"

"I'm not sure. Part of the fun will be in looking. Selling the house will free me up, Laura, and I want to help you, too."

"You always help me."

"I mean financially. This house should bring a nice sum, and I want to give half of it to you to use on a down payment for a house."

"Oh, Mom! You don't have to do that!"

"No, I don't have to, but I want to. I hope it will take some of the anxiety out of this part of your life. Then, perhaps, Lars can find a job with a less-high-powered firm. Perhaps he'll be able to practice the kind of law he likes. Or, you two might get divorced. You'll have money to buy a small house and start a new life."

"A new life," Laura murmured. Her lovely face was full of doubt.

"It will take a while to sell the house," Faye continued, trying to sound brisk. "Before I can give you the money from the house, I want to give you something else."

Laura looked up expectantly. "Okay."

"I want to give you and Lars a romantic weekend. I'll take care of Megan for three days, and you and Lars go wherever you want—within reason. Up to Maine to walk in the woods, or down to the Cape to stroll by the ocean. Someplace where you can wear pretty lingerie and take long afternoon naps, where you both can gorge yourself like gluttons on extravagant food and wines. Where you can rest and reconcile."

Now the tears exploded. Laura rushed across to give Faye a huge hug. "You're the best mom."

Faye hugged her back. She picked up Megan and laid her on the floor between them. Megan shrieked with pleasure, wriggling her arms and legs gleefully, like a beetle trying to flip over.

"Tell me, Mom," Laura said, sounding very grown-up all of a sudden. "Did Dad ever cheat on you?"

"Laura, you can't judge your marriage by mine."

"You're evading the question."

"No." Faye shook her head. "No, Jack never cheated on me." Bending down, she dug into the diaper bag, then handed Megan her brightly colored set of plastic keys. Megan cooed ecstatically at them and tried to stick them all in her mouth. "Who's Grandmother's beautiful baby girl?" *Don't let fear hold you back,* she remembered them agreeing at the HFC. And so, still grinning at Megan, Faye said, "But I cheated on your father."

"You did not!"

"I did."

"Mom!"

Faye leaned back in the cushions, looking up at the ceiling. "You were in first grade, and you loved school, and you were such an independent little thing."

"Yeah, well, look at me now," Laura snorted.

"Jack was overwhelmed with his work. I felt left behind. *Old.*" She chuckled. "I was only thirty. An old beau from college phoned me. He was in town for a conference, and I met him for drinks, and he was so *exciting*! Zeke led hiking tours all over the world, New Zealand one month, Switzerland the next. He was lean and tanned and the most glamorous thing I'd ever seen." Faye smiled up at the ceiling, remembering.

"Eew, Mom, so you *slept* with him?"

For her daughter's sake, Faye tamed her smile. "I did. Several times over the next few months, whenever he was in town. It was so *romantic*, Laura." She still could remember how it felt to get ready for a rendezvous, the sensuality of preparations, the perfumed soap, new silk lingerie, the anticipation as she drove toward the hotel. The thump in her body when she first saw him, the energy of his kisses, so different from the absentminded kisses of her husband. Zeke's need of her, the force with which he pushed her down on the hotel bed, pressing her legs open with his knees, shoving her skirt up, wrenching her panties down—the *urgency*. She'd felt wanton, carnal, tempting. He did not ask whether the plumber had been to the house, whether his mother had agreed to spend Christmas with them that year, or how Laura's teacher conference went. He did not ask her to rub his feet, he did not fart or belch in front of her, he did not ask her to inspect a worrisome mole, and if he had *had* a worrisome mole, Faye wouldn't have worried. It was as if there was another way to be a human being, completely different from the way Faye was doing it, and for a few minutes a month, she got to live that sensual, liberated life.

"Did Dad ever know?"

Her daughter's voice pulled the plug on her memories. "Yes. Someone from Jack's firm saw me coming out of the hotel with Zeke. She told Jack, who confronted me." Faye sighed. She hated remembering this part. "It was horrible. Your father was devastated. I was sick with guilt." Her daughter didn't need to know how close they'd come to divorcing. "But we got through it. We went to church. We saw a counselor. I started painting. Gradually, things got better, and after that, we were just more and more in love with each other with every passing year."

Laura made a soft, whimpering noise.

Faye turned to her. "Oh, darling, I didn't mean to upset you, I shouldn't have told you—"

"I'm not crying about you! I'm crying about me! Oh, Mom, what will I do if Lars wants a divorce?"

Faye took her daughter by her shoulders. "Do you love him, Laura?"

"With all my heart!"

"Can you forgive his affair?"

Laura looked away. "It will be hard."

"It will be harder if you wring your hands over a steaming pot of resentment," Faye pointed out sensibly.

"What if he doesn't want to go away for a romantic weekend with me?" Laura looked terrified.

"Maybe he'll be surprised and complimented if you ask," Faye pointed out.

"Oh, Mom." Laura hugged herself. "I wish you could ask him for me." But she grinned. "I know, I know. I've got to do it myself."

After Laura took Megan home, Faye walked through her wonderful house, turning lights on as she went. She looked in the refrigerator for some kind of treat—letting go of Laura had made her heart ache. She felt like a cast-aside stake, once the sapling stands tall and free. She was useless, except as a grandmother. Thank heavens for that.

Closing the refrigerator door, Faye sat down with a bowl of red grapes, plucked one from the stem, and rolled it between her fingers. It was cool and smooth, a lovely burgundy color, but she had no desire to paint it. She had no desire to seclude herself in her attic studio with a number of inanimate objects.

It was as if a part of herself, once as brilliant as an oil by Rembrandt, had faded into sepia and was disappearing altogether.

The phone rang. She snatched it up.

"Faye!" She sounded so happy it made Faye smile.

"Hello, Marilyn. How are you?"

"I'm great! And I owe it all to you! How can I ever thank you for arranging the wedding?"

"I had fun doing it. Have you heard from the honeymoon couple?"

"They phoned last night. They're hiking in Hawaii and having a wonderful time. Lila loves the beaches, and Teddy loves the volcanoes."

"Speaking of which, any eruptions from the Eastbrooks?"

"Oh, yes. Lila phoned them from Hawaii. They're furious, and Dr. Eastbrook threatened to hire a private detective to track down Mrs. Van Dyke."

"Uh-oh." A snake of fear slid down Faye's spine.

"Not to worry. Dora's so much happier now that she's started painting. She's eating more, her general health is better, and she's even thinking of going out to sit in a secluded spot on the grounds and paint. *That's* made

Mrs. Eastbrook so happy, she's told her husband not to pursue Mrs. Van Dyke."

"Whew." Faye's heart slowed down.

"Plus, Dora's asked Mrs. Eastbrook to find a private art tutor for her. This is like a miracle, I guess, because before you came, Dora was terrified of strangers."

"Speaking of strangers, did you ever find out who the man was you saw being so chummy with Lila at Mario's restaurant?"

"Lila's hairdresser. He's been her best friend since high school, and he's gay."

"What a relief!"

"I know. Everything's turned out beautifully, and we have you to thank for it, Faye. By the way, how's your daughter doing?"

Faye settled in a chair, put her feet up on the kitchen table, and described her most recent meeting with Laura. "Was it hard, letting go of Teddy?"

"Not really. We were never as close as you and Laura. Perhaps guys and their mothers aren't. On the other hand, he's being very protective of me since his father filed for a divorce, and he thinks I'm supercool for changing my appearance. Plus, Lila and I finally have lots to talk about. She loves giving me advice on clothes and makeup, and she wants me to go to the gym with her when she comes back from her honeymoon."

"The gym? But you're so slim!"

"True, but Lila tells me my posture's bad, I slump, and I need to work out or I'll start looking like a hunched-over witch with a hump on my back."

Faye laughed ruefully. "Young women can be brutal."

"It's all right. Actually, I'm grateful for Lila's advice. I really like Faraday, and I want to be attractive for him. I've been isolated too long. You and Alice and Shirley are bringing me up to speed. Which reminds me, Alice phoned. She's nervous about her date with Gideon. Afraid she might go to bed with him."

Faye laughed. "You both have dates tonight, right?"

"Right. And I've got to get ready. I just wanted to thank you again, Faye, for everything."

After saying good-bye to Marilyn, Faye wandered to the kitchen window and looked out. Flowers and newly budding trees lifted and fell in the gentle, intermittent breeze. Faye was restless. She turned from the window. Once again she experienced a sensation of emptiness inside, so vast and vague she didn't know whether she was hungry or melancholy, or both.

Faye fixed herself a cup of tea and called Shirley, simply because she knew Marilyn and Alice were out. Of the three other women, Shirley was the one with whom Faye felt least affinity. Shirley's thin, energetic presence made Faye feel fat by comparison. Plus, Shirley was kind of eccentric. On the other hand, Faye admired her for wanting, at sixty, to start a new business.

"Faye!" Shirley shouted into the phone. "I'm so glad you called! I've had the most amazing day! I attended this management seminar Alice forced me to go to, and it was *awesome*!"

"Tell me about it."

"Are you sure? Do you have time?"

"I'm sure. I'd love to hear about it."

"Good, you can tell me whether or not I'm making any sense."

"I know nothing about business—"

"Maybe not, but you're so much smarter than I am."

"Am not," Faye protested, laughing, but she couldn't help but feel complimented. "But go ahead."

"First of all, I've got notes on my five-year plan, want to hear them?"

"Absolutely." Faye settled at the kitchen table and sipped her tea. A few moments later, she rose, found the notebook she kept at the little antique desk where she paid her bills, and returned to the kitchen table, making notes as she listened.

After a while, Faye said, "Shirley, if you're planning to offer so many services and maintain this large a staff, you're going to need a pretty good-size building."

"I know, believe me, I've been thinking about that. But I met the nicest man at the conference. He told them this is a great time to buy a place because the economy's in the toilet, so it's a buyer's market." Shirley giggled. "Almost sounds like I know what I'm talking about it, doesn't it? I—"

"What man?" Faye asked.

"Jeez, Faye, chill! You sound like my mother! His name's Justin Quale, isn't that the classiest name? He's not a real estate broker, but his brother, Jake, is. Over lunch, Justin and I talked, and he says he can think of several places that might be perfect for my retreat. So tomorrow he's taking me to look at a few."

"Shirley," Faye said, "I'm going with you."

"Why?" Shirley inquired, her voice shrill. "Because you think I'm a moron?"

"Of course not—"

"You *do*! You do think I'm a moron! You think I'm going to take all that money you and everyone else is investing and give it to some man simply because he flirted with me, right?"

"Nonsense, I don't think that at all," Faye lied, crossing her fingers.

"You think I'm not capable of being a sensible businesswoman who makes shrewd judgments." Shirley's voice thickened with tears.

"Shirley, calm down."

"Here I was, thinking you and I were friends, that someone as classy as you would even stoop to being a friend to someone like me; here I am, thinking I've changed my life, I'm a brave new woman, I swallowed my fears and went to that seminar, and I thought people thought I was smart, but you think *they* think I'm just a naive, gullible little birdbrain who will give her money to the first man that—"

"Stop it, Shirley!" Faye shouted. She felt terrible! She'd never meant to humiliate Shirley, she had to do something to save Shirley's pride and their budding friendship. "I want to see it for my *own* purposes!"

Shirley hesitated, then asked in a small voice, "You do?"

"Yes," Faye affirmed in a ringing voice. "I do." She had no idea what she was talking about.

"What purposes?"

What purposes? Faye wondered desperately. She opened her mouth, and nothing came out.

"Faye?"

"Because—" Faye began, mumbling at first, and then speaking out triumphantly, "because I'm going to go back to school, get a degree in art therapy, and be the art therapist at your retreat."

"Why, Faye!" Shirley sounded dazzled with surprise. "What a brilliant idea!"

"Yes," Faye agreed, more dazzled than Shirley. "It *is* a brilliant idea."

"Cool. Then I'll see you tomorrow afternoon."

Faye hung up the phone and made a note on her calendar. The next day was Sunday. Well. She thought she might go to church. She hadn't been since Jack's death, and she realized now that she missed it all, the church and its rituals, the congregation and hymns, the flowers. She would go, definitely, and let her autumnal life be part of spring, part of the blue sky, the returning robins, the breeze with its scent of freshly mown grass, the warm sunlight pouring out like a benediction.

39

The doorbell rang. Terror shot from Alice's brain directly down to her stomach. She didn't know whether to answer the door or run to the bathroom and barf.

Snap out of it! she ordered herself, and opened the door. Gideon stood there, soigné in black trousers and a cream-and-black silk shirt that made his dark eyes gleam like jet.

"A little present." He held out a sheaf of flame red tulips. "They made me think of you."

She took them, burying her face in the resplendent blooms, using the moment to compose herself. She was so flustered by his compliment and his gift, she was absolutely tongue-tied.

"Thanks," she managed to squeak. "I'll put them in water."

She found a vase in the cupboard above the refrigerator and carried it to the sink.

"It's a great night out there," Gideon called from the living room, where he stood appreciating the view.

"Uh-huh." Alice was so *uncomfortable*, and she sort of itched all over. Was she breaking out in a rash? She felt prickly. Oh, God, *prick*ly. The clear cellophane cone around the flowers appeared to be made of some miracle material that would not respond to her efforts to tear it. She tried to slide it down the long thick bunch of stems, away from the tight bunch of petals. It was like trying to slip a condom off a penis.

Oh my God, couldn't she think of something other than sex? With trembling fingers, she dug scissors out of a drawer and sliced the cellophane paper so that it fell away from the flowers, but *then*, as she ripped open the little packet of powder that would keep the flowers fresh, a vision of opening a condom packet sprang to mind. She shook the powder into the water, and stirred, then gathered the stems in her hands and inserted them—*sex* again!—into the opening of the vase.

She was nearly hyperventilating as she carried the flowers out to the coffee table. "Would you like a drink?"

Gideon checked his watch. "I don't think we have time. The movie starts at seven-thirty."

"Fine. I'll just grab a wrap."

"You look beautiful tonight, Alice." Gideon's smile set off sparklers in her stomach.

"Thanks." She hurried to her bedroom, doing her best not to bump into the walls.

In her bedroom, she gave herself one last check in the mirror. She wore new, loose, cream silk trousers with an elastic waist, and a long-sleeved coral tunic top reaching nearly to her knees and cut deep at the bosom, displaying her abundant cleavage. For the first time in years, she didn't have to barricade her bust behind a panel of fabric. She crossed her arms below her breasts, cradled and displayed to advantage in their new resplendent lace bra, and smiled cockily. "Hello, girls. Nice to see you."

Then she squinted her eyes critically and bent closer to the mirror. From the rounded swell of her breasts fanned a series of lines upward across the loose skin of her chest. These wrinkles met with the row of rings circling her neck, forming a kind of upside-down triangle. Up close, her chest looked like something the National Geographic Channel would show to explain alluvial flows in deserts or dry stream beds.

Damn! Was she gorgeous or grotesque?

"Alice?" Gideon called from the living room.

Alice wrapped her pashmina scarf around her, crossing it over her chest. "Sorry. Couldn't find my scarf."

"It's pretty mild out tonight," Gideon told her, opening the front door.

"I often find the air-conditioning in the theaters too cold," she explained.

He held her hand as they walked through the city to the sumptuous new movie theaters near the new Ritz. As they passed an older woman with white hair, a hunched back, and a cane, Alice experienced a surge of pity mixed with fear—she was seeing the Ghost of Christmas Yet to Come, and reminded that she wasn't there yet. She straightened her shoulders and let the shawl slip, just a bit.

At the theater, Alice inaugurated her new Pee-Panic-Prevention Policy and refused refreshments. Gideon bought himself a big bag of popcorn and a Coke, and as the previews flashed before the screen, he munched away happily. Men don't worry about being unattractive when they're stuffing their faces, Alice thought wryly. Gideon was really chowing down.

Maybe he was nervous.

Maybe he was nervous because he was going to try to get her in bed later. After all, he'd brought her flamboyant flowers, he'd called her beautiful, and, walking over, he'd been uncharacteristically quiet. Come to think of it, he *had* planned to take her to another jazz club, but had phoned that morning to say he wanted to see a movie. True, it was a new thriller starring Denzel Washington, but still . . . The movie flickered across the screen while her thoughts wrestled with options. Did Gideon consider a movie more romantic? They *were* sitting there in the dark together. At the jazz club they'd not been able to talk very much, and when they did speak, they had to yell over the crowd. She'd come home hoarse and exhausted. Perhaps he had, too. Perhaps he needed to conserve his energy. Perhaps he was fueling up on popcorn for later exertions.

As if reading her thoughts, Gideon set his popcorn box on the floor, wiped his fingers on a paper napkin, and reached for her hand. The warmth and size of his hand around hers took her breath away. When had she last held hands with a man in a movie? It was so romantic!

Alice relaxed in her chair, inclining toward Gideon. He leaned toward her until their shoulders touched. Electricity zapped through her. *Wow,* Alice thought. Maybe there really was something going on between them. Her shoulder was suddenly as sensitive as the tips of her fingers.

Am I crazy? Am I desirable? An actress with a waist the size of Alice's ankle sauntered across the screen, nearly vanishing when she turned sideways. I'll never look like that again in my life, Alice mentally berated herself. Hell, I never looked like that *before* in my life. Gideon's arm lay partly on the armrest between them and partly against her ample abdomen, which also supported her breasts in their valiant bra. Sitting in the dark theater, she flushed, then rallied, and accidentally on purpose let the pashmina shawl slip way down. Now, in the silver light from the movie screen, the tops of her breasts rose like dolphins in the sea, sleek and rounded, while the wrinkles remained hidden in the dimness. She shifted her angle, giving them a little more exposure.

Ever since her conversation with Marilyn, Alice had thought of nothing but sex. How amazing that Marilyn, who had all the self-confidence of a dead chicken, had gone to bed so easily with Barton Baker and more amazingly, enjoyed herself! Of course, Marilyn didn't have to worry about being fat, plus she was only fifty-two.

Alice had tried, over the past few days, to diet, wanting to see just how much effort it took to lose five pounds. She didn't need to read diet books. Over the past thirty years, she'd tried every diet imaginable. She just stocked her refrigerator with diet drinks, fruit, lettuces, and lean meats and forced herself to take a long walk every day.

In five nights she went from hungry and hopeful to starving and stark raving mad. Thank God Alan had moved into his own place. He didn't have to hear her sobbing her heart out at the kitchen table, calling herself a failure, a big fat flop, a woman who'd lost her job and, worse, had been such a terrible mother that her son lost his job and his wife. For a few grisly moments, she'd considered killing her pathetic self. But she didn't have the energy. Besides, she wouldn't give those assholes at TransWorld the satisfaction.

So she'd dragged her sorry self down to a twenty-four-hour market, bought ham, cheese, bread, mayo, chips, ice cream, eggs, all the stuff the doctors promised would kill you. Back in her kitchen, she concocted a feast, remembering her mama, who had been a big woman, and her father, who'd been a huge man. Neither had died young. They'd been active until their eighties. That would be good enough for her. Especially, she decided as she ate, and the delicious taste and smells filled her senses and refreshed her soul, if she could figure out what to do with the next couple of decades.

So if Gideon Banks wanted a relationship with her, he'd better like her the way she was, and so far it seemed he did. Besides, he was a hefty boy himself. That belly of his—how would they manage to make love? Several images shot through her mind, making her giggle. Gideon turned his head her way, frowning. Up on the screen, someone had just been killed. Alice shifted in her seat and forced her attention on the movie.

When it ended, Gideon asked, "Would you like to stop somewhere for a late-night snack?"

"Why don't we just go back to my place," Alice suggested, hoping she didn't sound too brazen or imperious. Having spent her life barking out orders, she had to concentrate to talk normally. "My son brought over some strawberry angel food cake Jennifer D'Annucio made." Remembering he was diabetic, she added, "Not too much sugar."

"Sounds good."

The air of the May night was soft and full of fragrances. Everyone they passed was laughing or holding hands, and Gideon took Alice's as if it were a natural thing to do. At her condo, she slid the glass doors open and took their desserts out to the balcony. They sat together in a companionable silence, eating and watching the lights of all the boats sparkle on the water.

In the mellow night, Gideon spoke of his dead wife, their early years together, the love he carried for her, even now. Alice told Gideon about Mack and his charm and his infidelities, and then she told him about her long-term affair with Bill Weaver. Boldly, she added, “I haven’t slept with a man for many, many years.” That, she thought, should take care of any questions about AIDS and other STDs.

“Nor have I slept with a woman for a long time,” Gideon quietly confessed. Reaching out, he took her hand in his. “Haven’t wanted to. Until now.”

Have mercy! Alice thought. Her pulse did the jitterbug up and down her arteries. Here it was, *The Moment.* Damn, she thought, why did she bring him out here, where they were sitting in separate chairs? If they were on the sofa, it would be so easy to turn to each other . . .

Like an answer to her prayers, a breeze came up from the water, lifting the edges of their napkins and the hem of Alice’s loose silk trousers. Goose bumps sprouted across Alice's exposed cleavage, and she hoped Gideon assumed they were caused by the external touch of the chilly air and not the internal mechanisms of her own body.

Gideon said nothing. He seemed to have gone into a trance, staring at the water.

All right, then, Alice thought. He got us this far; I can nudge us along. "Let's go in." She stood, hugging herself. "It's gotten too cool out here."

She carried their empty plates to the kitchen. Gideon carried their cups of decaf to the coffee table and sat down on the sofa. Alice sat down next to him. Close. She turned toward him, her clothes making silky slithering noises as she moved. She imagined him lifting off her coral tunic, exposing her breasts in their new lace bra. She imagined . . .

"You're so beautiful, Alice," Gideon said. He put his arms around her and drew her to him. He kissed her mouth so softly it was like feathers brushing her skin. "Your breasts—" he whispered. "My God."

Alice took his hand in hers and laid it on her breast. *Boing* went her nipples. Her body lighted up like a pinball machine, lights flashing, bells ringing, flippers flapping, oh, heavenly days, she'd forgotten she could feel like this. *Jackpot!* she wanted to whoop.

But Gideon's face altered, he pulled away from her mouth, he removed his hand from her breast. He said, "Sorry, Alice. I think I'd better go." He stood up.

Alice stared up at him, stunned. "Go? Now? Why?"

Gideon walked toward the door. "I'll call you."

Alice jumped up. "But Gideon! My body's been asleep for twenty years, and you just woke it up. And you're *leaving*?"

"Well, now, Alice," Gideon mumbled, shoving his hands down into his pockets like a boy. "No need to get angry. No need to rush things, either. We scarcely know each other, after all."

Alice felt like he'd punched her in the stomach. "I didn't mean to rush things—"

"I'll call you," Gideon said again, and left.

Alice stood there with her mouth hanging open. She couldn't believe he'd gone. She couldn't believe he'd kissed her like that, then walked away! What the *hell* had happened? It was as if he was attracted to her, but once she put his hand on her breast, he was repelled. Did she have bad breath? Was she that horrible a kisser? Were her lips chapped? Were her breasts too big? Was she just too damned fat? But then, why had he asked her out in the first place?

One thing for sure, he wouldn't be asking her again. What had he said, no need for her to get so *angry*? Okay, so she'd shown him a bit of her bossy, angry side, but damn, he'd gotten her all riled up, he'd said he hadn't wanted to sleep with a woman until *now*. How the hell was she supposed to take that kind of remark?

And if he thought *that* was angry, he was one mistaken man.

She was so confused she wanted to tear her hair out. She was furious, frustrated, and humiliated. Her company didn't want her professionally, and now this really nice man didn't want her sexually.

Thank heavens for small blessings. Alan had moved into his own place, so she could collapse on the sofa. She lifted her hands to her face and let the sobs and wails rip from her throat, tears streaming down her cheek, falling plop plop plop on what she had, until then, thought of as her beautiful breasts.

Faraday's apartment was in a luxurious modern high-rise overlooking the Charles River.

Marilyn didn't know whether to gaze out the expansive windows at the Boston lights sparkling against the night sky or at the three walls of bookshelves in Faraday's living room. So many fascinating books! Her former self would have selected a pile, stacked them on the coffee table, and curled up on the sofa to read.

Interspersed among the books, in misshapen globs like petrified gnomes, were the rocks Faraday had brought home from his hikes in the most distant places of the globe. Dense, and mute, the rocks were books, too, their fossils and minerals inscribing a hieroglyphic diary of the universe.

Faraday approached her, a brandy snifter in each hand. He wore a soft blue cotton shirt with the sleeves rolled up over his massive forearms. "That," he told her, handing her a glass, "is colonial coral from Greenland, proof that once it was much warmer there."

"And this?" Marilyn asked, indicating a petrified black scarf of rock with iridescent purple tints.

"Pahoehoe," Faraday told her. "From a lava flow in Hawaii."

Marilyn sipped her brandy. Its amber heat made her whole body glow. "What's this?"

She pointed to a chunk of quartz veined with glittering crystals of transparent pale green.

"Apatite," Faraday said. He smiled. "Named from the Greek word for 'to deceive,' because it's so easily confused with a number of other minerals."

"Apatite," Marilyn mused. "So similar to appetite."

"Appetite," Faraday reminded her, " is from the Latin *appetitus*, meaning an eager desire for something."

"They sound the same." Marilyn took another sip of brandy, loving the flicker of flame in her throat. "I wonder if there's a kind of cosmic message there."

"In my case, not," Faraday said softly, moving closer to Marilyn. "I have no intention to deceive you about the fact that I eagerly desire you."

Faraday set his glass on the bookshelf, took Marilyn's from her, and put it there, too. Wrapping his arms around her, he drew her to him. "It would be very *gneiss* to take you to bed," he said softly, his breath warm against her cheek.

"I *zinc* I desire you, too," Marilyn quipped, giggling nervously.

She turned her head and lifted her mouth to his. She'd never kissed a man with a beard before, so her first reaction was surprise at the rough texture of his wiry red-and-white whiskers against her chin and cheeks. The contrast between his soft lips and the spiky whiskers was amazingly sexy, as if her entire face and not just her lips were being caressed.

Keeping one hand on the small of her back, Faraday supported her head with the other as he pressed his mouth more fiercely against hers, forcing her lips open, thrusting in his tongue. Her knees went weak.

"*Shale* I lead you to my bed?" Faraday whispered in her ear.

"Of *quartz*," Marilyn replied shakily.

Across the river, city lights twinkled, filling the bedroom with a gentle light that concealed as much as it revealed. The room was neat but cluttered with the treasures of a busy life, picture frames on the dresser, books and rocks on shelves. His closet door was open, revealing a tartan wool bathrobe on a hook.

He guided her toward his bed, then, keeping both hands on her hips, he sat down, turning her to face him.

"Undress for me," he murmured.

"Oh." She'd never undressed for a man before, not while he watched, and her habitual shyness stalled her ardor. Theodore's face reared up before her eyes, the pity in them as he begged her not to pretend she'd actually had an affair, not to be so *unseemly*.

"Get lost, Shorty," a vision of Alice snapped, and Theodore's face vanished. Marilyn thanked her clever neurons for chasing the older memories away.

"Marilyn," Faraday whispered. He took her hands and kissed the center of each palm.

Alice and Faye had assured her they'd give their back molars to be as slender as she was. And during dinner, before the lecture on the Burgess Shale, Faraday had asked her to accompany him next weekend when he went to a conference in Montreal. She'd be interested in the lectures, and the city was fascinating. He told her he wanted to take her hiking with him in Scotland over the summer, and in New Mexico next winter. So as she stood in the quiet room, their breath all that stirred the air, Marilyn felt secure enough to be brave.

Also, she felt unbelievably sexy. In this light, with this man, who was, she knew, perhaps five years older, she experienced a kind of pride in her body. Faraday's obvious desire provoked an unfamiliar inclination: She wanted to be flirtatious. She wanted to be *saucy*. She wished she were wearing that little French maid's outfit from the yogurt ad, and with that in mind, she raised her hands and began to unbutton her silk blouse. She let it hang open just enough to show hints of her lacy red bra while she unzipped her skirt and let it fall to the floor. She stepped out of it, and slowly drew her blouse off one arm and then the other, then dropped it.

"God, Marilyn, you are so beautiful," Faraday said, his voice thick with lust.

She stood there smiling, thrilled to be living a fantasy. She wore only silk hose fastened with a garter belt, high black heels, and a bra that lifted and flattered her small breasts. She'd worn no panties that night, and that fact alone had made her feel audaciously sensual during their meal.

Faraday pulled her to him, burying his face in her abdomen, the brush of his beard tickling her tender skin. She twisted in his embrace, trying not to giggle.

He moved slightly, bringing his head down to her thighs, and cupping her buttocks, he licked upward along her leg toward her crotch.

Marilyn nearly fell over backward. The moist touch of his tongue, the heat of his breath, the immediate cool tingle of air, sent a geyser of sensations shooting up inside. Then he raised his hands and grasped her breasts, pinching her nipples.

She groaned and leaned against him. *So this,* she thought, *is the famous foreplay. Oh, my!* He unfastened her bra and released her from it, so she wore only the hose, garter belt, and high heels.

"Undress me," he said.

She felt deliciously lewd as she knelt, nearly naked, to untie his wing-tipped shoes. She slipped them off, then tugged on his silk socks, releasing his bare feet, long and slim, to the air. She felt like a geisha. She felt like a sex object! She felt *fabulous*.

Rising, she bent over him to undo his tie, unbutton his shirt, and pull away his tweed jacket, its rough texture brushing her naked skin, making it tingle. He caressed her body with his eyes as she worked, unbuckling his belt, unzipping his trousers, then suddenly, he groaned and pulled her down on the bed. Impatiently he kicked off his pants.

"Hurry," he gasped, reaching into his bedside table and bringing out a condom.

Faraday ripped the foil with his teeth and stroked the condom down over his penis, then, naked and hairy and thick and hot, brought his body down on top of hers, and shoved himself into her, and she cried out.

He thrust once, twice, moaned, and ejaculated.

Hey! Marilyn thought.

He collapsed heavily against her.

Wait! All her senses screamed. *Don't stop now!* Every nerve in her body twanged with anticipation. It was as if she were perched on the end of a diving board, arms aimed in an arrow, body bent forward, pushing off with her toes, on the brink of diving into an ocean of delight, but all at once the ocean dried up into a pile of sand.

"You are amazing," Faraday murmured. He rolled off her, but kept his arm around her, and pulled her back against his front, holding her close.

She could feel his penis shrinking against her bum.

"I'll be right back." Faraday stalked off to the bathroom, shutting the door between them.

Maybe he'd want to make love again right away, like Barton had, Marilyn thought frantically.

She heard the toilet flush. Water ran in the sink. Light gleamed as Faraday opened the bathroom door. He slipped back into bed, pulling the covers up over them both, and snuggled close to her.

"Marilyn," he said, wrapping an arm

around her, "I've been wanting to make love to you for years."

Well, maybe that explained it, Marilyn thought. Maybe once he settled down, maybe the next time around.

"No other woman has aroused me like you do."

But what about *me*? her body pleaded, and she pressed her hips into his groin.

"Will you spend the night?" he asked.

"Oh." She hadn't even thought that far ahead. But why shouldn't she? No one was waiting for her at home.

"All right." She nudged her hips more forcefully. Faraday responded with a supersonic snore.

Well. Perhaps he'd awake in the night, feeling amorous. Certainly they could make love again in the morning. She wouldn't be able to fall asleep, not with her body still screaming to be satisfied. But she trusted Faraday not to break her heart or humiliate her, and her body would just have to learn to wait.

40

Tucked away in Faye's attic, inside a cedar chest, were handkerchiefs, dresser scarves, hand towels, pillowcases, and sheets, embroidered long ago by her grandmother and mother, and passed down to Faye to use "for good." Faye *had* used them, early in her marriage, then carefully folded them and forgotten about them in the rush of her busy life.

She rediscovered the beautiful handwork, sensual as dried roses, while sorting through the attic in preparation for putting the house on the market. She took the ivory damask napkins, embroidered thickly with ivory, pale blue, and peach, and with imagination, patience, a needle, and thread, concocted a sleeveless, hip-length top. She thought her grandmother would approve of her interpretation of "for good."

She was wearing it to the second Golden Moments meeting. She couldn't wait to show the other members of the HFC the ensemble she'd created. Her indigo blue rayon trousers had an elastic waist. Her lightweight, thigh-long, long-sleeved, indigo blue silk cardigan had deep pockets. Better, it had a modest mandarin collar that covered most of the rings looping her neck, but wasn't so high it would push her chin wattles up into one wobbling glandularesque goiter as most turtlenecks did. Beneath the cardigan, an azure long-sleeved shirt fell silkily over her stomachs, and beneath that was the sleeveless top, twined and knotted with gorgeous embroidery that twinkled out from the other shirts like a subliminal reminder to look beneath the surface for true beauty. She could remove the cardigan in a hot flash, and strip down to the top when she sizzled. Everything was simple, elegant, and washable.

"Mom! We're here!"

Faye winked at herself in the mirror, then hurried down to the front hall to meet Laura, who immediately thrust baby Megan into Faye's arms.

"I'll be back, Mom, with the rest of the stuff." Laura flew outside.

Faye bounced Megan, who clamped her fat little legs around Faye like a koala cub. As Faye sat down on the sofa, Megan sank against her as if she were made of pillows, sparking a memory in Faye of her own grandmother's soft, yielding, infinitely comfortable lap.

Laura returned, laden with bags of diapers, toys, clean clothes, jars of food, and containers of milk. Over her red silk dress, she wore an oversize shirt—obviously to protect the beautiful dress from baby spit. Her dark hair swung glossily to her shoulders. Her eyes sparkled. Her skin glowed. A slender, gold chain glimmered around her trim little ankle. And she hadn't even begun the three-day vacation.

Laura plopped herself down across from Faye. "I've written out her schedule. There's a list of phone numbers for her pediatrician, our hotel, the baby-sitter, and—"

Faye laughed. "Laura, you'll only be gone for three days. And I did raise a baby myself."

"You're right, Mom, I know, I just—" Laura stood up, then sat down and burst into tears. "You're so good to do this, Mom! And I'm so scared."

"Have the antidepressants kicked in yet?"

"I'm not sure. They said it would be two or three weeks, and it's only been one. But I do feel more optimistic—and Megan's doing fine on the formula, don't you think? Although today she seemed a little constipated. I hope she's not getting sick."

"She's perfectly healthy," Faye said decisively.

"Her bowel movements should be slightly runny and the color of—"

"Laura. We'll be *fine*."

Laura sniffed. "You're right." She shook her shining hair and smiled bravely. "Well, then, I guess I'll be off. Wish me luck."

"Good luck, darling. And you'd better redo your mascara."

Laura dashed to the bathroom, returning moments later looking flawless. She held Megan and cuddled her close, murmuring endearments to the baby, who babbled joyfully back. Then Laura handed Megan to Faye, who carried her to the door and stood waving Megan's fat little hand at Laura as she got into her car and drove away.

"Now," Faye said to her granddaughter, "we'll feed you dinner and get you dressed in your cutest clothes. You've got *work* to do, little girl!"

All night long, Alice obsessively replayed her date with Gideon. She tried to sleep, she wanted to sleep, she was fucking *desperate* for sleep. Instead, she tossed in her bed, reviewing their conversation, Gideon's delicious kiss and his abrupt departure, while every grisly emotion known to women galloped through her veins, anger and mortification neck and neck for the lead.

At three in the morning, she grabbed paper and pen and sat down at the kitchen table to write out the conversation, word for word. She brewed a cup of chamomile tea—a gift from Shirley—but let it sit cold and untasted on the table. At four, she gave up. She'd *never* understand what the hell had happened.

She went into the bathroom, turned on all the lights, and studied her reflection.

Bad idea. Who looks great after a night without sleep? She looked like a tired sixty-two-year-old woman, she fucking *was* a tired sixty-two-year-old woman, but she wasn't a *dog*. She wasn't *hideous*, she had all her hair, all her teeth, so what had sent Gideon running off like that?

The only explanation was that Gideon Banks was some kind of sadist who got off on leading women right up to the starting gate, then vanishing. She'd heard about men who did that—what was it called? *Seduce and abandon*. Yeah. But damn, she hadn't even gotten properly seduced!

She returned to bed, where she drifted into a restless sleep.

She woke at nine-thirty, head groggy, mouth gluey, eyes burning. *Nine-thirty.* When had she ever slept so late? Sleeping too much was a sign of depression, wasn't it? Well, hell, she had reason to be depressed. No job. No man.

As her oatmeal heated in the microwave, Alice leaned against the windows looking out. It was raining. Of course it was. And it was that dreary, relentless, monotonous rain that seemed eternal. Thank heavens she was holding a second Golden Moments meeting at her condo that night. If she didn't have that to look forward to, she'd probably just sit on the floor and weep.

Instead, she ate her oatmeal, carrying it with her as she padded barefoot, in her nightgown, around her condo. Everything was neat. Nothing out of place. Shipshape as a showcase. That was good, right?

She peered in at the second bedroom, which had been her home office until Alan arrived. She and Alan had carried her computer, printer, desk, and necessary office paraphernalia into her bedroom so that the fold-out sofa could be transformed into a bed for Alan. Now Alan had moved into his own place, leaving the bed folded back up into a sofa, his sheets washed, dried, and folded neatly on a chair. There was a big empty space where her desk had been.

Well, here was something she could accomplish. She set to work with enthusiasm, pleased to find she was still strong enough to wrestle the furniture through the doors by herself. When she was finished, she leaned against the doorjamb, panting, sweating, invigorated, pleased with her efforts. Her home workstation was ready for action.

Except she had nothing to do there. She no longer had a job. All this stuff was useless, like her. Useless, and *old*.

She crawled back into bed, pulled the covers to her ears, and fell asleep.

She woke at four that afternoon. The Golden Moments party started at seven-thirty. Tossing back the covers, she jumped from bed and headed for the shower. The hot water cleared her mind and cheered her. She pulled on the brown batik trousers and the brown tunic—she wanted to look professional, for Shirley's sake. Besides, she had very little left in her closet. She really had to go shopping.

Dressed, she whirled through her apartment, arranging chairs, setting out nuts and napkins, organizing the drinks on the counter between the kitchen and dining room. Alan was coming at seven with the canapés. It would be great to see him. She congratulated herself. With Alan, she'd done something right. He'd come to her when he needed help, then he'd pulled himself up by his own bootstraps. He planned to stay in the Boston area, and that was something *fine* she could count on: seeing her handsome, intelligent, clever son often.

Her hands were full of teacups when the phone rang. She let the machine pick up.

"Alice? It's Gideon."

The sadistic bastard.

"I'd like to talk to you. I was wondering whether you might like to have a drink tonight. Or dinner. Or coffee. Anything. Give me a call."

Right. Fool me once, Alice thought, shame on you. Fool me twice, shame on me. Alice glared at the machine. She wouldn't hurry to call him back. Let him suffer a bit. Let him wonder if something was wrong with *him*!

Shirley stared at herself in the mirror, not sure if she was happy or horrified.

"It's *fabulous*, darling!" Enrico said.

Shirley shot him a cynical look. Of course *Enrico* would think so. He was A) gay and B) her hairdresser.

She studied the floor. Her chair was surrounded by coils and curls of her signature gorgeous red hair. No one had told her to cut it. No one had even suggested it. She'd been studying photographs of successful businesswomen her age and realized most of them wore their hair pulled back and up, or cut short. Her own hair was too heavy to wear up. It always came loose anyway, filaments springing out around her face, like faulty wiring. So she'd thrown herself on Enrico's mercy, asking him to give her a style that would make her look intelligent.

"Oh, honey, I can make you look like a *genius*!" Enrico had trilled, and set to work.

Now, here she was with a crisp, layered cut, parted on the side, hanging in shiny shingles to her ears. He'd toned down the red with brown and blond tones and dried it straight, which made it shine. With her new bronze-tone lipstick and blusher, and without her violet eye shadow, she looked so smart she intimidated *herself*.

She didn't have time to change or mourn. She had to get over to Alice's for the second Golden Moments meeting. She wore bronze trousers and a matching top beneath one of Marilyn's blazers. With her new do, she looked pretty damn businesslike. *Too* professional? No time to worry about that, either. She was a woman on a *mission*!

Curled in a lopsided living room chair, Marilyn browsed through her favorite book about fossils. She knew she was taking comfort from these things in the way one draws comfort from a familiar blanket or song, but she thought she deserved such reassurances, because once she rose from her chair, everything around her seemed new and strange.

Many of the books and papers, once stacked around the house, Theodore had carted away to his temporary location in a rented apartment in Cambridge. Never before had Marilyn understood how all that clutter had consoled her, imparting the illusion that her life was full to overflowing. Now, being in any of the rooms of her house gave Marilyn a dizzying sense of vertigo, as if the heaps and piles had been balusters in a staircase that had vanished, leaving nothing to protect her from falling into a void.

Even the furniture seemed unfamiliar to her, sitting around naked in the emptying rooms, dust outlines emphasizing the new gaps. When she reached for a mug for her morning coffee, her hand closed on space—Theodore had taken most of the mugs away, leaving her with whatever was chipped. Without Theodore at home, the mailbox stayed empty. When Marilyn lifted the mailbox lid, she found only a compartment of air.

Never mind, she told herself. She was starting over. Her calendar was crammed with appointments to see new houses. Her clothes were new, her friends were new, and Faraday, who would be arriving at any moment to pick her up, was new, or she was seeing him in a new light, as a boyfriend and possibly even a suitor. Her newly awakened sexual desires quibbled, but her head and heart reminded her that Faraday was a terrifically nice man with whom she shared many interests. Just because he'd been too quick the first time they made love didn't mean he would always be.

But should she date him exclusively? It wasn't that hundreds of men, or even two, were pursuing her, it was more that Faraday was swamping her future with plans for hikes, exhibits, lectures, and trips, and while she knew she should enjoy his attention, she felt flustered by it.

And what about a house? Should she buy one in a nearby suburb with a yard where all her future grandchildren could play? She'd never had a yard before, and she wasn't certain she wanted one. Did she want to plant flowers? Or live more simply and travel?

She had no idea how to lead her life.

What did her revered scholar Richard Fortey advise? Looking down at the book in her hand, she read:

"But scientific work is interconnected: Like a spider's web, it is sensitive to movement in any part of the structure, and interweaving strands give it its strength."

Perhaps, Marilyn mused, that was also true for human relationships. All her life, she'd been too preoccupied with her husband, her son, and her own academic inquiries to find time for female friends, and besides, her sister Sharon usually seemed more than sufficient. But now Marilyn was involved in a different kind of alliance, with unique, unusual women. In her old life, she would have found Faye too artsy, Shirley too frivolous, and Alice would have just plain terrified her. Alice kind of terrified her even now. But these new friends provided her with energy, sympathy, and suggestions to live her life in ways she'd never think of by herself.

She'd ask them what they thought of Faraday—she heard a car pull into the drive. Goodness, he was early! Or was she late? Had she been daydreaming—

The front door opened and closed.

"Marilyn?"

Marilyn stood up. "Theodore?"

Her husband entered the room with the ponderous, cautious steps he always took, as if it were the belly he carried before him that contained his valuable, scientific brain. Sunlight fell through the window onto his shining bald head and sparked off the lenses of his glasses. He was uncharacteristically, casually, clad in gray flannels and a blue polo shirt, and the tufts of hair that usually bristled from his ears had disappeared, no doubt at the lovely Michelle's request.

Michelle! Marilyn eased toward the window and peered out. No one was in the car, or on the sidewalk. She sighed with relief. She really didn't want to face her husband's new lover. What would she say to her? "Congratulations on your pregnancy?"

"Did you come to pick up more books?" Marilyn asked.

"No," Theodore said, and to her surprise, he advanced toward her, reached out, and took her hand. "I'm here to tell you that I'm coming back."

Puzzled, Marilyn looked down at their hands, his pudgy one wrapped around her slender one.

"Coming back where?" she asked.

Theodore snorted at her stupidity. "*Here,* of course!"

"Oh! Well. Oh." Pulling her hand away, Marilyn thought frantically. "I suppose I can find another place to live, but really, Theodore, not tonight." She looked at her watch. Faraday would be here soon to take her to the Golden Moments meeting at Alice's. "Although"—an unexpected jolt of pleasure sparked through her—"if necessary, I suppose I could spend the night at Faraday's."

"Dammit, Marilyn, there's no need to be vengeful."

"Excuse me?"

"I'm prepared to be humble, but—"

A peal of laughter escaped Marilyn. "Theodore, when have *you* ever been humble!"

"Would you please allow me to finish a sentence!" Theodore's face was flushed. Why had she never noticed before, how the pouches beneath his eyes resembled the wads of chewing gum Teddy and his friends had once left on the rims of their plates.

Marilyn giggled. "I'll be quiet, Theodore."

"I've come to tell you I won't be divorcing you, after all." Theodore forced his mouth into a sickly smile.

"Theodore! What's happened!"

"You don't need to know the details. You need know only that I intend to move back here again and live with you as your husband."

"But Theodore—"

He waved his hand. "No need to thank me."

"But I wasn't intending to thank you! Good grief, Theodore, you can't just pretend nothing has happened! What about Michelle? What about your baby?"

Theodore squeezed his mouth so tight it looked like a tiny pursed anus. His face became increasingly scarlet.

"Theodore? Are you all right?"

"I could use a drink," he admitted through clenched teeth.

Marilyn fetched him a scotch and water. He was on the sofa, and when she handed him the drink, he patted the cushion next to him, but she took her vodka and tonic and settled in a chair across from him.

"Now what about Michelle and your baby? I so hope she hasn't lost it. I've always wanted Teddy to have a sibling."

Theodore's eyes bugged from his head. "Have you gone *insane*?"

Marilyn touched her temple. "I don't think so."

"What kind of woman hopes her husband's mistress doesn't lose his baby!" Theodore trumpeted.

Marilyn frowned, considering. *One who isn't jealous,* she realized.

"Look," Theodore said grumpily. "Michelle has not lost the goddamned baby."

"Theodore, that's no way to speak about—"

"She's keeping the *baby*. She *wants* the baby, because she wants to have a child with my *genes*! I tell you, Marilyn, the woman's a freak of nature! She wants the *child*, but she doesn't want me." His eyes bulged alarmingly.

Marilyn had to look away. In an attempt to keep herself from laughing, she pinched her nose the way she did when she tried not to sneeze. "Talk about designer genes," she snorted, reminding herself to tell the Hot Flash Club about her pun.

"It's not funny," Theodore snapped.

"No, of course it's not." Marilyn pulled

herself together. "I'm sorry, Theodore. I know you were anticipating a new and more vigorous life. I can understand, because—"

"It's best that it worked out this way, I suppose." Theodore's voice took on the philosophical tone he used when he lectured. "You and I have a marriage, after all, that is considered enviable by many. Michelle is only a graduate student, while you are a tenured professor with this university. You really are the more appropriate spouse for me, in spite of your age."

"Oh, but, Teddy, I can't continue to be your, um, *spouse.*" Marilyn cocked her head as she thought. "*Spouse* is a rather ugly word, isn't it? Like mouse. Or souse. I'd have to be soused as a mouse to remain your spouse." Another laugh escaped. "Sorry."

"Are you drunk?" Theodore roared.

"Not at all, Theodore! I've never been more sober. I'm just very—well, I guess I'd have to call it *happy.*" She rose, setting her glass on a copy of a journal containing Theodore's latest essay, even though—especially because—she knew it would leave a ring. A round, empty, unattractive, useless ring, like her marriage band.

"You can move back into the house, Theodore." Marilyn went to the window and looked out. "I have a party to go to, and I'm sure someone there will offer me a bed for the night. I'll come back tomorrow and fetch a few of my things, then we can make arrangements for appointments with the lawyers, and all the rest."

"Don't be ridiculous!" Even the top of Theodore's head was crimson. "I just told you, Marilyn, I'm coming home!"

But just then Marilyn saw, through the window, Faraday's car pull into the drive.

"I've got to go now, Theodore," Marilyn said. "If you think you'd be happier here in the house, then of course stay here. I'll make other arrangements."

Theodore rose, all five feet six inches trembling with frustration. "You can't just walk away! We have things to discuss."

Faraday walked toward the house, looking terribly handsome in his blazer and tartan tie.

Marilyn said coolly, "I apologize, Theodore. I had no idea you were coming over. You should have phoned first. I really have to go now." She grabbed up her purse, checked her hair in the mirror, and went to the front door. She wanted to forestall Faraday from coming into the house; Theodore might create an ugly scene.

But Theodore, incensed at her attitude,

came roaring down the hall after her, bellowing, "Marilyn!"

Abruptly, she rounded on him. "Stop it, Theodore, or you'll give yourself a heart attack!"

Theodore slammed to a halt, anxiously slapping a hand over his heart.

"Good-bye, Theodore," Marilyn said coolly. "You can stay here tonight, if you wish. Leave me a note about what you decide."

Theodore blinked. For the first time she could remember, he seemed at a loss for words.

Marilyn went out. She met Faraday on the sidewalk, where he grabbed her up and gave her such a long, passionate kiss, her toes tingled.

Too bad the preview lasted longer than the movie.

She'd ask her HFC friends about that; tonight, when she got the chance.

41

Alice's condo was wall-to-wall people.

The original crew was there: Dr. Donovan, the psychiatrist, and his wife Reya. Suzanne West, the astrologist. Tom Warren, the yoga pro. The beauticians Fred and Ted. They'd all brought friends of their own.

Marilyn had come with Faraday McAdam, a bull of a man so ruddy-faced and robust Alice could imagine him in kilt and shield, waving a sword as he charged after Mel Gibson in *Braveheart*. Shirley had driven two of her clients, old Nora Salter and shy Julie Martin, who, in the car, had begun to bond over a discussion of the stock market, and now sat whispering to each other on the sofa.

Bob Newcott, the rather slick-looking professor of the business management course Shirley was taking, had arrived, as well as three other couples taking the class, all of whom spoke little English and seemed most interested in the canapés Alan and Jennifer D'Annucio had made and were passing around on trays. Like Jennifer, Alan wore black pants and a white shirt. He'd gained back some of the weight he'd lost and carried himself proudly. All that baking and cooking with Jennifer was obviously good for him; Alice remembered he'd always liked messing around in the kitchen.

Faye sat on the sofa holding Megan, bobbing like a daffodil in her yellow frilly dress. Half the females in the room bent over her, cooing and smiling. What was it about babies that melted every woman's heart? No doubt the chemical reaction was caused by the same hormones that overheated and misfired when women hit fifty.

When she was sure everyone was there, Alice tapped a knife against a glass and called the room to order. She and Shirley presented a brief reprise of their Golden Moments pep talk, answered a few questions, then let the evening drift back into a flowing social mode where the real decisions would be made as people drank wine or sparkling water, munched crisp shrimp, bruschetta, and stuffed artichokes, exchanged business cards and jokes and gossip.

Alice wished they'd all go home, everyone

but the HFC. She needed desperately to talk to them about Gideon. In the kitchen, she found Jennifer filling the last tray with watercress cheese puffs, and remembered Faye's plan.

"You've been working all evening," Alice told Jennifer. "Let me take that."

"Oh, thanks!" Jennifer said brightly. She washed her hands, pushed her long black hair behind her ears, and sprinted out to the living room.

Alice followed, carrying the tray. People crowded toward her, grabbing up the puffs. Alice watched Jennifer squeeze into the group around the sofa.

"She is the cutest little baby I've ever seen!" Jennifer told Faye. "What's her name?" Jennifer crouched down with the fluid ease of a gymnast, in spite of her high heels, to be eye level with Megan, who reached out a dimpled hand for a lock of Jennifer's glossy black hair.

Faye doubled over, coughing like a consumptive in a blizzard. "Could you hold her?" she gasped. "Must get—water."

"Sure!" Jennifer lifted the baby from Faye's arms. Alice held her breath. Megan looked up at Jennifer and burst into her most winning, winsome smile, showing the glimmering beginning of one pearly tooth.

Bent and hacking, Faye headed through the crowd, flapping one hand to clear the way to the kitchen. Alice set the tray of puffs—only three were left—on a side table and hurried to join Faye. Shirley was in earnest conversation with a group of interested investors, but Alice caught Marilyn's eye. Marilyn left Faraday talking with Dr. Donovan and sped in.

"What's happening?" she asked.

Faye stood at the sink, running water into a glass. Part of the kitchen was open to the living room, divided by only a counter, so without turning around, she muttered, "Jennifer's holding Megan. She doesn't know who Megan is, doesn't know who I am."

"Looks like love," Marilyn reported softly. "She's smiling so much she's drooling."

"Megan or Jennifer?" Alice joked.

"That girl should have her own babies," Marilyn said.

"I couldn't agree more!" Faye exclaimed. "But she should have them with some other man than my daughter's husband!"

Alice interrupted impatiently. "Look, could we talk about *my* problem for just a moment?"

Faye turned around. "Absolutely!"

"What's up?" Marilyn asked.

"It's about sex," Alice murmured.

Faye and Marilyn drew close.

"This new man I've been seeing? Gideon Banks? I hardly know how to say this, it's so painful. But, um, I don't believe he finds me sexually attractive."

"What makes you think that?" Faye asked.

"Well, he, uh, we saw a movie, and came back here, and sat down on the sofa, and he kissed me, and then he basically got up and left!"

"Oh my goodness!" Marilyn cried, clapping her hands to her cheeks. "I haven't told you what happened with me and Faraday!" When Alice frowned at the interruption, she hurriedly added, "Wait, Alice, this might be relevant!" Leaning forward, she whispered, "Faraday delivered the most seductive, um, *enticements*, kissing and touching, and oh, it was delicious, and then he came inside, and came!"

Alice quirked an eyebrow. "And you're upset because?"

"I mean *instantly*," Marilyn clarified, glancing over her shoulder to be sure Faraday was still in the other room.

"That's premature ejaculation," Faye told her.

Alice nodded. "Yeah. That can be cured with time and patience. Unlike my problem, which is probably just that I'm too old and wrinkled—"

The doorbell rang. "I'll get it, Mom," Alan called.

"You're *not* old, and you have hardly any wrinkles," Faye began.

"If you want to see wrinkles," Marilyn whispered, "try looking at your crotch with a mirror. I've never done it before, and it's really pretty scary."

"Well, girl, why would you want to look there in the first place?" Alice demanded.

"Because I never have!" Marilyn told her. "I'm trying to contemplate all angles. I mean, I painted my toenails, colored my hair, and shaved my legs. I read about bikini waxes and heart-shaped trims, which reminds me, I researched merkins, you know, pubic wigs? And they do exist. They—"

"Never mind that!" Alice snapped. "At least you've got a man who wants to go to bed with you! I—"

A large handsome man entered the kitchen. "Alice?" His voice rumbled like thunder.

The three women jumped apart like schoolgirls caught smoking in the bathroom.

Alice recovered first. "Gideon!"

Gideon wore jeans and a red-and-white-striped rugby shirt, which did a fine job of showing off his wide shoulders and muscular arms. "Sorry to barge in on you like this. I didn't realize you were having a party."

"It's not a party, Gideon. It's a business meeting."

Laughter exploded from the living room, concluding with a baritone *har-har-har* and a soprano *tee-hee*.

"Right." Gideon frowned but remained, bullish and determined, like a football coach getting ready to chew out his most disappointing players. "I phoned, but you didn't return my call."

"Oh, I, uh," Alice stammered. This man made her feel so—so—so damned *googly*! She wanted to bat her eyelashes, giggle, and press her finger in a dimple in her cheek. What a mercy she had no dimples.

Gideon continued, "Look, I won't take much of your time, but I wanted to explain my behavior last night."

Alice stiffened defensively. "Not necessary."

"Alice! Please. Listen to me, just a moment, all right?" He moved closer.

Marilyn was observing Gideon with undisguised interest.

"Marilyn," Faye suggested brightly, "let's uncork some more wine."

"But it's all already un—" Marilyn began.

Faye grabbed Marilyn's arm and yanked her out of the kitchen.

As Marilyn and Faye left, Nora Salter toddled in. "Any more of those little crab things?" Her eyes raked appreciatively over Gideon.

"Maybe in the refrigerator," Alice said. To Gideon, she said, "Let's go to my room."

They stole away from the crowd, down the hall, and into her bedroom. Alice shut the door and leaned up against it.

Gideon looked around the room. The one chair in her bedroom was covered with clothing, so he sat down on her queen-size bed and patted the spread. "Sit here next to me, Alice. Please."

"Just say what you've got to say."

"All right then, Alice, but listen, dammit." He took a deep breath. "There's nothing more I'd like to do than take you to bed."

His bluntness caught her off guard.

"Right," she sniffed, crossing her arms over her breasts.

"But—"

Here it comes, she thought, *you're too old, too bossy, too fat, too ugly*—No, he wouldn't be that cruel. He'd couch his rejection in kinder language. Perhaps, "You remind me of my mother," or "I know I'd value you more as a friend." She struggled to control her facial muscles, but her lower lip quivered.

"I had a doctor's appointment yesterday. I have prostate cancer."

Alice gasped. In a second, the world turned right side up, then upside down again. She sat down on the bed next to him. "Oh, shit, Gideon, that's terrible."

"Yes, yes it is. I don't know how far advanced it is yet. They might have caught it early. Or maybe not. I've got to have a biopsy done. After that, well . . . Anyway, I don't think I've quite absorbed the news yet. I find myself pretty much preoccupied. That's why I asked if we could see a movie instead of going to the jazz club. I need a lot of time to take this in."

"Only natural." She put her hand on top of his.

"Last night, well, I am awfully attracted to you, Alice, I'm sure you're aware of that. From the first moment I saw you. When we kissed, when I touched your remarkable breast, well, that made all kinds of sensations explode in my body, and to be truthful, that scared me out of my wits. I mean, I am uninformed about prostate cancer. I don't think having sex will make the cancer spread, but any kind of commotion down there kind of alarms me. And I didn't want to be pathetic about it, and dump it all on you right when we were having such a great time, so I left."

"I'm glad you told me," Alice said softly. "And I don't think you're pathetic."

Gideon hesitated, then admitted in a very quiet voice, "Well, Alice, I *am* scared."

"Of course you are! It's only natural. But listen, Gideon, I know several men at TransContinent who've had prostate cancer, and they're just fine!"

"Uh-huh. But can they still have sex?"

"Well, I never talked with them about that."

"I've been scanning the information on the Internet," Gideon said. "A large percentage of men who have prostate cancer, and have the operation to remove it, end up impotent. That's a real possibility for me, Alice."

"That's tough."

"Tough for me. Certainly it means *you're* going to have to do some thinking. What kind of relationship are you looking for? Would you settle for companionship, if it comes to that? Or would sex be high on your list of priorities?"

Alice closed her eyes. Right then she felt like Gideon must have when he put his hand on her breast, attracted, yet terrified. She scarcely knew this man, and she wasn't good at wiping-the-fevered-brow stuff.

"Mom?"

She opened her eyes. Her son was peering into the room.

"Mom, there's someone here to see you."

"Alan, I'm busy right—"

"She says her name's Alison Cummings."

Alice's jaw dropped.

"I put her in your office," Alan informed her. "She said she won't take long."

Alice's brain dissolved into porridge.

"You go on," Gideon urged.

"Well. Maybe for a minute. There's lots of food and drinks in the living room. It's a Golden Moments party."

"I'll wait right here, if it's okay with you. I don't feel much like mingling."

"I'll hurry." Alice gave him a quick hug, which felt so warm and wonderful she could hardly pull herself away. She checked her reflection in the mirror and left the bedroom.

From the sounds in the living room, everyone was still having a good time. She crossed the hall and opened the door to her office.

Alison the Young and Beautiful waited there in all her sleek, slender glory. Clad in one of her figure-hugging red power suits, she stood straight and proud in her four-inch heels. Her youthful beauty radiated a kind of golden gleam, a light shield of protection. She seemed invulnerable and untouchable, and for the first time Alice understood how her own beauty in her earlier days might have kept people from becoming her friend, for why would someone so godlike need mortal alliances?

"Well?" Alice stayed in the doorway, ready to usher the other woman out of her office, her home, and her life.

Alison clasped her hands in front of her in a surprisingly beseeching manner. "Alice, I want you to come back to TransWorld. I need your help."

Alice was so surprised she burst out laughing.

"It's not *funny*," Alison protested. "I could lose my job if you don't help me."

"Why should I care?" Alice shot back.

"Look." Alison clenched her fists at her sides. "I was never after your job. *Barton Baker* was after your job!"

"He's *your* secretary!"

"True. He *doesn't* have my credentials, my experience, or my know-how! But he's sneaky and wildly ambitious!"

"And you're not."

"No!" Alison glared defiantly, then admitted, "Okay, I *am* ambitious. But I haven't resorted to duplicity. I certainly didn't tell him to sleep with Marilyn to find out what you were up to! That was all his own idea."

Alice shrugged. "Well, we paid him back."

"You did? How?"

"We sent that e-mail about his pectoral implants."

"*You* did?" Alison staggered backward, making a noise like a wounded duck.

"Are you okay?"

"You think that *hurt* him?"

"Embarrassed him, at least."

Alison shook her head so hard her entire body quaked. "Melvin Watertown and the other honchos are *impressed*! They think it shows Barton's devotion to the company, that he'll do whatever it takes to look young and virile! They want him to take over the position you held!"

Alice folded her arms over her chest and leaned against the doorjamb. "And you think I should care because?" She glanced down the hall to the living room, where the party was still in full flow.

"Because your TransContinent employees are going to get the shaft if you don't work with me on this. Barton wants to excise the whole bunch so all the Champion people have jobs! But *I* know, in the long run, that would be disastrous for the company. We need the expertise of both groups to make this merger work."

Alice squinted her eyes at Alison. What Alison said was true enough. *If* she really meant it. "What does Melvin Watertown think?"

"He says he was rash, letting you go like that. He's willing to eat humble pie, but first he asked me to make the first overture. Plus, he wants to be sure you and I think we can work together."

"And why would—"

"Because," Alison interrupted fervently, "I need friends! I just moved here! I don't know anyone! I'm all a—"

A shrill cry rose above the friendly chatter in the living room.

A woman cried, "She's Lars's daughter? *You*'re Laura's mother? But this is terrible! How could—I'm sorry—I never meant—Oh!"

Megan wailed.

"Wait here," Alice ordered Alison.

Alice rushed to the living room in time to see Jennifer D'Annucio shove Megan into Faye's arms, then stumble, scarlet-faced, from the room.

Alan pushed his way through the startled

guests, managing to grab Jennifer's arm just as she got to the front door. "Jennifer, what's wrong?"

Jennifer wheeled on him, black hair flying. "What's *wrong*? You lure me in so you can play this nasty trick on me? God, I'm so *humiliated*!"

"I don't understand!" Alan pleaded.

"Oh, *please* don't lie," Jennifer spat.

"I'm *not* lying." Alan looked desperate.

"You're telling me you had *no* idea that Lars Schneider's baby and mother-in-law were going to be here tonight!"

"Jennifer, I have no idea what you're talking about!"

"I don't believe you. You *had* to have known. You suckered me in so I would see that little baby and be confronted by Lars's mother-in-law. You wanted me to feel like a trashy home wrecker! Well, I *do*! I hope you're satisfied!"

"Are you *nuts*? Come on, Jennifer, calm down."

"I never want to talk to you again!" Jennifer jerked away from his grasp and slammed out the door.

The other guests clustered together, buzzing like a hive of demented bees. Faye, face flushed, head lowered to avoid eye contact, wound her way into the kitchen, little Megan on her shoulder, taking deep shuddering breaths. Faye's silk cardigan was wet with the baby's tears.

Alan saw Alice standing there staring. "What's going on, Mom?"

"This isn't the time—"

His eyes blazed. "Tell me now."

She knew full well how tenacious her son could be. "All right, but let's go where we can have some privacy." As they went past her office door, they passed Alison peering out, her eyes wide.

"Stay there," she ordered Alison.

Alison nodded with alacrity.

Across the hall, her bedroom door opened and Gideon looked out. "Are you all right?"

"Fine. I'll be back in a moment."

With Alison in her office and Gideon in her bedroom, the only private place left was the guest bathroom off the hall. She pulled Alan in and shut the door. Before, the bathroom had seemed spacious, but it didn't seem so then, with her huge, angry son in the room. Alice sat down on the bathtub rim.

Alan didn't sit. "Okay, so tell me." His voice was ominously low.

"Jennifer D'Annucio's having an affair with Lars Schneider."

"I know. What business is it of yours?" Alan demanded.

"Lars's wife, Laura, is my friend Faye's daughter. We thought that if Jennifer saw the baby, if she realized how much pain she could cause the helpless little creature, she'd break off with Lars."

"Who's *we*?" Alan asked.

"Doesn't matter. What does matter—"

"So you set Jennifer up."

"Hey, Alan, Jennifer's the one having—"

"In the first place," Alan said, biting his words off precisely, "Jennifer broke off with Lars this week. In the second place, I'm going to ask Jennifer to marry me."

Alice nearly fell over backward into the tub. "What?"

"As soon as I'm divorced from Genevieve Anne."

"But Alan, Jennifer's white!"

"I knew you'd say that!"

"Well, I'm not making it up!"

"You didn't like Genevieve Anne because she was too pretty, now you won't like Jennifer because she's white."

"I didn't say that, Alan."

"You're judgmental, Mother, and manipulative and *mean*!"

Alice's head was spinning. "Could we discuss this later?"

"I've got nothing more to say to you. *Ever.*" He bolted from the room.

Alice sprinted after him. "Alan—"

Her bedroom door was shut, but Alison gawked from Alice's study like a thoroughbred poking her head from a stall, yearning to join the race. In the living room, the guests had regrouped into chattering clusters. Faye was talking to Faraday and at the same time dangling a set of measuring spoons in front of Megan.

"Alan, wait," Alice pleaded.

Ignoring her, Alan stormed into the corridor, nearly colliding with a handsome man with silver hair tied back in a ponytail.

"Sorry," Alan muttered.

Ponytail watched Alan jab the DOWN button and disappear between the doors, which gasped pneumatically, as if in response to Alan's mood.

Ponytail turned to Alice. "Is this Alice Murray's home?"

"Yes," Alice sighed, thinking, *now what!*

"I'm Justin Quale. A friend of Shirley Gold's. She told me I might want to attend this meeting. I'm sorry I'm late."

"No problem. Come on in." Why hadn't

Shirley told her about *this* guy, Alice wondered. In his jeans, white polo shirt, and black blazer, he looked cool enough for Shirley and savvy enough to be an investor. "Shirley's over there. Excuse me, I've got—" It was too complicated to explain. Alison in one room, Gideon in the other—

She felt a hand on her arm. "Alice?"

She turned. "Marilyn? Are you okay?" Her friend looked flushed and shaky.

Marilyn tugged at the collar of her blouse. "I'm afraid I'm coming down with some horrible flu. I feel like I'm on fire. And my heart—"

Shirley joined them. "Are you all right, Marilyn?"

"I'm not sure."

Shirley touched Marilyn's forehead. "You'd better lie down. Can she use your bedroom, Alice?"

"Sure." Alice turned to lead the way.

"Hello, Shirley," Justin Quale stepped forward. "Sorry I'm late."

"Justin!" Shirley's face lit up. "I'm so glad you could make it. I need to check on something—Have a drink. I'll be right back."

Across the room, Faye rose, obviously wondering what the other three were up to. Adjusting Megan on her hip, she joined

Shirley and Marilyn as they followed Alice down the hall.

In the door to Alice's study stood Alison Cummings, gnawing her knuckles.

"You'd better go home," Alice told her. "I'm not going to be able to talk with you any more tonight."

"That's okay!" Alison insisted. "I think I'll stay! If you don't mind!"

Alice shrugged. "Fine. There's wine in the living room, and tea." She led the small group into her bedroom.

Gideon jumped up. "What happened?"

"Marilyn feels ill."

"Oh. Well, all right then. I'll leave."

Alice touched his arm. "Don't go home," she said softly. "Help yourself to some wine in the living room. I'll be out pretty soon."

When Gideon had gone out, Alice shut the door firmly. Marilyn stretched out on the bed, with Faye at her head and Shirley at her feet. Faye settled Megan to the middle of the bed.

"I'm going to take your pulse," Faye said. Everyone was quiet as Faye sat, fingers on Marilyn's wrist, eye on her watch. "Wow. Your heart's racing."

"I know," Marilyn replied. "Believe me, I can feel it."

Alice looked alarmed. "Should we call an ambulance?"

"Surely that's not necessary," Marilyn pleaded.

"I've got something that will help." Shirley went out of the room.

Marilyn was at the point of tears. "I'll be all right. In fact, I feel much better now."

As if in sympathy with Marilyn, Megan's lower lip quivered, then she began to wail.

Faye brought the baby to her shoulder and patted her back in little circles. "She's hungry. I've got to get her bottle." She left the bedroom.

Alice sank down next to Marilyn. She placed her own fingers on Marilyn's wrist. Marilyn's pulse was hopping around like a field of crickets.

"Was that Gideon Banks sitting on your bed when we came in?" Marilyn asked.

"It was."

"He's cute."

Alice wiggled her eyebrows. "Yeah, he is."

"Um, why was he is your bedroom? I thought you said he didn't find you attractive."

"Long story," Alice told her. "Wait till the others get back."

Shirley returned, bearing a mug. "Here," she told Marilyn. "Drink this."

Marilyn sat up, took the mug and peered into it. "What is it?"

"Just chamomile tea with a few drops of valerian."

"Valerian?" Alice asked suspiciously.

Shirley nodded. "An herbal supplement."

Marilyn grimaced. "Tastes awful."

"True, but it will settle your heart." Shirley folded her arms, watching Marilyn like a bossy nurse. "Drink it all."

Alice cocked her head. "You're sure it's safe?"

"Why, no!" Shirley retorted. "I just like giving experimental drugs to my friends!" She could see her reflection in the mirror above Alice's dresser. Her new haircut made her look so sleek, so intelligent, almost *formidable*. "*Of course* I'm sure. Valerian's been used for centuries. In medieval times it was called heal-all."

Alice was still skeptical. "You carry it around with you?"

"I carry quite a lot of stuff around, for my different massage clients." Removing her shoes, Shirley settled herself cross-legged on the bed, opened her capacious purse, and pulled out a large clear baggie full of teas, vials, and bottles.

"Good God, you've got an entire pharmacy there!" Alice exclaimed.

"It's all herbal, all natural, very mild," Shirley assured her.

Faye came back, holding Megan nestled close. Eyes closed, the baby was drinking enthusiastically from the bottle, grunting and sighing with pleasure. Faye went around to the other side of the bed and sank onto the velvet spread, arranging herself against the headboard next to Marilyn, kicking off her shoes and stretching out her legs. Alice grabbed some pillows and tucked them beneath Faye's arm.

"What did I miss?" Faye asked.

"Shirley gave Marilyn something called valerian," Alice said.

"I do feel calmer," Marilyn announced. "Alice, feel my pulse."

Alice put her fingers back on Marilyn's arm. Everyone was quiet. "It *is* slower and more steady," Alice announced.

"And your face isn't as red," Faye began, then laughed. "Marilyn! I'll bet you just had your first hot flash!"

Marilyn put her hands to her face. "My skin *is* cooling down. Goodness, if *that* was a hot flash, it was certainly powerful."

"Rest a few more minutes," Shirley suggested. "Let's see if you feel dizzy or nauseous."

"Good idea," Faye seconded.

"Okay," Marilyn agreed. She took another sip of tea.

Shirley asked, "So, Alice, tell us, who's the man you keep hidden in your bedroom?"

Alice grinned. "Gideon Banks."

"And he was shut in your bedroom during the party because—"

"He showed up without calling, that's all." Alice thought fast. Should she tell the others that Gideon had prostate cancer? Certainly it was private information, but how could she possibly make a decision, about going through all of whatever it might turn out to be, without discussing it with her friends? "Which reminds me, did you see that guy—I think he said his name's Justin Quale—come in a few minutes ago?"

Shirley blushed. "I saw him, but didn't get a chance to talk to him."

"And?" Alice prompted.

"He was in my management seminar, and his brother Jake's a Realtor. They've been showing me and Faye a few possible locations for the retreat."

"What does he do?" Marilyn asked.

"He's a retired professor of English. He can't decide whether to start his own business or join his brother's real estate firm."

"And he seems to think Shirley's pretty cute," Faye added.

"Why, Shirley, how exciting!" Marilyn said.

Shirley beamed. Then her face fell. "Poor Faye. We all have men waiting out there for us, except you."

"That's okay. I've got Megan." Faye cuddled the baby close. "Besides, I don't want a man. Although I *am* considering getting a dog. I'm thinking a yellow Lab. I'll name her Sunny."

"Listen, ladies." Shirley rustled around in her enormous purse. "I have something to show you. I didn't tell the group out there because I'm not certain about it yet, but I need your advice." She pulled out a sheaf of papers and photos. "Justin and Jake showed Faye and me this old estate out in Lincoln. It was a private school a hundred years ago. It's been on the market for a while, because it's too large for a single house and too small and isolated for most businesses. It might be perfect for my Golden Moments retreat. It's on thirty acres of land. There's a stream and a small pond, lots of old gardens. The cool thing is, it's got lots of large rooms. I was thinking, since you've all offered to invest money, that if you did, you could each select one of the rooms to be your personal refuge. In case, for example, Marilyn, let's say, your Cambridge house sells and you haven't found a new place to live yet, or if Faye starts teaching art therapy at the retreat and doesn't want to drive back to her house at night. What do you think?"

She passed the material around. The women bent over the xeroxed plans and photos of the buildings and grounds.

A knock sounded at the door. Alison's blond head appeared. "Aren't you coming out, Alice?"

"In a while," Alice answered. "I'm busy now."

"Okay. I'll wait. Uh, can I get you anything?"

Alice looked at the others, then at Alison. "We could use four glasses, a bottle of wine, and a bottle of Perrier."

"Coming right up." Alison went away.

Marilyn tapped a blueprint. "If I had a room there, maybe I wouldn't need to buy an entire house. If I travel as much with Faraday as he seems to think I will. And if we decide to live with each other . . . Of course, that's rushing things even to consider it, but this could be an intermediate place until I make other plans."

"Alice?" Shirley said.

Alice hesitated. "I don't know. I'm not

much for the countryside." She tossed the papers onto the bed. "I can't *think* properly right now. Everything's so messed up. Did you see? Alan roared off in a fury because you brought Megan here, plus he's in love with Jennifer!"

"He is?" Faye's face lit up. "That's wonderful!"

"For you, maybe," Alice retorted.

"Hey! Jennifer's a good kid!" Shirley insisted.

"She's white," Alice said.

"So are we," Shirley shot back.

Megan belched loudly, making everyone laugh.

Faye patted the baby's back. "It was so awful when Jennifer realized who I was, who Megan was. I didn't realize how upset she'd be."

"You did what was right," Alice asserted. "She wouldn't have been upset if she hadn't been guilty. Besides"—she sniffed—"she's got Alan to comfort her now."

"Alan and Jennifer are starting their own bakery business," Shirley announced.

"Oh, *please*!" Alice scoffed. "Alan has an MBA! He was vice president of an enormous corporation. Why would he settle for baking bread and living in the country?"

"Um, because it's what he wants?" Shirley suggested.

"How do you know that?" Alice demanded.

"We talked about it on the phone last night. This compound has a great kitchen. *If* the retreat works out, they'll use the kitchen for their bakery, supply daily goods for the retreat in payment, and sell the rest." She put her finger on the blueprint of the property. "They're talking about living in the gatehouse."

Alice closed her eyes and forced herself to take a deep breath. "Give me strength," she prayed.

"Anyway, we don't have to decide right now," Shirley said. "I just wanted to get the ball rolling."

Faye cradled Megan against her. "Still hungry?" Megan clasped the bottle in her fat baby hands and directed it toward her mouth, but her eyes closed drowsily, her head fell back, and she made a baby snore.

"I love your outfit," Shirley told Faye. "Especially the embroidery."

"Thanks. I'll make one for you if you'd like."

Shirley blinked. "You made it yourself? Wow."

"This is great." Marilyn wiggled her toes luxuriously. "It reminds me of camping out with my sister Sharon, lying on our sleeping bags, looking up at the stars, talking about the mysteries of the universe."

Alice chortled. "Reminds me of my high school sleepovers, talking about the mysteries of boys."

Faye looked around at them, all in their various states of reclining. "We're kind of like the Edward Burne-Jones painting *The Sleeping Beauty*. But with a baby."

Shirley ran her hands over the jewel-toned velvet bedspread. "I think it's like being on a magic carpet."

A knock sounded on the door. Gideon looked in. "How're you all doin'?"

Alice leaned back against the footboard. "We're got some business matters to finish. Alison's bringing us something to drink. But we could use some chocolate."

"Coming right up." He shut the door and went away.

"We'd better get busy," Alice prompted.

Marilyn punched her pillow into a more comfortable shape to lean on as she looked at the photos. Shirley tucked her feet beneath her while she read aloud from a checklist, comparing what her retreat needed and what this old estate had.

Faye carefully laid Megan on her tummy between her and Marilyn, brushing her fingers lightly over the pale brown fuzz on the baby's hot little head. The baby's cheeks were flushed, and when she exhaled, she made a sweet, high, sighing sound.

Another knock. Gideon and Alison entered, carrying trays of drinks, chocolate cake, forks, and napkins.

"Here, on the bed, is fine," Alice directed.

Alison set the tray down very slowly, her eyes working furiously as she tried to read the papers scattered there. "Need anything else?"

"No, thanks," Alice told her.

"Most of your guests are leaving," Alison warned.

"That's all right," Alice said.

"Do you mind if we wait?" Gideon asked.

"I don't mind if *you* wait," Alice said to him.

"Well, then, I'll hang around," Gideon said, and left the room.

"Me too," Alison said. She stood there a moment, looking rather wistful, then went out, leaving the door open a few inches.

"Shut the door!" all four women yelled.

Alison shut the door.

The women fell on the trays, dividing up the cake, pouring drinks, handing around plates and napkins.

"That reminds me of my mother's favorite

joke," Faye said. "A woman falls in love with a man from France. One night he comes to her house. He sits down with her on the sofa. He says, *'Je t'adore.'* She says, 'What?' He says, *'Je t'adore.'* She says, 'Shut the door yourself, I've had a long day.' "

The others laughed.

Alice moaned with pleasure at the rich chocolate. "This is as good as sex." She made a face. "In fact, it might be *instead of* sex for me."

Three heads shot up.

"Why?" Shirley asked.

"Do you think they can hear us?" Marilyn whispered.

"I'm sure they can't," Faye told her.

"We've given them plenty to talk about," Alice reminded them.

The four women looked at the door. Outside the room waited all the complications of men and money, business and health, grown children and childish colleagues. In here were a sleeping baby, friendship, and chocolate cake. Plus, the bed was comfortable, and they could keep their shoes off.

"I'd like to rest a little more," Marilyn decided.

"Good." Alice picked up her plate. "Because I'd like your advice about Gideon."

"And I want to tell you all about the art therapy courses I'm taking this summer," Faye said, licking her fork.

"And I didn't tell Shirley about my problem with Faraday," Marilyn said, adding hopefully, "Maybe you have an herbal solution for this problem!"

"What problem?" Shirley asked.

"I told Faye and Alice about it when we were in the kitchen and you were schmoozing potential investors." Marilyn dropped her voice. "It's about, um, sex."

"Oooh." Shirley grinned, squirming like a puppy. "This is the most fun I've ever had in bed without a man! Tell me!"

"Okay, then." Marilyn leaned forward.

The other three women bent closer.

Marilyn took a sip of her champagne, a fortifying bite of cake, then she began to talk.

ABOUT THE AUTHOR

NANCY THAYER is the author of thirteen novels. including *Custody, Between Husbands and Friends, An Act of Love, Three Women at the Water's Edge,* and *Everlasting,* which was a Main Dual selection of the Literary Guild. Her work has been translated into nearly a dozen languages. Her first Novel, *Stepping,* was made into a 13-part series for BBC Radio and her ghost novel, *Spirit Lost,* has been optioned and produced as a movie by United Image Entertainment. In 1981 she was a fellow at the Breadloaf Writers Conference. She has lived on Nantucket Island year round for nineteen years with her husband, Charley Walters.

Visit the author's web site at
www.nancythayer.com